EVERYONE LOVES JESSICA LEPE!

"This sparkling debut marks Lepe as a writer to watch when it comes to modern rom-coms." —*Kirkus*, Starred Review

"Jessica Lepe absolutely sparkles in this stunning debut that is equal parts heartfelt, funny, and deeply moving! I loved every page!"

—Lyssa Kay Adams, *USA Today* bestselling author of *A Very Merry Bromance*

"Voice-y and big-hearted, FLIRTY LITTLE SECRET delivers compassionate mental health rep, classic rom-com joy, and touching emotional depth."

—Chloe Liese, *USA Today* bestselling author of *Two Wrongs Make a Right*

"A heartfelt rom-com enriched by an honest portrayal of mental health issues, a beautiful blend of cultures, and the bonds of family. Jessica Lepe's moving debut reminds us of the importance of loving ourselves just as we are."

—Priscilla Oliveras, *USA Today* bestselling author of *West Side Love Story*

"FLIRTY LITTLE SECRET is an absolute dream of a romance! I was completely captivated by these realistic characters and the relatable struggles they both endure. As a former teacher, I really appreciated the authentic peek into the life of educators. With tons of wit and even more heart, Lepe's debut had me laughing one minute and crying the next. I will be anxiously awaiting Lepe's next book, I can't wait to see what she does next!"

—Falon Ballard, author of *Just My Type*

"Exquisitely inclusive, humorous, and original, Lepe's charming prose kept me enchanted from the clever opening post to the satisfying ending."   —Kelly Cain, author of *A Kiss from the Past*

"FLIRTY LITTLE SECRET is a masterfully done poignant tale of modern love, friendship, and intimacy that not only is a thrill to read but inspires you to be a little kinder and less judgmental to yourself and the world around you."

—Felicia Grossman, author of *Marry Me by Midnight*

"Hilarious, sexy, and brimming with heart."

—Yaffa S. Santos, author of *A Touch of Moonlight*

"A charming, heartfelt rom-com that will have you laughing, and rooting for the characters from the first few chapters. Jessica Lepe's debut is a must-read for romance fans!"

—Jaqueline Snow, author of *Snowed In for Christmas*

FLIRTY *little* SECRET

♥♥♥

JESSICA LEPE

FOREVER
NEW YORK BOSTON

Copyright © 2024 by Jessica Lepe
Reading group guide copyright © 2024 by Jessica Lepe and Hachette Book Group, Inc.
Cover design and illustration by Caitlin Sacks. Cover copyright © 2024 by Hachette Book Group, Inc.
Interior illustrations by Caitlin Sacks.

Forever
Hachette Book Group
1290 Avenue of the Americas, New York, NY 10104
read-forever.com
@readforeverpub

First Edition: March 2024

Forever is an imprint of Grand Central Publishing. The Forever name and logo are trademarks of Hachette Book Group, Inc.

The publisher is not responsible for websites (or their content) that are not owned by the publisher.

The Hachette Speakers Bureau provides a wide range of authors for speaking events. To find out more, go to hachettespeakersbureau.com or email HachetteSpeakers@hbgusa.com.

Forever books may be purchased in bulk for business, educational, or promotional use. For information, please contact your local bookseller or the Hachette Book Group Special Markets Department at special.markets@hbgusa.com.

Library of Congress Cataloging-in-Publication Data
Names: Lepe, Jessica, 1988- author.
Title: Flirty little secret / Jessica Lepe.
Description: First edition. | New York : Forever, 2024. | Series: Galindo sisters
Identifiers: LCCN 2023040986 | ISBN 9781538739341 (trade paperback) | ISBN 9781538739358 (ebook)
Subjects: LCGFT: Romance fiction. | Novels.
Classification: LCC PS3612.E598 F58 2024 | DDC 813/.6—dc23/eng/ 20230919
LC record available at https://lccn.loc.gov/2023040986

ISBNs: 9781538739341 (trade pbk.), 9781538739358 (ebook)

Interior book design by Marie Mundaca

Printed in the United States of America

LSC-C

Printing 2, 2024

To Mom, who always knew I could do it, even when I didn't. And when the load got too heavy, sat with me until I grew strong enough to carry it again. This book is for you.

CONTENT GUIDANCE

Dear Reader,

While I hope this romance will have you smiling and maybe even letting out a few laughs, please note this book does contain a main character who is both neurodivergent and depressed and lives with an anxiety disorder. This character also experiences an on-page panic attack and passive suicide ideation (no attempt). Ableist language is sometimes used regarding mental illness, and there is one scene with antisemitic and racial microaggressions. Reference is also made to the grooming and attempted sexual assault of a minor, but the incident itself occurs off-page. Cheating (past/off-page) is also referenced.

I strove to bring authenticity to this character who shares the same mental health diagnoses I do, but I know that my lived experience may be different from yours. Please read with care if these topics are sensitive to you.

Best,
Jessica

TheMissGuidedCounselor
Posted at 7:15 AM

Happy first day of school to all my teachers and admin! Today I'm sharing my top 5 tips to make this new school year your BEST one yet:

1. Embrace the Positivity: Sure, we all wish we were still on summer break, soaking in the sun and sleeping in late, but try not to dwell on what you are losing and focus instead on what you are gaining: a freshly wiped slate and chance to influence a whole new year of students!

2. Celebrate Your Success: Make sure to take time to celebrate all the amazing things you do each and every day.

3. Don't Try to Do It All: It can be easy to take on too much and want to be everything for everyone, but that is also the quickest way to burn out! Only say yes to the things that bring you happiness and real fulfillment.

4. Be Confident in Your Expertise: Many of us teachers and school professionals are nervous when starting a new year, especially those of us who are newer to the job. But try not to doubt

your skills and your knowledge—after all, it's what got you here in the first place!

5. Take the Time to Build Meaningful Relationships: Don't forget to set aside time to connect with your students, fellow teachers, and admin staff. Even a quick coffee each morning can blossom into a beautiful and supportive friendship. And let's face it, this job is hard enough as it is—shouldn't we all work together to make it easier for each other? So today, instead of heading straight to your classroom or office, stop by the teachers' lounge and pour yourself a nice big mug of hot coffee or tea and introduce yourself to someone new! You never know, you could meet your next best friend!

Liked by **BravesGuy93** and **others**

TheMissGuidedCounselor Back to school…more

View all comments

Chapter One

♡ *Fletcher*

LOOK, I KNOW THAT the first day at a new job usually tends to suck.

Especially when you're starting as a new teacher at a *new* school. And not just any school—but high school. Yes, the place you actively have nightmares about and spent both a decade and your annual health insurance deductible processing in therapy. That's where I work.

And starting a new job *anywhere* can be scary. You're fresh meat; everyone stares at you as you wander around, since you have no idea where the hell anything is; and you have to answer the same question a hundred times, maintaining a level of enthusiasm only matched by someone with a healthy dependency on cocaine. It's exhausting, but it's part of the deal of starting somewhere new. I accept it.

What I hadn't expected, however, was that my first day would also include getting a mug of boiling hot tea tossed directly onto my, for lack of a better word, dick. That...*that* had been a curveball.

And it's at this moment—mere seconds after the aforementioned tea has collided with my crotch, possibly rendering me infertile, it's *that* hot—that I see the culprit. Jet-black hair. Golden sepia skin. A quivering lower lip. All put together in a beautiful woman who is gaping at me with wide, horrified eyes on the brink of tears. And just like the tea had blindsided me a moment earlier, I'm struck a second time by her unique beauty. Even the sickly flickering fluorescent lights reveal a delicate softness in the curve of her crimson-flushed cheeks and thick black lashes that obscure the rich, dark umber of her eyes.

Sure, she may have castrated me, but there's something fascinating about this woman—beyond her incredible aim—that sends sparks of electricity straight through me, making me want to run my hand down her face and test that soft skin theory for myself.

Or maybe the hot liquid just burned some nerve endings and this is my body shutting down in response. Yeah, that makes much more sense for all these addled thoughts.

"Oh my God! I am so sorry!"

The voice does not match the hysterical person currently gaping at me with wide, panicked eyes. Probably because it's about five octaves higher than what I would imagine is her usual tenor. She leaps into action, ripping off her scarf, a vibrant purple and blue number made to look like the colorful feathers of a peacock. Falling to her knees, she presses it against my crotch, dabbing at the liquid stain. I suck in a sharp breath, willing my poor penis—if he managed to survive the tea attack—to not react to this very beautiful woman vigorously assaulting the front of my pants.

Out of the corner of my eye, I see a clock with the time: 7:21 a.m. I have been here exactly seven minutes and I am already getting my own peacock assaulted by a very determined woman and her peacock scarf.

Luckily, it only takes her a few seconds to realize she is giving me the world's worst and most traumatizing third-base hand job on the planet. All in the middle of the teachers' lounge. And if I thought her voice was high before, it just jumped to a range usually only accessible by dogs.

"I am so, so, so sorry!"

She jumps away, pulling the scarf with her, to reveal a giant wet spot that seems to have been made only worse by her earnest attempts.

Seeing the damage, her eyes widen to impossibly larger proportions that momentarily have me concerned they may just pop out of their sockets altogether.

She glances down at her hands, holding them out in front of her as if finally—*finally*—understanding how using them to blot out the tea from the front of my pants may not have been the most appropriate choice to make.

Strikingly chocolate-brown eyes filled with moisture and regret lock on mine. "I am so sorry and I will just leave you to"— she waves her hand over my stained crotch—"to this *situation* that I am very sorry I have left you in but I have to go because I have a very important meeting I just remembered and—"

She doesn't bother finishing the sentence before she rushes out of the lounge, repeating her apology as she flees, her voice carrying into the hallway before the door unceremoniously slams shut.

The entire room is silent, and I can feel every set of eyes watching me, most of them looking directly at my crotch. So much for blending in.

I look down at my pants, wondering what the hell I'm going to do. I had packed a first aid kit, an entire box of protein bars, and three cans of Red Bull for my first day of school but had neglected to pack a spare pair of pants. Getting tea spilled on me hadn't really crossed my mind as something I should be preparing for.

My bad.

I think my best move would be to find the nearest men's room, make sure my dick is still intact and functioning, and figure out how I can teach my first-period class from behind my desk as I wait for my pants to dry and collect whatever remaining dignity I have left.

I frantically scan the lounge only to find a crowd of gaping faces staring at me. As much as I hated my old job, I never had to stand in front of my colleagues looking like I had wet my poor khakis. For the briefest of seconds, I wonder if this is perhaps a sign from the universe that I made the wrong choice in leaving and that maybe this is a cruel fated bitch slap.

I grab a stack of napkins and blot my pants, but the water has set in, and they do nothing but accessorize my crotch stain with tiny specks of white. I had forgotten that I was no longer teaching at a fancy private school, that this was a public school. And public schools have cheap, single-ply napkins—the kind that shed crumbs of white paper the minute they encounter moisture.

So, in addition to the wet stain, it now looks like I have dandruff of the pubic hair variety.

A giant hand claps me on the shoulder. "Welcome to Harview High!"

I turn to find a man with a flaming red beard and a wide,

toothy smile on a pale ivory face peppered with freckles. He easily towers over me, but the combination of his playful smile, yellow and pink polka-dot bow tie, and thick accent make him seem far less intimidating and more like a jolly Scottish giant with a unique sense of fashion.

He holds out his hand. "The name is Brodie. I'm the phys ed teacher here. I'm also the badminton coach. You must be the new history teacher, aye?"

I shake his hand. "That's me. I'm Fletcher."

"Fletcher," he says, rolling the *r* at the end of my name for a few extra syllables. "Nice to meet you." He gestures toward the door with his chin. "Why don't we venture over to the locker rooms? They've got some hand dryers there so we can dry off your trousers before the first bell."

I gladly accept his offer—mostly to dry my pants, but also to get the hell out of that lounge and all the noticeable stares and whispers—and follow him out of the teachers' lounge, strategically holding my bag over my front even though every person in here has gotten a clear view of my soaked khaki-clad member.

As the door swings closed behind us, the chatter in the lounge fervently picks up again. I have no doubt they are all discussing whatever it is that just happened. I wish them luck—I'm still trying to put the pieces together. One minute I was going to make myself a cup of coffee, the next I had my new colleague on her knees scrubbing my groin.

Definitely *not* how I pictured today going.

Brodie confidently navigates through the hallway, pointing out different classrooms for me and greeting the students beginning to trickle in. Meanwhile, I'm extra diligent about keeping my bag positioned in front of me, hiding the wet stain. Even as a thirty-year-old man, I'm still terrified of teenagers. Especially ones that have cell phones with cameras permanently attached to their hands, who could post a picture of me looking like I had pissed myself on my first day on the job. That would be a fun one for the yearbook.

We finally reach the empty locker room, where we are greeted by both the overwhelming smell of dirty socks mixed with wet towels and a line of hand dryers flanking the tiled wall by the toilet stalls. Jackpot.

He sits on one of the benches, stretching his long legs and crossing them at the ankle. I can only assume he's going to sit here while I dry my crotch. Our friendship is progressing quickly.

Brodie is a talker. He barely takes a breath between sentences as he impressively navigates from one topic to the next. Like how he's currently ranking the area's different Mexican restaurants by the quality of their nacho cheese.

"You can't have too liquidy of a cheese," he explains with the same seriousness you would expect in a conversation about the geopolitical conflicts of the Middle East, "because then the cheese will saturate into the chip, and the chip will lose its crispness. And you really need a firm chip to scoop up the rest of the fillings. That is why Rancho Chico will always be number one in my book. As a matter of fact, that's where I took the boys when we had won the badminton regionals." He shakes his head. "Too bad we didn't win that year. I really thought we had it in us."

I try to keep up, but I am far too focused on getting these damn pants dry. I continue to swing, thrusting my hips upward as I prop my hands on my back to arch toward the hot air blowing from the dryers.

Brodie pauses and eyes me curiously. "Mate, you're going about this all wrong," he calls out. "You need to take off the trousers and hold them up."

Okay, so undressing in front of my colleagues was *also* something I had not expected when I woke up this morning. But Brodie's right—this is not a great method, and it kind of feels like I'm steaming my balls, and the poor pair have already been through enough today. But I've got less than fifteen minutes before I have to report to my first class, and I need this stain gone. So the pants—*trousers*—have got to go.

I kick off my shoes and then unbuckle and slide my pants down to my ankles before bending over and picking them up. I'm not wearing my finest boxers—a plain gray pair from the ten-pack that I get from Target—and I feel oddly self-conscious in front of this giant man who is surprisingly comfortable with this entire situation.

"And that is why you want to volunteer for the winter bake sale," he continues, even though I had tuned out the change in topic trying to hold my pants up to the dryer. "Try to avoid the Spring Fling if you can. The kids get too frisky with the changing weather and mostly the chaperone duties are watching out for any emerging boners." Brodie chuckles, shaking his head as if having a discussion about students' boners while I am half naked is a completely normal thing to do on a Monday morning. "Don't want to have another 2014. Did I tell you about that?" He doesn't wait for me to answer before diving in, telling me about the three girls in the junior class who had all made a pregnancy pact because they wanted to get on the *Teen Mom* TV show.

Luckily my pants are starting to dry, the splotch of water beginning to disappear under the heat. Thank God.

"It's working, eh?" Brodie asks.

"Looks like it. Thanks for the help. It would have been brutal to have this stain on my first day."

He nods, fully understanding. "My first day I tripped and fell down in front of the whole cafeteria. For weeks, every time a student would see me, they would shout 'timber!' and try to get me to topple over again. I guess seeing a full-grown man tumble to the ground is an amusing sight."

I try to picture what this man—who had to be at least six foot five—would look like falling to the ground. It had to be a hell of a journey down.

"Well, you seem to be doing fine now by the looks of it. Were you a teacher back in Scotland, too?"

He arches his brow and smiles. "You got the accent right. Attaboy! Most people I meet ask me if I come from the same place as Harry Potter. But, no, wasn't a teacher back home."

I look down to see my pants fully dry—giant wet splotch completely invisible—and I slip them back on. "How did you end up here then?"

He gets a wistful look and his eyes dart up to the ceiling. "Followed a girl here. But she unfortunately passed two years ago."

Shit. Great job, Fletch.

"Oh, man, I am so sorry."

He wipes the back of his hand across his cheek to swipe a stray tear and rises to his feet, dwarfing me again. "She was a beautiful, wonderful woman, and she gave me the most precious little daughter." He digs his phone out of his back pocket and shows me the lock screen. A pretty girl, with bright green eyes and the same fiery red hair as her father, smiles, holding a small golden retriever puppy.

"She's adorable."

He swells at the compliment and tucks his phone back into his pocket. "Arabella. My pride and joy. But enough about me. What brings you to our little corner of Harview? Rumor has it you were a teacher at one of those fancy schmancy schools."

I inwardly cringe at the question. How do I explain leaving Kenton, one of the most prestigious schools in the world, from which half a dozen or so senior politicians, top CEOs, and even a president graduated, to come and teach at a public school in Massachusetts? I force a smile. "Uh, I had some family that needed me back home."

Brodie nods knowingly. "I hear you. Is it cancer? I stayed with my uncle a few years back when he fought testicular cancer. Poor guy."

It is becoming abundantly clear that besides his nonstop talking, Brodie has zero boundaries. "Uh, not cancer," I answer. "My father actually left my mom."

Brodie covers his mouth with a loud gasp.

"For his secretary," I add, eliciting another loud, dramatic gasp.

"Who is now pregnant with his kid." I toss in that last bit and enjoy a surprisingly high-pitched third gasp paired with Brodie's hand clutching his chest. I bite back a smile, feeling only the tiniest bit of guilt for using my tragic family drama for entertainment.

"Mate, that's heavy," Brodie says, shaking his head. He places a meaty hand on my shoulder, a somber expression on his face. "If you need anything, I'm here for you. Anything at all. I just got one of those new kitchen gadgets. What do they call them? Oh, the Instant Pot! I can make you anything you need. Yogurt, applesauce, even a whole roasted chicken!"

I suppress a laugh, not wanting to offend Brodie. He's so sincere, a far cry from my colleagues back at Kenton Prep, who were often cold and competitive. "Thank you, but I'm staying at my mom's for a bit, and she's a great cook," I add to reassure him, which is mainly true. Except for the fact my mother hasn't cooked, really hasn't done much of *anything*, since discovering the affair.

Brodie nods and drops his hand from my shoulder. "You're a good one, Fletch. Now, we should be getting on. I'll show you to your classroom so you can get situated before the bell."

Now fully clothed, I thank him for his offer and follow him down the hallway, which has swelled with students. Luckily, Brodie is so big, the crowd naturally parts for him, and I take full advantage, following behind until we stop outside of a classroom.

"This is your stop," he says, waving his hand to the door. "Try not to get any more drinks spilled on you today. Or any more hands on your willy!" The last word he calls out as he walks away, sending the hallway of students into a fit of laughter as they stream into their classrooms—including mine.

Yep, this day definitely sucks.

Chapter Two

♡ *Lucy*

I'LL NEED A NEW name. A dye job. Colored contacts (as a *Twilight*-obsessed millennial, I *have* always wanted violet eyes). Oh, and a whole new identity. Might need to burn off my fingerprints, too, to ensure that my body can never be tracked back to the old Lucy Galindo. That should cover everything I'll need to escape and start a life somewhere else. Oh, I'll need Wi-Fi, too. And ideally somewhere that Amazon delivers because I have unfortunately created a lifestyle for myself where I am entirely dependent on them to survive.

"Lucy?"

The sound of Nia's voice tears me away from the elaborate fantasy life I had been carefully constructing in my head: a fabulous rent-controlled brownstone with brick walls and hardwood floors in Harlem. (Do they have brownstones in Harlem? I'll have to look that up later.) My neighbor will be this crotchety old man who teaches me how to play chess, but in the process bestows upon me all these valuable life lessons. Oh, and a bookstore across the street that also has a café attached where they host a variety of open mic nights where I can show off my mastery of the ukulele.

"Hello? Lucy!" Nia calls out again.

Shit. Fantasy gone.

I pop my head out of my hiding place and wave her forward, granting her formal permission to enter our sacred space. She pushes aside the thick blue wrestling mats and ducks under the volleyball net until she's on the other side, claiming the comfortable armchair across from mine.

My first year as guidance counselor here, I discovered a long, awkward hallway behind the gym that housed abandoned and forgotten equipment that no one really wanted to deal with. It didn't really lead anywhere, and because there was so much crap shoved in, no one had realized that the hallway extended to the right a whole seven feet, leading to a single closet that had just enough space for two comfortable armchairs, a corner piled high with pillows, and a small tribute to my queen, RBG.

On days where I just need to lie on the floor, question my entire existence, and bask in the myriad poor decisions I've made in life to bring me to this point, this is where I go. This is my sanctuary: my space to come and cry when I am overwhelmed, or stressed, or angry, or any of the plethora of emotions I cycle through any given week. Nia never cries, but she does enjoy the secret space for camping out during her free periods and watching *Great British Baking Show* reruns while she hides from her students.

So I am the primary occupant of what we have aptly named the cry closet. Because I cry...a lot. Not like every day, or even every week. But I do enjoy a biweekly or so cathartic cleansing of my tear ducts. Sometimes I have really great reasons for crying—like that time we lost a student to cancer, or when Lily Applegate, the coolest girl in tenth grade, told me that my flared jeans and chain belt made me look like a Dollar Tree J.Lo.

And then some days, I don't have much of a reason to cry. It could be because of something as simple as stubbing my toe in the doorframe or dropping a pile of papers—nothing that any other person would deem more than a mere annoyance. But for me and my clinical chronic depression with a heaping side of anxiety, rain clouds are always trailing a few feet behind. And from time to time, they catch up with me, and those minor inconveniences of life begin to feel...*overwhelming*.

In those moments, crying is all I can manage to do. So it's nice to have a quiet place, with a stash of snacks and a strong Wi-Fi connection, on those days.

"You doing okay?" Nia asks. Her voice is doing that kind of singsong thing that she does when she doesn't know how to comfort me. Nia is a math teacher and the complete and total opposite of me in every single way imaginable. Where I like to cry and journal my feelings and attend weekend retreats on healing my inner child, Nia spends her free time watching documentaries about Pythagorean identities and going on long runs, which she finds "relaxing"—a concept I entirely do not understand.

As Nia's eyes narrow, assessing me with that big, beautiful brain of hers, I look down at my fingers knotted together in my lap. Nia knows me well enough to know I'm not doing okay. I think I am still in shock, considering I am not bawling my eyes out in humiliation. I have no doubt the tears will come later—possibly tonight—when I finally process my day over a glass of wine and two Lean Cuisines, because honestly, who ever gets full from just one?

But still, I nod and hold up my phone, where I have my Notes app open. "Totally fine," I lie with a false peppiness. "I'm just working on a draft for an upcoming post now."

I'm doing my best to channel my humiliation through my online alter ego, @TheMissGuidedCounselor, who is the voice of guidance and wisdom for almost half a million followers on Instagram. As an overwhelmed and self-conscious grad student, I had started the account to share some of the advice I wished someone would give me, as well as grow my own confidence in my counseling skills. Two years and hundreds of posts later, @TheMissGuidedCounselor always knows the right words to say, the perfect advice to give.

As @TheMissGuidedCounselor, I am confident, brilliant, witty, and wise. She's a curated version of myself that highlights all my best parts...and just ignores all the other baggage. Which is why she is also anonymous.

Well, *mostly* anonymous. As my best friend, Nia knows about my secret, though I know she has her misgivings about it.

Because if anyone ever discovered that *I* was the one behind the account, @TheMissGuidedCounselor would lose all credibility. Lucy Galindo—with her biweekly panic attacks and eight different alarm clocks with reminders to take her anti-anxiety and depression medication—would not inspire *anyone*.

She is everything I wish I could be in real life, and she would, most definitely, *never* accidentally grope a teacher.

Nia doesn't look the least bit convinced by the false cheer in my voice and leans against the doorframe, crossing her arms at her chest. "And what is this post about exactly?"

I clear my throat. "Five ways to recover—gracefully, of course—from an embarrassing work incident."

The edges of Nia's lips quirk into a smile. "And what number on your list is 'hide in a closet at work'?"

I shoot her an annoyed look and pocket my phone.

"@TheMissGuidedCounselor wouldn't hide in a closet, Nia. Which is why *she's* the one with the Instagram account, not me."

Nia rolls her eyes. "I'd much rather have you be the face of *your* account. Perfection is boring."

"Says the perfect person," I grumble in return. "Anyway, can we please not argue about this again? I need to know if everyone is still talking about this morning."

Nia forces an unnatural smile to her face so I know the next few words coming out of her mouth will be lies. "Oh, no, it was totally not a big deal."

Yep, she's lying. Nia is a terrible liar.

I drop my head into my hands and groan. I have no doubt my accidental fondling will be the talk of the teachers' lounge for the next few days, at least until someone catches the freshman biology teacher, Ms. Tanner, practicing her TikTok dances in the choir room.

I am such a klutz, always tripping over my own feet or embarrassing myself in some way or another, though today definitely topped the list. I try so hard to fit in, but I only can ever seem to stand out. And not in the good way.

"I can never go back out there," I moan before dropping my head into my hands, despondent.

Nia leans over the upholstered chair I had scored from a yard sale and snuck in on a Saturday to add to the closet—not an easy feat at all—and reaches for my hands, pulling me up to my feet.

"You are an amazing badass bitch. And you're an awesome guidance counselor and help out so many people. You are hilarious and have so much heart. *And* you have an incredible ass. Ten outta ten." She pulls me into a hug—a rarity from Nia.

"You smell so good," I say, inhaling her cinnamon scent. "I wish I could unzip your body and crawl inside and hang out with you there."

Nia pulls away, shaking her head as she bites back a smile. "Some of these things you say *seriously* concern me."

"Yeah," I say with a long sigh. "Me, too."

Chapter Three

♡ *Fletcher*

I HAVE NEVER FELT more relieved than when I see the clock hit three p.m. Between the tea-scorching crotch incident this morning and countless snickers from the students as I got lost in the halls, I'm ready to get the hell out of here.

As the last of my students trickle out of my classroom, I grab my phone and unlock it to check if I have any notifications, smiling when I see a message from @TheMissGuidedCounselor. After I started following her online a year ago, we became fast friends. I found her when I was about to start my third year at Kenton, where every morning I was waking up with my stomach full of dread. No matter how much I loved teaching, I hated working there: the constant battles between the powerless teachers and condescending parents, the overentitled students, and the administration who cared only about raising more and more money.

It had begun to remind me of the life I had fought so hard to escape—the one where I had been basically born and bred to work in the wealth management fund my father had founded and oversaw with an iron fist. The same job where, after handing in my resignation letter, my father had shouted me out of his office, telling me I was making the worst mistake of my life to pursue teaching.

And then one night, wide awake at two in the morning, questioning whether my father *had* been right all along, I saw something that, well, changed my life. And on Instagram of all places.

I had been scrolling through my feed, something I admittedly did a lot when my anxiety about the day to come would twist my stomach into such a tight knot it was impossible to sleep, when I saw a post about how we only have one life and we need to live it in a way that will make us, and no one else, feel proud and fulfilled. I'm still not sure if it was the simplicity of those words—or the humor, kindness, and empathy in the ensuing caption—but that post spoke to me. I instantly began following the account @TheMissGuidedCounselor.

It was her advice that solidified my decision that I needed a change. I had initially taken the job at Kenton thinking that working at such a world-famous, prestigious school would impress my father. And even though I was miserable there, a small part of me *still* thought if I stuck it out long enough, my father would finally—*finally*—stop seeing me as the family disappointment who had walked away from a high-six-figure salary to pursue a "meaningless" career.

Before finally drifting off to sleep, I was messaging her, asking for her advice, a lightness on my shoulders that I hadn't felt in years. And when I had woken in the morning, @TheMissGuidedCounselor had already responded, encouraging me to see that it was okay to not be happy and to want more for myself.

Talking with @TheMissGuidedCounselor was the first time I had finally met someone who just…got it. Who understood

the inspiring highs and frustrating lows that came with educating the next generation. Who was passionate about her work
because it fed her soul. She got it—and she got me. She'd made
it all make sense.

Just because my first school placement had been a nightmare, that didn't mean I had made the wrong decision about
following my dream. It didn't mean my father had been right.
Though, in a weird way, it was his actions that finally gave me
the opportunity to leave Kenton for good. After all, if he hadn't
abandoned his wife of thirty-four years and blown up our entire
family, I never would have moved back home and transferred to
Harview.

Thanks, Dad.

My phone buzzes again, but before I can open her message,
a familiar face bursts into my classroom.

"You survived your first day!"

I drop my phone onto my desk as Brodie leans against the
whiteboard behind my desk. "How did it go?"

"It was definitely eventful. Thanks again so much for your
help earlier. Especially the whole announcing to the hallway
that my 'willy' had been violated."

Brodie laughs and wraps his arm around me, like we've
been old friends for years now. "This job is hard enough as it
is. Us teachers have to look out for one another. That was just
my friendly way of welcoming ye. And hey, at least you got the
worst of your shit on the first day. Can only get better from here,
right?"

I'm about to agree when I hear a *tap-tap* on the metal doorframe of my classroom. When I look up, I see the *only* thing in
the world that could make this day even worse.

What is *she* doing here?

"Fuck." The word slips out of my mouth and though it's a whisper, Brodie is close enough to hear it. He turns and presumably also sees the blond woman standing at the door, a strained smile on her red-lined lips. The same red lips that five years earlier had shattered my world with a single sentence: "I don't think I'm in love with you anymore."

Which is always hard to hear, of course, from the woman you love.

But then she followed that crushing blow by confessing she had fallen in love with another man. Who she had been cheating on me with for two months. Another harsh slap of painful reality across the face. But it wasn't until she revealed *who* that man was—my older brother—that the betrayal had felt less like a slap to the face and more like a knife twisting into my back, painfully severing every nerve ending until all my insides had collapsed into each other in one jumbled, messy clump of organs.

Yeah, it had been a shitty breakup.

And seeing her again feels like I've been cruelly shoved back into my twenty-five-year-old body, suffering through my first heartbreak—the moment that had me questioning everything in my life and ultimately led me to pursue teaching.

"Well, if it isn't Aldrich Fletcher in the flesh." My ex, Georgia Flannigan, strides in, her heels clicking loudly on the linoleum floor. The sound echoes, and I wonder if this will be the last sound I hear before I die, because I doubt my body can handle any more humiliation today. "When I saw the roster of this year's teachers, I couldn't believe it. I had to come see it for myself."

She walks up and sits on the edge of one of the student's desks in the first row. I catch a familiar whiff of her perfume, flooding me with another wave of memories I thought I had locked away forever. There had been a time in my life when I had craved the smell of that perfume and the woman who wore it. But that had been another time and another Fletcher. And while I have matured, acquiring a few stray gray hairs or so, she hasn't aged a day. She's just as beautiful—even more so, actually—than the last time I saw her. When she catches me looking her over, her smile widens, and she arches a perfectly manicured blond brow.

Brodie shoots me a curious look. "You two know each other?"

Georgia swivels her head from him to me, clearly waiting for me to answer. And though I teach history, the kind that Georgia and I share is not one I want to get into.

When I don't answer right away, Georgia turns back to Brodie, a tight-lipped smile on her face. "We actually used to date," she says, selectively skipping over the part where she dumped me for my brother.

Brodie drops into the empty seat behind my desk, his mouth agape. He's already seen my boxers this morning; might as well get a look at all my other dirty laundry. But I have other plans for myself: mainly getting the hell out of here as soon as humanly possible.

"Well, it's great seeing you again, Georgia," I say as I hoist my bag over my shoulder. "And thanks again for your help earlier, Brodie."

But Georgia stands and takes a step forward, blocking my exit to the door. "It's been years. We should catch up!"

I pause mid-step. Sure, enough time has passed that I've mostly gotten over our breakup, but it's still not a period of my life I want to revisit. Especially not now, and especially not here with Brodie. Although he doesn't look bothered; I think he's actually enjoying the drama. I guess, in a small way, I can repay him for his help earlier with the entertainment of my failed past relationship.

When she sees my hesitation, she takes a step forward. "Just dinner. Between friends." When I don't immediately respond, she adds, "For old time's sake."

I steal a glance at Brodie, who is watching with rapt attention. I'm not the greatest when it comes to confrontation. It's mostly a hazard of my upper-class New England breeding. When issues arose, my family would ignore them, preferring to pretend they didn't exist so as to keep "appearances up." Years later and I still struggle with expressing my actual feelings and opinions, which is why I so strongly value my online friendships, like with @TheMissGuidedCounselor.

Behind a computer screen, I can think before I reply—and there's no judgment if I'm insecure and unsure. I don't have to be the Fletcher who constantly worries about rocking the boat and upsetting the delicate dance my family all does to avoid confronting reality. In the safety of my DMs, I can express how angry I am at my father for abandoning his wife and my frustration at my mother's helplessness in the aftermath. I can rant about how my sister is self-centered and indifferent, and how my brother has chosen complete complacency toward our father in the interest of keeping his cushy job at the family business. And @TheMissGuidedCounselor would never judge me for any of it.

But I'm not @BravesGuy93 now. I'm plain old Fletcher—

and he just wants to get the hell out of here and run his sweaty palms under some icy cold water.

I draw my lips into a firm line, internally debating. I already have way too much on my shoulders. The last thing I need in my life is more drama. And yes, while going to dinner with my ex who dumped me for my brother is not my idea of a fun night, it's a hell of a lot easier than saying no and risking any workplace awkwardness. I came to Harview to fall back in love with teaching again, and I won't be able to if I am always sneaking down hallways or darting into the bathroom to avoid my ex. What was more painful? Dinner with Georgia or another year of dreading coming in to work each day?

"Maybe we can talk about it later?" I relent, wanting this conversation to end and for me to feel the cool autumn breeze on the back of my neck, where anxious sweat has already begun to pool. "I have to head out."

She smiles wider, masking any annoyance at my not-quite rejection. "Sure, sounds great."

She leaves with a half-wave, disappearing out the door and into the hall.

When she's out of earshot, Brodie turns toward me. His eyes are wide. "*She* was *your* girlfriend?" His face is a mask of utter confusion as he grazes his eyes over me in an astonished assessment that is beginning to make me feel a bit self-conscious. I nod, and he lets out a low whistle, shaking his head. "You are indeed a lucky man."

I pinch the bridge of my nose, feeling a headache coming on. And I know it's only going to get worse when I get home and find my mother holed up in her room, having not left her bed all day, and Liv, draped on the couch with her fingers covered in orange Cheetos dust, probably still hungover from the night before.

"You are going to have a good year at Harview," Brodie says, grinning. "I can sense these things. Now let's get you out of here. Work-life balance is very important, you know! I learned that from Miss Lucy. She's very good at giving advice, when she's not spilling her tea all over you!" He laughs and playfully elbows my side.

"Lucy?" I pause packing up my bag, my interest piqued by his mention of the gorgeous, tea-wielding woman from this morning.

He nods, a twinkle of excitement in his eye at my interest. "The guidance counselor. Pretty lady, eh?" His face darkens as he quickly shakes his head. "Well, no, I don't mean that. I know we're not supposed to comment on our colleagues' appearances. Though she is. Pretty, I mean." His cheeks turn a bright shade of red as he stumbles over his words. "But she gives great advice. Helps me a lot. Much cheaper than the therapist I hired after my wife died! Fifty dollars each visit. Can you believe it? And that's *with* my insurance! Anyways, we should get moving!"

Before I have the chance to respond—though what I would even say, I'm not entirely sure—he wraps his arm around my shoulder and starts half-dragging me out of the classroom.

I let him, distracted now by his mention of Lucy. *Lucy.* I like the way her name rolled off the tongue. Short and sweet—kind of like her. And Brodie was right—she was pretty. Beautiful. And memorable, that was for sure. Especially the way we met—her on her knees, drying me off with her scarf as she mumbles a string of apologies in this high-pitched voice, staring up at me with those big brown eyes. That is *not* a woman you easily forget.

As we reach the parking lot, I deftly slide out of Brodie's grasp and wave goodbye, digging my phone out of my pocket to feign a call. While I don't like lying, I have a feeling that if I don't, I will be stuck with Brodie in the parking lot until school starts up again tomorrow morning.

When he's out of sight, I pull out my keys and head toward my car, which I'd parked out of view at the far end of the lot. While I love my Audi hybrid, I feel uncomfortable driving a car that cost the equivalent of most of my colleagues' salaries to school every day. I had bought it when I was still working for my father at the family's hedge fund management firm and thought dropping six figures on a car was not only normal but expected. After all, we dealt in wealth management. Our lifestyles needed to reflect that—ridiculously overpriced cars and all.

I quickly pull out of the school lot and drive home, taking a minute to myself in the driveway before braving whatever chaos awaits.

The minute I do step inside, my sister, Liv, grabs me, a panicked expression on her face. "Mom is on another ice cream bender. You need to intervene. I just can't handle her right now."

I sigh and drop my bag on the floor. Back to reality.

"Fine, I'll handle it," I tell Liv, who looks instantly relieved as she disappears into the living room, her fingers tapping on her phone screen, probably already making plans to bolt from any responsibilities again for the next few days.

I suppress a sigh of annoyance at watching her eager retreat. I can't be too angry, considering we come from a family that has mastered the art of sweeping everything under expensive imported rugs. But I can't let my mom down, not when she's stuck in this depressive and self-destructive spiral. The worst part is, I don't know how to help her. As much as I would love to, I can't unbreak her heart.

I walk toward the kitchen, where I find my mother perched on a stool at the white marble kitchen island, shoveling down some neon pink strawberry ice cream chased by shots of Kahlúa. The combination makes my stomach churn, but it seems to be working for her.

Two days ago, my mother had left the denial stage of her grief over the end of her marriage and comfortably settled into the anger stage. While the progress is admirable, it's come with a lot of collateral damage. For one, the fire department was called after a neighbor spotted a quickly growing fire in our back-yard. My mother had piled up everything she could find of my father's—from errant mismatched socks to his old boxes from college—and lit the damn thing up. Luckily I had pulled into the driveway the exact moment the fire trucks had and was able to defuse the situation by promising that the Fletcher Founda-tion, the family's charitable foundation, would love to sponsor a table at their annual fundraiser.

Since that incident, Liv and I have taken shifts checking on our mother, who insists she is "perfectly fine" and has taken to calling herself a liberated woman. It doesn't take a shrink to tell us that our mother is one very close step to a complete breakdown.

It makes me really fucking hate my dad.

I guess you could also say I'm in the anger stage right there with her. My father has always been a distant man, reserved and slow to offer praise. When I was growing up, he was constantly at the office or on business trips, which we all accepted because we knew those long hours were what paid for our nice house with the indoor pool and our private-school educations. My mother's mantra for us growing up had been "now, let's not bother your father," while shuffling us out of his office.

And still…I never thought he would do this. Walk out on his wife of thirty-four years to shack up with his secretary turned mistress. It was too clichéd to feel real. Yet here we were.

But like my mother, I am not yet ready to advance to the bargaining or depression stages of grief. Really, I'm hoping to kind of just skip over those and move on to acceptance. My dad is an asshole: I accept this.

Only I'm not quite there yet.

I step into the kitchen and take the seat next to my mom, draping my arm around her. She leans into me, offering me a weak smile. After a long moment, she pulls away and looks up at me, her brow furrowed. "Hey, Aldy." My mother is the only one allowed to use that particular nickname for Aldrich. "How was your first day?"

I shrug. "Nothing special. You doing okay today?"

She shakes her head and pulls my hand into hers. "I don't want this," she says, gesturing toward herself, "to screw you up about falling in love. Don't get cynical and jaded on me, okay?"

I suppress the urge to let out a sigh. We've had this conversation *many* times already, despite my constantly reassuring her that I am perfectly fine. After Georgia cheated on me, I had admittedly fallen into a similar self-destructive cycle.

Like I said, we Fletchers have a tendency to avoid our problems and pretend they simply do not exist. So, when the inevitable crash with reality *does* happen, we don't tend to handle it well. We run away, deflect, and turn to anger (or sometimes ice cream and Kahlúa). And I can see that same fear in my mother's eyes now that I've moved back home—she's worried I'm going to run away, hide away from all the chaos as our family falls apart like I always have. And as much as I try to reassure her that I won't, I know there is a part of her that has doubts.

Because there's a part of me that does, too. Am I really strong enough to stand here and weather this storm with her?

"I won't let that happen, Mom. I promise. Besides, I *just* started a new job, I have enough going on without needing to worry about finding a girlfriend."

My mom eyes me, scanning my face as a sad smile crosses her lips. "Okay, Aldy." She slides out of her seat and blows out a sigh. "I think tonight calls for a hot bath and a good book." She leans over and presses a kiss to my cheek. "I'm very proud of you. Have I told you that recently?"

I chuckle, shaking my head. "Well, it's been at least thirteen hours, so you're slacking, Mom."

She squeezes my arm. "I'm going to get through this. I don't want you to worry about me."

"I'm not," I lie.

My mother leans over and presses a kiss to my forehead before trudging out of the kitchen. Her blond hair is matted to the back of her head, and she's been wearing the same clothes for three days now.

My stomach sinks as I watch her go. I returned home to help my mom put the pieces of her life back together, and I'm failing miserably. Putting together the pieces my father's betrayal broke is harder than I anticipated, and I'm becoming less and less sure I am capable of the task.

Whenever I begin to doubt myself, though, I turn to @The-MissGuidedCounselor. So I slide my phone out of my pocket and open up our latest string of messages. She has an unwavering faith in me that, in moments like this, is sometimes the only thing that keeps me from sinking into the same pit of despair my mother is currently in. It's a lot of pressure to be the one holding together all these broken pieces, balancing each one delicately enough to not allow their jagged edges to cut me. But @The-MissGuidedCounselor *gets* it, like she gets everything about me.

> **BravesGuy93**   **4:49 PM**
> Hey
> You got time to talk? Having a rough time with my mom again.

Her response only takes a minute, and when I see her words float up my screen, heaviness lifts off my shoulders.

> **TheMissGuidedCounselor**   **4:50 PM**
> I've always got time for you.

TheMissGuidedCounselor
Posted at 1:15 PM

Have you ever had an embarrassing incident at work? Maybe a student caught you secretly recording the newest TikTok dance in your classroom during your lunch break. Or perhaps you accidentally bumped into a colleague and spilled your pasta Bolognese all over their crisp white shirt. Whatever the situation, just remember to keep a good sense of humor and give yourself the grace to accept you aren't perfect and keep on smiling—chances are, no one even noticed your little mishap!

After all, mistakes are what make us human ♥

Liked by **BravesGuy93** and **others**

TheMissGuidedCounselor What do you...more

View all comments

Chapter Four

♡ Lucy

"ARE YOU SURE HE'S gone?"

Nia rolls her eyes but nods. "He just drove away. Trust me, you're in the clear." She grips my shoulders and lightly shakes me. "You can leave your office now. You're already like ten minutes late."

My stomach clenches with guilt. I'm *never* late. I hate being late. It is mostly due to my anxiety, but you would think that growing up in both a Mexican and Moroccan family, two cultures that have *very* flexible relationships with time, I would have mellowed out by the ripe old age of twenty-eight. I have not.

I decide to trust Nia that the new teacher has exited the building and grab my bag and gigantic binder. She escorts me down the hall, hyping me up for my least favorite responsibility as a guidance counselor: my weekly Konfident Kids Klub meetings.

It's the main reason I dread every single Monday. I mean, Mondays are bad enough and then you add in me being forced to read from a horribly outdated textbook from the 1990s to a room of teenage girls desperate to be anywhere else. About 99 percent of them were sent to me as punishment—the rest have been forced to attend by their horribly confused parents, who actually think this forty-minute curriculum will instill confidence in their child, who is a fumbling, awkward mess solely because they are fifteen years old. Who isn't a fumbling, awkward mess at fifteen?

When we arrive outside the door of the small theater rehearsal room we meet in, Nia wiggles her eyebrows. "Got your hood and tiki torch ready?"

I groan and shoot Nia an annoyed look. To her credit, she shoots me a remorseful smile before slithering down the hallway back to her classroom. It's bad enough that I am forced to lead this club, but why the hell did the school have to use a curriculum with the initials KKK? It's now a terrible running joke for the whole school, and while I have *begged*—well, via email—for the board to change the curriculum, their argument is that we don't have the budget.

So here I am, stuck for another twenty-eight minutes as the teacher in charge of Konfident Kids Klub, or, as the students secretly call me—which I unfortunately learned last year and likewise tried to stop (well, emailed teachers to tell their students)—the "grand wizard" of the most awkward and delinquent children of my high school. Lovely.

I enter the room and greet my hodgepodge group of students, who have already assembled the chairs into our curriculum-mandated "semicircle of trust." While I recognize most of them from last year, I'm pleasantly surprised to spot a few new faces who have joined or who otherwise got very lost and mistakenly ended up here.

Not coincidentally (nor for the first time), none of the students have set out a chair for me—I'm not included in the semicircle of trust. Not that I can blame them—I am, after all, the one forcing this outdated, boring, and cringe-worthy curriculum on them. But still, it would be nice if they tried. I mean, theoretically, shouldn't the forty minutes I hold them hostage each week give them at least a small dose of Stockholm syndrome?

Like, just enough to maybe include me in the semicircle of trust or at least for one of them to offer to read aloud from the binder so we're not all stuck listening to *me* drone on about antiquated nineties references and the importance of not having underage sex?

I pull over a chair, smile, and sit down. None of the students are talking to each other, preferring to stare at their phones. If it were up to me, this group would consist of us sharing memes while I assure them all that life after high school is infinitely better because you don't have to live with your parents and you can stay up as late as you want and people don't shove you into lockers anymore. But as I reflect on that, I realize that even though I *did* move out, I only managed to make it forty feet or so to the house across the street.

And I still eat most of my meals at our family restaurant or my parents' house.

And while, yes, I can stay up as late as I want, I rarely make it past eleven.

Damn. Has my life improved *at all* since leaving high school a freaking decade ago? Who am I to be teaching confidence when I am the biggest, most unconfident mess of them all?

"Uh, Ms. Galindo?"

The sound of a student's voice pulls me out of my head. I look over to see her concerned face. "Are you okay?"

Well, *that* is a loaded question. Truthfully, I am still mildly traumatized from this morning. After all, I am the very definition of a wallflower, and wallflowers are meant to lurk in the shadows and be ignored, not be thrust into the center of the teachers' lounge attacking the hot new teacher. That went against the very laws of nature.

Before I can even stop myself, I burst into tears.

Full on, body-heaving ugly tears. Remember that Kim Kardashian meme where she's crying over her failed seventy-two-day marriage to Kris Humphries? Yep, that's me, just with a lot less mascara and a hell of a lot less dignity.

And while I want to stop, and quite frankly know I *need* to stop, I can't. That whole "I'm a crier" thing? Yeah, I wasn't exaggerating. For the first half of my life, my frequent crying episodes—followed by intense periods of silence when I would lock myself away in my room for hours—were dismissed as the travails of a young girl who was perhaps just a tad too emotional. I was a mystery to my parents. They had endured *real* struggles in their lives—like poverty, settling into a new country without any family, and literally walking twenty miles in the snow to get to school (the last was actually a complete lie—it took my sisters and me far too long to realize that it never snows in Rabat).

They had never felt the crushing weight of being so sad that simply taking a shower felt like an insurmountable task.

After all, I couldn't quite decipher the why myself. My world was perfect: I had countless relatives, two loving parents, and two sisters, who all adored me. I did well in school, and while I wasn't the most popular, I had a small circle of friends. I had hobbies and liked to sing in the shower and spend hours reading outdoors.

Yet, for most of my life, I felt like I was wearing a mask that hid the scared, broken girl behind it. Eventually, wearing it joined the list of things that felt too overwhelming, and I just became a person who didn't necessarily want to die, but rather wanted to just…cease existing. In my wildest fantasies, I would get in a car accident with a drunken Kennedy and spend a year or so in a coma before waking up to a cool five million in hush money. But how do you explain that fantasy to *anyone* without sounding utterly insane?

The worst part of being diagnosed with depression and anxiety is that even when I do everything "right"—take my medications and drink my water and eat somewhat healthily and force myself to exercise a few times a week—I can still succumb to that rain cloud that lurks just a few steps behind me at all times. My life is an endless walk across a never-ending tightrope. I know that if I fall, I have a loving family to catch me.

But my family can't always be there.

Today, my safety net consists of eleven high school students—half of whom look utterly traumatized at the sight of their school's guidance counselor falling apart at the seams.

A tentative hand pats me on my back. And then another. I look up to see my ragtag horde circling me. They don't say much, but those tiny and awkward supportive pats on my back give me the strength I need to swipe my hand across my face, wiping away my tears. "Thank you, all. I'm so sorry I am such a mess today."

And while I wish I could leave it there, grab our twenty-pound binder, and continue with this week's lesson, which might be about anything from saying no to drugs by using a fun rap that rhymes the words *reefer* and *geezer* (both words I had to translate to my students) to role-playing how to inform a teacher that they need a "sanitary napkin" for "menstruation purposes," I am not *just* Lucy here. I'm Ms. Galindo, guidance counselor *and* this group's "konfident" leader. I need to pull my shit together.

"So," I start, clearing my throat. "I'm sorry for my little, well, meltdown. Sometimes when I get overwhelmed or even when I'm really angry or frustrated, my body's reaction is to cry. Weirdly enough, crying sometimes helps make me feel better, and even though I'm not afraid to admit I'm a little embarrassed to have cried in front of all of you, I'm feeling a lot better and really grateful to you for comforting me."

I force a pained smile to my face as eleven blank faces stare back at me. Apparently seeing their guidance counselor bawling out of nowhere has not fazed them in the slightest. These kids terrify me.

"Uh, Ms. Galindo?" Trina Monaghan says, breaking the uncomfortable silence. A sophomore, she suffers from a severe case of middle-child syndrome, something I know *very* well myself. Her older sister, Kelly, is the head of the cheerleading squad and one of the most popular girls in the senior class and her younger sister, Monica, skipped three grades and is a quasi-genius. Trina, though she can't see it, is an amazing artist, a fantastic writer, and has more empathy in her little finger than most people have in their entire bodies.

For all of those reasons—and because her mom owns a bakery and Trina sneaks me weekly treats—Trina happens to be one of my favorite students, and I'm excited to see her back this year.

"Yes, Trina?"

She bites down on her lip and shares a glance with another

student to her right. "Do you think we could maybe, I don't know, like, skip the binder today? Since it's the first day of school?" To my surprise, the other students murmur in quiet consent.

"Really?" I mean I know that *I* hate the binder. It's antiquated, and the examples are borderline ridiculous, but everyone always seemed to go along with it. I flip to the chapter we should be covering today—*Setting Healthy Boundaries Is Da Bomb!*—and slam the binder shut. "No, you're right. We can take a break this week. Is there something you wanted to talk about instead?"

She giggles nervously. "Uh, anything else. Like literally anything."

I laugh and drop the binder to the ground, where it lands with a loud thud. "Okay, literally anything. I can do that."

"Why were you crying?" Rachel, one of the sophomores, asks with a slight lisp (thanks to the thousands of dollars of dentistry currently in her mouth).

The other students lean in with interest. I should have known better when I had agreed to "literally anything." I've walked into this, leaving myself wide open.

Maybe we do need to revisit *Setting Healthy Boundaries Is Da Bomb!* because clearly my students have zero issues delving into my personal life. Which, to be fair, they had been unwilling participants in a mere few seconds ago.

I wave my hand, forcing an unaffected, casual smile on my face. "Oh, you know. Long day!"

Trina hums, shaking her head. "You said that the semicircle of trust was a safe place where we could be honest with each other."

"Yeah, and you're always making us share *our* feelings," Rachel adds.

"Well, yeah," I admit. "But I am really fine. I just had a moment of…like a moment of *bleghness*." My smile, and my entire façade, is fading—and fast. And these girls know it.

They stare me down, engulfing me in an intimidating veil of silence, where all I can do is try to think of a way to telekinetically set off the fire alarm. But instead, I crack. In less than five seconds.

"I just had a hard day today and embarrassed myself, and I can't stop thinking about it and feeling worse."

Trina leans forward, dropping her elbows on her knees. The other students look equally rapt and engaged. I have never once been able to hold their attention like this, and it feels good, but also terrifying. These are the youth of tomorrow; I cannot risk totally traumatizing them even more.

"So what happened?" she asks.

I pause, choosing my words more carefully. "I, well, I had an embarrassing encounter with the new—in front of someone new, and I'm embarrassed about it."

"Oh, do you mean when you groped the new history teacher?" Poppy asks. The seemingly sweet sophomore—who I have never heard say more than five words—has now called me out for spilling boiling hot tea on the new history teacher and then idiotically trying to clean it up. While I am immensely proud to see Poppy engaging in conversation with her peers, did it have to be at this very moment and on this very topic?

The other students look admiringly upon Poppy, and I feel kind of like a sacrificial lamb.

I wonder if this is how Isaac felt right before he realized his dad was going to stab him in the gut. Like he was obviously pissed his dad was going to murder him, but he must have been a *little* proud his dad was following God's instructions so well?

Yeah, that analogy might be a stretch.

"I did not grope anyone!" I clarify, my voice coming out in a shriek and totally sounding guilty. "And let's remember, groping is *bad*. We should not be groping anyone, and if we are groped upon, we need to tell a safe adult right away. Like me. So, please do *not* grope, but if you are groped, tell me right away."

Oh my God, could I be messing this up any more? I need to *stop* talking about groping before Chris Hansen bursts into this classroom. "Anyway, who is saying that I grope—err…inappropriately touched the new history teacher?"

"Everyone," they answer in unison.

"Oh, shit," I mutter before slapping a hand over my mouth. Although I did allow swearing in our semicircle of trust, I need to be a role model for my students. And right now, I'm gloriously failing at the task. "I just…it happened this morning in the teachers' lounge! How do all the students already know?"

They all shrug.

"I mean, stuff gets around, I guess," Trina responds. "It's high school."

"Okay, well…" I pinch the bridge of my nose, collecting my thoughts. This is new territory for me, since I've never been popular enough—in high school or in adulthood—to be the source of any kind of gossip. One of the benefits, after all, of being a wallflower is that your presence tends to go unnoticed, something which I *very* much appreciate.

"Look, I get that gossip can be fun. Trust me, no one devoured a *J-14* faster than your girl right here."

The girls shoot each other quizzical looks at my apparently archaic reference to *J-14*, a pivotal cultural touchpoint in my youth that means nothing to the next generation.

"It was a celebrity gossip magazine," I clarify. "Anyways, while gossip *can* be fun, it can also be really hurtful and embarrassing. Who here would want one of their most vulnerable or humiliating moments to be shared with *everyone* they know?" I look around the room to see a group of bashful teens, cheeks tinged red with a mixture of embarrassment and discomfort.

"And I know it can be really hard to not join in," I continue, "especially with how easy it is to share something with a single tap of your finger on social media, but we have to try to remember that there is a real human being on the end of that gossip. Someone who might get hurt. And I know it can be awkward to confront someone who is spreading gossip, so I'm not asking you to do that." I hold up my two palms. "All I ask is that *before* you share any hot gossip you've heard, take a minute to ask yourself if those words might hurt or embarrass someone and if that is something *you* want to be a part of."

The girls are all silent for a long moment, and I'm hopeful they're taking the time to digest my words instead of being completely tuned out like they are 95 percent of the time during these meetings.

"Wait, but if it's true, like if you *did* grope the new teacher, doesn't that mean it's not a rumor? Like aren't we just sharing facts?" Rachel asks.

I fight against the urge to toss this binder out the window, with me following closely behind. This is a learning opportunity, after all. Let's not crank up the gossip mill again by jumping out the second-floor window.

"Okay, well, that's a good question, Rachel. So let's say something is true—which it very clearly is *not*," I rush to add. "Then it's still not a kind thing to do, because we are embarrassing someone. Well, embarrassing me."

The girls all look at me, little light bulbs going off simultaneously above their heads.

"We're sorry, Ms. Galindo," Trina says, a contrite expression on her face as she bites down on her bottom lip. "I mean, I didn't mean to spread that whole groping thing. I heard it from Daphne and Ricardo, but then I only told John about it. Well, Shondra was there, but I don't know if she was listening." Trina glances down before looking back up at me, a nervous and guilty smile on her face. "Oh, and I might have maybe, sort of, also talked about it at lunch."

At least they all look remorseful. And who could blame them? When I was their age, teacher gossip had been the most exciting topic of conversation. *Was Mr. Monroe dating Ms. Chernov? And didn't you see Mrs. Rogoff totally steal that cookie from the cafeteria?*

I shake my head and smile at my students. "It's okay. What's done is done. But I hope we can all learn a valuable lesson from this in that spreading rumors, or even the truth, can hurt people."

The girls all nod thoughtfully as they consider my words. I feel victorious, having imparted an important life lesson on the impressionable youth of tomorrow. The next time they hear some new rumor crop up again, they will stand up tall and refuse to pass it along, having learned this invaluable life lesson I have bestowed upon them.

I deserve a medal for this. I am a goddamn national treasure.

Trina tilts her head to the side and looks at me. "Wait, so you admit that what happened was true then?"

I look down at the binder and then wistfully out the window, silently calculating whether a broken leg would be *more* painful than this moment.

Yeah, it's a toss-up.

TheMissGuidedCounselor
Posted at 7:22 AM

Five Ways to Feel More Confident at Work:

1. Stop Comparing Yourself to Others: There is a reason why people say comparison is the thief of joy. Look, we are all on different journeys with different resources, abilities, responsibilities, and more. Don't be unfair to yourself by comparing your path to someone else's!

2. Remember Your Strengths: What is it that only *you* can bring to the table? What is your "special sauce"? Keep a running list—on your phone or on sticky notes—of all your positive strengths and take the time to remind yourself how amazing you are!

3. Wear Something You Feel Confident In: Grab your power suit and your favorite (sensible) heels or stylish oxfords and let your clothing help boost your confidence. When you look good, you feel good!

4. Speak Up and Ask Questions: A lot of people think asking questions indicates that they don't know what they are doing. However, speaking up and asking for help can strengthen your understanding!

5. Set Goals and Celebrate Successes: Set small, actionable, and measurable goals that will help guide you to becoming the confident leader you know is inside you! And make sure to take the time to celebrate, recognizing that each goal you meet is leveling up your confidence—and your career!

Have an amazing day at school and remember: "With confidence, you have won before you have started" (Marcus Garvey)

Liked by **BravesGuy93** and **others**

TheMissGuidedCounselor Here to…more

View all comments

TheMissGuidedCounselor
Today at 8:03 AM

BravesGuy93
I need some clarity from your post this morning. Specifically, is six inches too high to be considered a "sensible" heel?

TheMissGuidedCounselor
It is my humble opinion that a six-inch heel is the *least* sensible heel size there is. You are practically asking to break an ankle wearing something that high. May I suggest a more modest two- or three-inch heel with an orthopedic insert?

BravesGuy93
Mm, I like to live on the edge. I think I'll go with the six-inchers.

TheMissGuidedCounselor
Your funeral. Anyway, you ready for another exciting day at work?

BravesGuy93
You mean more exciting than embarrassing myself in front of all the new teachers AND running into

my ex-girlfriend who completely shattered my heart with a spiked baseball bat?

TheMissGuidedCounselor
Ouch, that's a brutal visual!
And yes, it will definitely be hard to top that first day, but from what little you shared, it sounds like you managed to escape relatively unscathed.
You sure you don't want to talk about what happened? I bet it was not at all as embarrassing as you thought it was.

BravesGuy93
No, but thanks.
And I'm sure you're right that it wasn't probably that bad.
I just feel like I have a lot on my plate with starting this new job and then when I got home, my mom was having a rough day and even though I tried comforting her with all those ideas you gave me, it felt like nothing I said was working.
It's hard not to feel like moving back home and transferring to this new job might have been a horrible mistake.

TheMissGuidedCounselor
Ugh, I'm sorry.
Transitions are always hard, and
you also have no time to process
all these changes because you are
busy supporting your mom.
And I am sure your words have
more of an impact than you realize.
Sometimes just holding space for
her and letting her feel safe to cry in
your presence can do so much more
than words can.
You're an amazing son and friend,
and I'm here for whatever you need.

BravesGuy93
Thanks for the pep talk. I'm so
thankful to have you as a friend.
And truthfully, my first day here
wasn't so terrible. If anything it
was...pretty memorable.

 TheMissGuidedCounselor
Memorable in a good way or a
bad way?

BravesGuy93
I think time will tell, but I can't help
but feel it was in a good way.

Chapter Five

 *Lucy*

IN THE GALINDO HOUSEHOLD, most meals come with a healthy dose of unsolicited, and often unhelpful, advice. And thanks to a moment of vulnerability when I had arrived home yesterday and called my sisters in a panic, I am now the subject of the aforementioned unwanted advice over an impressive breakfast spread of scrambled eggs mixed with chorizo, fried beans smothered with crumbled cotija cheese, and an alarmingly tall stack of pancakes.

At my side, my younger sister, Julieta, grips my shoulders as she locks our eyes, a stern expression on her face. "Okay, repeat after me: I am a warrior. I am strong. I am a secure, confident, and independent woman."

I groan but mumble out the affirmations, knowing that if I don't, my sister will hold me captive. Beside me, my mother frowns and shakes her head before leaning over to pour more potatoes from her plate onto mine. "You need to eat."

I restrain from rolling my eyes. My mother's solution to most problems is a hearty serving of food—preferably carbs. But I don't think my stomach can handle much this morning—not when I have to go back to work and face the entire school, which will, no doubt, be abuzz about how quiet little Ms. Galindo felt up the hot new history teacher.

I have worked very hard these last few years to be as anonymous as possible. And now, thanks to my clumsiness and preference for hot beverages, all that has been ruined.

"I think she's panicking again. Look how red her cheeks are getting."

I glare at my older sister, Amira, sitting beside my aunt on the other side of the table. Both watch me with concerned frowns, as if silently calculating how close I am to collapsing into a pile of tears.

"I am not panicking," I bite out. I'm lying. I'm totally panicking. And everyone here knows it.

Julieta reaches for my hands and gives them a gentle squeeze, calming me slightly. "We know this is hard for you, and we're both very proud of you."

I love both my sisters, but I have such a gushy soft spot for our youngest, Julieta. She was the surprise baby, and I grew up coddling her like my very own baby doll. She returned the favor by always having my back. Julieta is also quiet like me, an astute observer of everyone else around her, and is able to discern a lot about people just from the way they act. It is an incredibly valuable skill, because she is usually the first person who can see when the heavy weight of my depression becomes too hard for me to carry, meaning she's sure to be at my house with open arms and warm chocolate chip cookies.

Julieta's words remind me I am at a crossroads. I can let the floodgate of tears pour out of me, or I can hold them back, put on a brave face, and not waste sacred PTO on hiding from the inevitable jokes that will come my way today. As tempting as it sounds to hide in bed all day, I know that it will just sink me deeper into this sandpit.

So I force a smile and nod. "I'm okay. I'm just nervous about all the gossip."

"If anyone tries to say anything, tell them they are banned from the restaurant!" my mother declares. She really thinks denying random strangers access to our family restaurant is a fierce enough punishment to scare anyone from bullying her middle child.

"No!" my aunt cries. "Don't say that! We can't afford to lose so many customers."

I groan and drop my head to the table as my mother and aunt begin to vehemently argue about the financial implications of banning my future hypothetical bullies versus allowing them to order takeout. It's soon clear that—due to the potential volume of lost customers—they are leaning toward takeout only.

I look up when I feel Julieta tugging me out of my chair. "Okay, well, Lulu needs to get off to work," she cheerfully announces, "so Amira and I are going to walk her to her car."

My mother rushes to give me a dozen kisses before resuming her argument with my aunt, and my sisters and I slip outside to walk back across the street to my house. Each step closer feels like another step toward my grave.

When we reach my car, Julieta turns me to face her. "You're going to be okay, you know."

Her smile almost convinces me that she might be right. Sure, half the school faculty will probably ridicule me today, but I could survive it—just like I survived much harder obstacles that have come my way: with the support of my family, my anti-anxiety PRN, and the expired Halloween candy I keep stashed in my freezer.

I nod. "Thank you both for coming last night and staying over."

"Anytime. Your bed is way comfier than mine." Amira presses a quick kiss to my cheek, turns, then spins back around instead of leaving. Unclasping the gold bracelet around her wrist, she transfers it to mine. "Hold on to this for a while. It will help you keep anyone who tries to make fun of you in check."

I glance down and raise a brow at the small gold filigree charm of an upward-facing palm, with the mirrored symmetry of two fingers pointed outward. "A hamsa?"

"Yes, to ward off any evil bitches from messing with you."

I finger the charm. If only it were that easy. "Thanks, Amira. Now, I need to get going."

I slide into the driver's seat, and as I pull out of my driveway, I see the two of them arguing. I love my sisters, but sometimes I also get the urge to strangle them. In a loving, sisterly way, of course.

The drive is less than five minutes. It takes me twice that amount of time to motivate myself to leave my car. When I reach the school's entrance, I steel myself, taking a second to adjust my skirt and iron out invisible wrinkles with my hand before pushing the gray doors and stepping inside.

I look down at the hamsa dangling from my wrist. "I hope you're up for this, buddy."

I will *not* let yesterday's teapocalypse send me down a spiral of self-loathing and shame. People have accidents all the time, and in the grand scheme of things, this wasn't even *that* bad. No one was (seriously) injured, and as far as I know, there was no video evidence to post online and share eight million times. I refuse to end this day eating pizza over my kitchen sink like some divorced dad who doesn't know how to wash dishes. I am better than that.

Though I do think I will order pizza tonight, because I have a coupon floating around in my kitchen's junk drawer that expires next week.

Nope, I am *not* letting anyone get to me today. I am going to face all the jokes and jabs this morning, and hopefully everyone will just get it out of their system so I can make it through the rest of my day. The stakes are too high: there's pizza involved now. I push open the door to the teachers' lounge and do a quick assessment of the room.

To the left, sitting at a round table, are all the foreign language teachers. They like to get together and remark on how cultured they are. While they do tend to bring the tastiest foods to the staff potlucks, that entire table is pretty much the embodiment of that one girl who went to France for a semester and came back wearing a beret and insisting on saying croissant the "right" way, confusing the poor cashiers at Dunkin' Donuts.

At the next table beside them are the boss babes. These are the teachers who wear maxi skirts with chevrons and sell essential oils or hot dog–patterned leggings or dildos in their free time and call themselves small business owners. You always have to be careful when talking with them, because they will inevitably try to recruit you to join their "tribe" (which, *ugh*, talk about gross and appropriative language) that is really just either a pyramid scheme or a cult in the making. Sometimes both. Despite my love of buying sex toys from my colleagues—I mean, you see this is ludicrous, right?—I tend to steer far, far away unless they are offering free samples.

I *never* pass on free samples.

Next to them is the table I like to avoid at all costs, mostly because the people there serve as a constant reminder of everything I lack. You know that knot in your stomach you get when scrolling through Instagram, seeing all the perfectly toned bikini bodies prancing along white beaches in some exotic location? Well, that's basically how I feel every time I see them: the Pinterest Posse. They're the teachers with flawless skincare routines and polished nails who decorate their classrooms to rival any spread in *Architectural Digest*. And their queen B is the stunningly perfect Georgia Flannigan.

If Barbie came to life and rode a Peloton bike six days a week, she would be Georgia. She has long blond hair that, even under fluorescent lighting, always seems to be shiny and soft, unlike the mess of tight coils that I usually gather haphazardly in a bun at the top of my head, held precariously together by a neon pink pencil I found in my desk drawer. Her skin has zero pores and is the shade of porcelain that looks like it's never been touched by the sun.

And unlike me—and Lizzie McGuire—she never repeats a single outfit, showing up each day in clothes perfectly tailored to her model-ready, size 2 body. All the female students idolize her, ranking her outfits every day. She has never received below a 7.5.

I'm always too scared to ask what my ranking is, or if my weekly rotation of Ann Taylor discount blazers is even worth ranking. My fragile self-esteem doesn't need any more damage. But a quick scan of my matching black pencil skirt, shell, and blazer—with my peacock scarf, which is now a literal accessory to my crime—confirms I am not going to be on any best-dressed list. I mean, I look like a server from Olive Garden.

Basically, these are the teachers who would never trip over their own two feet and accidentally fondle someone.

Behind their table is the coffee bar. And by coffee bar, I mean a single hot water kettle and packets of instant coffee and expired Earl Grey. I bring my own tea bags and have my chamomile tea stashed in my pocket. My mug—the same culprit from yesterday's incident—is in my hand. My plan is to hold my head up high and get this damn tea. After all, I am a warrior. I am strong. I am a secure, confident, and independent woman and whatever else Julieta had forced me to say earlier this morning.

With a renewed sense of purpose, I stroll toward the coffee bar in the tame two-inch heels I dug out of my closet this morning. While I don't own a power suit, I thought it was probably a good idea to at least try to take my own advice. Though if anything, these heels make me feel even less confident as they loudly clack across the tiled floor.

Too late to change shoes now.

Pretending that I don't even notice the entire teachers' lounge watching me with wide-eyed amusement, I *click-clack* my way across the room to fill up my mug with hot water and exchange a few pleasantries with Tania, the art teacher, and Brodie, the gym teacher/badminton coach with the swoon-worthy Scottish brogue. When done, I exhale a breath of relief: I am victorious! All I have to do now is dump the tea bag wrapper, fake a phone call, and dart out of the teachers' lounge, and I am in the clear!

Prepared to lie low until whatever new scandal hits the school later today.

But before I can escape, a hand wraps around my arm, long, slender fingers with perfectly polished red nails. She even has a gold sparkly accent nail. See what I mean? A living, breathing Pinterest board.

"Oh, Lucy," Georgia coos, "I was thinking about you all last night. Wondering how on earth you must be feeling"—she leans in to whisper, even though everyone can still very clearly hear her—"after that little incident yesterday!"

As if on cue, the rest of her table tut sympathetically. I wonder if they all met up earlier this morning to rehearse.

I force a tight-lipped smile, repeating the words I had memorized and rehearsed in front of the mirror last night. "You are so kind to worry, but I can assure you I'm perfectly fine." I hold up my mug of tea and widen my smile, this time displaying all my teeth because I read an article once that it makes you look more believable.

Dakota, the sophomore English teacher—Georgia's best friend, likely due to their shared childhood trauma of being named after US states—frowns. "Oh, Lucy, it's okay to be embarrassed. I mean, if it were me"—she presses her hand to her chest—"I don't think I would ever recover. I would want to just die! Like literally, seriously just die!"

Subtle, Dakota.

I wish I had something clever to say, but my mind is blank. My best comebacks only manifest days later, when I'm in the shower, replaying the conversation in my head for the hundredth time. It is so unfair how I can be so witty online behind a keyboard but absolutely speechless in real life.

But to my complete and utter shock, it's *Georgia* who speaks up, breathing out a huff of annoyance. "Please, Dakota, didn't you accidentally flash the entire PTA when you had your skirt tucked into your underwear at the spring fundraiser last year? I would think *that* would be more mortifying."

Dakota and I are both stunned into silence at Georgia's snappy remark. Based on my accumulated knowledge of Georgia, I am fairly confident she is *not* defending me. But still, I can't help but feel the teensiest bit grateful at her humbling Dakota and taking some of the attention off me.

I can sense the tension percolating between the two, and as much as I would love to witness whatever comes next, I am worried that I could easily be collateral damage. It's time to retreat.

But before I can come up with an excuse—*any* excuse—to leave, a shadow lands beside me, and when I turn to look, I see the very victim of my assault by tea and reason for my extreme IBS last night.

To my surprise, he smiles at me, and I take a good second to soak in being its focus. Cause it's a great smile. Like, *really* great. Everything about him is great, now that I'm looking. Perfect teeth. Friendly brown eyes. A not too big but still pronounced nose and cute wavy brown hair that looks super fun to run your hands through. He looks like he plays golf on the weekend and pops his Ralph Lauren collar while drinking "brewskis."

"Sorry I didn't get a chance to introduce myself yesterday. I'm Fletcher," he says, looking directly at me and not at the gorgeous specimen of a human being to my side as he extends his hand.

My mouth drops open as I gape at him in response. This is not right. He's breaking some unspoken rule in which you must greet people in order of hotness. Kinda like how they do it in the royal household with titles but based on waist and hip circumference.

Still, I offer my hand, sliding it into his. He has surprisingly soft hands, much warmer than Georgia's cold fish-like tentacles. It feels good. Familiar, in a kind of weird way.

Our hands linger just a second too long, veering dangerously close to being as inappropriate as my fondling of his junk a short twenty-four hours ago, and I quickly pull my hand away.

"I'm really sorry about yesterday," I tell him.

I like the way the corners of his eyes crinkle when he smiles. It's kind of disarming, which must explain why the next sentence leaves the safe recesses of my thoughts that I keep under strict lock and key between 7:20 a.m. and 2:45 p.m. and travels out of my mouth. "You know, usually a guy buys me dinner before I'm on my knees like that."

Fletcher's eyes bug open, and Georgia loudly gasps at my side. In my two years here, I don't think I've ever made a joke—certainly not a sexual one. Definitely not with half my coworkers as the audience.

And absolutely never in front of one of the hottest guys I've ever laid eyes on.

Shit. Shit. *Shit.*

But before I can apologize again, Fletcher is laughing. *Hysterically.* Like, full-bodied, bent-over laughing. Despite thinking it impossible, I'm actually even more horrified now.

"Sorry," he says between a burst of laughter, probably noticing the traumatized expression on my face. "I'm sorry. That was just really funny."

How the hell did I allow myself to even say that? It was so... inappropriate! This is *not* me—Ms. Galindo the wallflower, who keeps her head down and hides in abandoned storage closets. This was the unfiltered, unchaperoned voice in my head that I never let out unless I'm with my sisters or Nia.

He and his stupid adorable smile and dreamy brown eyes had to have made me do this.

"I have to go and uh, go." I mumble out a goodbye—at least I think that's what I say—and scurry out the door, running directly into Nia and only narrowly avoiding another teapocalypse.

She takes a step back and gestures to my mug. "*That* is a lethal weapon."

I shake my head in response. "Nope, my mouth is."

Chapter Six

♡ Lucy

"JUST SO I'M UNDERSTANDING this clearly, you want to drop out of high school because DJ Breezy Buzz Boo liked one of your pictures on Instagram?"

The student across from me smiles and pumps her fist in victory. "Yes! Finally, you get it!"

I hold up my hand.

I absolutely do *not* get it. If anything, the only revelation I'm having is that I shouldn't have stayed up so late watching cat videos on TikTok because I am way too tired to be having this conversation. At least it's Friday, and after our family dinner tonight, I can pass out and sleep in tomorrow. Though, knowing me, I will probably still stay up far too late watching even more cat videos.

But I also brought this upon myself when I spotted Sophia in the hall five minutes ago and cornered her. I have been hoping to pin her down early in the school year to keep her focused on her academics. As much as she tries to hide it, Sophia is academically gifted, and if she slacks off like she did last year, she could be seriously jeopardizing her chances of getting into a good school or scoring a free ride at the college of her choice.

Except apparently, I am already too late because she is now explaining—or at least trying to—how she is swapping out a college degree for a chance to be an Instagram influencer.

"I *don't* think I quite get it, Sophia. I'm still lost as to how DJ Breezy Boo Boo liking your picture means you don't need to go to college."

She blows out a long, dramatic sigh and leans against the metal lockers. "It's DJ Breezy Buzz Boo. And Ms. G, he has like twelve *million* followers. And after he liked my photo, I got three thousand more followers! If I can get fifty thousand more followers, I can have Instagram be my job."

"How will Instagram be your job?" I ask, my curiosity admittedly a tad piqued, both as Lucy and as @TheMiss GuidedCounselor.

Sophia rolls her eyes. Evidently, I am missing something here.

"Because then people and companies will send me stuff for free and pay me to post about it. I'll be an *influencer.*" She stresses the last word, staring me down as if challenging me to ask *So what's an influencer?*

But the joke's on her. I'm hip and I know what influencers are. They are the reason I had to spend thirty minutes on the phone with my credit card company over the weekend, trying to cancel that shoe subscription box I bought after seeing ten thousand ads on my social media feed. *Suck on that, Sophia.*

"Sophia, the odds of that happening are very, very, very, even microscopically small. And it's not a sure bet. A college degree *is*. Influencers come and go, but a degree in accounting is forever." I want to mime dropping the mic to the floor because that advice was simply poetic. Unfortunately, all it does is earn me another eye roll from Sophia.

"I just don't think I can commit to college right now. I feel like this opportunity is too important for me to pass up."

I squint and squeeze the bridge of my nose. I feel a headache coming. "But, Sophia, what opportunity has *really* come? I mean, sure you got DJ Breezy Wheezy Boo to like your photo, but that's not necessarily an opportunity. What will you do if no companies offer to sponsor you?"

She lifts her shoulder. "I guess I could try to get on some reality show. That would definitely help grow my platform. You know, like a dating show." Her face lights up with excitement. "Maybe something where I live on a yacht with like six billionaires that all compete for my love. Like we can hold an auction, and whoever bids the highest wins my heart and I get to walk away with a check. We can call it *Sailing into Love*."

Great, the headache has now fully arrived, settling into the middle of my forehead with a resounding thud. "Okay, look, Sophia, you clearly have an…entrepreneurial spirit. Why don't we discuss how we can channel your unique ideas in ways that don't seem like the plot for *Taken*?"

"Fiiiiiine," she whines. "But I have AP Chem in five, so I need to go."

She pushes off the wall of lockers and adjusts her skirt. I have to wonder how a student with four AP classes and a perfect GPA wants to throw that all away to live on a yacht with six billionaires. Well, I mean, I get *that*, but Sophia has her pick of any Ivy League, and she wants to throw that away? But just as she's about to leave, though, a brilliant idea pops into my head and I jump in front of her.

"I want you to join the Konfident Kids Klub," I tell her.

She laughs, assuming I'm joking. But when my expression

doesn't change, her eyes widen into large saucers. "Oh my God, you're serious?"

I hold up my hand. "Just hear me out. You have more confidence in you than the whole group combined. And I think it might be good for them to hear from you and how you are chasing your dreams no matter how much I try to dissuade you!"

She pops a stick of gum in her mouth and shakes her head. "No way. I like you Ms. G, but not *that* much. Joining the KKK is social suicide."

I expel a sigh, wishing my club didn't have such a negative reputation, though what could I expect from something called the Konfident Kids Klub?

"Please think about it?" I ask, bordering on begging.

She purses her lips and gifts me with one final eye roll before darting out of my way just as the bell rings for next period. As she leaves, I spot Fletcher walking toward me with a very confused and concerned look on his face.

When he reaches me, he gives me a tilted, nervous smile. "Did I just hear you trying to recruit students into the KKK?"

I internally groan. How is it that I only seem to embarrass myself in front of this man? First, I practically maim his balls with my tea, then I make an inappropriate blowjob joke, and now he thinks I'm recruiting students for a hate group. If making terrible first impressions was an Olympic sport, I would be taking home the gold.

"It's the Konfident Kids Klub," I explain. "A torturous forty minutes every week where I impart my wisdom to the youth of tomorrow through forced role-plays and oversharing. It's obviously *the* place to be every Monday from three to three forty."

"So not a hate group then?" he clarifies.

"Not really. I mean, all our members, myself included, do have a little self-hatred, but nothing we can't resolve with forty minutes of role-plays once a week."

Fletcher laughs. "That's funny. You've got a great sense of humor."

The compliment is unexpected, but not totally unwelcome. Especially coming from Fletcher, who looks like one of those old-school Abercrombie models from my *Teen* magazine, whose abs I would frantically scratch to get a smell of the cologne sample. It makes my stomach clench a bit, and I'm not entirely sure what that means.

Probably just the tuna from lunch.

I scrunch my nose. "Thanks. Just another day in the life of a high school guidance counselor." I add a little curtsy, though I have absolutely no idea why other than the fact that despite being a trained social worker, my actual social skills are only slightly above those of a feral child who has spent their entire life living in the woods.

"Fun job?" he asks, seeming genuinely interested, which confuses me because no one has ever asked me if being a guidance counselor for high school students is fun because the assumed answer is "No, actually, it's quite traumatic."

"Sometimes, I suppose. Most days." Fletcher and his nice smile and perfect, fluffy brown hair are too distracting for me to answer properly.

"Uh, so how are you liking Harview?" I ask, switching the topic of conversation back to him. I don't like talking about myself, anyway, mostly because I never know what to say. I don't have many hobbies besides bingeing Netflix and stalking celebrities on Instagram, and any free time I *do* have is spent at either of my two jobs or with my family.

"Great! I am really enjoying the students," he answers enthusiastically—enough for me to actually believe him. "It's very different from where I was working before."

"Oh, really? Where did you teach?"

He suddenly looks a bit embarrassed and his cheeks flush to a soft pink. "It was this school called Kenton."

My brows shoot to the top of my head. "Kenton? Isn't that the private boarding school in New York that costs like a hundred thousand a year? How did you score that gig?"

He coughs into his hand. "I actually graduated from there, so I had a bit of an in when a position opened."

I stare at him wide-eyed. What the hell is a Kenton grad doing working *here*? It's probably rude to ask, but I figure Fletcher and I have moved beyond polite conversation considering we've already made it to second base. (Or was it technically third base? I can never remember.)

There's also something oddly familiar about Fletcher, though it's hard for me to pin down exactly what that is and why I feel so comfortable with him. I mean, I made a *blowjob* joke in front of him a mere few seconds after shaking his hand. It's as if there's something about Fletcher's, well, *essence*, that acts like some antidote to my social anxiety and overthinking. When I'm around him, those carefully constructed walls I've built around myself seem to disintegrate as easily as the single-ply toilet paper in our bathrooms. And while it scares me a bit, how comfortable and at ease I feel around him, I also find it exciting. Like the thrill of sneaking store-bought snacks into a movie theater.

"So can I ask why you're here? And not like having high tea with the future secretary of commerce?"

He laughs and scrubs a hand over his jaw. "I needed to come home for some family stuff, and when I heard that there was a position open, I jumped at it."

"Wow, that is very impressive," I say, quite proud at how I am suppressing the urge to pepper him with questions about Kenton. Mostly about the food, if I'm being honest. I bet the cafeteria is *amazing*.

"It's a lot less impressive than you may think, believe me."

I choke back a laugh. "Um, I very much doubt that."

"Well, my father would vehemently disagree with you," he responds with a practiced smile that tells me there's more truth in that statement than he is letting on.

"Really? If my kid taught at Kenton, I would be bragging about it to everyone I met. Seriously, I would find a way to work it into every conversation."

He lets out a forced laugh. "Well, my father is *definitely* not bragging about his son, the teacher. He expected me to work in the family business like my older brother. And I tried it for a bit, but it wasn't right for me."

He lifts his brows in a "what can you do?" kind of way as he shoves his hands into his pockets, and it's then that I see how revealing that small piece of information was probably not as easy as he tried to make it seem. How it left him feeling vulnerable and a bit exposed, and my heart squeezes a bit in my chest in solidarity and understanding.

At that moment, a piece of advice I had shared a few months back as @TheMissGuidedCounselor pops into my head—and out my mouth. "I think it takes a lot of courage to choose a path that goes against the expectations of the people we respect."

I so rarely get to channel my inner @TheMissGuided-Counselor in the real world that I am actually kind of proud of myself. In person, I usually feel so clumsy and awkward that my succinct little motivational quotes and helpful lists never get the chance to see the light of day. Most of the time I offer half-rambling advice, veering off to some tangential story that only makes sense once I remember to circle back and explain.

If I weren't nervously holding my hands together now, I would give myself a congratulatory high five.

To his credit, Fletcher looks equally impressed by my words. "I don't know if my father would call it courageous," he says after a pause. His eyes have glossed over, as if captured by a faraway memory. One that, judging by the way Fletcher's casual smile falls from his face, was probably not a happy one. "I think his choice words were 'unbelievably stupid.'"

I wince. Fletcher's dad sounds scary. "Just because he doesn't agree with your choices doesn't make them stupid," I respond, feeling a bit defensive on Fletcher's behalf. "You're your own person, and you're allowed to choose a different path for yourself."

Cheesy? Yes, but I believe it. And judging from the look on Fletcher's face right now, it looks like he could benefit from believing it, too.

He doesn't say anything for a long moment and then looks at me, rather intensely, before breaking eye contact to glance down at his shoes, almost bashful. "How much do I owe you for this therapy session?" he asks, looking back up with a playful smile.

I smile and shake my head. "Nothing. I'm on the clock."

"You're easy to talk to," Fletcher says, surprising me yet again.

I'm not the biggest fan of compliments, mostly because I suck at receiving them. Especially when a gorgeous man with deep brown eyes, a perfect smile, and white teeth that look like tiny Chiclets is the one complimenting me. "Well, that's what I get paid the big bucks for," I joke, pointing my fingers into little air guns and firing them—until I realize how ridiculous I look and drop my hands, interlocking my fingers so they don't go rogue on me again.

Fletcher opens his mouth to respond, but right before he can say anything more, the bell rings. He smiles apologetically and shoves his hands into his pockets. "I have to get to my next class, but I'll see you around?"

I nod, wisely deciding *not* to speak, because I'm not sure my voice has returned to normal yet. So instead, I play it cool, staring at his butt as he turns around, heading down the hall back to his classroom. It's nice, a close second to his smile. Everything about Fletcher is nice, which worries me. Thanks to my *very* unimpressive success rate with the opposite sex, I tend to let my walls down too eagerly and fall fast. And hard. And I can't do that with a brand-new coworker, no matter how tempted I am to run my fingers through his fluffy brown hair.

A lifetime of dating apps and reality TV has shown me that cool, nice guys like Fletcher never seem to stick around for long.

It usually takes about seven to twelve business days for my neuroses to start showing. My anxiety will pop in first, and most men mistake it as a cute quirk, not realizing how much of the iceberg lies beneath the surface. Then there's the fun stuff, like biweekly identity crises, weekends spent in bed because having a brain on overdrive is exhausting, and crying spells brought on by the smallest of things—or even nothing at all. I was just way too much work and gave mediocre blowjobs, and those two facts alone were usually enough of a red flag for any suitors to strap on their running shoes and bolt.

I sigh and watch the students mill about the hallway for a few seconds before pushing off the locker and returning to my office. Already I was wasting valuable real estate in my head daydreaming about Fletcher and his dimpled smile. But Fletcher *and* his dimples would both need to be ignored and forgotten. There is no way I will let myself fall for someone who I would have to suffer through seeing *every* day at work once it went wrong.

Nope, not worth it. There is a reason I keep a respectable distance from my colleagues. And Fletcher cannot be the exception.

Absolutely not.

TheMissGuidedCounselor
Posted at 3:22 AM

Let's talk about taking risks. It can be scary putting yourself out there and trying something new, but without risk there is no growth.

I am challenging all of you today to step outside your comfort zone and do one thing that challenges, intimidates, or even scares you. Whether it's signing up for that 5K or asking out the hot history teacher, try one thing to put yourself out there, and report back here when you're done so we can celebrate your achievement!

Liked by **BravesGuy93** and **others**

TheMissGuidedCounselor I've been…more

View all comments

TheMissGuidedCounselor
Today at 3:35 AM

BravesGuy93
Hot history teacher? Trying to tell
me something there, MissGuided?

TheMissGuidedCounselor
Please, the only reason I used hot
history teacher was my appreciation
for alliteration. Nothing more.

BravesGuy93
I remain unconvinced…
I think this is you desperately trying
to tell me you're in love with me.

TheMissGuidedCounselor
And I think this is you trying to tell
me you're suffering from delusions.

BravesGuy93
Well, in the spirit of stepping outside
of my comfort zone…
What if we just did it?
Finally met up?

TheMissGuidedCounselor
We talked about this…

BravesGuy93
I know, I know.
Just…ever since I've started this
new job and been back home, it's
been making me think about the
relationships in my life. And you've
been such a rock for me these last
few months.
I just want the chance to meet you. I
value our friendship so much.

TheMissGuidedCounselor
I value our friendship, too.
Talking to you is the bright spot of
my day.
And I know you've been going through
so much lately, and so much change
with starting at a new school and
helping your mom through the divorce.
But I can't risk losing everything
I've built up here. I know it probably
doesn't make any sense to you, but
this account is my safe place. It lets
me be the person I want to be and
believe I can be. I can't lose that.

BravesGuy93
Trust me, I get it.
I'm sorry. It wasn't right of me to push.

I just really like you and would like to meet you one day. But if that's not an option, then I definitely don't want to lose this friendship so if you need me to drop it, I'll drop it.

 TheMissGuidedCounselor
I need you to drop it.

BravesGuy93
Consider it dropped.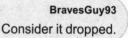

Chapter Seven

 *Fletcher*

"OKAY, FOLKS, LET'S ALL settle down! We have a jam-packed and exciting day ahead of us!"

The room comes to a hush as Principal Padmesh twirls the mic in his hand. He's wearing an oversized football jersey over light-wash dad jeans as he paces the stage in the auditorium.

"To kick off our fun day of professional development," he starts, his voice brimming with far too much excitement for eight fifteen on a Wednesday morning, "we are going to do some icebreakers!"

He pauses, clearly expecting his audience of exhausted and undercaffeinated faculty to jump to our feet in a round of enthusiastic applause. When he accepts that his fantasy will not be happening, he frowns. But he hasn't given up yet. "Well, let's begin! Under each of your seats is a sticker label with a word written on it."

We all bend down to retrieve our stickers. Brodie looks at his and loudly asks, "Why does mine say paintbrush?"

"Really?" the teacher beside him says. "Mine just says scissors."

"No!" Padmesh shouts into the mic, his voice echoing in

the auditorium. "*Don't* look at your sticker! The point of the ice-breaker is to find the matching pair of school supplies. Clever, right?"

He pauses, waiting for us to all enthusiastically agree.

When we do not, he continues, "We will be placing our stickers on our backs, and then we will use our skills of *communication*"—he holds up his hand, waving it excitedly as he overenunciates each syllable in the word—"to help our colleagues identify the object on the sticker, and then find their match!"

"What's the match for a paintbrush?" Brodie asks.

"An easel, duh," the art teacher shouts out.

"Wait, why wouldn't it be paint?" one of the biology teachers chimes in. "You can't use a paintbrush without the paint."

"Okay! Okay!" Padmesh taps onto the mic, and we all cringe at the sound of screeching feedback. "Let's not give too much away! Remember, we are utilizing our *creative communication skills*!" Again, he draws out each syllable in the words, as if hoping that if he says them loudly and slowly enough, the skills will seep into our brains through audial osmosis.

Everyone grumbles as we stick our labels on our backs and begin going about finding our matches. Most of us had read what was on our sticker before Padmesh had warned us not to, so we all mill about—using zero creative communication skills—to find our matches. My sticker has the word *pencil*, so I roam around the auditorium until I find one of the Spanish teachers with the word *eraser* stuck to her back.

Unsure of what to do, we stand together as we watch Brodie helplessly search for his match for ten more minutes until Padmesh realizes that particular sticker is missing and the activity ends, with Brodie grumbling about how now he will never know if the match to paintbrush is an easel or paint.

And it's still only nine in the morning.

Next, we get an allotted ten-minute coffee and restroom break before Padmesh informs us that we will be breaking into small groups to play a less-fun version of Desert Island. For this activity, we will receive a list of fifteen available items we can bring with us to our deserted island to help us survive, but as a group we must decide on only five of them. Padmesh explains this will help with not only our creative communication skills but also encourage collaboration.

There is a strong sentiment of doubt in the air.

"Okay, so we are going to break off alphabetically by last name," Padmesh announces. He calls through a list of names and when he reaches *F*, I inwardly groan as I'm paired with the name preceding Fletcher: Flannigan.

Since finding me that first day of school, Georgia has been popping into my classroom, stopping me in the halls, and joining me at lunch to chat about "the good old times," of which we both seem to have wildly different recollections. While it was nice to know *someone* here, it was hard to see so much of Georgia, especially after all this time. After she had broken up with me, she had dated my brother for approximately three months before *he* had ended things by leaving her for some girl in the fund's accounting department. I had thankfully been long gone by the time their relationship had imploded, having quit to start graduate school across the country.

When Padmesh finishes announcing the teams, he explains the rules and informs us we will have one hour to complete our decisions. An hour feels a bit excessive, but I think he had been counting on our first icebreaker taking longer and the professional development breakout lectures don't start until ten thirty.

As everyone drifts to find their groups, I take advantage of the lull to pull out my phone and see if I have any messages from @TheMissGuidedCounselor. I don't feel great about how our conversation from earlier this morning ended. I knew I shouldn't have pressed the issue about wanting to meet up with her, but I couldn't help myself. @TheMissGuidedCounselor was my closest friend and really, my only confidante, and I couldn't help wanting to meet her and be able to talk—without a keyboard. I understood why she was so protective of her identity—as much as @TheMissGuidedCounselor was loved by her followers, there was never any escaping the trolls or internet bullies who could leave cruel and hurtful messages on her posts. And though she never mentioned it, I'm sure they found their way into her DMs as well. Sharing advice on the internet, *especially* as a woman, meant you were going to get your unfair share of harassment. I couldn't deny, though, that it still hurt, and left me a bit frustrated, that she didn't want to meet in person. But I needed to put those feelings aside and respect her decision and appreciate the friendship we *did* have—which felt just as real and valid as any of the other friendships in my life. More so, in some ways, because of how easy it was to talk with her about anything behind our two anonymous profiles.

Unfortunately there are no new messages waiting for me from her, and my stomach tightens into a nervous knot, wondering if I overstepped and she was possibly angry with me. As I type out another message, I'm interrupted when a way-too-chipper voice for this early in the morning says, "Looks like fate has brought us together again, right?"

I force a smile and nod noncommittally as Georgia slides into the empty seat beside mine. Thankfully I don't need to respond as another teacher—who looks young enough to be a student—arrives, introducing himself as Donovan before sitting down in the folding chair beside Georgia and closing his eyes. "Just letting you know now, I plan to sleep through this whole thing."

A familiar voice follows. "I think I'm with this group."

I look up to see Lucy, who claims the free chair beside Donovan. I think he's already fallen asleep.

I scoot up in my seat, a bit more enthused now. In my short but *very* memorable time knowing Lucy, I've found her to have a dry sense of humor that doesn't quite match her shy and reclusive personality. I'm thankful she's in our group, since at least it will mean this activity will be slightly less dull.

We all sit in silence for a few minutes, waiting for Padmesh to deliver the sheets listing the mystery items. When we get our copies, Georgia starts reading them out loud: flashlight, bug spray, lighter, tarp, knife, fishing net, radio, first aid kit, flint, inflatable raft, hammock, a box of matches, sunscreen, a satellite phone, and a single flare.

"So what five items do we all want to keep?" she asks, looking up to the group.

"How about we keep the knife, the lighter, satellite phone, inflatable raft, and hammock?" I propose.

"Sounds great," Georgia replies with a wide smile. "Anyone want to add or change anything?"

Lucy shakes her head, and Donovan continues to sleep.

We've reached a consensus. I look down at my watch. Forty-eight minutes to go.

Another long silence stretches over us as we all sit, avoiding eye contact. A few seats away, I hear another group get in a spirited debate on whether to keep sunscreen or bug spray, then see one teacher pulling out her phone to list all the different types of venomous insects that live in tropical climates.

I accidentally make eye contact with Lucy and instantly look away.

If I let myself, I know I would continue to stare. There's something that keeps tugging me toward her, even when I know I should be staying away. Between starting a new job and everything going on with my family, I don't know if I have anything left to pursue a relationship. Especially with a colleague. Thanks to a few dating mishaps at Kenton, I've learned that dating coworkers is usually a catastrophically terrible decision.

And whenever I *do* forget, @TheMissGuidedCounselor always swoops in to not-so-gently remind me.

We make eye contact a second time, and Lucy lets out a nervous chuckle as she quickly shifts her focus down to her feet. We need something to distract us, otherwise this silence will be the death of me.

"How about we play the *real* Desert Island?" I impulsively ask, desperate to kill this awkwardness. "While we wait for everyone else to finally finish?"

"Yes!" Georgia says, clapping her hands. "Great idea, Fletcher."

"Lucy," I say, aiming a smile her way, "you in?"

I don't bother asking the now fully asleep Donovan.

She nods and I drop my elbows on my thighs, leaning forward. "Okay, first up: books. You're deserted on an island and can only bring one book for the entire time. What do you bring? Georgia?"

"Um, I guess it would be *Eat, Pray, Love*. So inspirational."

I nod, even if I have no idea what the book is about, and we turn our attention to Lucy, who bites down on her lip as she thinks. "*Anxious People*. By Fredrik Backman."

I raise a brow and jerk back to look at her. "Seriously? My pick is *A Man Called Ove*."

"I loved that one, too." Her face lights up with excitement. "But *Anxious People* won my heart. Have you read it?"

I shake my head. "Not yet. You think it's better than *Ove*?"

"Different, but more…" She pauses, tilting her head to the side. "It spoke to me differently, I guess. That's what I love about Backman: his stories are simple, but the writing is so layered, and there's so much meaning packed into every sentence."

Nodding vigorously, I pick up where she left off. "Yes, and the way he infuses his humor, but also manages to make it light-hearted is one of the reasons I love his writing."

"Oh, absolutely and I love how—"

"Okay," Georgia interrupts with a tight-lipped smile and a wave of her hands. "We all can see how much you love these books!" She forces a laugh. "Anyway, let's keep going. If you could bring one celebrity with you to the island, who would you bring? Fletcher?"

"Oh, um, I have no idea." I thrust a hand through my hair. I look back over at Lucy. "Who would *you* bring?"

"Bear Grylls, obviously," she answers with a smirk. "I'm not planning on dying out there."

"Clearly the obvious choice," I agree, returning her smile. "Though I think I would pick Mykel Hawke over Grylls."

Lucy's jaw drops. "What? Sure, Hawke has the edge with his military training, but Grylls's survival skills are unmatched. I mean, the man slept in a *deer carcass*."

"Yeah, but—"

"I'm so sorry," Georgia interrupts again, a strained smile on her lips. "But what are you talking about?"

"Oh, sorry," Lucy apologizes with a sheepish grin. "So, they're both survivalists and had different reality TV shows where they would try to survive out in the wild. Bear Grylls was on *Man vs. Wild* and Mykel Hawke was on *Man, Woman, Wild*."

Georgia frowns. "And those are two different shows? They sound the same."

Lucy lifts her shoulder in a shrug. "They pretty much are the same thing." She shoots me a playful smirk. "Except for Bear Grylls being, of course, far superior."

Before I can respond, Georgia lets out another forced laugh and claps her hands together. "Well, why don't we all agree that living out in the wild is just a ridiculous concept to start with and move on. How about a favorite movie? Lucy, why don't you go first?"

Lucy sucks in her bottom lip and bites down. She stares up at the ceiling, as if sifting through an invisible catalogue of movies, and I take advantage of her distracted state to study her. To take in her ink-black hair, which falls just below her shoulders, held back by a simple gold clip. To appreciate the warmth in her dark brown eyes, the round curve of her jaw, her graceful, slender neck adorned with a simple gold chain necklace.

Every minute I spend with Lucy sinks me deeper and deeper

into a growing fascination that makes me question whether breaking my no-coworkers rule would be worth it.

"Okay, so I think I have my pick. Well…" She pauses and a shy grin crosses her face. "I had a four-way tie, *but* if I can only bring one, it's got to be *Legally Blonde*."

"*Legally Blonde*? I am very curious as to the methodology that makes it your favorite movie," I respond with a teasing smile. "Please, state your case."

Lucy rolls her eyes as she straightens in her chair. "Most people write it off as some silly or superficial film, but it actually has a lot of great messages. For one, there are countless examples of positive female relationships. Also, Elle proves you don't need to change yourself to succeed in the world. She grows, but not at the expense of losing herself. And," she finishes, "she's consistently positive, always choosing to see the good in people."

I nod, impressed. "Maybe I'll have to give it a rewatch. I'm curious—what were your other picks in your four-way tie?"

"Uh-uh!" Georgia tuts before Lucy can answer. "You can only pick one! Fletcher, why don't you go next?" she asks, her unwavering smile beginning to twitch.

"Sure." I scrub a hand over my jaw as I think. "I would have to say *Good Will Hunting*."

"Oh my gosh! What a coincidence—that was what *I* was going to pick!" Georgia squeals excitedly.

Lucy grins and waggles her brow. "How do you like them apples?"

"What?" Georgia asks, her forehead furrowed in confusion.

"Oh, it's a line," Lucy says, "from the movie?"

"Right. Of course, I knew that!" She responds and swats

me playfully on the arm. "Isn't it so weird how much we have in common?"

"Um, yeah," I respond, though I'm still distracted by Lucy, wanting to know more about her—and not just her favorite books or movies, but how she looks in the morning, her hair tousled from sleeping. Or the way her body would feel against mine.

Shit. This is getting bad. I shift in my seat, placing my hands over my lap to hide the evidence of my wandering thoughts.

Thankfully Padmesh chooses this moment to come check on the progress of our group. Lucy kicks Donovan's shin to wake him, and we all report that we've happily learned a great deal of creative communication skills.

"Okay, it looks like all the groups have finished their tasks!" Padmesh announces, taking his place back on the stage facing the auditorium. "Very impressive!"

He glances down at his watch and frowns. "It looks like we still have thirty minutes before our first breakout sessions." When we all stare back at him, he sighs in defeat. "Why don't we all take that time to relax before we continue through the rest of the day?"

Before he can finish, half the faculty has leapt out of their chairs and migrated toward the exits at the back of the room. Including Lucy, who joins her friend, the math teacher, as they follow the crowd into the hall.

I can't help but feel a small sting of disappointment watching her go. Every minute with Lucy was like inhaling a fresh breath of air. She was so familiar, yet unlike anyone I've ever known, and the paradox only piqued my interest in her more.

"Uh, did you hear anything I just said?"

I turn to see Georgia watching me, her eyes following where mine had just been. Her jaw ticks with annoyance, but she wears a tight-lipped smile.

"Sorry," I answer. "What were you saying?"

She pauses, then squares her shoulders. "I was asking if you had plans for this weekend. I thought maybe we could catch up. You know, for old time's sake?"

I rock back on my heels and quickly scan the room. I cannot believe Georgia is bringing this up. At school. *Again.*

I want to tell her no—to tell her to stop trying to open a door that I've long since closed. But the words can't seem to form a coherent sentence in in my head. Sweat starts collecting in my palms, and I fight the urge to wipe them down the side of my khakis. Biting back a bitter laugh, I think of the advice @TheMissGuidedCounselor has repeated to me at least a dozen times over the past year of our friendship: "No is a full sentence."

But as much as I wish I could just spit that word out—*no*—I can't. I know that Georgia, despite @TheMissGuidedCounselor's advice, will keep pressing me. She'll want to know why I'm turning her down. She'll frown, probably pout, and then I'll give in, tying myself to a date that I never wanted in the first place.

I can see her growing frustration as she crosses her arms at her chest, tapping her heel on the carpeted floor, waiting for my response. But it's too early—and I'm too unprepared, and sweaty now, to handle this conversation. So when I see her open her mouth, I quickly interrupt.

"Look, I need to run to the restroom before the next session, so let's, well, talk later?" I lift my hand in a hasty goodbye, not waiting for her response, and rush toward the back of the auditorium.

I'm grateful for the reprieve—and for the chance to ask @TheMissGuidedCounselor to help me craft a response for when Georgia inevitably brings this subject up yet again. Like she has informed me on *several* occasions, I will gladly tap dance around a subject rather than tackle it head-on. In fact, she once said the only thing that could outrun my fear of telling someone no was a cheetah on steroids.

And she wasn't wrong, considering I was now hiding in the men's bathroom to avoid telling my ex-girlfriend I had zero interest in getting back together.

It was past time for me to work on saying no. And I would. Just…later.

Chapter Eight

♡ *Lucy*

"YOU LOOK LIKE YOU'RE hate-fucking your fork with your tongue, Lulu."

I drop my fork and find Amira watching me with amusement from behind the bar. She's been working there all night, likely surpassing me tenfold in tips even though all my older sister knows how to make is a Shirley Temple and a screwdriver.

But her bartending skills aren't why customers keep coming back to our family's Mexican-Moroccan fusion restaurant, Come Con Gana, dropping crisp twenty-dollar bills on the counter for their badly mixed gin and tonics. Nope, you can thank Amira's perfect, perky boobs, killer smile, and gorgeous face, plus lush, full eyelashes and plump lips—the kind of face a Kardashian would pay handsomely for.

Not that anyone seems to mind. I've seen the effect of Amira flashing her dimpled smile: people just turn into goo.

Tonight her thick black curls are divided into two high pigtails on the sides of her head. She's wearing a black tank that seems molded to her body and a sprinkle of gold eyeshadow on her lids. On anyone else, the combination would look ridiculous, but on Amira it looks edgy and sexy. Really, anything Amira does looks edgy and sexy.

And she *never* looks like she's hate-fucking a forkful of tilapia.

"Not today, Amira. I'm in a mood."

She laughs. "Yeah, no shit. What's going on?"

"None of your business," I grumble. I look over my shoulder at the nearly empty restaurant. "Do you think we'll get out of here early tonight?"

Amira rolls her eyes. "Why? Do you have a hot booty call you need to rush off to?"

"Why does *everything* need to be about sex with you?" I moan.

She leans forward so that her perfect boobs are right in my face. "Because, Lulu, sex is the best. Which you would know if you let your little pucha free every once in a while."

I want to argue with her, but in this particular instance, she isn't far off.

Truthfully, the reason for my grumpy mood is Fletcher. I cannot get him off my mind, and I find myself becoming one of those people I always used to pity, the ones whose moods and emotions depend on whether they've had any interaction with someone they find attractive.

I am *not* that person—yet I have mentally catalogued every single interaction I have had with Fletcher in the eight days since we bonded over Fredrik Backman, replaying them in my head each evening, frame by frame. From our jokes on professional development day, to spontaneous hallway hellos, to random visits to my office, to him sitting next to Nia and me at the mandatory school assembly on...some topic I can't even remember,

Fletcher is quickly becoming someone I look forward to seeing each day, and I don't know how to feel about that.

Every time I *do* see Fletcher, those obnoxious little butterflies start to flutter and my long-neglected nether regions tingle in tandem. It has been so long since I've even been interested in anyone that I am *almost* positive my hymen has regenerated and closed up shop. So yeah, maybe Amira is right and my pucha does need to be freed.

Not that I would *ever* admit that to her. You couldn't waterboard that information out of me.

"I am perfectly fine," I spit out, stabbing my fork into the last chunk of fish.

"Clearly," she responds, rolling her eyes.

But before I can retaliate, Julieta slides over to the bar, dropping her head dramatically onto the lacquered counter.

"I am so bored," she says with a loud groan—the dramatic effects fitting for our youngest sister.

I pat her on the back as Amira and I share a knowing smile. Julieta's passion is cooking, which I assume she must have inherited from our mother and aunt, since the cooking gene skipped so gloriously over both me and Amira.

After all, this restaurant is their love child.

Though my sisters and I hadn't yet been born, we all know the genesis of the family restaurant thanks to the thousands of times our parents have reminded us: soon after my parents' marriage, my mother and my father's youngest sister discovered that they were both amazing cooks. My mother and Tante Mirielle spent hours in my mother's tiny apartment kitchen, fighting over recipes and ingredients.

My aunt had only arrived in the States a few months prior,

so her English wasn't yet the best. She and my mother would argue in a combination of the English my aunt had learned from TV and Ladino—the hybrid Spanish-Hebrew language used by the Sephardic Moroccan Jews who had been part of the Megurashim, the expulsion of Jews from the Iberian Peninsula to North Africa during the Spanish Inquisition.

Between those scraps of English and Spanish, and the occasional curse words in French from my aunt, the two discovered they only needed one language to communicate: food. And it was their love of food that brought them to a non-homicidal level of friendship—and eventually, to them opening Come Con Gana. The name played on the old Ladino phrase to "eat with a good appetite," which everyone who walked through our restaurant's doors obviously did.

The restaurant actually worked out really well for my sisters and me, because we all had reliable employment from the age of eight. Child labor laws, as I had learned at a young age, did not apply to those of us at Come Con Gana.

Which is how I'd ended up here, twenty years later, on the third hour of my waitressing shift, shoving down another bite of saffron fish dusted with cilantro and a squeeze of lime. It's still early on a Thursday night, and I plan on taking full advantage of the lull to stuff in as much free food as I can: a nice perk for all those years of unpaid labor.

But Julieta wanted more than kitchen scraps; she wanted to be *in* the kitchen, inventing new recipes and improving the ones on our current menu with her expert cooking skills garnered by years of following our mother around the kitchen and hours spent poring over cooking videos on YouTube. Unfortunately, Julieta has been banished to the front hostess stand, where she can only seat tables and manage the takeout orders. She hates it, but our mother is insistent that she "put in her time" to earn her place in the back kitchen with her and our aunt.

And, in full transparency, there *were* two separate occasions where Julieta had accidentally set the kitchen on fire. Julieta, my mother had decided, needed to first learn every facet of the restaurant if she was serious about taking it over one day. And that started by showing our guests to their tables and bringing them their takeout orders.

All of which is why Julieta is currently banging her head against the counter, eliciting a string of curses from Amira.

"Can you two please get your shit together?" Amira hisses. "You are scaring all my customers away." She shoots a nervous glance over her shoulder at the string of men—of all ages, shapes, and sizes—occupying every available barstool despite the rest of the restaurant being nearly empty. Though I don't look at our financials, I'm pretty sure the success of Come Con Gana is due less to our amazing food and more to Amira's ability to flirt with any adult human with a pulse.

"But I'm *so* bored," Julieta whines.

"Out!" Amira yells, grabbing the towel tucked into her waistband and twisting it in the air like a whip. I jump with a yelp but am a second too late, the towel slapping across my hand, leaving an angry red welt.

Thanks to the spriteliness of her youth, Julieta escapes unscathed and we both flee to the front hostess stand, where we can bitch about Amira and catalogue our grievances against her, adding assault by towel to the ever-growing list of who has been harmed the worst.

I typically always win thanks to the time during Josh

Feldman's bowling-themed bar mitzvah party, where Amira had been so distracted by the newly braces-less Josh that she accidentally dropped a bowling ball on my foot. Julieta comes in a close second from when Amira once stole her favorite Michael Kors white satin dress—which she had scored at TJMaxx for more than half off—only for Amira to return with the dress covered in red, splotchy stains thanks to fruit punch Four Loko. Julieta had been devastated and went nearly two weeks without saying a single word to Amira.

And honestly, I totally understood. I love my sisters and would literally slice open my body to give them an extra kidney if they ever needed it. But over my literal dead body will they ever borrow *any* of my clothes.

We've recapped Amira's transgressions through the early 2010s when the front door to the restaurant opens, inviting in the balmy autumn air and the familiar face of the person responsible for my sour mood this evening.

Well, besides Amira.

With a speed that should absolutely qualify me for a sport at an Olympic level, I jump up from my slouch over the hostess stand and adjust the hem of my shirt. In my panic, I strike an unnaturally stiff pose, jutting my hip out to the side in a valiant (but failed) effort to accentuate my hips. Heterosexual males in my species are biologically attracted to wide birthing hips, right? From the corner of my eye, I see surprise then horror cross Julieta's face as she processes what she's just witnessed—and will, undoubtedly, question me about relentlessly at a later time and date.

"Fletcher, what a surprise," I say, inwardly cringing at how high and pitchy my voice sounds.

"Lucy, hi." He smiles and instantly the butterflies living in the terrarium inside me start fluttering all at once, sending shivers of excitement up my spine. The electric sizzle I get when I'm around Fletcher feels like something out of a movie—or at the very least, a concerning new symptom of my previously diagnosed IBS.

"So, um, how can I help you?"

Fletcher tilts his head to the side, inspecting me as his eyes wander down to the embroidered pink, yellow, and blue Come Con Gana logo on my lapel. "You work here?"

I nod, my cheeks flushing with embarrassment. Being a teacher—or school professional in general—in America frequently means having one, two, or even three jobs. Most of my colleagues at Harview have similar second jobs, but for some reason it always feels a little embarrassing when I run into someone from my school at the restaurant. *Especially* if that someone is a student who I recently had in my office for some uncomfortable reason, like the time I had to serve Jake Chu's parents with a completely straight face after having met with them only a day earlier to discuss Jake's suspension for poking holes in the free condoms we provided on a table outside of my office.

Thankfully, I think Jake's parents had been even more embarrassed, judging by the *massive* tip they had left me for my *very* below-average service.

"Did you need a table? Or—" I let the question linger and this time, it's Fletcher who blushes a bright hue of pink.

"Just picking up a takeout order for my mom," he says. "Mary Fletcher."

"I'll go check in the back!" Julieta declares, sprinting away and reminding me why she is my favorite sister.

"So, how long have you worked here?"

I shrug. "Since I was a little kid. It's a family restaurant. My mom and my aunt's, actually. So they've been making me work since I was practically a fetus."

Fletcher's eyes widen. "That's incredible. This is one of my mom's favorite restaurants, and we've gotten takeout from here a lot since I've moved. The food is always amazing. You must be such an incredible cook."

I deflate at the comment.

No, I am most definitely *not* an incredible cook. And it's something I've always felt guilty about. After all, I grew up with all these incredible chefs who would retreat into the kitchen with no more than a handful of ingredients and glass jars filled with bright, colorful spices—only to later emerge with platters piled high with spiced chicken, fragrant dishes of stewed meats, and magical-tasting sticky desserts.

And what do I have to show for that free lifetime education? A freezer stuffed with microwavable meals and a pantry boasting at least seven different kinds of macaroni and cheese. Really, I'm not incredible at *anything* culinary—especially anything that involves knives, measuring, or knowing the difference between a skillet and a saucepan.

"Actually, my sister Julieta—the one who just ran away—she's the incredible cook. I'm mediocre at best," I say, forcing my lips into what I hope is a pleasant grin.

Fletcher's easy smile turns downward into a frown as he shakes his head. "I don't think 'Lucy Galindo' and 'mediocre' ever belong in the same sentence."

My chest tightens and my stomach does a violent somersault, and I am again confused if it is because of Fletcher or some undiagnosed disease. Considering that WebMD will likely just tell me it's a rare, incurable form of cancer, I decide to conclude that whatever weird sensations are happening in my body at this moment are thanks to Fletcher.

And the way he says my name, dragging out the *Lu* in *Lucy*, like he's savoring the vowel on his tongue. And the way he's looking at me, his smile a bit guileless, like he sincerely believes that there is absolutely, positively nothing mediocre about me.

Because I'm so lost in those beautiful brown eyes, I make the fatal error of not paying attention to Amira when she strolls out from the back of the restaurant, her eyes locking on Fletcher in the same way as a wolf spying the hare it plans to kill for its afternoon snack.

"Well, well, well, is there any other way we can *service* you tonight?" She elbows me playfully, her eyes lit with mischief. "May I suggest adding a dessert to your order? We actually have a new item on the menu. Organic, locally sourced, and *very* tasty. We call it pucha, and I believe it's available to take out or eat in, isn't that right, Lucy?"

Blood thrums as heat rushes up my body.

Rage replaces the light, flirty feelings Fletcher had sparked, and even as I know that I could be looking at twenty to life for murdering my sister, the thought does not bother me one single bit. Prison could work for me—I thrive with structure and have a very extensive list of books I've been meaning to read.

But before I murder Amira, I need Fletcher to get out of here. Witnesses complicate things, and I don't want to ruin whatever—possibly misguided—positive impression Fletcher has of me.

"Unfortunately, that's all sold out," I rush to explain, not allowing Fletcher the opportunity to respond. I see Julieta returning with his meal. "But, um, it looks like you have plenty of food and really, our desserts are not that great. Terrible, even." I rip the white plastic bag from her hands and shove it toward Fletcher. "So, well, thanks for the order and for catching up, and I'll see you at school tomorrow, right?"

Fletcher's face drops a bit, but thankfully he doesn't say anything as he lifts his hand in a wave and leaves through the front door.

Only when the heavy thud of the door confirms his exit and I am confident that he is gone do I turn to Amira and lunge, my hands primed to wring her neck.

She yelps as she ducks out of my grip, and Julieta tucks her arms beneath mine to pull me away from Amira.

"I am going to kill you!" I squeal. "I've already humiliated myself in front of him once, and I do *not* need your help doing it again!"

Realization crosses over Amira's face as her mouth drops open. "Wait, *that* hottie was the tea guy?"

I let out a grunt and hold up my hands palms out, declaring a momentary truce. "Yes, you idiot. That was *him*. And if he didn't think I was a total weirdo then, he absolutely does now!"

To her credit, Amira looks regretful. "I didn't know, Lucy. I just saw you chatting up some hot guy, and you looked so cute and comfortable together, which, to be fair, is *not* your default state. I was just trying to, you know, move things along!"

"Well, if my pucha never sees the light of day now, we know whose fault it is!" I shout at her, for once grateful the restaurant is empty.

She cringes and bites down on her lip. "I'm so sorry, Lulu.

Trust me," she says, placing her hand over her heart. "No one wants you to get laid more than I do. Is there anything I can do to fix this?"

I let out another long, loud groan and cover my face with my hands. "No, please, for the love of God, do not try to *fix* anything. Let's just pretend this never happened and hope he slips and falls on the way to his car and gets short-term amnesia."

Julieta gives my shoulders a comforting squeeze, and I drop my head to rest on her shoulder.

"It's fine, Lulu. I doubt he had any clue what *Amira*"—she lifts her head to glare at our sister—"was even saying. And you know Amira, in her very own unique and unhelpful way, just wants the best for you. Like I do. We love you, and honestly, it looked like you two were *really* hitting it off."

I lift up my head. "You think so? Did I look awkward? Or did he look, I don't know, bored?"

Julieta shakes her head. "No, Amira and I were watching from back here." She points to the column that separates the lobby from the main dining room. "And you two were totally vibing."

"You should have seen the way he was looking at you," Amira chimes in, sidling up to my side, an apologetic smile on her face. "Like you were the most beautiful, interesting person in the world. Which, of course, you are. Because you're amazing. And *so* forgiving and understanding."

I shoot her an annoyed look. "I am not forgiving you for this for at least another week."

Amira purses her lips and tilts her head to the side. "How about I cover closing for you tonight and we make it two days?"

I narrow my eyes at her but finally relent with a nod. "Deal."

Chapter Nine

 *Fletcher*

THE BELL RINGS AND I let out a sigh, smiling.

I've officially made it three weeks at Harview High. An unfamiliar lightness settles over me as I think back to how stressed and miserable I was back at Kenton. How my afternoons were plagued by angry parents pounding on my classroom door, demanding to know why their precious child failed a paper they never turned in. How the principal would always side with the parents, encouraging us teachers to do what was "necessary" to keep them happy.

"Remember where the money comes from, Aldrich," he used to say. As if I could forget—I couldn't tell you how many times I had a student tell me "I pay your salary!" as justification for their abhorrent behavior.

That lightness quickly dissipates when I see a certain someone stand in the doorway as I'm shoving my water bottle into my bag.

"Georgia," I say, forcing a smile. "How can I help you?"

She perches on the edge of my desk, crossing her left ankle over her right. "Well, I wanted to circle back about us grabbing dinner together. I figure you've had enough time to settle in and sort out your schedule. Don't you agree?"

I know this tactic of hers—she frames her question in a way that gives you no choice but to say yes. Something I used to find charming. Now? Not so much.

I blow out a sigh and shake my head. "I don't think that's the best idea, Georgia."

"Look, Fletcher," she says, her voice softening and losing some of its false peppiness. "I know I messed up by breaking up with you. I was dumb and naïve and thought that I was in love with your brother, which turned out to be…just a terrible decision. I know that now, trust me. And now that you're back, I feel like it's fate that reunited us. Don't you think we should give us a shot?"

No—no way in hell do I have any interest in pursuing a relationship again with Georgia. While I had been heartbroken over her leaving me, I now realize that we were never meant to be. Seeing how easily she had moved on—how callously she had cheated on me—had been the wake-up call I had desperately needed, opening my eyes to the type of relationships I had centered in my life. Superficial and shallow, they were based solely off what my family's name and money could offer.

More than that, it had shown me how trapped I'd felt by my father's expectations. My entire life I'd been told that I would work at the family hedge fund, adding to and caring for Fletcher Management's exclusive roster of clients (i.e., anyone with at least a ten-figure net worth).

So naturally, when I quit, my father had been livid. But after my brother's betrayal—and how easily my father forgave him, which, given the last year, doesn't surprise me anymore—I was perfectly content leaving the family business. I had no desire to see his face.

It took me almost a year to speak to my brother again and another year to forgive him—and even now, our relationship isn't exactly great. Flying across the country to go to grad school had made it easier to move on, but my father still resented how I "fled" from the business and our family.

Not that he has much of a leg to stand on now, considering that his whole affair situation did far more damage than my quitting ever did.

So, do I believe fate brought me back to Harview? Sure, maybe. But that doesn't mean I have any desire to give Georgia another shot. I'm no longer the same man who fell for her—those feelings have long disappeared, along with the person I used to be.

"I don't think that's the best idea, Georgia," I say again. I bite my tongue to stop myself from continuing—of reminding her of how *she* had been the one to leave me. At how easily she had closed the door on our relationship.

My palms start to itch as I feel the first few droplets of sweat gather at the base of my neck. Because even though Georgia had been the one to break my heart years ago, I don't have it in me to do the same to her.

Especially since we're going to be working together for the next eight months. "Look, I'm not in a place to be pursuing a relationship, and I don't want to mix my dating life with my work life."

She assesses me, her eyes narrowing. "You don't want to date your colleagues? Or do you just not want to date *me*?"

I thrust a hand through my hair. I should have practiced this conversation with @TheMissGuidedCounselor. With a few keystrokes, she would have prepared a speech for me that was respectful, kind, and firm. Unfortunately, I am without her guidance today, but the least I can do is try to channel her words. If she were standing here right now, what would she say?

Be respectful. Be kind. Be firm.

"Look, Georgia, it's not you," I assure her. "It's a rule I've made for myself. I prefer to keep my private life and my work life separate."

There. That should do it, right?

She eyes me suspiciously for a long moment. "So you would *never* date a coworker?"

Georgia's trying to trap me, and we both know it.

If I don't say yes, she'll continue asking why I won't give her a second chance, and I'll have to explain why I'm not interested. And that will mean getting too honest and truthful—and an even *more* uncomfortable discussion.

Have I mentioned I'm not great at confrontation?

But if I say that's right—*all* coworkers are off limits—then we never need to have that talk. Not dating coworkers is a pretty standard policy for most people, and it would end this whole uncomfortable dance Georgia and I have been engaged in these last few weeks. Only it wouldn't be the truth. Because there is a particular coworker at Harview I *am* very interested in dating.

Just not Georgia.

But if I do say yes, what happens if I do pursue Lucy? Would Georgia find a way to sabotage any chance I have? God, what if she shows Lucy the photos of when I had convinced myself frosted tips à la Guy Fieri was actually a good look for me? What if she reveals all my faults to Lucy, scaring her away?

Think, Fletcher, *think*. What would @TheMissGuided-Counselor do?

Well, that's an easy one to answer. She would tell Georgia the truth: "I am not interested in dating you. Not because I don't date coworkers but because I don't think we are compatible. Also, it really fucking sucked when you cheated on me, and I would prefer to move on from that dark chapter in my life. I harbor no ill will, though, and wish you the best of luck in your future dating endeavors."

But when I try to open my mouth to repeat those words myself, they don't come out. Instead, all I can manage is "I…I am, um, well, not—um, yes."

I mentally kick myself. Could I come off as any less coherent?

Her blue eyes pierce mine. "Really? Because it looks like you and Lucy are…getting along well."

Shit. Lucy is a subject I *definitely* do not want to be getting into right now. I force myself to look unaffected as I shake my head. "She's been a good friend, helping me get situated here."

"So you would never want to date her?" she pushes.

Fear rises again at the thought of Georgia finding a way to sabotage me if I say yes. And I can't risk it. These feelings that have started to develop are so fresh and exciting—I don't want anything to risk this spark between us. So while @TheMissGuidedCounselor may not agree, I think in this case, the most prudent thing to do is to lie.

Both to get me out of this conversation and get Georgia out of the way for me to give this chemistry with Lucy a fair shot.

"No," I finally say, rubbing my eyes as I feel a headache coming on. "I would never date Lucy. Can we move on now?"

After a long moment, she finally says, "Well, it's good to know where you stand." She pushes off the desk and smooths a wrinkle from her skirt. "I guess that's that, then." With a small wave of her hand, she walks out of the room, her heels clicking on the linoleum floor.

I blow out a relieved breath and sink back to my seat. Not wanting to risk a potentially awkward second encounter as we both walk to the parking lot, I decide to loiter in my office a bit longer. I dig my phone from my bag to scroll through Instagram and am instantly inundated with pictures of old friends and colleagues smiling bright for the camera, showing off their perfect families and lives.

Against my better interest, I navigate over to check on *her*. My father's mistress, who I follow anonymously on my burner account. She tends to post a few times a week, and she's recently shared a new photo where she is standing in front of a chalkboard countdown to the baby's birthdate. Apparently, my future baby sibling is the size of a cantaloupe.

It's weird, thinking that in just a few months I will have a new sibling that will be thirty years younger than me. And proof of the affair that ripped my family apart.

I don't blame them, though, his mistress and her cantaloupe. A small part of me even hopes to have some kind of relationship with them. After all, their father will be practically geriatric—they'll need a fun uncle to take them out and play with them. And as angry as I am with my father, I know that, for the sake of this baby, we will need to find a way to coexist. We haven't spoken more than a few dozen words all summer, ever since I had confronted him about the affair, needing to hear the truth from him for myself. He's attempted to reach out more with a phone call or two every week, but I decline them all. While I know I need to shed this anger at some point, returning home each day to my heartbroken mother makes that hard to do.

I zoom in on the picture. She has a name—Amelia—but it's hard for me to think of her as anything other than the other woman. She's so young; she can't be that much older than me. And she looks so happy. Is she in love with my father? Or excited about having a baby with eighteen years of seven-figure child support?

I hate that I've become this jaded, but money has a way of doing that to you. When I was growing up, it was always hard to weed out who wanted to be my friend because they liked me and who wanted me for my wallet. That's why I love being @BravesGuy93. When I'm him, I can know that I'm liked for being me—my real, authentic self—and not for being the son of a billionaire hedge fund manager.

It's the same being around Lucy—I feel so comfortable around her. Like just being in her presence makes me feel safe to voice all the chaos and worries in my head, because I know she won't judge me for them, but instead take all those knots of tangled, anxious feelings and hold them tenderly in her hands, unfurling them until they're nothing more than harmless individual ribbons that don't feel so overwhelming any more.

She's unlike anyone I have ever met, and this pull to her I feel only keeps me wanting more. More of her quirky sense of humor, more of watching her scrunch her nose when she laughs, more of wondering what it would feel like to kiss her lips and feel her body beneath mine.

I have it *bad*.

I've found myself looking for excuses to run into her, timing my free periods to walk by her office and stop for a chat. I just want…*more* of her. And even now that I know Georgia's watching and could make trouble, more is all I can think about. My thoughts are a mess, and if there's one person who can sort through it all with me, it's @TheMissGuidedCounselor.

I open up our latest DM exchange.

BravesGuy93   4:13 PM
Hey I think I may need some of that all-knowing wisdom of yours… again 😊

TheMissGuidedCounselor   4:14 PM
Be careful, I might start charging you! I recently learned from a student I can apparently be making a much more lucrative career here on Instagram if I just shared a few more pictures of my butt. I could be a living, breathing influencer!

BravesGuy93   4:15 PM
Well, by all means, do NOT let me stop you. And, if you ever would like to send a few butt pictures for me to first vet and professionally assess, I would be happy to take on that burden.

TheMissGuidedCounselor   4:15 PM
How gracious of you.

Anyway, stop deflecting. What advice do you need? My brain is fried and I need some new content for the 'Gram, so give me something good I can recycle later!

BravesGuy93   4:16 PM

Really? Using your poor friend's life woes for content? You should be absolutely ashamed.

TheMissGuidedCounselor   4:17 PM

Oh, I am. Now spill so I can start drafting my next post…

BravesGuy93   4:18 PM

Ugh, fine.

Since we've—well, you've—already established you have zero interest in meeting me offline and falling in love with my boyish good looks and ability to pull off salmon-colored shorts, I have unfortunately had to move on and, well, I think I found someone.

TheMissGuidedCounselor   4:19 PM

…

Can you clarify what the problem is? This sounds good?

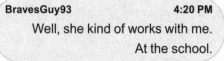

BravesGuy93   4:20 PM

Well, she kind of works with me.

At the school.

TheMissGuidedCounselor   4:20 PM

😎 Seriously?

BravesGuy93   4:21 PM

Yes, seriously. What happened to

your "judgment-free zone"?

TheMissGuidedCounselor   4:22 PM

Did we not learn from your

"extracurricular" lessons in French the

last time you asked out a coworker?

She has me there. Back at Kenton, I had asked out one of the French teachers, thinking it would be harmless since we were in different departments. But very early on, I could tell we weren't very compatible. Trouble is, she had felt differently. And it had led to an extremely awkward year where I would frequently find soggy, moldy baguettes shoved into my mail cubby.

I write back:

BravesGuy93   4:23 PM

This is different.

She is different.

TheMissGuidedCounselor   4:23 PM

How? Concrete examples, please.

My fingers hover above my phone before I start rapidly typing away.

> **BravesGuy93**   **4:24 PM**
> She's funny.
> Way funnier than you, actually.
> And she's beautiful.
> Super gorgeous brown eyes that
> just, I don't know, pull you in.
> And I like the way she laughs.
> It's cute.

 TheMissGuidedCounselor   **4:26 PM**
> Now I KNOW you're lying.

> **BravesGuy93**   **4:27 PM**
> Really? And how is that?

 TheMissGuidedCounselor   **4:28 PM**
> It's impossible there is someone out
> there funnier than me.

I roll my eyes, but I'm biting back a smile.

> **BravesGuy93**   **4:28 PM**
> It's true, better believe it. You would
> probably like her, too. She's a
> guidance counselor like you.

 TheMissGuidedCounselor   **4:30 PM**
> HA. No way!

Guidance counselors are all weirdos (present company excluded, obviously). But I want to get to the juicy stuff. What's the issue exactly? Sure, it's probably not the smartest idea to date a coworker, but it's been done before. And it sounds like you really like her.

I hesitate before writing back, knowing she will likely send another round of eye roll emojis. All deserved.

BravesGuy93   4:31 PM

Well, it's a bit more complicated because my ex-girlfriend also happens to work here. And she was just in my classroom asking for us to get back together.

As expected, I get my dozen or so eye roll emojis.

TheMissGuidedCounselor   4:33 PM

🙄🙄🙄🙄🙄🙄🙄🙄🙄🙄🙄🙄🙄🙄

How is your life more dramatic than a telenovela? Let me guess—do you also have an evil twin determined to kill you? A secret baby? Have you ever had amnesia and forgotten your aforementioned evil twin and secret baby?

I laugh, feeling a lightness settling over my shoulders. My chats with @TheMissGuidedCounselor always make me feel better and leave me with a much-needed smile on my face.

Behind the computer screen as @BravesGuy93, I could be honest about my feelings. Sure, I didn't share the super personal details about my life, and I avoided talking about my family's wealth, which made me uncomfortable, but I shared how I felt about those things. How I was often angry at my father's selfishness. Disappointed by my brother's complacency. Annoyed at my little sister's self-centeredness and frustrated by my mother's inability to stand up for herself. And @TheMissGuidedCounselor just…*got* it. Never judged me for my feelings, even as she held me accountable and challenged me. Encouraging me to not sit, helpless at my emotions, but to do something about them.

Without her, I would still be the same miserable teacher at Kenton. Without her, I never would have transferred to Harview. Never would have met Lucy.

I type out my response with a relaxed smile that feels foreign on my face.

> **BravesGuy93**   **4:35 PM**
> How is it that you always seem to make all my problems seem not that big and scary at all?

> **TheMissGuidedCounselor**   **4:36 PM**
> Duh, it's how I make the big bucks. Did you not see the part where I told you I was an ~influencer~?

BravesGuy93   4:37 PM

Oh, how could I forget?
Anyway, I think the coast is clear.
Any parting words of wisdom before
I head out for the day?

TheMissGuidedCounselor   4:38 PM
Yeah.
This woman actually sounds like
she would be amazing for you.
Don't mess it up.

TheMissGuidedCounselor
Posted at 7:44 PM

Are you crushing on someone in your professional life? Here are 3 questions to ask yourself before taking things a step further.

1. Don't feel embarrassed or ashamed or guilty about your crush! You spend more time at work than you do in most other places in your life, and it's only natural you might find someone you have a romantic interest in. Ditching negative feelings about your crush will help you make smarter and less-emotional choices about whether or not you want to pursue things further.

2. Make sure you have a full understanding of what would happen if you did take things to the next level. How would you feel about other teachers knowing about your relationship? Or even scarier, your students? And what happens if the relationship doesn't work out? Would you be okay working so closely with your ex? Make sure you have a firm grasp on these important questions before making any decisions.

3. And remember, in the wise words of the incomparable Taylor Swift: "Even if it ends badly, it's worth it if it made you feel something. It taught you something."

Liked by **BravesGuy93** and **others**

TheMissGuidedCounselor Let's talk…more

View all comments

TheMissGuidedCounselor
Today at 9:17 PM

BravesGuy93
Well, don't I feel called out by your post today.

 TheMissGuidedCounselor
Look at you and your big ego. You know, *not* everything is always about you.

BravesGuy93
😵😵😵
I don't believe it. Does THE famous @TheMissGuidedCounselor have a crush on someone?
Wait, is it me?
You can tell me, you know. I promise I will not freak out and immediately purchase a plane ticket to meet you and fully woo you in person.
How do you feel about a ukulele serenade?
And do you have any food allergies I should know about?

TheMissGuidedCounselor
Okay, buddy, let's slow down. Your ego is becoming concerningly overinflated, you know.

BravesGuy93
So, I'm taking it this post was not about your secret love for me...

TheMissGuidedCounselor
I am afraid not. Besides, don't you think you have your hands full enough with that little love triangle you've walked yourself into your first week of school?

BravesGuy93
Ouch, but fair. So, spill. I'm always the one with the dating drama. Who's the lucky guy?

TheMissGuidedCounselor
He's just...someone I have met and felt a bit of a, oh, I don't know, a spark with.

BravesGuy93
I'm going to need some more details here.

TheMissGuidedCounselor

Can't. I'm heading off to dinner and need to get off my phone before my sister snatches it out of my hands.

BravesGuy93

Fine, leave me hanging. I guess I'll just have to imagine for myself what kind of guy is special enough to catch the infamous MissGuided's attention…

Chapter Ten

♡ *Lucy*

"MORE."

My sister arches her brow but doesn't say anything as she fills my glass to the rim with the dark red wine. She barely has time to snatch her hand away before I am pouring the wine down my throat. I'm not a drinker, and *technically* I shouldn't be drinking with my current med regimen, but that's why I need to chug this Merlot before my father, who conveniently happens to be a psychiatrist, comes barreling through the door, listing the side effects of drinking while on antidepressants like the ending credits of *every* drug commercial on TV.

"So, uh, what's with all this?" Julieta asks when I finish shotgunning my glass.

I swipe my mouth with the back of my hand and lift my shoulder. "Rough week."

Julieta opens her mouth to respond, but Amira's late arrival interrupts her.

Sauntering into the dining room, Amira collapses into an empty seat with a loud sigh before turning her attention to me. "So am I forgiven yet?" she asks with a hopeful smile.

"Tomorrow," I say, gesturing for Julieta to refill my glass. "*If* I'm feeling generous."

Amira lets out a low whistle. "Someone's in a mood. Did you see the *hot tea* today? Get it? Instead of hottie, it's 'hot' and 'tea,' like because of the whole tea—"

"We get it," Julieta and I answer at the same time.

I sigh. "And I saw him for a few minutes, and thankfully it wasn't *too* awkward. No thanks to you," I add, shooting her a pointed look.

"Okay, so then what's with this gloomy mood? And your newly acquired drinking habit?" Amira asks.

I wish I knew how to answer in a way that made sense. Why *am* I so gloomy?

Well, because of Fletcher and this stupid, annoying crush I can't shake off, no matter how badly I want to. Today, when we bumped into each other outside my office, he had enthusiastically shared how much he and his mom had enjoyed the takeout from the restaurant and while the conversation had been…nice, I hadn't been able to help but want more. Fletcher is quickly becoming an addiction, and I keep needing another hit.

It feels foolish to admit how I'm disappointed when we don't get to talk for more than five minutes. When I don't see his smile, or hear his laugh, or uncover some new fact about his life. Why do I care so much? I've only known Fletcher for three weeks, and while he's always nice, he is clearly just interested in being friends. After all, Fletcher is nice to everyone—always laughing with other teachers and high-fiving his students. And while, yes, he did make it a point to sit with me and Nia for lunch most days, that could just be because Nia always packs extra candy in her lunch and shares it. Maybe he just *really* likes Skittles? It doesn't mean he's interested in anything more.

Right?

This wouldn't be the first time I mistakenly conflated simple conversations with what was in my head, thinking they meant more than they did. It's one of my favorite pastimes and the reason why I convinced myself I had been in a long-distance relationship with Tom Wheeler for almost a year in eighth grade when he moved to Oregon and gave me a hug that, for me, had meant we were practically engaged.

"Girls, time to come light the candles!"

At my aunt's call, my sisters and I rise from the table and join the women of our family in the living room.

My mother, my tante Mirelle, her two daughters, Sarah and Yael, and Yael's daughter, Bella, crowd into the kitchen alongside Julieta, who pulls off her stained apron as she stands by the kitchen counter. There two tall white candles stand in elegant blue and white ceramic candlesticks. My aunt smiles when she sees me and places a matchbox in my hand. She rarely passes off the Friday-evening prayer to anyone else, preferring to stick to our family tradition of having the oldest woman in the house perform the mitzvah of lighting the candles.

I must really be looking terrible if even my aunt notices I need a pick-me-up.

I strike a match against the coarse sandpaper on the side of the box. A flame jumps on its tip, and I light the two candles before lifting my hands, fanning them over the flames and toward my face three times as I "guide" in the Sabbath.

"Baruch ata Adonai Eloheinu melech ha'olam, asher kid'shanu b'mitzvotav v'tzivanu l'hadlik ner shel Shabbat," I recite, and an echo of "amens" follows. There's always a peaceful shift after we light our candles, the weariness and stress of the week fading to the background. Arms wrap around each other, and kisses press into cheeks as we all wish each other "Shabbat Shalom."

Friday nights are sacred in our home. Each week, we gather—sometimes just my immediate family, sometimes more. My parents have a habit of inviting strangers to our table, particularly if they are Jewish and of "marriageable" age for their daughters. No matter how many, we always find a way to fit everyone into the dining room, and the leaves of the table always seem to stretch long enough to fit whoever wanders into our home.

Then, for the next few hours, we eat and talk and eat some more. There is always singing—usually after a bottle or two of wine. Inevitably, the children will get bored and start running around the house before they pile in the middle of the living room, a jacket or rogue blanket covering them.

It's a familiar but comforting pattern.

After the women finish welcoming Shabbat and exchanging hugs and kisses, my mother shuffles around the house, collecting the stray men as we bring the assorted food out to the table. Tonight dinner looks like whitefish, cooked in a rich sauce with tomato, chickpeas, lemon, and my aunt's secret mixture of ras el hanout spices. A vat of couscous, drizzled with olive oil and parsley, and a chopped salad of cucumbers, chickpeas, and red onions joins the fish.

And then, like most every other week, there is our dafina, a stew of red meat with chickpeas and potatoes, sweetened with honey and cinnamon as it cooks throughout the day, bathing the house in the sweet smell that wraps around me like a soft, warm blanket on even the chilliest of nights. The recipe has been passed down for generations, with tiny tweaks and changes throughout the years as it's been shared with all the women of the family.

That tradition temporarily came to an abrupt halt when Julieta cooked a vegan version and horrified the entire family with her tofu "lamb," getting herself banished from the kitchen for three weeks.

As we all sit down, my father takes his place at the head of the table and lifts up a gold-etched cup teeming with wine. We all rise as he recites the Hebrew prayer in his accent laced with French and Arabic. The harmonious blend of all three languages is a lyrical melody that is uniquely his. In a sea of voices, my father's always stands apart.

His voice is home.

And Shabbat dinner is, too. Our weekly dinners are one of the few constants in my life and though, at times, I resented the obligation (like when I missed the infamous tenth-grade scandal of Ricky O'Reilly skinny-dipping in Jenny Freedman's pool), I've come to appreciate it more in my adult years. Shabbat is more than a weekly dinner: it's the opportunity to end the week and begin a new one with a clean slate.

With the lighting of our Shabbat candles, I can always start again, no matter what happened during the days before. It's the "reverse" Uno card for Jews.

My father takes a long sip from the wine and then picks up the challah, freshly baked this morning from our cousin's bakery, reciting another prayer before ripping off a piece to share with everyone around the table. Right as the challah reaches me, a series of loud beeps echoes in the room from my phone, which I had forgotten to silence.

"Someone's popular," Amira remarks before shoving a piece in her mouth.

Before I can respond, my phone goes off again, and I slide it out of my pocket to turn off the ringer. I smile when I see the series of Instagram messages from @BravesGuy93, who apparently has a lot of free time on his hands tonight.

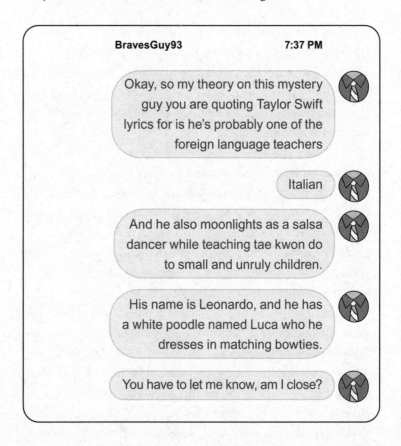

BravesGuy93   7:37 PM

Okay, so my theory on this mystery guy you are quoting Taylor Swift lyrics for is he's probably one of the foreign language teachers

Italian

And he also moonlights as a salsa dancer while teaching tae kwon do to small and unruly children.

His name is Leonardo, and he has a white poodle named Luca who he dresses in matching bowties.

You have to let me know, am I close?

"Oh, who is making you smile like that, Lulu?" Amira teases from across the table.

At the sound of my name, I jerk my head up to find my entire immediate family staring at me.

"Uh, a friend," I stammer.

Amira balks. "Nia is making you smile like *that*?"

"I have lots of friends besides Nia," I argue for absolutely no reason other than to maintain a tiny shred of dignity.

We all know I don't have any other friends.

"He's a friend from online," I add impulsively. "You don't know him."

I realize that I've just done the adult version of "You wouldn't know my boyfriend. He goes to a different school." It lands pretty much the same as it did when I told my friends about Mario, the football-playing, six-foot-tall pescatarian boyfriend I had for two years in high school that they were never able to meet because of his strict parents, Tony and Martha.

Sadly, I had to kill Mario off in a tragic surfing accident because the pressure was growing too high—and it was getting too expensive to send myself flowers.

RIP Mario.

My confession opens the floodgate of questions.

"Oh, kinky! Is he like a sugar daddy?" Amira asks.

"You didn't give him your Social Security number, right, Lulu?" Papa follows.

"Does his mother know he's messaging girls online?" Amá says.

I glance longingly at the Shabbat candles at the center of the table. A strategic kick and they'd tip over, catching the linen tablecloth on fire, and in the chaos, I could slip away. But arson seems a bit extreme, even for me.

I hold up my hand. "This is not a big deal. We just talk

online sometimes." Okay, practically every day, but they don't need to know that.

Julieta rests her chin on her hand. "So what's his name? Where's he from?"

You would think that, as friends for a year now, I *would* know these things about him. Instead, what I do know is his favorite food (his mom's lasagna), the top five celebrities he thinks are hottest, and his weird aversion to hot fudge.

But his name?

Where he lives?

Yeah, I don't know that.

And worse, I don't know how to explain that to my family.

"We keep most of those details private."

Despite us chatting well into the night, I don't even know what @BravesGuy93 looks like or where he lives. I know it's because I'm so protective of my identity as @TheMissGuidedCounselor.

I never dare let details of my life as Lucy seep into my online space—at least not on my Instagram feed, which is perfectly curated and designed thanks to the hours I spend tediously designing each graphic post on my Canva account. Every font has to be perfectly aligned to the center, each caption spell-checked twice, and the color scheme dependent on the content of the post (navy blue for inspirational quotes, peach for lists, and a pale robin's-egg blue for advice).

Because while Lucy is flawed, a little messy, clumsy, and awkward, @TheMissGuidedCounselor is the exact opposite. She is concise, wise, and professional. She always knows *exactly* what to do—unlike IRL Lucy, who takes the entire day to craft a single email, contemplating if the ratio of exclamation marks to periods is too high. And @TheMissGuidedCounselor would definitely *not* be waiting around for the hot history teacher to decide whether he wanted to ask her out or not—she would ask *him* out, dazzling him with her wit and exceptional graphic design skills.

"Okay, so what *do* you two talk about then?" asks Amira, and the thick, dark-brown eyebrows shared by all my family members lift in anticipation around the table.

"Just about our lives and how our days go. He's a teacher, so he gets what work is like. We talk about our families—mostly about how insane all of you are." I purposefully glare at Amira. "And unlike you all, he respects my boundaries."

"Well, why don't you meet up, then, if you get along so well? Maybe he can come over for dinner?" my mother asks, the excitement barely contained on her face.

I decide to spare my mother a lecture on the dangers of inviting strangers from the internet over for dinner, especially considering this guy probably lives halfway across the country—or worse, in Florida.

But still, my mom's question reminds me how protective I feel over my friendship with @BravesGuy93. While I've succeeded at keeping @TheMissGuidedCounselor the perfect guidance counselor that I aspire to be, I've allowed myself to be a little more Lucy in my DMs with @BravesGuy93.

Thanks to the hours and hours we spend messaging, I've grown comfortable with him. Let him see the slightly less curated parts of myself. But still, I wasn't brave enough to show him *everything*. It's why I pushed him away when he asked for us to meet in person. As much as I love our friendship and how freely I can speak with him, I have to keep that wall up.

A wall that I won't let down for him—*can't* let down for him. I'm so unlike @TheMissGuidedCounselor in real life that

I know if we ever do meet, he'll be woefully underwhelmed and disappointed. That's what I'm hiding from him—the knowledge that Lucy in real life would never, ever be enough.

Because if we did cross that line, break all my rules? If he finally saw me—*all* of me?

I know the answer to that question even without asking it.

He would run.

Or, I guess, in this case, ghost. Which is, unfortunately, something I have dealt with quite a bit as a millennial hoping to find love by swiping right. Time and time again, I've put myself out there and laid bare all my mismatched puzzle pieces, hoping that there would be a man willing enough to try to fit them together. A few came close, but inevitably, they disappeared.

And while my family, Nia, and a half dozen or so therapists have tried to convince me otherwise, the truth is, it always feels like I'm too much work, and even more heartbreaking: I'm not worth the effort.

I'm not enough for any person to fully love.

And no matter how much everyone in my life denies it, sometimes it's hard to hear their voices when the ones in my head, telling me how worthless and unlovable I am, are often the loudest.

That thought kicks me straight in the gut, and within seconds, my eyes are watering. I pinch my eyes closed, wishing I wasn't so damn transparent.

"Oh, Lulu." Julieta's hand reaches for mine. "What's wrong?"

I suck in a breath and shrug. "I don't know, really. I guess it's just been a long time since I even thought I had feelings like this for someone, and it's just so overwhelming because there is no way a man like Fletcher would ever want to be with someone like me.

And it makes me wonder if any man will ever want to be with me *ever* or if I am going to just be alone for the rest of my life."

I let out a gasp before turning to my sister and wrapping my arms around her. I need a hug right now, and Julieta always smells really good (her double Ds also make a soft landing place for my cheeks). She doesn't rush me, just pets my hair. The rest of the room is quiet, filling me with guilt.

It's just like little depressed Lulu to ruin a nice family dinner with one of her episodes.

I pull away and swipe my tears away with the back of my hand. "I'm sorry. I'll just go home so everyone can finish dinner."

"No, no," my mother says, reaching across the table to take my hand. "You stay right here with us."

Between sobs, I say, "I don't want to ruin dinner."

"You never ruin anything for us," Papa says, his voice a gentle and calming timbre that always comforts me. "You make it better. You make everything better, Lulu. And this boy—your online friend—they would be lucky to have someone like you in their life. You are a fighter, Lulu. You've gotten yourself out of your dark times before. You'll do it again."

"But what if…" I pause and swallow, fears rising one after the other. "What if I'm not enough for someone to love? I mean, I don't even know who the hell I am!"

"What do you mean you don't know who you are, mija?"

"Well, for starters, I barely speak any Spanish, and I know this is like heresy, but I don't like chicharrónes. They give me really bad gas—not to mention all the Jewish guilt for eating pork."

The words are spilling out of me like a flood.

"But I also don't feel like super Moroccan because I don't

speak French really well, either, and I only know curse words in Arabic. And all the other Moroccans in town are Muslim, and they're cool, but I don't really fit in with them, either. And all the other Jews are Ashkenazi and they think we're the weird Sephardic family that eats rice at Passover.

"And even here!" I add, waving my arm across the table. "You're all normal and don't have any kind of mental health issues, while I live in a constant existential crisis!"

The room grows silent.

I've never spoken with my family so candidly about the anxiety I carry around my identity. My sisters always seem to spring so easily back and forth between our two families, something that always sends my stomach sinking. But I always feel like I have to wear a mask, tempering my Jewish self while in the presence of the Mexican side or hiding my Mexican self when at synagogue.

I know both sides of our family wholeheartedly embrace all the parts of us, but that same measure of comfort doesn't exist with my Jewish peers. I always feel like I'm on the outside looking in: a viewer instead of a participant. I'm never *quite* Jewish enough because my father is a Sephardi Jew from Morocco, and I didn't grow up watching *Seinfeld* or eating gefilte fish, and our skin is just a little *too* dark. And despite having a mikveh well before my bat mitzvah, I'm *still* not Jewish enough for some because my mother isn't Jewish.

Basically, my head is a constant battle of never feeling good enough for anyone.

My father leans forward. "Lulu, of course you belong here. In this family, in your mother's family and in mine. You belong, and not because of your DNA or what languages you speak or food you like, but because you are our daughter, and we love you."

"But didn't it make you upset when that rabbi called you an Arab and said you're not a real Jew? Or Amá, weren't you angry when you couldn't stand on the bima for Amira's bat mitzvah?"

My father's eyes soften, and he slowly shakes his head. "Lulu, there are always going to be people in this world who try to separate and divide. They look for differences, rather than the things that bring us together." He reaches for my mother's hand and cradles it in his. "When we met, your mother and I were from two different countries, cultures, religions, languages—on paper we had nothing in common. And if we had accepted that, we would never have fallen in love or had you girls. And what a tragedy that would be, eh?"

He pauses and levels his gaze to mine. "You don't need anyone's permission to be who you are, Lulu. You tell the world who you are."

"But what if I don't know who I am?"

My father smiles and waves his hand. "You have your whole life to figure that out. You know," he says, turning his attention back to my sisters around the table, "this reminds me of when your mother and my sister decided to open a restaurant together."

My sisters and I all reflexively groan. Remember when I said my parents would remind us of the origins of the family restaurant thousands of times?

Yeah, I wasn't lying.

My father glares at us before continuing, "They could communicate only in pieces of Spanish and English. And they would argue for hours because they were both too stubborn and could never find the words to resolve their conflicts. But when they cooked? It was pure magic." Pinching his fingers together, he makes a loud kissing sound.

"Food was their language and what brought them together. When they cooked, they created something amazing. They told the world, through their food, who they were. You'll find your way, Lulu, to share who you are. I have no doubt."

I swipe away an errant tear as Julieta gives my hand another squeeze.

"And don't think that we," she says, gesturing to Amira, "don't also struggle with how we feel about our identities. You remember that time I studied in a seminary for a year and kept kosher and shomer Shabbat? I was so desperate to feel some kind of spiritual connection and thought that was, like, the only way to do it. I felt I had something to prove to everyone back home, like that I was Jewish enough because I wore long skirts and didn't rip my toilet paper on Shabbat." She laughs.

"And do you think it's easy for me," Amira adds, a playful smile on her lips, "when I am *this* gorgeous and have all the moms at the synagogue *begging* me to marry their sons? It's exhausting!"

Julieta shakes her head. *Ignore her*, she mouths silently to me.

"Look, we all struggle in our own ways," Amira says, her tone turning slightly more serious. "You are not abnormal. You're amazing, and you are enough. I want you to know that, and if some guy doesn't see that? Then he's not the one for you."

I dab at my eyes with my napkin, doing my best to keep my tears from spilling down my cheeks. I can't lie—it's draining to feel this shame at my inability to reconcile all these pieces of me.

For as long as I can remember, I've been a walking identity crisis who overanalyzed everything, someone with love handles and sideburns, who cried too much and felt things too deeply. Too self-conscious and afraid of being rejected, too used to sitting on the sidelines.

But it's a lonely way to live.

No wonder I'm always exhausted—siloing all these different parts of me is a lot of work. But maybe all these mismatched puzzle pieces don't mean I am broken or not enough.

Maybe it just means that putting together my puzzle takes a little extra willpower and grit. Maybe some industrial, builder-grade glue.

I never put myself out there because I couldn't chance getting hurt, but now I'm beginning to wonder if Fletcher might be worth that risk. Even worth the hurt. I like the way he makes me feel, the way he looks at me, the way he laughs at my silly, clumsy jokes.

I like how I feel when I'm around him.

And maybe that's enough for now. Maybe it's enough to just *want* to try, knowing it won't be easy and that it's okay if I mess up along the way. Because while I can live with mistakes, I don't want to live with regret.

Chapter Eleven

 *Lucy*

SOMETHING SUSPICIOUS IS GOING on with the Konfident Kids Klub.

For one, they've neglected to set up our semicircle of trust prior to the start of our Monday meeting. They *always* set it up, purposefully not including my chair as if to remind me that I am not part of the semicircle. Which, to be honest, should not hurt my feelings as much as it does considering I am over a decade older than all these kids.

They're also completely ignoring me. Most of the time, they have the decency to pretend to respect my very limited authority, but today they are all talking over each other, phones out as they all discuss something in excited whispers.

My curiosity is killing me—and we need to get through another chapter in this giant binder I have lugged with me—so I drop it on the top of a nearby table, where it lands with a deafening thud.

The chatter stops and I have everyone's full attention. "Who wants to spill about what's gotten you all so excited?"

The girls all share another round of side glances, communicating in the unknown language of near-invisible eye movements and imperceptible shrugs. Clearly, I have killed their excitement.

"Come on," I continue, my voice taking on a dangerous level of desperation that I know will lose me whatever little respect I may have with them. "What's the tea?"

I've taken a risk using the slang of the youth, but I am hoping it pays off and they see me as someone cool enough to share whatever has them so excited. It's very important for my job that I stay attuned to the current trends to help me relate to my students, so they feel comfortable confiding in me.

Also, I'm nosy.

Sadly, no one bites, so I turn up the heat. I see Trina shifting uncomfortably in her seat, and I know I have my weakest link. When she makes the mistake of making eye contact with me, I pounce. "Trina, what's going on?"

She shares a furtive glance with Nicola, seated beside her, and they both erupt into a fit of giggles. "Sophia is going to be famous!" she gushes, her cheeks flushing a bright pink.

"What do you mean Sophia is going to be famous?" I ask, a knot beginning to form in my stomach as I visualize Sophia lounging on some yacht.

"She is going to be in DJ Breezy Buzz Boo's new music video!" Nicola squeals excitedly.

Instantly my stomach sinks. More than that, it catapults out of my body and lands on the floor in a squishy, gross mess. When we spoke the other day, I wrongly thought I had talked her out of this ridiculous, reckless fantasy of hers.

But I was so wrong.

A combination of fear, worry, and anger wrap around me so tightly it feels like my chest is closing in on itself. "Where is she right now? Does anyone know?" I ask, failing, despite my best efforts, to temper the alarm in my voice.

The room is silent, and my frustration seeps into my words. "Listen, Sophia could be in danger right now, so if you know something, I need you to tell me. *Now.*"

There's a long pause, until Trina breaks and hands me her phone. "She posted on her Instagram Story an hour ago."

I glance down at the phone to see Sophia, taking a selfie in some dirty bathroom mirror. Across the photo, in big pink letters, the caption reads: My last pic before I'm famous!

"Who has Sophia's cell phone number?" I demand. When no one responds, I repeat the question more firmly. Nicola pulls out her phone and reads me the number, which I copy down into my cell phone.

"You all wait here for me," I instruct as I step out into the hall. The students are all somber, my reaction hopefully finally showing them how serious the situation really is. As soon as the door closes behind me, I am dialing Sophia's number. She doesn't answer on the first or second try, but finally picks up on the third.

"Sophia? This is Ms. Galindo. Are you okay?"

I hear sniffles over the sound of loud music and raucous laughter. "I think I made a mistake," Sophia says, her voice barely audible with all the background noise.

"It's okay, Sophia. I just need you to tell me where you are, and I'll come get you."

I hear more sniffles.

"I don't know where I am."

"Okay, can you ask someone there? I can send over an Uber to pick you up."

"I'm scared," she confesses, her voice shaky. She's muffled and it sounds like she's trying not to be overheard. Dread washes over me, but I ignore it, thinking through what I need to do.

"Send me a pin of where you are, and I'll come get you. Don't go anywhere, okay? I'm coming."

"Thank you," she whispers, then adds, "Please hurry."

I disconnect the call and open the door. "I have to leave early," I tell the girls as I pick up my bag. They all watch me, silent and guilt-stricken, and I'm hoping the gravity of Sophia's dangerous situation is finally sinking in. "We'll talk about this next week."

I don't wait for a response as I rush out the door. My phone is in one hand as I dig through my purse to find my keys with the other. My heart hammers in my chest, panic squeezing my insides as each second passes without hearing from her—until my phone dings and I get a pin of her location.

She's in the city. I *hate* driving in the city, mostly because I can't parallel park and I find one-way streets confusing, but I need to get over that to help Sophia.

I try to open the door leading to the back parking lot with my hip, but the door doesn't open—it pushes into me and I tumble backward, spilling the contents of my purse all over the floor. On all fours, I ignore whoever opened the door on me and start snatching up my belongings and shoving them back in my bag.

"Oh, shoot!"

I look up to see Fletcher's familiar face. "Are you okay?" he asks. "I'm so sorry, I didn't see you. I forgot my thermos, so I was running back to get it and…Are you okay?"

I jump to my feet, finally having located my keys. "I'm fine, but Sophia's in trouble and I need to go into Boston to get her and I think it's all my fault. I mean, I didn't think she was going to seriously try to meet up with him! But now she has, and she's scared and needs my help and I'm not a very good driver." The words rush out of my mouth, betraying the panic I am trying to quell.

Fletcher's hands wrap around my arms. "Hey, hey. Slow down. What happened?"

I take a calming breath. "Sophia met up with some guy she met online. A DJ she told me about. And she's with him now, but she needs me to come get her."

Fletcher nods and reaches for my hand. "I'll drive."

"This is it! We're here."

I point to a nondescript red-brick building and Fletcher slides behind a car, killing the engine. I look out my window, trying to see if I can spot anyone, but the street is empty and the windows of the building are all shielded by dark blinds. There's no sign outside except for a small and rusted bronze plate listing the building number, 322.

I pick up my phone and dial Sophia's number again. It rings and rings, but she doesn't answer. I try again, and then a third and fourth time before turning to Fletcher, panic rising. "She's not answering."

Fletcher nods and unbuckles his seat belt. "I'll go in and get her. You wait here."

"What?" I jump out of the car and follow him. "No way!"

"Who knows where the hell we are, Lucy? It might not be safe and—"

"I'm coming," I say, cutting him off. "Now let's go in."

I'm putting on a bit of a brave front because in any other circumstance, I would have *much* rather preferred waiting in the car. But this is my student, and I've known her now for two years. She's a good kid who made a really stupid decision. My only hope is that she wasn't harmed in doing so.

Fletcher pushes open the door, and we step into a dark entryway that feeds into a long, narrow hall. It looks like a run-down office building without many tenants. Most of the placards on the doors are empty, and as we round a corner, a staircase leads to a second floor. We don't speak as we ascend the stairs, but around halfway up, we hear a thumping bass. It's so loud that it rattles the neglected paintings hung over shabby, faded floral wallpaper.

The overwhelming smell of marijuana accompanies the sound.

This isn't the type of place Sophia should be. With her grades and grit, she has a promising future ahead of her. We pass a door with an OUT OF SERVICE sign hanging on for dear life by a single strip of yellowed tape. Near the end of the hall, the last door is slightly ajar.

Fletcher looks over at me and I nod. *This is it.*

He pushes open the door, and I follow very closely behind him. The room is dimly lit and filled with half a dozen mismatched couches that leave very little space to move. On them are a few couples, including one aggressively making out on stained blue pillows. A scarf covers a lamp in the corner, which I suppose gives a dimmed light effect, but really just looks like a fire hazard to me. No one seems to be paying any attention to us, despite Fletcher and I clearly not fitting in with the crowd, considering our clothes aren't ripped and our faces are free of any piercings.

We don't see Sophia, though, so we continue to another large room with surprisingly zero furniture. It's like whoever dragged the couches into the first room ran out of energy to bring a few more in here.

Fletcher and I share a look. *Where the hell are we?*

Beyond another doorway, the "music" grows louder and louder until we find a twenty-something white guy with green dreads sitting in front of a laptop in a dark room. The light from the screen illuminates his face as he brings a vape to his mouth, inhales, and then blows it out.

I hate him already.

Sophia isn't here, either, and I'm starting to sweat. Where the hell is she? Turns out Fletcher is a tad more comfortable engaging, because while I was looking around for anyone who looks like Sophia, he walked straight up to the green-dreaded man.

"I'm looking for a girl. Sophia. Where is she?"

Green Dreads just offers him a blank, unresponsive stare. I feel like I should be contributing more, so I ask the gaggle of girls sitting on the floor if they've seen her. They all shrug in response, perfectly unbothered by the fact that a sixteen-year-old girl is scared and lost.

To my surprise, Fletcher holds up his cell phone and loudly announces. "I'm calling the cops in five seconds unless someone tells me where the hell Sophia is right now."

The girls all rush out of the room, but Green Dreads just takes another puff from his vape, looking unbothered. "I told you, man, I have no idea who you're talking about."

I take a step forward.

I'm angry now.

I slam his laptop closed, which finally draws a reaction. But before he can protest, I hold up my hand, silencing him. I am wearing sensible flats with Dr. Scholl's orthopedic inserts and a black turtleneck. I am *not* a woman to be messed with. "Are you DJ Buzzy Bee?"

He sneers. "It's DJ Breezy Buzz Boo."

Fletcher groans at my side. Together we look like two disappointed and disapproving parents, which normally I would say isn't the best look for me. But for DJ Douche, it works. I imagine he's seen this look many a time before from his own poor parents.

When he moves to pick up his vape again, I snatch it from the table before he can.

"This," I say, holding it in front of him, "is going to annihilate your lungs, eating them from the inside out until they disintegrate into tiny little useless pieces of tissue that you hack into a cheap single-ply napkin at whatever hospital you end up dying at by your fortieth birthday because you never got a job with benefits because you wanted to play pretend DJ. You are *destroying* your brain synapses, and I swear to God if you do not tell me where Sophia is in the next five seconds, I will run this over with my car until it is nothing but tiny shards of plastic."

He hesitates a moment before exhaling on a sharp breath as he eyes his vape, then me, and then the vape again.

I win out.

He throws up his hands in defeat. "Fine! I don't know where she is. She kept messaging me to meet up, so I gave her this address and she hung out for a bit, but then freaked out and ditched. Someone said she was hiding in one of the bathrooms though."

I shake my head and slam his vape onto the table. "I am *very* disappointed in you," I say before turning and looking for the nearest bathroom. I am a woman on a mission to find my student, and I am throwing open any door I can spot now, but all we are finding are more empty rooms and more people making terrible life choices. Fletcher stays right by my side, and when we exhaust all the doors, I turn to face him. "What now?"

He bites down on his lip as he thinks. My stomach is a tight coil of nerves. *Where the hell is she?*

Fletcher looks up, his eyes widening with feverish emotion. "We must have passed the bathrooms." He grabs my hand, and we rush back through all the rooms, slamming doors behind us until we're at the one marked OUT OF SERVICE. I try for the knob, but it's locked. I tap on the door.

"Sophia? Are you in there? It's Ms. Galindo."

To my relief, the particle board door bursts open and Sophia tumbles out. Mascara stains her cheeks, and she reaches her arms out to pull me in for a hug. She sobs against me, and I look over her shoulder to find Fletcher watching us, relief written all over his face. I'm sure I look the same. The past hour of panic, fear, and guilt has taken its toll on me. I'm exhausted.

I pull away from Sophia. "Let's get you home, okay?"

She nods and uses the back of her hand to wipe away tears. I drape my arm around her, leading her back to Fletcher's car—which thankfully does not have a ticket because he super illegally parked.

We spend most of the drive back in silence. Sophia doesn't need a lecture right now, and truthfully, I'm too drained to even attempt one. When we're back in town, we first drop Sophia at home. Her mother and I quickly set up a family meeting for the following day, and then Fletcher drives us back to the now nearly empty parking lot of the school.

"You going to be okay?" Fletcher asks as he pulls up beside my car.

I nod. I'm not, but I don't want him to know that, so I force a smile. "Just tired."

He nods understandingly and gives my shoulder a gentle squeeze. "See you tomorrow," he says, dropping his hand, and I instantly miss the warmth and comfort from his touch.

Because he is a gentleman, he waits to make sure I get into my car before he leaves.

And because I'm a liar, I wait until his taillights fade into the distance before I lean over my steering wheel and sob, both with relief and with the overwhelming fear that, despite today's positive outcome, I'm not okay. It's *my* fault Sophia was in this position—clearly I overestimated my counseling skills, arrogantly assuming that Sophia hadn't truly been serious about pursuing her reality TV dreams. And because of that, Sophia had followed through on her quest for social media stardom, putting herself in danger. Because of *me*.

I let out another sob and angrily swipe at the tears now cascading down my cheeks. My cup is empty; my spoons are spent.

And all I have the energy to do is cry.

TheMissGuidedCounselor
Posted at 10:37 PM

Have you ever experienced a day that totally drained you physically, emotionally, and psychologically?

As teachers and school staff, we give so much of ourselves each and every day to our students, parents, and fellow colleagues. But it is so important to take the time to refill our own cups before returning to work to take care of everyone else. Burnout is the number one reason more than half of our nation's schoolteachers want to leave the field, so prioritizing our own self-care is so important. I want to encourage you all to remember that as we continue on this school year.

Need some ideas? Here are 5 ways to practice self-care after an emotionally taxing day:

1. Take the time to reflect without dwelling on what went wrong. It's important to process and validate your emotions, *without* focusing just on the negative. My suggestion? Try spending a few minutes journaling your feelings to get all those thoughts and emotions out of your head and onto paper.

2. Make the space to appreciate everything you did right. It is so easy to get caught up in what went wrong, so try to capture all that went right and honor those things as well.

3. Do an activity that will make you feel better. Whether it's a face mask, a long walk, or a stop at your favorite bakery on the way home—find one way to treat yourself. Try to end your day on a high note by doing something that makes you feel good.

4. Get some sleep. Seriously. Chances are your body needs it, and in order to conquer the next day, it's always a good idea to have a well-rested body *and* mind.

5. Know that just because today was hard, it doesn't mean tomorrow will be, too. It's okay to have a bad day, and those are the days that help us appreciate the good ones even more. Try to remember that one bad day doesn't mean the rest of the year will be the same. And don't forget—you've got this ♥

♡ ◯ ◁   ⊓

Liked by **BravesGuy93** and **others**

TheMissGuidedCounselor I want…more

View all comments

TheMissGuidedCounselor
Today at 11:01 PM

> **BravesGuy93**
> Excellent—and weirdly,
> timely—post today.
> As always.

 TheMissGuidedCounselor
Thanks.

> **BravesGuy93**
> Everything okay?

 TheMissGuidedCounselor
Yeah.

> **BravesGuy93**
> You sure?
> You know, I'm always here if you
> ever need to talk…

 TheMissGuidedCounselor
I know.
I'm sorry for being so short. It's just
that…well, today kind of sucked.

> **BravesGuy93**
> Shit, I'm sorry. Do you want to talk
> about it?

TheMissGuidedCounselor
I don't know.
I'm so exhausted and I just feel so…
drained.
Like a dried-up, wrung-out sponge
that's well past its prime, with dried
crumbs of old, moldy food stuck
alongside its edges.

BravesGuy93
That's certainly a visual.

TheMissGuidedCounselor
Sorry for being such a downer.

BravesGuy93
Never apologize for that.
We're friends—through the good
and the bad. And if you ever want to
talk about it, I'm here for you. Like
you have always been for me.

TheMissGuidedCounselor
Thanks. That, well, means a lot.
I think I'm just not really ready to
put into words what I'm feeling,
so maybe I'll take a raincheck on
talking about it?

BravesGuy93
I'm here whenever you're ready.

But in the meantime, why don't you take some advice from my good friend @TheMissGuidedCounselor and head to sleep? Tomorrow's a new day, and I promise to have at least five new memes waiting for you when you wake up to put a smile on your face by 7AM.

 TheMissGuidedCounselor
You're the best.
Night xx

BravesGuy93
Good night.

Chapter Twelve

♡ *Fletcher*

I STARE DOWN AT my phone, disappointed to see my messages to @TheMissGuidedCounselor from this morning still unanswered. As promised, I had rounded up some funny memes, twelve in total, sending them all to her in rapid succession. But she hadn't responded or even opened my messages, which was unusual for her.

As much as I wish I could check on her, the only way we communicate is through Instagram, so if she's not checking her messages, there's really not much I can do. Which sucks. A lot.

And to make things worse, I think there's something up with Lucy.

She's been avoiding me all day, and the one time I did catch her, she rushed off with the excuse that she needed to make a phone call. Yesterday afternoon was intense, and I want to check in and make sure she's doing okay, but every time I try to pin her down, she disappears.

I know it has to do with chasing down Sophia in Boston. She had been fearless storming into that building. Even more so when she confronted that idiot who lured Sophia out there in the first place. But when we had gotten back in the car, she changed. A sadness had quietly settled over her, and when we parted ways, she had looked like she was on the verge of tears. I should have stayed with her and am angry I didn't.

The end of the day can't come fast enough, and as soon as the final bell rings, I scoop up my jacket and bag and push through the students. I pass Lucy's office just as she opens her door, ushering out Sophia and a woman I can only assume is Sophia's mom. Sophia's cheeks are a blotchy red, matching her mother's. Looking almost as miserable as Sophia, Lucy waves goodbye to them both and closes her door before she can spot me.

I contemplate knocking to check in on her, but before I can make my way over, the door swings back open and she slips out, head low, as she darts down the main hallway. From my vantage point, I see her march quickly past both the teachers' lounge and restroom, and something in my gut urges me to follow her. Her brisk, purposeful strides and the way her head hasn't lifted once are sending little SOS signals to my brain, confirming that something is *definitely* up with Lucy.

And while I don't want to stalk her, I *do* want to make sure she's okay. At least with her, unlike @TheMissGuidedCounselor, I may actually be able to help.

I follow, almost catching up until she rounds the corner to the double doors leading to the gym. The gym is empty save for a few students playing a pickup game of basketball. Lucy doesn't look anywhere but straight ahead, and despite my being a good foot taller, I'm jogging to keep up with her. She keeps her pace fast and purposeful, moving toward the hall behind the gym that leads to the locker rooms and Brodie's office.

When she approaches another set of double doors, I call out her name. Despite her short stature, she's clearly outpacing me, and this is a part of the school building I'm not familiar with.

At the sound, she turns around with a sharp gasp.

My heart tugs when I see the moisture gathered in her eyes. "Fletcher, what are you—"

"I'm sorry," I hurry to explain. "I didn't mean to follow you like this. I just…I haven't seen you all day, and then I saw you rushing out of your office and wanted to try to grab you to talk. See how you were doing."

A tear breaks loose and starts to snake its way down her cheek. She glances over my shoulder then lets out a resigned sigh. "I can't talk here. Follow me."

She turns around and continues, slower now, until the end of the hallway, where there is a large pile of what can only be called abandoned junk. Stacks of old volleyball nets and deflated basketballs—a graveyard of broken and discarded gym equipment.

To my surprise, Lucy pushes between two stacks of mats and ducks under a torn volleyball net like she's done this a hundred times before. I clumsily follow behind her and am surprised to see a few feet of hallway behind the pile—and a door. Lucy walks up and pulls it open, revealing either a small office or a generously sized closet.

At first glance, the inside looks like an adult-sized fort. A pile of pillows claims one corner beside a basket filled with soft, plush blankets. A small table sits against the back wall with battery-operated candles and a twelve-inch waterfall on top, beside a framed picture of Ruth Bader Ginsburg.

Lucy shuts the door behind us then dumps her bag onto the floor and collapses into a large overstuffed electric-blue chair, dropping her head into her hands. Her body shakes as she starts to sob. Uncontrollable cries flow out of her, and the sight rips a hole through my chest.

I crouch beside her, placing my hand tentatively on her back as her chest heaves. I don't know what to say. I've never seen someone cry like this. I mean, my mother cries all the time lately, but it's always more subdued—a gentler cry that is usually remedied with her sleeping pills or a strong drink.

This is the crying of someone suffering. I just don't know what from.

I go with my instincts, murmuring reassuring words as I rub circles on her back. "It'll be okay. I'm here. I'm going to stay with you." She continues to cry, but after a few moments, her body doesn't shake as much, and her cries grow softer. She uncovers her face but doesn't look at me. Her hands land lifelessly in her lap.

"Are you okay?" I know it's probably not the most tactful or best question to be asking, but it's the one I need to know the answer to so I can help.

She sighs and balls her hands into fists as she cracks her knuckles. "Do I look okay?" she responds softly.

I shake my head, sinking to sit on the floor. "No, you don't. Did something happen with Sophia? I saw you finishing up a meeting with her and her mom."

She inhales a long breath, then exhales. She squeezes her eyes closed, as if trying to shut everything out. "I failed her. I wasn't there for her."

I pause for a moment before responding. I don't understand, and it frustrates me because if I understood, I could help. "What do you mean? You were the one who saved her last night."

She shakes her head and looks down at me. Her eyes look tired and defeated. "It doesn't matter. She told me two weeks ago that she didn't want to go to college because she wanted to follow this DJ Breezy Buzz whatever around or become a yacht billionaire's girlfriend, and I didn't think she was serious. I didn't think she would run off like that. And if I had, I could have…"

She chokes back a sob. "I could have stopped her."

"This isn't on you, Lucy. You can't control the decisions that she makes."

Her lips tremble as she takes another steadying breath. "You know why she locked herself in the bathroom? That…that monster had tried to attack her. She had been so excited to meet him, and he tried to kiss her, and she pulled away, and then he pinned her against the wall and tried to…She pushed him away and ran, but she was so scared and she didn't know where she was."

She sobs again, and a torrent of tears stream down her face. I wipe them away with my thumb and hold my palm to her cheek.

"I'm so sorry she had to go through that. But she's lucky you found her and brought her home safely."

"You don't understand," she says, shaking her head. "I should have never let her get to that point. I thought I had gotten through to her. I thought I was good at my job, but it's not true!"

Her voice grows louder and more frantic with every word. "I don't even know why I pretend to be good at this, thinking that I can help these kids when I'm probably more messed up than all of them! And because of that, I failed one of my students and put her in danger."

It stuns me that Lucy thinks she's responsible for what happened with Sophia. How can she even believe that, after everything she does for her students? I don't understand how she can put all of this on her shoulders, and it hurts me to see her so angry with herself.

I move in front of her, so she can see my face when I tell her that none of this is her fault. I only hope she will believe me. "You didn't know this was going to happen. There was nothing you could do to stop Sophia."

She shakes her head. "You don't know that. I should have checked in with her more. I'm so bad at this job, and I feel like such a failure at everything. I can't do anything right."

The anger in her voice—the anger at herself—confuses me. The only person at fault here is that adult predator who lured a sixteen-year-old girl to that hovel. And yet, Lucy's guilt is ripping her apart, and there seems to be nothing I can say that can convince her none of this is her fault.

"Hey, you are a damn good guidance counselor. No one cares for these kids more than you do."

"It's not true. They barely even notice I'm there half the time. And even then, they just think I'm this out-of-touch idiot. Which I probably am. It was a mistake to ever think I could handle this." Another sob escapes her lips, and she folds herself in half, drawing her legs against her chest.

My heart breaks seeing her like this. I wish I could take her pain away, or lessen it in some way, but I don't know how to comfort her. And it makes me feel powerless. Like I'm failing Lucy, who is clearly in so much pain as she splits herself open to me, bravely baring every hurting piece of her. It's like I'm holding my mother again, as she sobs, collapsed in my arms, mourning the loss of her marriage and the life she had known.

I had felt just as weak and useless then.

I try to remember how @TheMissGuidedCounselor had comforted me after, reassuring me that sometimes holding space for someone's pain is a gift all in itself. That words of love and comfort don't need to be flowery or eloquent, only sincere. So even though I might not know what to say to Lucy, maybe there is someone who *does*. If she were here, what would @TheMissGuidedCounselor say?

I lean back on my heels so I can look her in the eyes. "I'm so sorry you're going through this right now. I can see how much pain you're in, and your feelings are valid." I swallow, taking a deep breath to steady myself, and continue. "And it's okay you're feeling this way, not that you need my permission to feel, well, anything."

I wipe my sweaty palms against my pants, worrying that like always the right words won't find their way out of my mouth. "But I also want to gently challenge them—your very valid feelings—and share that I think you're being a little unfair to yourself. I know it can be hard to see that, though, so if there is anything I can do, or say, to make you feel better, please let me know."

I blow out a breath, hoping my words don't sound wooden or insincere because I do mean them. Because my words are all I have, even if they feel so painfully inadequate right now.

"You sound like a therapist," she remarks, offering me a crooked smile. "Worse even, you sound like *me*."

I let out a relieved chuckle at her joke and give her knee a gentle squeeze. "I'm going to take that as a compliment, then."

She shakes her head, her shoulders drooping in defeat. "Fletcher, I'm a depressed, anxious guidance counselor with ADHD who pretends to have her shit together, when in reality, it feels like most days I'm drowning. I feel like I'm cosplaying adulthood and faking it to everyone around me. I'm a fraud." She waves a hand over herself. "How am I supposed to help anyone when I am so clearly a mess?"

I want to reach out and grab her hands, hold them so tightly that she'll be able to feel the depth of the feelings I have for her already. But my gut tells me now isn't the right moment. That what Lucy needs now isn't physical touch, but a space where she can let herself fall apart and, hopefully, pull herself back together.

"Do you ever think that maybe your mental health struggles make you a better guidance counselor? I mean, who better to understand the challenges that come with mental illness than someone who lives with it?"

She lifts her shoulder in a shrug. "I don't know. It's hard not to wonder," she says, her voice so soft I have to lean in, "why God even put me on this planet when I can barely function in it, and if I even want to keep fighting these feelings anymore."

Her words are a knife twisting in my gut, and I swallow back my initial reaction of shock. Up until now, the Lucy I've known has always seemed so…different from the one sitting in front of me. A little anxious, sure, but she's always exuded a quiet kind of confidence. And her humor always has me laughing—even days later when I replay our conversations in my head.

While I want to correct her, tell her she *is* meant to be on this earth because it is so fucking clear how much of a positive impact she has on everyone around her, I know that's probably not a feeling that can be fixed right now. Even if nothing about this is fair: neither the blame she is placing on herself nor her feelings of worthlessness and shame nor her mental illness.

Because if I've learned anything from @TheMissGuided-Counselor, I also know it's not my job to battle with Lucy's depression for her, but to offer to be by her side while she wages the war for herself.

Unable to hold back, I reach for her hands and wrap mine around them. Her tears slice through my skin like tiny slivers of glass. "I know nothing I say right now will matter, and we're still getting to know each other, but I am really grateful I've met you. And I really hope we can continue to get to know each other more."

Lucy levels her gaze on mine, waving a hand over her body. "Fletcher, look at me. I'm a mess. The smallest things can send me into a spiral, and I go days or even weeks where I can hardly function. I'm almost thirty and barely moved out of my parents' house because I was so scared to be away from my family, who I depend on for everything. I'm just this burden of a person who just takes and takes and takes."

"Lucy, I *am* looking at you. And nothing I see is scaring me away. If anything, it makes me want to get to know you better. As friends, if you want, or"—my hands tighten around hers as I push back familiar fear—"maybe something more, which I would like, but this feels like a terribly inconvenient time to hit on you."

My chest loosens as Lucy lets out a little chuckle, a small smile peeking through the tears still streaming down her cheeks.

"Look, Lucy, I want it all—the good and the bad. I like how easy it is to be around you, and I'm okay if it's sometimes hard, too. It's *all* worth it to me."

She shakes her head. "You don't know what you're saying. Did you know I'm on three different types of meds? And two of them basically kill my sex drive, so even though I *want* to have sex, or think I should want it, it takes me like twice as long to even get in the mood. Are you prepared for a life of spending like thirty minutes of foreplay *every* time you want to have sex? I saw that you have a remote starter for your car, which means that spending ten minutes in the morning to heat your car probably feels like a tedious chore to you." She sobs again and pulls her hands from mine, throwing them in the air. "I don't have a remote starter. I am like a very old, beat-up sedan that takes two hours to heat up."

She doesn't give me a chance to respond before continuing.

"And I get sad from the stupidest things. One time I just could not get the stupid fitted sheet on my bed and I slept on the couch for a week because I was so embarrassed and ashamed that I couldn't even accomplish something so obviously simple."

She groans and covers her face. "Anything is a trigger for me. Stress, but then also not being productive. Exhaustion, but also sleeping too much. Low self-esteem, but also when I'm feeling good about myself because I know it's not going to last. I am a mess of a human being."

I shake my head. "You are not a mess of a human being, Lucy. You are—"

"I'm depressed, Fletcher," she interrupts. "And not in the '*One Day at a Time* got canceled way before their time' depressed. I'm *depressed* depressed."

I nod and give her a warm smile that I hope she finds reassuring—because nothing she's said is making me like her any less. If anything, I'm in awe that she is so kind and funny even with how hard life can be for her. "Yeah, I kind of put that together." I lift a shoulder. "And if you're trying to scare me off, it's not working very well."

Lucy laughs humorlessly. "You still haven't seen me at my worst. This," she says, waving her hand over herself. "This is nothing."

"Okay, so we'll cross that bridge when it comes. And hopefully, you'll still have me around when it does. Because I don't want to leave, Lucy. We all have our shit, and while I may not fully understand what you're going through, I want to be there for you. Be *with* you. So please don't push me out the door before you even give me a chance."

She exhales a shaky breath. "After that entire sad monologue, you *still* like me?"

I grin and nod. "I do."

"You heard the part about the thirty minutes of foreplay, right?"

I lift my shoulder in a nonchalant shrug. "I like a good challenge."

Lucy lets out a bark of laughter, and the edges of her lips curl into a small smile. "Fletcher, I don't think you have any clue what you are getting into."

I smile and give her hand a gentle squeeze. "Well, let's find out, shall we?"

Chapter Thirteen

♡ *Lucy*

WHEN I CHECK MY cubby the next day, like I do every morning before I venture into the adjacent teachers' lounge, I find a flyer requesting chaperones for the upcoming dance, a white mesh bag of loose-leaf tea, and some kind of purple plastic dinosaur with a note attached around its long neck:

I THINK YOU'RE TEA-RIFIC.
—FLETCHER

A very unladylike snort escapes as I investigate this little silicon dinosaur and discover it's a tea diffuser. It's cute and, yes, a little cheesy, but it's also sweet and thoughtful, and I have a weakness for bad puns.

After my closet confidential yesterday afternoon, Fletcher had patiently waited until my tears had dried, then dug his phone out of his pocket to show me some funny TikToks his class had shared with him earlier to kill time until the rest of the students and teachers left the building. Even though he assured me I looked "positively radiant," I knew that I was likely a blotchy, eyeliner-smudged mess. I told him I appreciated him staying late with me. And when I felt comfortable enough to leave, he walked me back to my office to grab my bag and keys.

While a part of me was still a little embarrassed at how completely I had unraveled in front of him, I couldn't help but also feel a measure of...lightness. I like Fletcher. *A lot.* And vomiting out all my insecurities, flaws, and defects before we even had our first date had me feeling surprisingly...relieved. It was a bold (and unintentional) strategy, to be sure, but also a relief. Now that he knows *everything*, it's up to Fletcher to decide if he wants to pursue anything more than friendship.

I hope he does. I mean, he *did* tell me he wanted to be more than friends yesterday but didn't want to hit on me while I was having a mental breakdown in a closet, which if that isn't an example of modern-day chivalry, I don't know what is.

And I want Fletcher to ask me out. Desperately. Over these past few weeks he's quickly come to occupy my thoughts to the point where I'm about to scribble his name with hearts in the margins of my notebook. I know I need to stop obsessing over him, but it feels nice to have a crush on someone who is age appropriate and not a member of a boy band.

And getting a note like this in my cubby? It's perfect. It's as if I am living out my high school fantasy of having the hot, popular guy noticing me and sliding little love notes in my locker. Except I'm an almost thirty-year-old woman with a faded, peeling GUIDANCE COUNSELOR sticker on my cubby.

I carefully detach the note, sliding it into my pocket, and carry the tea bag and diffuser over to the lounge, where Fletcher is sipping his coffee and smiling way too cheerily for this early in the morning.

I grab my mug and fill it with hot water before sitting down in the empty chair beside Fletcher. I gesture toward my mug. "Thanks for the gift." I scrunch my nose and offer him a shy smile. "And the terrible pun."

Fletcher's eyes crinkle in the corner as he laughs. "I couldn't help myself." He fidgets with the handle on the side of his thermos, looking a bit nervous. My own hands keep busy as I carefully pack the loose-leaf tea, which smells heavenly, into the little dinosaur's body before dunking it into my hot water.

The silence grows longer between us. I am far too awkward, and *way* too undercaffeinated to lead this conversation right now. And seeing Fletcher look so uncomfortable is making me anxious. And when Fletcher catches me watching his fingers as he continues to play with his mug handle, he stops and looks back up to me with a hesitant smile. "So, how was the rest of your afternoon yesterday?"

At the mention of yesterday, my cheeks heat a bit, but I try to combat the feelings of embarrassment at what had happened. Yes, I would have *obviously* preferred to not have a complete panic attack in front of my crush, but it happened. There was nothing I could do to change it.

"Good," I say. "I went home and heated up some leftovers and ended up binge-watching organization videos on YouTube, which led me to ordering a new set of plastic organization bins online all before passing out promptly at nine o'clock."

He lets out a low whistle. "Sounds like a wild night."

I chuckle and stir the long neck of the dinosaur in my tea, watching the color turn into a soft hue of pink. "Oh, most nights are in my house. My neighbors call the police on me at least once a week just from noise complaints alone."

"Oh, of course. From all the house parties you host, I'm sure?"

"Well, no, it's mostly because I like to pretend that I'm an opera singer and belt out Mariah Carey songs, which, I guess, to my neighbors sounds like I'm getting viciously murdered."

Fletcher's mouth drops open, and he barks out a laugh. Shaking his head, he shoots me one of those smiles that sends my stomach leaping into Olympic-level somersaults.

"I never know what's going to come out of your mouth, but it always seems to cheer me up," he says, grinning from ear to ear.

My cheeks heat up at the compliment, and I look down, thankful the teachers' lounge is relatively empty of any audience to witness this moment between Fletcher and me that feels so special, I wish I could freeze it and lock it away somewhere safe and precious.

"So, any plans for this weekend?" he asks, looking up at me as he toys with a paper napkin.

"Just working at the restaurant and enjoying my new bins. I have my whole pantry makeover planned and bought these special waterproof labels so I can have an aesthetically pleasing pantry and pretend I have my life together." I wink and shoot him a self-satisfied smile. "Impressive, eh?"

Fletcher nods approvingly. "Coming from someone still living with their mom, I am *very* impressed."

"You still live with your mom?" The question jumps out of my mouth before I have the chance to realize it's pretty rude of me to ask.

Luckily, Fletcher doesn't seem offended. "Well, when I got

the job at Harview, it happened pretty quickly. So I haven't had a chance yet to find my own place, but I'm working on it."

"Well, good for you. When I moved out, I only managed to move across the street from my parents."

"Are you close with your family?"

I nod. "Very. As you've seen, we all work together and pretty much spend all our free time together. We also have a lot of cousins that live around here, and we *always* have family visiting, so our house is basically an Airbnb."

"That must be nice," he muses. "I didn't grow up with a lot of family around."

"Yeah, it *can* be nice. Though sometimes it can feel kind of…" I pause, searching for the right word. "Overwhelming. Remember, you met my sister Amira. Imagine that 24/7."

Fletcher grins and lets out a playful, dramatic shudder.

"Let's just say," I continue, "it was good when I could finally get my own place and not be crammed into a room with my sisters. And so I could, of course, spend entire weekends organizing my pantry, which no one besides me will ever see."

He laughs, and those adorable dimples in his cheeks make my heart start pounding dangerously fast. "I wouldn't expect you to have a control freak side, especially about a pantry. It's cute."

I think Fletcher has called me cute. Or maybe he called my pantry cute. I'm not quite sure, and my brain cannot handle this kind of compliment. Not when it's coming from this gorgeous-looking man who clearly irons his shirts and has dimples and perfectly coiffed hair. The last time I was called cute, it was by a drunk man loitering at the gas station at three in the afternoon while I pumped my gas.

So instead of accepting his compliment like a normal functioning human being, or possibly even complimenting him back, I do *this*.

"Oh, I exercise control in all things, Ms. Steele."

Yep, I quoted a movie based on a BDSM *Twilight* fan fiction. This is…not my proudest moment. If Amira were here to witness this, she would immediately disown me.

He arches his brow, utterly confused.

I suppress the urge to run as heat rises over my chest and up to my cheeks. I have to remember that a very small portion of grown adults are able to recognize *Fifty Shades of Grey* references, and Fletcher is not one of them.

"Oh, it's just a line from *Fifty Shades of Grey*," I mumble. "It's embarrassing, but it's one of my favorite movies. One of the other movies from my four-way tie." I refrain from mentioning that the reason it's one of my favorite movies is because I love Dakota Johnson and her stunning perfectly symmetrical boobs.

Fletcher nods, and my stomach twists into an anxious coil. He's probably thinking I'm this major dork and will never want to speak with me—

"Would you like to have dinner—?"

But before he can finish the question, the door to the teachers' lounge swings open and a group of teachers walk in. I watch as Fletcher glances at the new arrivals and a pained smile crosses his face as he rises from his chair. "I'm so sorry, Lucy, but I just remembered I have something I need to take care of. Let's talk soon?"

He's halfway out the door before I even have the chance to answer him. Or to interrogate him further. Was he about to ask me out on a date? Or was he just curious if I liked dinner, which was a perfectly platonic question to ask a colleague, I suppose.

As if sent by the angels themselves, the door to the lounge swings open again and in walks Nia. I wave her over, probably looking insanely desperate, because she practically runs, even before grabbing the very last stale donut that was left over from last night's PTA meeting.

"Are you okay?" she asks, claiming Fletcher's empty seat, her concern etched into her face.

"I think Fletcher was going to ask *me*"—I lean forward, closing the gap between us—"on a date!" I hiss.

Nia's eyes turn into wide saucers. "What do you mean? Did he—"

"Well, he asked if I would like to have dinner," I interrupt.

Nia scoots forward in her seat. "Okay, and how are we confused here? Clearly he's asking you out on a dinner date."

"No, you don't understand. His exact words were 'Would you like to have dinner?' That could mean a whole host of things."

Nia rolls her eyes so far back I worry they might disappear. "What on earth could 'would you like to have dinner' also mean?"

"Well, maybe he was just asking if I *like* to have dinner. Like do I enjoy dinner itself as a meal, or am I more of a breakfast person. He could just be very interested in my opinions on all the different mealtimes. I mean, you have breakfast, brunch, lunch, linner—"

Nia reaches across the table and grabs me by my shoulders. "You have got to stop with the self-doubt. Obviously he is interested in you and not your opinions on whatever the hell linner is! He very clearly has asked you out on a date! How much more proof do you need that this guy is into you?"

"I don't know. A notarized letter?" I joke and drop my face into my hands. "I guess I just don't see why he's...attracted to me. I mean, less than twenty-four hours ago, I was sobbing in the cry closet with him about how I have no sex drive and I cry over fitted sheets! No way is he actually attracted to that unless he's some kind of masochist."

Before I can finish, Nia swats my hand and points her finger accusingly at me. "Stop that right now. That man would be lucky to date you. You are a catch. You have an amazing ass, and you're hilarious and sweet and empathetic. You're like a really warm pair of socks on a cold, rainy day."

"Socks on a rainy day with a nice ass? Yeah, I'm the total package."

Nia shakes her head. "Uh-uh," she tuts. "I am not going to let you feel sorry for yourself."

"But aren't you the least bit curious why he's still interested in me after seeing me completely fall apart?" I push. "I mean, you've seen me when I'm, well, you know, and it's not pretty. My face gets all hot and sweat just drips off me and snot pours out of me like I'm an erupting volcano. It's not a pretty sight."

"Okay, *fine*. I'll admit your sweat and snot volcano is not your most attractive state, *but*"—she holds up her finger—"it's still a big part of you. And the fact that he didn't run away or blow you off should prove that he likes you for you—*all* the parts of you. Sweat and snot volcano and all."

Nia reaches across the table and squeezes my hand.

I don't deserve Nia and her amazing friendship. Her learning about my anxiety and depression cocktail had been an accident. She had found me crying in my car in the parking lot and just let herself into the passenger side despite us never having had a conversation of more than a dozen words. In a moment of weakness, I confessed that the reason I was crying was because of no reason at all. And just the fact that I was crying for no reason made me sob even harder.

Depression carries a heaviness that few people understand, and while most days I can carry that load, there are also days when I can't. And on those days, the shame of feeling despondent despite everything in my life being completely fine is the hardest burden to carry. After all, I was a middle-class girl who had a stable childhood with parents who loved each other and sisters who adored me. The only trauma I had experienced was seeing my grandmother lose her battle against cancer and getting rejected by Harry Tremont in front of the entire sophomore class. On paper, I had nothing to be depressed about, and yet there would be periods of time when I would be so sad, I was unable to leave my bed for days. And in a rare moment of vulnerability, I had spilled that all out to Nia. That day, in that baby-blue Hyundai littered with empty cans of Diet Coke and candy wrappers, I had made a friend.

I bite down on my lip and look up at a cracked ceiling with the flickering overhead light, willing myself not to cry. I look back at Nia and shake my head. "Have I told you lately that I love you?"

Nia laughs and shakes her head. "Nope, but you can make it up to me by buying me dinner at Come Con Gana tonight!"

"Deal. I'm working practically every day this week. I have to pay off my air fryer. So, with my subpar waitressing skills, I should be able to muster enough money to pay it off in, oh, eight months?"

Nia shakes her head. "I told you the air fryer wouldn't be worth it. Just use your damn oven. And, please cut yourself some slack. Now don't get me wrong—you definitely are a bad waitress. But you have that adorable scared face that scores you those nice pity tips."

I roll my eyes but take the quasi-compliment. "So you think he was asking me? On a date?"

Nia nods, cupping my face with her hands. "I think you two are going to get dinner, and it will be amazing. I can't wait to overanalyze and dissect every single minute with you immediately after, okay?"

I nod, grateful for such a strong friendship with Nia. That girl is definitely going to get an appetizer with her meal tonight.

Chapter Fourteen

 *Fletcher*

"LET'S PLEASE ALL REMEMBER not to park our cars by the kitchen's loading dock, okay? We have received our final warning from the delivery drivers, and we cannot afford to anger them anymore." Principal Padmesh pauses to survey all the teachers and school administration gathered in the auditorium. When no one even nods in acknowledgment, he does his best to hide his disappointment that we are not as invested in this gravely serious issue as he is.

With a foreboding look, he continues, "Otherwise, the drivers will leave the milk on the loading dock instead of bringing it inside, and then we will have to bring in the milk again like we did two years ago. It was a very unpleasant time for us, so let's not repeat it. Does everyone understand?"

A few of us finally murmur in agreement, but the majority have completely checked out. We're nearing the end of our monthly faculty meeting, and Principal Padmesh is desperately trying to run through the dozen or so items on his agenda before we all nod off to sleep.

He sighs and looks down at the sheet on his clipboard before scrubbing a hand over his face. "Okay, next item. Nia's math competition team, the Denominators, have made it to regionals, and our very own Harview High will be hosting the competition this coming Saturday! Now, Nia, is there anything you need from the staff? Why don't you say a few words?"

Nia rises from her seat next to Lucy, who I noticed had snuck in a few minutes late to the meeting.

"Well, it's a great opportunity," Nia says, clearly proud, "especially for our juniors and seniors, because we have a few admissions counselors from the local colleges who like to come and scope out the students. And we *should* be all set on volunteers, between the PTA and our lovely guidance counselor"— she playfully nudges Lucy with her knee—"helping out." She pauses, tilting her head. "So, yeah, I think that's it? Though if you want to come by, we wouldn't say no to extra help, and the kids always appreciate the support!"

Before she even can even sit back down, my hand is shooting in the air. Volunteering for her best friend's math competition would *definitely* give me the chance to properly ask Lucy on a date. I had, admittedly, panicked yesterday when Georgia walked into the teachers' lounge *just* as I was about to finish asking Lucy out for dinner. I was scared she would stroll over and find a way to sabotage whatever was just beginning between us—especially because I had made that reckless agreement with her to not date my coworkers. I may have fallen into her trap, but the last thing I wanted was to drag Lucy down with me.

Padmesh arches his brow but calls on me. "Yes, Fletcher?"

"I would like to volunteer." I look toward Nia, who eyes me a bit suspiciously before a toothy grin takes over her face. Lucy's looking away, so I'm not able to see her reaction. "I mean, if you need more volunteers. I volunteer."

Padmesh looks delighted at my enthusiasm—I've clearly earned me some nice brownie points with my new boss, which doesn't hurt—and he claps his hands together. "Wonderful! I love seeing the passion for our students in their extracurriculars. Now, before we go, I am just going to pass out—"

"I volunteer, too!"

I swing my head around to find Georgia, a few rows back, her hand high up in the air. Padmesh—along with half the faculty—shares a bewildered look.

I suppress a groan as my stomach tightens into a knot. Spending a Saturday in a gym packed with math nerds is not her usual MO. Sure, the Georgia I knew liked to volunteer—it had been one of the things I admired about her. She'd been generous with her time, often visiting the local hospital to sing with her choir or deliver toys to sick children.

But volunteering at a math tournament is definitely not her style, and I can't help but think that this is Georgia trying to find another way for us to talk—despite how clearly I have been avoiding her. And how am I supposed to properly ask Lucy out if Georgia is hovering over us the whole time? I utter a curse under my breath at how my "brilliant" plan has *already* been foiled.

A bright smile spreads across Padmesh's face. "Wonderful! Anyone else?" He looks around the room, clearly expecting several more teachers to volunteer. The poor guy thinks that Georgia and I have volunteered out of our love of mathematics-themed competitions and school spirit.

He doesn't know we both have less-than-pure motives.

When no one else raises a hand, Padmesh returns to the agenda, handing out a packet with updates on the upcoming statewide standardized tests. Half of them end up in the recycling bin before we even leave the auditorium.

I try to catch up with Lucy, but she and Nia were among the first ones out, and with everyone rushing toward the same two doors that lead back out into the hallway, I lose sight of her.

My stomach grumbles, and I decide I should be heading home anyway. But before I can escape, a hand wraps around my forearm, stopping me. I swing around and swallow back a groan of annoyance. *She found me.*

"Yes, Georgia?"

"Why have you been avoiding me?" she asks, her voice so low it comes out as a hiss.

I twist my wrist and gently pull her hand off me. "I haven't been avoiding you."

She props her hands on her hips and pins me with her stare. "Really? Because every time I try to talk to you, you conveniently have a meeting to rush off to, or you suddenly remember a student you need to meet with."

Well, she has me there.

"I'm sorry," I say, raking a clammy hand through my hair. "I've just been busy. And I really need to go. Goodbye, Georgia," I say, turning to walk away. I have no doubt she'll try again tomorrow, but I tell myself at least then I'll have prepared how to tell her that I am firmly over our relationship and ready to move on, and suggest she do the same.

"Not too busy to be taking out Lucy, though?"

At the mention of Lucy's name, I bite back a sigh and reluctantly turn around. "What are you talking about?"

"Lucy," she says, crossing her arms. "I saw you both in the

teachers' lounge, and I heard you asking *her* out on a date. What happened to your 'I don't date colleagues' speech?"

"It's…complicated," I answer, rubbing the heel of my palm against my forehead as a headache starts to take hold.

"Complicated?" she repeats, her voice growing thin and shrill. "Less than two weeks ago, you told me you would *never* want to date Lucy and suddenly, you're asking her out—but you won't even give *me* a second chance despite your so-called declaration about not dating coworkers? How does that make any sense, Fletcher?"

"Georgia," I start, trying to keep my tone gentle but firm, despite the sweat uncomfortably gathering at the base of my neck. Thankfully, we're alone in the hallway, but that doesn't mean everyone has left—and the only thing that would make this worse would be someone overhearing us. "Look, can we not do this now?"

"You're right," she says, pressing her lips together in a pout. "Maybe we should just wait until Saturday and find a spot with more privacy."

Shit. The last thing I want is to spend my Saturday juggling avoiding Georgia while trying to ask Lucy out on a date. "Georgia, I don't think that's a good—"

"Don't you think," she interrupts as she takes a step closer toward me, her eyes locking on mine, "it's fate that brought you here to the very same school where I work? Don't you think this is some, I don't know, sign that we should be together? We worked well together, didn't we?"

She takes another step closer, reaching for my hands, and I can see the moisture welling in the corner of her eyes. "I don't want to lose you a second time."

The smell of Georgia's perfume overwhelms me, and my throat feels like it's filled with cotton. She's too close, and I'm starting to feel like a trapped animal—but the cage is one I constructed myself. I had no one else to blame for Georgia thinking we could have a second chance.

And because I didn't want to hurt or disappoint her—or, to be honest, *face* her hurt or disappointment—Georgia now mistakes my silence as agreement and moves even closer, lifting her hand to rest on my forearm, giving it a firm squeeze.

"You feel it, too, don't you?" she murmurs as she closes whatever distance remains between us and presses her mouth against mine.

Time comes to a halting stop as Georgia's hand wraps around the back of my head, pulling me closer. I'm so taken aback that I react far too slowly, stumbling backward far too many seconds later, nearly taking her with me, before lifting my arms to disentangle myself from her grip.

"Asshole."

I turn around to find Nia glaring at me, her hands propped on her hips as anger radiates off her body. Behind her, Lucy stands frozen as her eyes, the same ones I'm always captivated by—especially how they always seem to light up when they see me—fill with disappointment and hurt.

"Wait, this isn't—"

But before I can finish, Nia holds up her hand, warning me off with an angry glare. She wraps her arm around Lucy and leads her down the hall to the doors to the outside.

I drag my hands over my face and groan, letting out a string of mumbled expletives.

Georgia is staring at me, her mouth hanging open as her

eyes widen into large saucers. "Oh," she whispers, taking a step back. "You really like her, don't you?"

I blow out a breath. "What are you talking about, Georgia?"

She gestures to the hallway that Lucy just disappeared down. "Lucy. You *like* her, don't you? I mean…" She waves her hand over me. "I thought you were playing hard to get, but you genuinely have feelings for her, don't you?"

I hesitate a moment before nodding. While I'm angry at Georgia for the kiss, none of this would have happened if I had only been honest with her from the beginning.

"Okay, wow. Well, I'm going to leave, because this is all a bit too much humiliation for me to endure in one day," she says before she quickly gathers her things and disappears down the now empty hallway.

And then I am alone, my actions weighing on my shoulders like a heavy boulder—until my phone rings.

Dad

When I see his name flash across the screen, I hit Ignore like usual, but I can't help the uncomfortable thought that follows. We're a family that fears confrontation—we would rather bury our uncomfortable truths than risk bringing them into the light. But was this how he'd felt when my mom discovered his affair? Was this how he'd justified his actions, lying to my mother and avoiding the inevitable? Was I that different, telling myself I was sparing Georgia from rejection—and myself from her scorn—when really, I'd been keeping my life comfortable?

Instead, I allowed those I care about—like Lucy—to get hurt.

My decision to lie had been cowardly and selfish—lies

meant to make my life easier without any consideration of how those lies would inevitably hurt the people around me.

I needed to make this right.

Watching Lucy walk away, the disappointment and sadness written all over her face, had felt like a knife twisting in the pit of my gut. Georgia had been right about one thing—I do have feelings for Lucy. Strong ones. And now that I know what it feels like to see her walk away, I'll do anything to prevent it from happening a second time.

TheMissGuidedCounselor
Posted at 5:34 PM

"Sometimes we create our own heartbreaks through expectation."

Liked by **BravesGuy93** and **others**

TheMissGuidedCounselor Author unknown

View all comments

Chapter Fifteen

♡ *Lucy*

"I THINK WE SHOULD murder him."

"Oh my God, Amira, that is so extreme," Julieta admonishes.

Amira claps her hands enthusiastically. "I heard they do this chemical castration procedure. We could try that."

"No, that won't work. They have to take a pill like every day," Nia pipes in as she mindlessly scrolls through her phone.

"Oh," Amira responds, looking dejected. "I kind of thought we just threw some acid on his junk and it kind of just shriveled up." She looks up, with a renewed sense of optimism. "Can we just order it online? Like through the black market?"

Nia shrugs. "Probably."

I groan and grab a pillow off my couch to swallow my scream. Why do I ever let anyone know what is going on in my life? Not only did I have to endure the humiliation of watching Fletcher kissing Georgia, but now I have to listen to my sisters and my best friend try to plot his death to "avenge my honor" *Sopranos* style on a Friday night. I thought I was the mentally ill one, but at least I'm not plotting how to cut off someone's appendage.

"Can we all please stop?" I finally beg after the discussion turns to securing alibis. "We should not be conspiring to commit an assault. *Especially* on Shabbat." Seriously, there *had* to be something in the Torah about not castrating someone on the day of rest.

"Ooh, good thinking, Lulu!" Amira says. "If we don't want the premeditated charge, we should just spontaneously do it. I'm free Sunday afternoon, does that work for everyone?"

Julieta shakes her head. "I have my friend's bridal shower. Can we push it to Monday?"

"Does Monday work for everyone?" Amira asks.

This time, I don't bother to use the pillow to muffle the sound of my scream. When I'm done, I'm rewarded with—finally—silence.

"We are *not*"—I lock eyes with Amira, Julieta, and Nia—"going to be committing any kind of illegal crimes against Fletcher, or anyone else for that matter. I am perfectly fine. If Fletcher wants to go kissing other teachers at the school, he is welcome to."

It hurts to say those words, and my heart battles my brain, but the last thing I want is for my sisters and Nia to know how bad it felt seeing Fletcher kissing Georgia. How my stomach had twisted itself into a dozen knots, and how my heart had felt like it was being squeezed through one of those Orange Julius industrial juicers.

Thankfully, no one challenges me, allowing me to keep a tiny shred of whatever lingering dignity I have. I reach down to the side of the couch, where I find my Stanley Cup glass now half empty since filling it with the wine bottle we pilfered from my parents' house after Shabbat dinner. After helping to finish washing the dishes, my sisters had followed me back to my house, where Nia was meeting me to watch a movie and talk shit about Fletcher, like the very best friend she is.

"Also, any time you want to leave, feel free to show your-selves out," I grumble, waving my hand at the door.

"Lu, it's not even nine o'clock," Amira says. "Besides, we still need to put on the face masks I brought over. They're seventy percent liquid gold and are supposed to make our pores completely disappear." She digs in her purse and extracts a small black Sephora bag. She pulls out a mask and then chucks the bag to Julieta, who is sitting on the small love seat beside her. I catch the bag next, pulling out my mask before passing it to Nia, who has made a comfortable spot for herself on the floor of my living room.

I inspect the mask and then unlock my phone to look up the unfamiliar brand. My jaw drops open as I spot it on the Sephora website.

"Amira, this mask is like eighty dollars!" I exclaim.

"Oh my God, Amira," Julieta chimes in. "How are you able to spend like three hundred bucks on face masks?"

Amira rolls her eyes. "You need to calm down. I used my Plan B money."

"Plan B money?" Nia asks, propping herself up on her elbows, clearly intrigued.

"Yeah—after I sleep with a guy, I tell him 'Oh no! I think the condom broke!' and he freaks out, but then I reassure him that I'll just take Plan B. But"—she holds up her finger as a mischievous smile crosses her face—"I tell him I don't have the money to buy it. And usually he coughs it up, but sometimes I have to do the whole 'maybe I'll keep it and we can get married' bit, and then he hands over the cash like an ATM. And because most men are idiots, I tell him it costs like a hundred bucks."

We all stare open-mouthed at her for several seconds.

"Wait," Julieta says, her brow furrowed with deep lines. "I thought you were on birth control."

Amira smiles and holds up her arm, poking at her birth control implant.

Julieta shakes her head. "So you just shake down these guys for their money? To buy face masks?"

Amira shrugs. "Capitalism, baby." She rips open the top of the face mask sheet. "Everything is a commodity. And if I am going to sleep with these mediocre men, I might as well get something out of it." Seeing the horror-struck expressions on all our faces, she holds up her hands. "Hey, if they're good in bed, I give them a discount."

"I am horrified, but also somewhat impressed. It says that Selena Gomez swears by this mask!" I say, reading through the product description page. As I continue scrolling, I get a notification on my phone and instantly a smile crosses my face.

You have a new message from @BravesGuy93

This is *exactly* what I need.

Here is a man who has never come close to disappointing me. @BravesGuy93 is always cheering me on in my comments, defending me against the inevitable trolls, and popping into my DMs to check how my day is going or share a funny anecdote from his day.

He appreciates me. He values me. He *likes* me.

And sure, maybe he doesn't know the 100 percent real me, but he knows the Lucy I *aspire* to be, and isn't that pretty much the same thing? With the three and a half glasses of wine in my system, it feels like the same thing, at least.

And I am in the mood to be appreciated. Not just by Amira

and Julieta, who are obligated to like me in case they ever need an organ donation, or Nia, who is my friend because I forced my company on her and I'm somewhat convinced she just stuck around thanks to a bad case of Stockholm syndrome.

I *like* being admired as @TheMissGuidedCounselor.

After all, @TheMissGuidedCounselor has hundreds of thousands of followers—while plain old Lucy doesn't even have enough friends to get the "bring eight friends, get the ninth one free" promotion at Smithy's Arcade. @TheMissGuidedCounselor is never awkward or at a loss for words; she gives good and helpful advice; she's funny and engaging and witty. She's everything I can't be in the real world, where I need a regimented schedule of antidepressants and therapy because my very existence is a source of anxiety for me.

"What is going on with Miss Lucy over there? That smile on your face is concerning me," Amira says.

"It's her Cheesecake Factory smile," Julieta chimes in. "The same face she makes when she sees the cheesecake display."

"Oh, you're right!" Amira responds, clapping her hands. "Are you looking at cheesecake? Should we order some in?"

"No!" I shout back, a tad too aggressively. My sister's commentary is seriously ruining any excitement I had at chatting with @BravesGuy93. "I just…it's none of your business. In fact, I am going to the other room. I have…an assignment I forgot I needed to work on."

I stumble to my feet and grab my wine off the floor, draining the contents in a single sip. The rational side of my brain knows I will wake up tomorrow absolutely regretting this. "I trust you'll see yourselves out. Nia, you're welcome to the guest bedroom. But you two can go back to Amá and Papa's to sleep."

Amira snorts and shakes her head as she jumps off the couch she was sharing with Julieta to claim my abandoned seat. "I'll be taking this couch, thank you very much," she declares, spreading her legs across the space, claiming it.

I roll my eyes but know not to argue with her.

I head into my bedroom and collapse onto the bed. Now that I'm finally alone, though, thoughts of Fletcher and Georgia begin invading my brain again, and I wish I could turn it off for even five minutes. This is why I hate being alone—I'm never truly by myself: my overly negative and intrusive thoughts are always there with me.

I need a distraction.

Now that I've had two too many glasses of wine, I'm feeling bold. And yes, a bit horny, too. I can't help it—wine makes me slutty. And while my brain keeps fantasizing about Fletcher and his perfectly coiffed hair, reality reminds me that I need to get over him.

Maybe seeing Fletcher with Georgia was a sign from the universe that I need to just get laid, like my sisters clearly think.

But because I am lazy and fearful of all men thanks to a childhood obsession with *Law & Order*, cybersex will have to do. After all, cybersex is the same as real-life sex, right? Except way less clean-up afterward and zero anxieties about UTIs.

But instead of heading to the variety of dating apps installed on my phone to find a potential cybersex partner, I find myself opening the new message from @BravesGuy93.

Love the uber depressing quote on the 'gram today. Why no impressively verbose and articulate caption to accompany it?

And am I correct in seeing that you have included NO hashtags? Is everything okay?

I love that he noticed the irregularity from my usual posts and slid into my DMs to check in on me. I love how thoughtful and caring and sweet @BravesGuy93 is. I love how he always finds a way to make me laugh, whether with an embarrassingly bad joke or a string of random memes. I love how he asks for my advice and is always so grateful when I offer it, taking the time to ruminate over my words and report back with the outcome. I love how comfortable I am with him and how easy our friendship is.

I love how he doesn't pretend that he likes me and then kisses another woman in plain *freaking* sight!

But do I want to risk the comfortable, stable friendship I have with @BravesGuy93 *just* because I'm feeling lonely and desperate for one person on this planet to want to sleep with me…even if it is virtual?

Well, lonely and desperate is pretty much my brand.

And I feel comfortable with @BravesGuy93—though not enough, the sober part of me reminds me, to risk meeting in person. And yes, he thinks I am someone I am most definitely not. Plus @TheMissGuidedCounselor would *never* sext strangers online. She's an elegant lady who remembers to moisturize each day and probably has a Roth IRA, whatever that is.

But pretending to be perfect all the time is exhausting. And I don't want to be perfect tonight. I just want to feel better than I do now. Since the wine isn't doing the job, maybe something—or well, someone—else will.

I have nothing to lose, I reason. My dignity is in tatters, and if I truly embarrass myself, it's not like I *really* know him. Absolute worst-case scenario, I'll just tell him my phone was hacked by a horny stranger and we can laugh it off.

I'm too lonely and tipsy to change paths now, so I quickly tiptoe to my door to make sure it's locked and then jump back into bed, propping my head up on my pillow as I lean over to light a vanilla-scented candle on my nightstand to set the mood for my first foray into sexting. I stretch my arms out, crack my knuckles, and settle into a comfortable position.

Time to get it on.

> **TheMissGuidedCounselor**   8:42 PM
> Hey, you up?

> **BravesGuy93**   8:43 PM
> Considering that it's 8:43pm on a
> Friday night, yes, I am up.

> **TheMissGuidedCounselor**   8:43 PM
> Great!
> How is your penis? Is it erect?

Sure, it's a little forward, but I like to be in my pj's, face washed and asleep by 10 p.m. at the *absolute* latest, so we have to get this show on the road.

> **BravesGuy93**   8:45 PM
> Uh, not currently.
> But I could get it there.

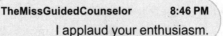

TheMissGuidedCounselor   8:46 PM

I applaud your enthusiasm.

BravesGuy93   8:47 PM

Well, I need to catch up a little here.

This is a little…unexpected.

But definitely not unwelcome,

trust me.

It could be the wine—or the loneliness—but that "definitely not unwelcome" bit makes the little butterflies in my stomach flap their little butterfly wings, sending a surge of liquid heat to my core.

What can I say? I'm a romantic.

TheMissGuidedCounselor   8:48 PM

Wonderful

So I guess just let me know when

you're ready to send me over some

dick pics?

It feels a bit unnatural to actually *ask* for dick pics. After all, a primary attribute of the dick pic is that it's usually unsolicited. But, seeing as I am not up to speed on the etiquette of sexting and dick pics, I am in uncharted territory.

BravesGuy93   8:49 PM

Well

To be fair, I might need something to

help me get started…

I know what that "..." means. Every woman on this planet knows what "..." means. We freaking invented "..."!

"..." means @BravesGuy93 needs motivation to get his penis up and running. I'm sure I can do that. I can probably just grab a sexy pic offline and crop it, tell him it's me. Or I can grab my Kindle and plagiarize a few lines from one of the hundreds of romance novels stored on it.

Maybe I should see what he's in the mood for first before starting.

> **TheMissGuidedCounselor**   8:52 PM
> Do you want, like, a picture
> of my boobs?
> Or do you want me to tell you I'm
> like super wet and want my pussy to
> gobble your penis?

I'm not sure if gobble is sexy, but I throw it out there to try. Fifty-fifty chance, right?

> **BravesGuy93**   8:53 PM
> Dear god no
> No, I don't want any of that.
> Well
> I like the boobs idea but no, I do not
> want my dick gobbled.

> **TheMissGuidedCounselor**   8:54 PM
> Is gobbled not sexy anymore?

> **BravesGuy93**   8:54 PM
> Gobbled was NEVER sexy.

Sorry to break the news.

Bummer. I loved the way "gobbled" rolled off the tongue.

TheMissGuidedCounselor   8:55 PM
Boobs still sexy?

BravesGuy93   8:55 PM
Boobs are still very much in play.
And trust me, I would LOVE to see
your boobs.
Like LOOOOOVE.
But...is everything okay?

TheMissGuidedCounselor   8:56 PM
Yep! Perfectly fine!

BravesGuy93   8:57 PM
Really?
Because you went from "we can't
share any personal details about
our lives under any condition
whatsoever" to "let me show you my
boobs" really fast.
So spill. What's really going on?
We can always do boobs later.

I pause, my fingers hovering above the keyboard. He's right.
I've kept a strict boundary between us because it's what I need to
protect myself. I'm a therapist, we *love* boundaries. And showing

my boobs is definitely crossing the boundary line *I've* been careful to enforce.

TheMissGuidedCounselor   8:59 PM
Well, there may be a few things that
are upsetting me as of late.

BravesGuy93   9:00 PM
Yeah, that's what I thought…
What's going on? Is it family stuff?

TheMissGuidedCounselor   9:03 PM
No, nothing like that.
It's kind of stupid. I feel
embarrassed.

BravesGuy93   9:04 PM
More embarrassed than asking to
gobble my penis?

I laugh but I'm also mildly mortified. Nothing like being called out for asking to gobble your friend's penis to sober you the hell up.

TheMissGuidedCounselor   9:06 PM
Can we please never mention this
conversation ever again?

BravesGuy93   9:07 PM
Deal
So what's going on?

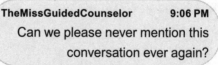

Chapter Sixteen

 Fletcher

 TheMissGuidedCounselor   9:10 PM
Okay, so you have to promise not to
judge.

I smile and quickly type back, parroting the words she has told me at least a dozen or so times in our year of friendship. As expected, she responds with the emoji rolling its eyes.

BravesGuy93   9:10 PM
Our DMs are a judgment-free zone,
remember?

 TheMissGuidedCounselor   9:11 PM
🙄
Right, okay
Well, there's this guy at work.
A teacher.
And I am kind of crushing on him.
Badly.

My fingers hover over the keyboard, my interest piqued. Usually @TheMissGuidedCounselor is the one giving *me* the advice, so it feels a bit odd to be on the other side of the conversation. I sincerely doubt I am anywhere near qualified to be offering advice, especially dating advice, considering that my current status is the personification of "it's complicated."

God, if I had *just* been honest with Georgia from the beginning, none of this would have happened.

The kiss. Lucy seeing the stupid kiss.

Instead, I would probably be passed out in my bed, getting in some extra sleep before the math competition tomorrow, planning how to finally, properly finish asking Lucy out on that date. Now, however, I will need to explain this whole mess of a situation and hope that she gives me another chance.

Not that I have a good reason for her—I have no one to blame but me and me alone.

I write back, refocusing on our conversation and off my own problems. It's so rare that @TheMissGuidedCounselor ever needs my help or advice, and this is the perfect opportunity to pay her back for all the help she's given me this last year. The least I can do is set aside my own crap and give her my full attention.

> **BravesGuy93**   9:13 PM
> Okay
> What's the problem?
> I'm assuming if he's managed to
> win you over, he has to be a pretty
> amazing guy.

> **TheMissGuidedCounselor**   9:14 PM
> Well, he is.
> Or well, I thought he was.

And I thought he liked me, and we had good chemistry, and he told me he liked me…

Which is big for me considering the last time that happened was…

Well, a long time ago.

She doesn't continue, and I read over her words again, wondering what I'm missing. This situation doesn't sound too terrible. When she doesn't say more, I write back.

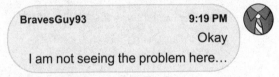

BravesGuy93   9:19 PM

Okay

I am not seeing the problem here…

Her response comes two minutes later.

TheMissGuidedCounselor   9:21 PM

Sorry, my annoying sister was trying to break down my door and interrupted me.

I chuckle. Though @TheMissGuidedCounselor doesn't share too many personal details, I *have* heard about her sisters and how they are a constant source of annoyance for her, though it's clear she adores them.

TheMissGuidedCounselor   9:22 PM

Anyway, yes, he's perfect.

Amazing.

Like he doesn't look exactly like a Hemsworth, but definitely a close relation.

Like a cousin or illegitimate half brother.

And he's really, really sweet.

For example, I was having a rough day at work and he was super supportive when he could have totally freaked out and left me by myself.

And he even got me a little gift the next day, which was the SWEETEST thing ever.

BravesGuy93   9:25 PM

Still failing to see the problem here...

TheMissGuidedCounselor   9:25 PM

I'm trying to explain.

But it's embarrassing and I am still kind of drunk, I think.

Though the whole failed attempt at sexting definitely sobered me up.

Ugh, this is so humiliating to share...

The three bouncing dots to the right of her profile picture pause, then resume pulsing before stopping again, and I can tell that she's holding back from whatever it is she wants to share. Which, admittedly, has my curiosity piqued even more.

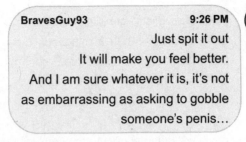

BravesGuy93   9:26 PM
Just spit it out
It will make you feel better.
And I am sure whatever it is, it's not
as embarrassing as asking to gobble
someone's penis…

TheMissGuidedCounselor   9:27 PM
😶😶😶😶😶

Those three dots are bouncing again. This time, she types everything into a giant paragraph so when it finally sends, I have to scroll back to the top of my screen to read the entire message.

TheMissGuidedCounselor   9:32 PM
Ugh fine. So, now that you're caught
up on how I THOUGHT this guy was,
well, perfect, you can see how it's all
gone to hell. After school today we
had this whole staff assembly, and
then as it's ending, I'm walking back
to my office with a friend to grab my
bag and then…I see him. Kissing
another teacher at our school. And
not just any teacher, of course, but
the one teacher at my school who,
for whatever reason, hates my guts.
And, of course, she is stunning.
Perfect hair, perfect skin, perfect
everything. Which is not the point, but

just makes this whole thing cut a bit deeper because them kissing looked like an ad for some expensive French perfume. They just looked so right together. And now I can't get that stupid kiss out of my head, and now I am questioning every interaction I've had with him because if he really did like me, then why is he kissing some other woman? And even though my friend keeps telling me I shouldn't be embarrassed, I can't help but feel humiliated. I'm more embarrassed about how long I've been building this guy up in my head and thinking we could have a real shot at something.

I have to read her message three or four times before it finally penetrates my brain.

This...this couldn't be a coincidence. No, no there was no way.

My chest tightens as I scroll back up and reread our conversation.

Well, there's this guy...
A teacher...
I was having a rough day at work and he was super supportive when he could have totally freaked out and left me by myself...

And he even got me a little gift the next day, which was the SWEETEST thing ever...

No, these aren't coincidences. I drop my phone on the couch, practically tossing it as if that can stop the revelation slamming into me like a runaway train.

Lucy is @TheMissGuidedCounselor. @TheMissGuidedCounselor *is* Lucy.

I drop my head into my hands as my brain struggles to process this situation.

The woman who has been my emotional support through one of the worst years of my life, holding my hand, guiding me through it all with her wisdom and humor and kindness, who I have only ever talked to online, completely anonymous, is *also* the woman I am starting to fall for in the real world.

How could this have happened?

Hundreds of our exchanges start to fly through my head, like a slideshow on steroids, as I try to reconcile the two women. But as I mentally sift through some of the messages we've sent, the similarities start to strike me—their senses of humor and how they both see the world, perfectly marrying the tragedy of any situation with the comedy.

There are obvious differences, of course.

@TheMissGuidedCounselor has always presented a very curated and professional aesthetic. Her posts are fun and witty even as they offer tangible and relatable advice. In her DMs, though, she lets some of her walls down. Her humor is sharper, a bit darker; her messages are less polished.

She feels more real there...More like *Lucy*.

Of course, they are the same person.

No wonder I've been so drawn to Lucy—she's the *same* woman who I message with, sometimes for hours, every day. I almost laugh, thinking of how Georgia kept talking about fate. But this can't just be a coincidence. I have never believed much in all that, but this has to mean something, doesn't it?

How else would anyone be able to explain this?

I let out a groan staring guiltily at the phone, lying precariously on the edge of the couch. She's waiting for me to respond. Lucy is waiting for @BravesGuy93, her friend and confidant, to respond—not knowing that the guy who she's currently complaining about is the same guy she's talking to.

This is too complicated and overwhelming, and my heart feels like it's about to explode right out of my chest. But I can't just leave Lucy hanging, I need to respond to her. Especially when she's being so open and vulnerable with me and *especially* now that I know how awful she feels—because of me.

Think, Fletcher, *think*.

How would I respond to this as @BravesGuy93? If I didn't know the other side of the story—that the kiss Lucy witnessed hadn't been one I wanted? My stomach sinks as I realize that @BravesGuy93 would advise Lucy to move on from this loser. He would tell her she deserves more than some guy who makes fancy promises but then doesn't back up his words with his actions.

To find someone who truly deserves the incredible woman she is.

But because I'm selfish and don't want her to move on, I want to tell Lucy to give this guy—*me*—another shot. But that feels gross and manipulative, especially since she doesn't know I would be giving her advice that benefits me and my desires.

I stare down at the screen, cursing my inaction and hoping she isn't taking it personally that my response is so delayed. She's already had enough to deal with today.

Do I confess now? Panic rises, and my palms start to sweat. No, no that won't work. I can't confess now, not when she's already hurt—and also drunk. What if she blocks me online before I can explain? She could also freeze me out offline. I'd lose not only one of my closest friends, but someone who I've started to develop strong feelings for. *Really* strong feelings.

Shit, this really is a mess.

I need to respond. Be supportive, like always—but keep it simple and offer no advice. That would be crossing a very clear boundary in an already terrible situation.

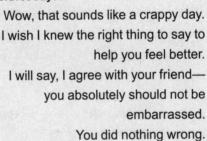

BravesGuy93   9:40 PM
Wow, that sounds like a crappy day.
I wish I knew the right thing to say to help you feel better.
I will say, I agree with your friend— you absolutely should not be embarrassed.
You did nothing wrong.

My response feels so sterile and inadequate. But it's better than *not* responding, right? My phone almost slips out of my clammy hands when her response pops up a moment later.

TheMissGuidedCounselor   9:41 PM
Well, thank you.
It's hard to not feel completely

> humiliated though because I had
> totally built up this guy in my head
> and really thought he liked me.
> And part of me feels so pathetic,
> wishing he would turn up outside my
> window with a boom box.

I read over her response, confused. A boom box? Is that actually something she would want from me? I shouldn't, but...I need more details.

> BravesGuy93   9:42 PM
> Boom box? How does that help fix
>   things?

Yes, I'm fishing for clues on how to make things better. And yes, that is probably—*definitely*—violating some boundaries, but I'm desperate for clues how to make things better and if a boom box can do it, then I'm willing to try.

> TheMissGuidedCounselor   9:43 PM
> We really need to work on your
> knowledge of critical pop culture
> history. Haven't you ever seen Say Anything?
> Lloyd Dobler, on his mission to show
> Diane how much he means to her,
> stands outside of her bedroom blasting
> the Peter Gabriel song that was
> playing the first time they made love.
> It's, like, a literal cultural touchpoint

and THE prime example of the grand gesture.

BravesGuy93   9:43 PM
Grand gesture?

TheMissGuidedCounselor   9:44 PM
Wow, you really are clueless.
Watch literally ANY romcom! I am going to send you a list and assign you homework.
The grand gesture is an elaborate (aka the "grand" in grand gesture) act meant to show the other person how much they mean to you. So Lloyd with the boom box.
Oh, and another personal favorite. Never Been Kissed.
Drew Barrymore apologizing to the guy from Alias for pretending to be a high school student and then asking for a kiss on the pitcher's mound.
Which now that I'm writing it sounds weird, but you need to see the whole movie to get it.
Oh and OF COURSE, any time someone runs through an airport.
You just need to suspend your belief in the TSA temporarily.

> Which reminds me, Crazy Rich
> Asians.
> The airplane scene? With the ring?
> I cried for a solid hour.

I literally have no idea what any of these movies are, but I make a mental note to look them all up later.

> **TheMissGuidedCounselor**   9:53 PM
> Okay, so now I want to go watch a
> romcom to make me feel better. I'm
> going to sign off for the night...
> But, thanks. Not just for this—for
> everything. I'm so lucky to have you
> as a friend.
> And sorry about my very pathetic
> sexting attempt earlier. I think I've
> done enough to humiliate myself
> today so I'm going to head to sleep.
> Talk tomorrow?

I type out a quick good night and sink deeper into the couch cushion, dropping my phone beside me. Pressing the heels of my hands into my forehead, I let out a long groan. How? How did I manage to pick the *same* school as my completely anonymous online best friend?

What were the odds? They had to be nearly impossible, right?

But I can't dwell on that. I *need* to focus on how to tell Lucy

I am @BravesGuy93. And how to tell her in a way that won't cause her to panic or shut me out.

As @TheMissGuidedCounselor, Lucy has always been intensely protective of her anonymity, so much so she refuses to voice chat, send pictures, or even share first names. The anonymity, she explained, gives her the freedom to be truly authentic with me, something she can't do in her offline world.

It made sense to me—even when I longed for more. As someone raised to hide their emotions for the sake of appearances, our friendship has also given me the space to open up in ways I've never been able to before. It's what makes our connection so meaningful; we could be completely honest with each other.

But all of that could—*would*—change when I tell her who I am.

Would Lucy still want me, knowing that the shield of anonymity that protected her and allowed her to be so open with me would be completely shattered? Or would I just be a painful reminder of how that special space she had created for herself had been violated?

How had my life turned so complicated? In the span of a single night, the woman I'm falling for has also become one of my closest friends. Which means that the stakes can't be higher. Lucy is too important for me to lose. Because this—*us*—is the most real I've ever felt.

Which means that I need to explain the kiss to Lucy *before* I confess who I really am. I can't risk her pushing me away—I can't risk losing her before we've even had a chance to start. I have to tell her. I know I do. But first I need her not to hate me as Fletcher.

Then…then I can tell her the truth.

Chapter Seventeen

 *Fletcher*

I'M AT THE SCHOOL a good thirty minutes before registration for the math competition is set to begin. But despite arriving so early, I am still beat out by the alarmingly energetic PTA moms who, with extra-large coffees in hand, have already unloaded all the tables and moved on to hanging signs.

I look around, hoping to find Lucy. I'm worried she'll bail on today, knowing that both Georgia and I have also volunteered.

I hope she doesn't. I need to talk to her.

Even if I don't know what to say at this point. *Sorry you saw me kissing Georgia—that had been a complete misunderstanding. Oh, also, that guy you've been messaging with, anonymously, on Instagram? The one you already said you don't want to meet in person? Yeah, that's me. Isn't that the best news ever?*

God, this was all so complicated.

Only as I lay awake all last night, I found myself wondering how I *didn't* see the truth earlier. Because now that I know Lucy is the voice behind @TheMissGuidedCounselor, it's as if puzzle pieces are slipping into the place, and I can finally step back to see the whole, completed picture. After all, Lucy's humor, sensitivity, and empathy are the reason I started falling for her in real life—and why I cherish our friendship online.

I wander down the hall to the auditorium, trying to spot the familiar shape of the woman who has occupied my every thought since I first laid eyes on her. A few students are already milling around, looking about as awake as you would assume for seven thirty on a Saturday morning.

A loud screech pulls my attention to the stage where I find Padmesh and Lucy playing with the mics to adjust the sound. I take advantage of Lucy not yet spotting me to study her. She's wearing the same neon green T-shirt as all the other volunteers and students. On the front, in bold black letters, it reads DENOMINATORS.

A few other students who I don't recognize are wearing navy-blue shirts with white text that say ALGEBROS. There are too many math puns around me; I am officially out of my element. I watch as Lucy sorts through a box on one of the two six-foot tables on the stage, pulling out spare parts to assemble what looks like a second microphone.

"Testing, testing! Can anyone hear me?" Padmesh looks over the auditorium. When he spots me, he waves enthusiastically. "Testing! Fletcher, can you hear me?"

At the sound of my name, Lucy drops her mic into the box, where it emits another long, loud screech. She fumbles for it as I flash Padmesh a thumbs-up.

He holds up the mic again. "Lucy, say something so we can see if Fletcher hears it."

She swallows—loudly enough for the mic to pick it up. "Test, test," she mumbles.

Padmesh steps toward her. "No, Lucy, hold the mic like this," he says, demonstrating himself.

She sighs. "Test, test," she repeats, her voice louder.

I lift my hand and give her a thumbs-up, but she's already passed the microphone to Padmesh and is retreating from the stage. I jog toward the steps back down to the auditorium to meet her. When she sees me, she lets out a frustrated grunt.

"Can we talk?"

She forces a fake cheery smile to her face. "I have to set up the snack table."

"Great," I respond. "I can help."

She lets out an annoyed huff of air and breezes past me. I follow her, not surprised at how quickly she's walking. She's almost clearing a jog when I finally catch up to her at the snack table—which is fully assembled, stocked, and staffed by a pair of chatting PTA moms.

Lucy freezes before spinning on her heel to face me. "I just remembered that I was supposed to help Nia with this thing over there." She points vaguely down the hall.

"Okay, I can help with that, too," I offer.

She pauses, and it's as if I can see the gears inside of her head turning, desperately searching for an excuse. "Actually, it's in the girls' locker room. We...have to help the girls warm up for the competition."

I arch my brow, both amused and wondering how far she'll take this. "What kind of warm-ups are needed for a math competition?"

"Vocal warm-ups. We massage the throat." She demonstrates on herself, thoroughly committing to this elaborate lie.

She's about to make a run for it, but I wrap my hand around her wrist. "Please, just give me five minutes?"

She responds with a terse nod and finally faces me, her hands twisting together in front of her. "I'll give you one."

I'll take it.

"I know you saw Georgia kissing me, but that's all it was. And I didn't *want* her to kiss me." When she doesn't respond, I thrust a hand through my hair.

"Look, we dated years ago. I was in my twenties, and I thought we were happy together, but then she tells me one day that she's no longer in love with me and is leaving me for my brother. The breakup devastated me, and I ended up pretty much running away, quitting my job in finance to go to grad school and become a teacher." The words spill quickly out of my mouth now, my desperation for her to understand fueling me forward.

"And I moved on. By the time I started here, I'd honestly realized that Georgia and I had been incompatible, but she didn't feel the same and thought there was a chance for us to get back together. Which is my fault—I wasn't clear or direct enough with her.

"Sometimes when I'm in uncomfortable situations," I say, shoving my dampening hands deep into my pockets, "I avoid them because I don't handle them well. Or I just say what I think the other person wants to hear to avoid making things awkward. But I know that it's not the best way to handle things. It's actually a really bad way to handle things."

Aiming my gaze on hers, hoping she will see my sincerity, I continue. "Please believe me when I say I didn't know she was going to kiss me. I didn't *want* her to kiss me. And you have every right to be angry, but I wanted you to know the truth and I hope you give me a second chance because I really feel like there is something here"—I pull my hands out of my pockets to gesture between us—"and I think we owe it to ourselves to explore it more."

I'm desperate for Lucy to understand and give me just one more chance—even if it does hurt for these memories to resurface. This isn't a time in my life I liked to revisit. But if I am going to tell Lucy the truth, she deserves to know the whole truth.

Lucy takes a long moment before responding, heightening the pit of dread growing and twisting in my gut. Finally, she raises her eyes to look at me, her lips drawn into a tight line.

She lets out a long breath. "That is…intense. I can't imagine my sisters ever hurting me like that. And if I'm being honest, I can also be afraid of conflict and do everything in my power to avoid confrontation."

Her lips curl up in a shy smile as she lifts her shoulder. "Like pretending I need to massage teenagers' throats to prepare them for a math competition."

I let out a relieved laugh and shove a hand through my hair. The weight on my shoulders lifts, though not entirely. I doubt it will fully leave until I tell Lucy everything, but I don't want to risk revealing all of that now. I can't—not when I see the way she's looking at me, with that hopeful, sweet smile that makes my chest constrict and my body feel things I'm not sure it's ever felt before.

God, I *want* this woman.

"Well, maybe we can work on that whole avoidance thing

together?" I ask, returning her smile. "Because I really, really like you, Lucy. And I want to see where this can go."

"You do?" she asks, her voice barely above a whisper.

I nod. "Enough to risk humiliating myself here by asking if I have a chance at getting you to agree to have dinner with me?"

She bites down on her lip, hesitating the briefest of moments before answering. "I think—"

But before she can continue, she's interrupted by a frantic Padmesh, carrying a giant red buzzer in his hands, the power cord trailing behind him, dragging on the tiled floor.

"Fletcher! Lucy!" he shouts as he runs by. "The competition is almost about to start!"

I fight back the urge to throw my hands up in the air and ask the universe why it's decided to mess up my entire life, over and over again, *especially* when it comes to Lucy.

"We're coming!" Lucy calls out to him.

He pauses and frowns when he sees me. "You"—he points at me—"you need a T-shirt! For school pride. And we want to take a photo for the Facebook!"

"Uh, sure. I'll get right on that," I assure him as he continues his jog back to the auditorium.

"Shirts?" I ask, looking at Lucy for direction.

She grimaces and gestures down the hall. "They're in Nia's room. Follow me."

Chapter Eighteen

 *Lucy*

WE WALK DOWN THE hall in silence until we reach Nia's classroom. I helped her unload the box of T-shirts this morning and know there are a few left over. Hopefully there is one in Fletcher's size. If not, crop tops are in fashion now anyway, so he should be fine.

I rummage through the box, checking the tags and find a lone XXXL in a sea of smalls. "So, I think I found one. Might be a bit big, but it's—"

My words catch in my throat when I turn around to find Fletcher completely naked from the waist up, waiting for his new shirt.

He offers me a knee-weakening smile. "Thank you."

I can't help myself. I *have* to look. I mean, this guy's body is mind-boggling. I knew six-packs existed, but more in a theoretical sense. I've never had the chance to see one in person. He even has that *V* of abdominal muscles that I thought were kind of like ligers, a real-life animal that sounds more like a mythical creature.

But there Fletcher was, my very own liger.

"Uh, are you okay, Lucy?"

Fletcher's voice rudely interrupts my blatant drooling over his body, and I know I *should* feel ashamed, but I'm not in the slightest. No wonder Georgia was losing her mind over this man. He looks like the love child of a Renaissance-era sculpture and Channing Tatum circa his *Magic Mike* era.

"Um, yes. Sorry," I respond, forcing myself to look up at his amused face. I reluctantly toss him the shirt. "Here you go."

He turns the shirt over, about to slide it on when I say, "Wait."

I know it's wrong of me, and possibly very inappropriate, but I may never get to see a half-naked Fletcher again, and I feel like Future Lucy would be *very* disappointed if I didn't take full advantage of this moment. Sure, Fletcher just said that he feels like there's something between us, but he could change his mind. There's also the chance that whatever *is* happening between us fizzles into nothing, and I do *not* want to be ninety-six years old, sitting on my deathbed, regretting that I didn't at least take a full minute to ogle Fletcher's six-pack.

"Did you need something, Lucy?" Fletcher asks, an amused smile on his face, one that I barely notice because my attention is focused a few inches lower.

I shake my head and finally tear my eyes away. Heat flushes my cheeks and rushes down the rest of my body, pooling in my center and sending tingles of electricity from the tips of my toes all the way up to the haphazard bun sitting at the top of my head.

"I just wanted to, well, clarify if you really did want to go on a date? With me?" I ask, my voice coming out much less like the seductress I was aiming for and more like I sucked down a tank of helium.

He nods and waits until my eyes lock with his. "I really, *really* do," he says. "I want the chance to show you that I think we could be something pretty special. That I think you're special, and I would be lucky to be with you."

He takes a step closer, and I hold every muscle in my body taut in anticipation as the distance between us closes.

"You make me laugh, Lucy. Like, really laugh in a way that makes me feel like a kid again. I love figuring out how your brain works and how you see the world. I love how vulnerable you are, and how you let me feel it's okay to also be vulnerable with you."

He takes another step and reaches out to tuck an errant curl behind my ear. He's so close, I feel his breath when he exhales. It smells like mint, and something sugary sweet, like he popped a handful of Skittles earlier this morning. And when he looks at me, with those hazelnut-brown eyes, my knees start to buckle, and I already know I'm going to kiss him.

I can't help myself. I'm a weak woman, and I've never kissed a liger before.

I close the distance between us, pressing my body flush against Fletcher's, my soft curves to his solid, chiseled chest. I'm wearing my Chuck Taylors today, so I don't have the height advantage and Fletcher is a good foot taller. I place my hands on his arms, leaning up on my toes to kiss him.

Only when my lips are on his does he react.

His hands instantly are in my hair, pulling me closer. I try to taste that tangy minty Skittle freshness, and when I do, he grunts and moves his hands to my butt, lifting me with ease to sit on Nia's desk. His hands fall on either side of me, caging me as he leans forward to deepen our kiss. I fling my arms around his neck to keep myself from collapsing onto the desk. Fletcher's lips leave mine and travel down to my neck, which he kisses and nips with his teeth.

The sight of the muscles rippling in his forearms has me practically panting. He has some *nice* forearms. I'm a sucker for arms and have an entire Pinterest board dedicated to Chris Evans's perfect forearms, but Fletcher's come a *very* close second.

But enough admiring—I want his mouth back on mine.

I wrap my legs around his waist, pulling him against me. His hard length connects with my core, and I drop my head back at the delicious friction. His lips find mine again, kissing me with an urgency that sucks the breath straight out of my lungs. Like a man starved, Fletcher devours my lips, caressing them open with his tongue to continue his conquest. He kisses me like this is not only our first kiss, but our hundredth—our thousandth. He kisses with a passion that tells the story of someone who not only wants me but *craves* me. And I have absolutely zero complaints.

Until he pulls back, his eyes locking on mine. "Am I going too fast? Are you okay?"

And as much as I love him asking, I want his lips to get back to work, so I respond by dragging his face back to mine, answering with a needy kiss. This time, he gently leans forward, pushing me onto my back, shoving the box of shirts to the floor. His left hand slips under my shirt, and I buck at the touch. His palm travels up until he reaches my bra, his lips never leaving mine. His thumb brushes over my nipple, and I groan into his mouth. He seems to love the reaction because he does it again, thrusting against me as he does so.

There are too many sensations, too much pleasure,

and I wonder if it would be possible to have an orgasm from dry-humping on my best friend's desk.

But before I can test that theory, I hear the door to the classroom open and a voice cry "Oh—oopsy daisy!"

Fletcher immediately pulls his hand out from under my shirt and separates from me. We both turn to find Brodie watching us in shock, his cheeks stained a bright cherry red.

"Nia sent me here to get my shirt," he mumbles.

I push up into a sitting position and smooth out my hair. Fletcher, still shirtless, holds the T-shirt I had given him strategically over his very obvious hard-on.

"Of course. I was just actually getting a T-shirt for Fletcher. Padmesh wanted him to have one for the group photo, so we came in here and got one." The words spill clumsily out of my mouth and my cheeks heat with embarrassment, though, thankfully they're not as bright red as Brodie's.

Brodie looks even more uncomfortable, his eyes darting around the room, looking at anything *but* us. "Oh, yes, absolutely, makes complete sense," he rambles to the poster of Isaac Newton behind us.

Fletcher reaches into the box and tosses him a shirt. "I didn't know you were volunteering today."

Brodie's cheeks turn a dark crimson. "Well, after I saw everyone else volunteering, I worried I might be missing out on something. And I have terrible FOMO, as the kids call it. You know, fear of missing out. Ever since I didn't join my cousins to go to the Dundee footie match back in ninety-eight. They hadn't won anything in over a decade, but the one time I didn't go, they won. It was terrible, so now I try to never miss out on things."

He sighs and shakes his head. "But I honestly don't get this whole math competition that you all seemed so excited about. So far, *very* underwhelming."

Fletcher and I share a look, unsure of how to respond. Truthfully, I'm never quite sure how to respond to Brodie, but luckily, he does most of the talking so I never need to.

"So, um, we'll see you out there?" Fletcher asks when Brodie doesn't turn to leave.

Brodie's eyebrows shoot to the top of his head. "Oh, right! Of course!" He spins on his heel and turns back around. "Also, Padmesh is looking for you both. He needs help grabbing some ice from the cafeteria."

"Right, of course!" I slide off the desk and adjust my shirt. "We will be out in a minute."

Once Brodie stumbles out of the classroom, Fletcher and I share a look before bursting into laughter.

"I think we traumatized him," Fletcher says, a playful smile on his face, as he shrugs into the three-sizes-too-big T-shirt, which *should* look ridiculous, but because he is a gorgeous human specimen, he kind of pulls it off. He tucks the shirt into his pants. "Ready to go?"

"Yes," I answer. "But you may need a few more minutes." Fletcher follows my gaze down to his protruding, and very obvious, erection.

He chuckles nervously. "Yeah, that might be a good idea. But I may need you to leave first."

"Why?" I ask, worried that I may have done something wrong to upset him.

He gestures to his tented jeans. "This is your fault," he says with a teasing smile, "and if you keep standing there, I don't know if I'll be able to think of anything else."

I don't know what to say. I don't know if a man has ever confessed that my mere presence was enough to inspire an erection, especially when I was fully dressed and wearing an ill-fitting, oversized math competition T-shirt.

"But before you go," he calls out as I reach the door, "about that date?"

I bite back a laugh but nod. If these five minutes alone in Nia's classroom are any indication, an actual date with Fletcher will probably be life-altering.

"Next week? Saturday?"

I nod again and then open the door. I'm walking on cloud nine, basking in the dry-humping afterglow and Fletcher's penile affections.

"I'll see you out there," I say, waving a hand in goodbye. I blush when I capture his still fully tented pants. "And, uh, good luck with your penis."

BravesGuy93
Today at 5:30 PM

TheMissGuidedCounselor
Hey! I CANNOT believe I am saying this, but I think I need some dating advice.
I have a date tonight and my stomach is twisted up in knots and I am beginning to panic a bit.

Today at 5:49 PM

TheMissGuidedCounselor
Okay, so maybe I am past the "beginning to panic" and more "fully stressing out now"

Today at 6:26 PM

TheMissGuidedCounselor
Guess you're busy—forget I said anything!
I'm sure it will be fine.
I mean, of course, it will be fine. Everything's fine.
Everything will be amazing.
I just need to get out of my own head.
Wish you had some of those ridiculous memes you could send me right about now that could distract me.

But you're probably busy.
It's Saturday night after all.
Anyway, I am perfectly fine!
Hope you're doing okay, too. I know
you've been busy. Feels like it's
been forever since we chatted.
Talk soon?

Chapter Nineteen

 *Lucy*

THIS DATE IS DOOMED.

While I remain a skeptical believer in fate, I am now fairly convinced that whatever entity *is* up there, whether it's an old white guy with a long beard or Alanis Morissette, does not want this date with Fletcher to happen.

Why else would the thing that controls the heat on my shower—you know, the twisty thing that when you turn it magically makes hot water pour from my overpriced showerhead with eucalyptus draped over top—completely fall off and land on my toe at just the precise angle to leave a nasty cut that is now covered with a hot-pink Bratz Band-Aid?

And because I refuse to shower unless I am boiling, I had to end my very intense date grooming preparation early and finish shaving my left leg while balancing quite precariously on the ledge of my bathroom sink.

And then, when I went to make tea to calm the anxious knot in my stomach, I discovered I only had one rumpled, very unappealing, and slightly soggy tea bag left, with not even a single squirt of honey to help sweeten it up.

I mean, if a bleeding toe and empty tea stash were signs

from the universe, shouldn't I gracefully bow out now? Claim a migraine and shoot off an apologetic text?

I glance down at my phone and let out an audible groan. Fletcher is set to pick me up in less than ten minutes. Canceling now would just be downright rude and the final nail in my very short, practically nonexistent dating history with Fletcher. And I like Fletcher—a lot. I would also *really* like to get laid before my twenty-ninth birthday in two months.

I scroll over to Instagram and check my DMs for the eightieth time today. It looks like @BravesGuy93 has *still* not responded to my last few messages even though he has clearly seen them. I am torn between feeling worried and disappointed. If anyone could quickly ease my anxiety over this date, it would be him. It's always so easy for him to make me laugh and based on how much I am panicking right now, I could *really* use the laugh.

I close the app with a disappointed sigh. I'll have to worry about him later, because I need to calm the hell down before Fletcher gets here.

I try to think rationally for a few solid minutes, taking in deep gulps of air. Rational Lucy knows that the handle for the hot water thingamajig has been loose for a while and that the search results for "how to fix handle thingy in shower" have been hanging out in one of the thirty-seven tabs on my Safari browser for a few weeks now.

And that my lack of groceries is simply a direct result of me putting off going to the store because I *had* planned to be one of those organized adults who has a whiteboard to meal-plan and uses up those random ingredients—like the three cans of coconut milk and the bottle of ranch dressing that is probably bar mitzvah eligible this year—to make delicious, unique Pinterest-worthy recipes.

Really, all I need to make that happen is time to audit all the current canned goods in my pantry, list all of the splotchy frost-bitten lumps of *something* in my freezer, look up recipes, and, well, buy a whiteboard. But because I keep waiting for the day when all those things will magically materialize, I've neglected to actually buy food for myself.

Which on most days isn't truly an issue—I *do* work at a restaurant. And considering it's my family's restaurant, no one ever chastises me for clocking in with empty Tupperware containers and filling them with steaming couscous and a generous helping of marinated chicken smothered in a balsamic glaze at the end of my shift.

But for the basics, like tea and milk and sugar, I'm generally on my own. And damn did I need to go to the grocery store.

But that would have to be a problem for Later Lucy. Because Right Now Lucy needs to finish getting ready for this date and talking myself off the precarious ledge of anxiety.

And if Right Now Lucy is being truly honest with herself, she'll admit that the reason she thinks this whole date is a disaster before it's even begun is not because of the shower turning-thing breaking off or because the inside of her refrigerator currently resembles the insides of a long-neglected frat house, but because she is nervous.

She should also probably stop talking about herself in the third person.

God, I'm *really* nervous.

And not like those adorable dainty-little-butterflies-fluttering-in-my-tummy nerves. More like spider-monkeys-leaping-from-tree-to-tree-in-the-pit-of-my-stomach nervous.

I have not been on a date I was excited for in a *very* long time.

I have a bad tendency to agree to a date whenever asked, even if I don't very much like the guy. I always ignore the red flags and tell myself I'm being judgmental, and I should be grateful that I'm even getting asked out on a date. But with Fletcher I never feel that way. It's nice to be going out with someone I am attracted to on both a physical and emotional level. More than nice.

I mean, this dating thing is stressful. The anxiety can be, at times, completely overwhelming. Not only do you have to spend a good hour primping and shaving *everything* "just in case," but then you have to actually sit through the date. That somehow always means coming up with appropriate questions that don't make me sound like I am interrogating them Olivia Benson style *and* finding a way to act interested when they break down their fantasy football picks for the season.

It is a *lot* of work.

And I am of course overanalyzing everything—wondering if he's silently judging me for ordering the salad instead of a burger, or the burger instead of the salad. Does he plan on kissing me, and do I even *want* him to kiss me, because if I do then that means definitely no onions on the salad. Or the burger. And what if the night does go well and I want to invite him in? Will he judge me for having sex on a first date? Should I play it cool and wait until the third date? Fifth date?

There are far too many questions and variables that all together are too mentally exhausting to work through.

What's *not* mentally exhausting? Netflix and a vibrator.

The doorbell rings, pulling me away from my endless thoughts, and I let out a loud curse.

I am nowhere near emotionally prepared enough for this date. Between all the drama of the new school year and the change of routine from a summer spent sleeping in till long past noon to rising early every day, between school and my shifts at the restaurant, I've been struggling. My mental health can sometimes feel like a never-ending roller coaster of highs and lows. I need to take a break from the roller coaster and feel my feet on solid ground.

A part of me wonders if I should even be dating, but I should probably save that to process with Tiffany during my weekly therapy sessions. Thankfully I have one coming up on Wednesday, which just happens to be the monthly double feature with my psychiatrist, Dr. Zhou, *and* Tiffany.

It's a special treat because I get to sit across from Dr. Zhou and answer a set of routine questions to assure him that I am adequately depressed enough to require a re-up of my meds, but not *so* depressed that I would end my life and then have my devastated parents sue him. And like most who have been around the block, I know to follow the unspoken agreement between psychiatrist and patient where I parrot back reassuring responses even if they're a teensy bit not true so Dr. Zhou feels good and I don't get thrown into a "grippy sock vacation" aka an inpatient stay (and yes, I learned this lesson the hard way thanks to divulging that I sometimes fantasize about jumping off a bridge but honestly who doesn't from time to time?).

But when Dr. Zhou is satisfied enough, I'm gifted with thirty more days of happy pills. Then I pop over to the office next door to sit with Tiffany for exactly fifty minutes—she has a timer that goes off at the exact *second* our session ends, so I try to time my breakdowns accordingly.

Maybe Tiffany will be more flexible with her time if I have spicy date details to share—but that means actually going on this date.

Part of me knows that if I don't push myself and give this attraction to Fletcher an honest shot, I will always regret it. Something about the way he makes me feel quiets the anxious voices in my head. A simple smile makes me want to try to make this work, to swallow down all these insecurities and fears—and not open the door with my stomach in a knot, tears brimming in the corners of my eyes and an impending panic attack elevating my heart rate to two hundred beats a minute.

I sneak a look out the window from my bedroom on the second floor and see Fletcher at my doorstep.

Shit, he's actually here.

I don't think I've ever had a date come to my actual doorstep—I usually just get the "I'm here" text—bonus points if there's a smiley face emoji.

I expel a breath and nod at my reflection in the mirror.

"You've got this," I say to the woman standing in front of me. And even if I don't, I did spend two freaking hours watching makeup tutorials on YouTube, and this cat eye needs to be seen by the world and admired. Sure, the stress about my shower and lack of groceries and the million other pesky things I need to do are bouncing around my head with the gusto of a flying trapeze artist, and it feels impossible to quiet those never-ending lists, but I need to try.

At the very least, for the sake of my cobweb-covered vagina, I *need* to try.

Dabbing the moisture from my eyes with a rumpled piece of toilet paper, I carefully and slowly descend my stairs, these heels making my ankles quiver like a newborn giraffe who has just been cruelly thrust into the world and expected to walk in thirty minutes flat.

I finally reach the landing, and I can walk a bit more gracefully to open the front door, where I find Fletcher looking absolutely delicious in every single way. He's wearing dark pants—not jeans, another plus!—and a crisp white button-down tucked in with a fitted blazer over top; more preppy than my usual taste, but I definitely don't hate it on him. In his hands is a bouquet of pink and purple tulips.

It's all so perfect, and I wonder if now would be an appropriate time for me to swoon. I've never swooned before, so I am not entirely sure when during a date is appropriate. Already I am beginning to question if this is real life or if I have somehow been transported into a romance movie where I am the lead character.

Even if the night ends here, it would be absolutely perfect just because I got to see date-night Fletcher looking surprisingly sexy in a blazer, handing me flowers, and looking at me like I am a hunk of meat he can't wait to sink his teeth into.

I smell the tulips, even though tulips have no smell, because that's what they do in the movies, and I could possibly be in one right now, so I'm going with it. "Thank you for the tulips. They're lovely. Let me just put them in water." I spin back around and scurry to the kitchen to grab a vase.

Then I realize I never invited Fletcher in and he's still standing on my doorstep.

Great. Good job, Lucy.

I quickly rush back to the door. "Sorry to make you stand there. That was super rude of me, I should have invited you in so—"

"It's fine, Lucy," he cuts in with a gentle smile, looking completely unbothered.

And I don't know why, but somehow those three words—*it's fine, Lucy*—cut through me like a hot knife through cake.

Is it the cadence? The deep timbre? The way the corner of his mouth arches into a reassuring smile? Whatever it is, it is enough to shatter what pitiful, decaying wall I'd built to hold back the tears threatening to spill from earlier. The wall that was supposed to hide all my messy parts: the depression, the anxiety, the total lack of organization both in my brain and in my life. The wall that I do my best to never let down but have already done so too many times in front of Fletcher.

As the hot, messy tears spill, snaking down the roundness of my cheeks, Fletcher's easy smile disappears. "Lucy, what's wrong?"

Well, *that's* a loaded question, isn't it? Quite literally, well, *nothing's* wrong.

Sure, my shower broke, but that's fixable. And yes, I desperately need to go to the grocery store, but I can do that tomorrow if I wake up early. These are *not* problems, but thanks to my anxiety-ridden brain, I've made them into problems. Big ones. Ones that are stressful enough to make me cry in front of the man I really, *really* like, who must have some kind of masochistic streak since he wants to take *me* out to dinner.

"I'm *so* sorry," I say, swiping the back of my hand over my eye and letting out a frustrated grunt when I see the smeared black from my eyeliner and mascara trailed across my skin. "If you want to go, you can. I mean, you should." I hiccup. "I'll be okay."

I don't want him to go. But I also don't want him to stay and see me like *this*. But if he does go, I want it to be because I offered him the out first. So therefore, it's not *really* rejection and I can't feel that terribly about it.

Lucy Logic 101.

"Don't be sorry, Lucy," he says, crinkles creasing the corners of his eyes as he locks his gaze on mine. "And I don't want to go. Just tell me what's going on. Did something happen?"

The firmness in his voice reassures me enough to take a long steadying breath. I like the way he says my name. I like it better how he makes that uncontrollably spinning tornado inside of me instantly transform into a harmless summer breeze. I wonder how he can calm me so easily when it usually takes a milligram of Ativan to accomplish the task.

I shake my head. "Nothing really happened. I just, well, I'm overwhelmed by some things. My shower thing broke. I'm completely out of groceries. And I think I'm having a little panic attack. Kind of like the closet, but a sequel." I offer a weak chuckle to try to lighten the mood, but it only causes the lines across Fletcher's forehead to crease even deeper.

"Okay," he says, nodding seriously. "So, last time your panic attack was about Sophia, so did something happen or—"

"Nothing bad," I rush to reassure him. "Just…" My voice trails off as I try to find a way to explain how these little life inconveniences have needled their way in my brain to becoming big, tear-inducing problems.

"Okay, well, I have ADHD, in addition to my depression and anxiety, or as my mother calls them 'my mental health bendiciones' and, anyway, I get easily overwhelmed by things. And they may be little things, like stuff that could take less than an hour—or even five minutes—but because I've built them up in my head to be these big tasks, I get paralyzed when I need to do them. And then I feel terrible about myself for *not* dealing with them because here I am, an actual adult human being who *should* be able to deal with this stuff, but I can't. So then it starts this shame cycle and those tiny things are now gigantic."

I let out a long sigh and brave a glance at Fletcher, who miraculously is still standing in my entryway. "Does any of that make sense?"

"I think so. I mean, you've kind of described my little sister, Liv, to a T. She will put off things, like paying a bill or calling to make an appointment, for weeks." He lifts his arm to scratch the back of his head, a hint of a blush on his cheeks. "I admit, sometimes I kind of thought she was being disorganized or irresponsible, but now I think she just got overwhelmed like how you described."

"Does your sister also have ADHD?" I ask.

He nods. "I always thought it was just about being hyper, but now that I'm back to living with her, I'm seeing that it's so much more than that." He chuckles. "I kind of want to go home and apologize to her for being so judgmental in the past. The way you just explained it now? Totally helped me see it from a different perspective."

I soak in his words. *I* changed his opinion enough to make him want to apologize to his sister?

Something about that helps calmness settle over me, and

my racing heart begins to slow. When you have ADHD and a disorganized brain, it can often feel like you're the only one who lives like this. The shame and stigma make it hard to talk about—though for whatever reason, whenever I'm around Fletcher, my filter disappears and I just word-vomit all the mess I usually try so hard to hide.

And instead of running away, he accepts it. He takes it, considers it, thoughtfully reflects on it, and accepts it like a gift. Like *I'm* a gift.

"Well, now that I've completely ruined our date," I say with a weak smile, "should we get going? You mentioned you would be making reservations. Did I make us totally late for dinner?"

He looks down at his watch and shrugs. "We can still make it." He pauses, his eyes narrowing as a smile crosses his lips. "But I'm wondering if you might be up for something else tonight?"

I match his smile with a more cautious one of my own. "Sure. What did you have in mind?"

He glances down and, spotting my shoes, points. "Well, first we'll need a change in footwear."

Chapter Twenty

 *Lucy*

"WELL, THIS IS CERTAINLY one of the more unique dates I've been on."

Fletcher smiles at my comment and my stomach does a little somersault. He has a really nice smile that looks like the result of either really good genes or very expensive dental work.

"I'll take it that that's a good thing, right?"

I nod. "Very good."

"Great. Now, let's try to find someone in an orange vest, because I have no idea where I'm supposed to be looking."

I gawk at him. "You want to find a store associate to help you?"

He arches a brow. "Yes, why?"

"You're a man…in a home improvement store. Don't you want to assert your masculine prowess by doing everything yourself and not admitting you need help, even if it takes hours longer?"

Fletcher cocks a brow. "I don't know what kind of men you're used to, but I am not afraid to admit when I am out of my depth. And I am *definitely* out of my depth here."

Within a few minutes, we chase down and corner a sales

associate and I'm handing them my phone with my search history for the part I am 99 percent sure I need for my shower. The part is located within five minutes, and Fletcher and I listen intently as orange-vested Jacob tells us exactly how to install the piece. He even texts Fletcher a YouTube tutorial, so when we check out, I make sure to pocket my receipt and fill out the customer feedback survey because Jacob deserves it.

Exactly fifteen minutes after pulling into our parking spot, we're back inside the car.

Fifteen minutes.

For months, I've put off fixing my shower, knowing it would inevitably break during the most inconvenient time, adding it to the hundred-item to-do list that exists solely in my head. And all it took was fifteen minutes.

I fight against the twin feelings of shame and embarrassment, trying to acknowledge that yes, even though the task itself did only take fifteen minutes, the process of getting here was *not* simple.

In fact, it feels like the simpler a task, the longer it takes for me to physically do it. A phone call to schedule my annual doctor's appointment? That should take me about, oh, I don't know, three to six weeks. Running to the post office for stamps to mail this census form that is probably eight years past due? Well, that involves at least an hour pep talk. Plus, I need to go right when it opens so I can snag one of the enviable three front spots so I don't have to parallel park. And I need to go on a weekday because the guy who works on Saturday is kind of mean.

So much brainpower for such simple tasks. The mental gymnastics I use to convince myself I'll do them later could qualify me for the Olympic gymnastics team ten times over.

"So, where do you usually like to get your groceries?"

Fletcher's question pulls me from the self-pity rabbit hole I was dangerously veering toward, and I shoot him a quizzical look. "Groceries?"

He nods. "You mentioned needing groceries, so I thought that could be our next stop."

My chest clenches with emotion. Fletcher is being so... sweet.

"I've already taken more than enough of your time," I object. "Can we still make those dinner reservations? I feel bad that—"

"Please do not feel bad," Fletcher gently interrupts. "Plans are flexible. And all I want is to spend time with you. I honestly couldn't care less where or how." He pauses, considering. "But you're probably hungry, so let's grab something to eat."

I nod. "I am a little hungry." I look down at my Converse high-tops and lift up my foot. "But I'm probably a little underdressed for whatever you had planned."

Fletcher shrugs and starts to reverse out of the parking spot. "Actually I was thinking of this nice little local spot. Food is fantastic. It's like a Moroccan-Mexican fusion restaurant. Come Con...something. Have you heard of it?"

I give his arm a playful punch. "If you take me anywhere near there, I will absolutely tuck and roll out of this car. I don't care how fast you are driving. I love my family, but not in my dating life."

Fletcher cocks a grin. "What a shame, but I guess we'll have to settle for something else. How do you feel about sushi?"

I let out a breath of relief. "Sushi sounds amazing."

"Well, I think that does it."

Fletcher presses a button, and the trunk door starts to close. I do my best to temper how impressed I am at the fanciness of the tech. I'm equally impressed by his ability to squeeze all my groceries into his trunk. Considering I haven't been to the store since the school year started, I was running seriously low on essentials, and thankfully Fletcher was not at all fazed by my excitement at the sale for a jumbo thirty-six-roll pack of toilet paper.

I follow Fletcher into the car and claim my seat, sliding the seat belt over my hips. "Thanks for, well, everything tonight. I've had a really nice time."

I mean it. Tonight has been amazing—one of the best dates I've ever been on—which is odd considering the majority of the date involved us running errands.

After we finished dinner, Fletcher insisted we go to the local supermarket to stock up, remembering how stressed I was about my upsetting lack of tea and sugar. I tried to convince him he didn't need to go with me, but then he parroted my earlier words back at me with a teasing smile. "Didn't you say that if you keep putting it off, you'll never do it?"

And, of course, he was right. If I don't do it in that moment, I probably won't for at least another few days. Possibly longer.

And then the guilt and shame and embarrassment will set in, so isn't it worth it to just do it now? And let's be honest, taking the hot guy I have a crush on to do my least favorite adult chore (next to taxes) is not a terrible way to spend a Saturday evening. I had *fun* going shopping with Fletcher. As we wandered through the aisles, debating the validity of the "organic" label on a box of cheese crackers, I had felt so domestic, like

Fletcher and I were just another boring old couple getting our weekly groceries together.

I liked it. A lot. It showed me what a future with Fletcher could be like and how easy it is when we are together.

But now that we are sitting in Fletcher's car, the nervous butterflies in my stomach are starting to flutter again. Because now we are going to my house, and considering how much food I just bought, Fletcher will probably, like the gentleman he is, insist on helping me carry them inside. Which will mean he'll then be *inside* my house. Which will *then* mean he'll be a mere ten feet away from my bedroom, which could mean…all kinds of things.

And according to my sisters, I'm in *desperate* need of getting laid. And Fletcher is an ideal—if not perfect—candidate for the job.

As we turn onto my street, I allow myself to feel excited about the rest of the evening. To not lose myself in thoughts of what-if and list all the things that could go wrong. Maybe this *could* be perfect, maybe this will be exactly what I need. Maybe—

"*Shit.*"

Fletcher turns to look at me, clearly startled by the loud expletive. "Is everything okay?"

I groan and drop my head into my hands as Fletcher pulls his car behind mine in the driveway, quickly putting it into park. "Did I do something?"

I shake my head then let out a frustrated sigh. "It's my family," I explain, gesturing behind us to where, across the street, they're sitting comfortably in lawn chairs.

My *entire* family. Clearly waiting for me and Fletcher to return from our date.

I glance at the clock on Fletcher's dashboard and inwardly curse. It's almost nine at night! Does no one in my family have anything better to do on a Saturday evening?

Fletcher turns to look and lets out a nervous chuckle when he sees the parade of people parked on my parents' lawn, watching the car like we are the latest feature at the local drive-in theater.

"Maybe they just wanted to make sure you got home safely?"

I let out another loud, long groan and shake my head. On the rare occasion I *do* go out on a date, my father subtly writes down their license plate number from behind the safety of his living room curtain—this action has been previously authorized by me. My father and I share a slight paranoia thanks to our subscription to the ID network and our penchant for *Dateline*. While my mother and sisters find our obsession a bit absurd, my father and I took advantage of a Groupon deal to get our photos professionally done, so in the event that we do go missing, we'll have nice pictures to share with the media.

Never underestimate the power of a good photo—it can really make or break whether you get a prime spot on the evening news.

But my entire family camping out in the front yard to check out my date? That has not been authorized.

I get out of the car, ready to storm over and lecture them all for this gross invasion of privacy, but they all start to wave enthusiastically. All nine of them: my mother, my father, both of my sisters, three of my aunts, one cousin, and interestingly enough, our neighbor, Mrs. Greenfield. She looks like she was unsuspectingly roped into this and now deeply regrets it.

"So that's your family?" Fletcher gets out of the car and comes to my side, a hint of confusion in his voice.

I nod and pinch my eyes closed, hoping that when I reopen them, this will all be a terrible mirage I hallucinated because I am severely dehydrated. In my head, I am reminding myself to write each and every one of them out of my will. My sole beneficiary will now be our very uncomfortable-looking neighbor, because she at least has the decency to look mildly embarrassed.

"Do you want to go say hello?" Fletcher asks, probably questioning whether he should just run away now and Venmo me later for all my groceries he's driven off with.

I place my hand on his arm. "Look, I'll level with you. Those people are about thirty percent of my immediate family. And because we've now been spotted, we kind of have to go over and I need to introduce you to everyone and say hello, and then before we go, we have to say goodbye to everyone individually again and the whole thing is going to take at least half an hour and if you have somewhere you need to go…"

I half expect him to disentangle his arm from my hand and drive away, thinking how he's dodged a bullet the entire ride back home.

Instead, he laughs and gently tugs me forward. "We've got nothing but time. Let me go meet my future in-laws."

I stifle a laugh and shake my head. "I suggest *meeting* them before making such a bold assumption. Trust me, if I had the choice to—"

"You're telling me," he interrupts, "if you had the chance to marry into your family, you wouldn't? From everything you've told me…" He pauses, a red hue staining his cheeks. "Well, you haven't told me too much, but what from what I've gathered, your family seems kind of amazing."

The sudden change in Fletcher takes me aback, from the

seriousness in his tone to the sadness that crosses over him, flipping his casual smile into a tilted frown. Admittedly I don't know much about Fletcher's family (other than the fact that his dad *does* seem a tad bit judgmental), but he's right.

Of course, he's right.

I *am* lucky to have such an amazing and supportive family—even if they have a very murky understanding of how boundaries work, no matter how many times (with visual demonstrations!) I've tried to explain the concept to them.

"Okay, let's do it. But keep your answers short and vague. Don't mention anything mildly interesting about yourself; otherwise they'll keep you there forever, interrogating you. And stay away from topics of food, politics, religion, baseball, anything to do with cruise ships, or boats or submarines—long story—and then we should be able to make it out in under twenty minutes."

Fletcher nods and grabs my hand, dragging me across the street. Everyone rises from their chairs to form a circle around us, and I suck in a giant gulp of air. "This is Fletcher."

I start individually introducing everyone, and I can see the gears turning in his head as he tries to remember everyone's names and their relation to me.

Good luck. I still get confused sometimes.

When Tía Rosa has engaged Fletcher in a spirited discussion about his car and where he bought it and for how much—because, again, boundaries are not a thing that exist in my family—I drag Julieta to the side by the elbow.

"How could you let this happen?" I hiss.

"I'm sorry. But when Papa wrote down his license plate when he picked you up, he mentioned that Fletcher had a *really* nice car. Naturally, that piqued Amá's interest, so she decided to wait on the front deck until you got back so she could see, but then Tía Rosa and Tía Luisa stopped by to catch up on the gossip and they, of course, insisted on staying, too. But there wasn't enough room on the porch, so they moved to the front lawn. That's when Papa grabbed the lawn chairs out of the garage. And then, well, Tante Mirielle was here with Yael to drop off the tablecloths for the party tomorrow, so they also decided to stay, and well, then it kind of devolved from there."

She at least looks a tiny bit remorseful. The rest of my family? Not so much.

I find Fletcher, who's handling this surprisingly well, now talking with my father, who is very interested in his Audi.

"Papa, we need to go. I have groceries I need to bring in to the fridge."

"Groceries?" my mother asks, a horrified expression on her face. "Why do you have groceries?"

"Because we went to the grocery store," I reply and suppress a smile at seeing the confused look on my mother's and aunt's faces as they wrap their heads around the fact that my date tonight involved a grocery store.

I know they have more questions, but I forcefully initiate the usual series of goodbyes until fifteen minutes later, my hand is wrapped around Fletcher's as I, quite literally, drag him out of my mother's clutches, despite her already inviting him to the next two weeks' worth of family events.

When we get back into my driveway, I insist on loading my arms up with as many plastic bags as possible to avoid the possibility of having to go back outside a second time and facing another round of interrogation. Only when the door closes behind us do I finally let out a sigh of relief.

"I am so sorry," I say.

He shakes his head and gives my hand a reassuring squeeze. "It was cool to meet your family."

I groan.

"They're usually not this…involved when I go out on dates. Not that I go on a ton of dates," I quickly add. "But they usually respect the fact that I am an adult woman and do not need to introduce every guy I'm dating to all of them."

This is a lie. My family absolutely does not respect the fact that I am an adult woman, but that's something to unpack another day.

"Well, I liked meeting them. And I'm excited about the next family lunch. Your mom promised to make me her famous tamales."

Of course she did. "Really, you are under no obligation to—"

"I *want* to," he interrupts, covering my hand with his. "As long as I'm with you, then yeah, I want to."

BravesGuy93
Today at 2:03 PM

> **TheMissGuidedCounselor**
> Okay, I am officially getting concerned. It's been like a week since we talked.
> Is everything okay?

BravesGuy93
Yeah, I'm sorry.
I've just been super busy.

> **TheMissGuidedCounselor**
> He lives!
> How are you?
> I was beginning to wonder if I should fill out a missing persons report except I realized I didn't know your name, or where you live, or what you look like 😄

BravesGuy93
Sorry I've been so MIA.

> **TheMissGuidedCounselor**
> It's okay, I get it.
> I feel like there's so much to catch up on. Are you still loving the new job?
> Oh, and what's the latest gossip on

you and the guidance counselor at your school?

BravesGuy93
Actually, I have to run.
I'm so sorry.

TheMissGuidedCounselor
Okay, sure. No worries.
Talk soon, I hope?

Chapter Twenty-One

 *Lucy*

I MAKE IT LESS than three steps into Come Con Gana before my sisters descend upon me like vultures on a decaying carcass.

"How was the rest of your date last night?"

"Did you put out?"

"Are you officially boyfriend and girlfriend now?"

The questions come in rapid succession, and I hold up my hand to calm them all down. "Can I sit before you all interrogate me, please?"

Julieta grabs my hand and half drags me to the end of the bar. Amira follows and slides behind the counter. I shrug out of my jacket and look toward Amira. "Aren't you going to ask me what I want to drink?"

Amira rolls her eyes. "I only ask that to *paying* customers who are going to tip me. You are neither." She crosses her arms at her chest. "Now, spill. You finally have something worth sharing, and we want details."

"Fine, but I do want some water." I clutch my throat. "I'm *so* parched, and if I am going to tell you all about my date, I'm going to need moisture."

Amira rolls her eyes again but complies and shoves a

half-filled glass of lukewarm water at me. I take my time sipping, relishing *finally* being the one with an interesting dating life. Only when I put the glass down, I realize I don't exactly know where to start. "Um, well, what do you want to know?"

Amira throws her hands up in the air. "Dear God, woman! Just start at the beginning!"

"Okay! Fine. Well, full disclosure, the date didn't really start off well. I had a bit of a panic attack. I think it was because it was my first date in ages, and I like Fletcher. Like *really* like him." I wince at the memory but continue. "Anyways, he saw how I was panicking and was really sweet about it. And I kind of just word-vomited out everything that was making me anxious, and he was totally unfazed. He just said we could cancel our dinner plans and then took me on some errands to Home Depot and the grocery store."

"Ahh, he is so dreamy." Julieta sighs and rests her chin dreamily on her hands.

"You're just saying that because you've never been on a date," Amira says before turning her attention back to me. "So get to the good stuff! Did he rail you in the back seat in the parking lot? Or did you wait until you got back to your house?"

Julieta and I groan in response. "Amira! It wasn't that kind of date. We barely even kissed. Just a really sweet, kind of dreamy eight-seconder on my doorstep before he left for the night."

"Really?" Amira asks. "So you went to Home Depot, the grocery store, and then...that's it?"

"Well," I respond, feeling a bit deflated. "We grabbed some dinner, too, but yes. And yeah, I know it's not the most exciting date, but it still felt really special. Being with him...I don't know how to describe it. It's just so...easy."

Amira rolls her eyes. "Well, to his credit, it's not the worst date you've been on. Let's not forget about Trey Michaelson."

I groan at the memory: that date had ended with a very unenthusiastic hand job in the Wendy's parking lot in exchange for a vanilla Frosty.

"No, let's *please* forget about Trey Michaelson," I plead, regretting that I am physically incapable of not sharing every single detail of my life with my sisters.

"So do you think you'll go out with him again?" Julieta asks, thankfully changing the subject.

I nod, a smile overtaking my face. "We're meeting up again next Saturday. Low-key date with Chinese takeout at my house." I pin them with my stare. "So you both are ordered to stay far, far away."

Amira claps her hands and jumps up and down. "Lulu's going to get laid!" she sings, way too loudly—enough so that the couple sitting at the other end of the bar turns to glare at us.

"Oh my God! This is so great, Lulu. I'm so happy for you!" Julieta exclaims.

Amira pulls out her phone. "Do you want me to see if my wax girl can get you in?"

I drop my head into my hands. I love my sisters, but times like these make me fantasize about life as an only child.

"I don't know if I can do it, though," I say with a groan, dropping my head onto the bar.

"What? Why?" Julieta asks.

I look at them from between my fingers. "Ugh, I don't even know! I don't know what's wrong with me!"

"Is it because you need to wax?" Amira asks. "If my girl is busy, I can try to get you in with my backup. She can *probably* get you in before Saturday. I'll just explain that my little sister needs to get some action. She'll get it."

I turn to Amira and pin her with my stare. "I am fine and do not 'need to get laid,' thank you very much. And I do *not* need a wax!"

Amira holds up her phone. "It's okay, I just texted her, and she's free tomorrow night at six. Clara can cover the first half of your shift for you."

I gape at her. "How the hell did you manage to arrange all of that in the past five seconds?"

Amira eyes me, clearly confused, and gestures to her phone. "It's texting, Lulu. It's not rocket science."

"Okay, whatever. You all need to butt out of my life a little! I respect all of your privacy!"

Amira snorts and props her hands on her hips. "Excuse me? You ran background checks on my last three boyfriends."

"Um, that is totally different," I argue, holding up my hand. "That was for your own personal safety."

Amira shakes her head. "Well, it is also a matter of *our*"— she gestures to Julieta—"personal safety that you get laid soon."

"How is me getting laid related to your personal safety?" I ask.

"Because when you're having a dry spell, you can get really...how do I say this?" Amira starts. "You get bitchy."

"What she means is you get a little...wound up tight," Julieta adds. My mouth drops open, and she wraps my hand in hers. "Lulu, we love you. We want the best for you, and this guy sounds amazing."

"And rich! After all, he *did* go to Kenton, and he drives an Audi!" Amira adds with a wiggle of her brow.

"Right! And rich. Which is awesome, because you are a terrible waitress and super in debt," Julieta adds with a playful smile.

"What does that have to do with anything?" I ask.

Amira looks at me like I have two heads. "Duh, if you get married or knocked up, you'll be set for life."

Julieta's eyes widen and she nods in agreement. "Right. Don't sign any prenups until you have Tío look it over first."

I snap my hand out of Amira's and push off the barstool. "Okay, you are both officially insane. I am *not* going to get pregnant or married or anything! Okay? None of this is going anywhere! Perfect, gorgeous people like Fletcher do *not* fall in love with insecure, crazy, and ugly women like me!" My voice cracks as the words tumble straight out of that terrible vulnerable part of my head and out of my mouth.

My sisters fall into a silence that stretches for what feels like eternity.

"What the hell did you just say?" Amira asks, her tone sharp and angry.

I look at her, startled. "What?"

Amira squares her shoulders and pins me with her eyes. "You are my sister, and I love you more than anyone in this world possibly can. But even you do not get to call yourself ugly, or insecure, and *especially* not crazy. You are *none* of those things, and I don't care how perfect or rich or gorgeous this Fletcher guy is. He would be beyond lucky to have a woman like you."

She pulls a dishrag out from behind the bar, spins it into a tight spiral, and then promptly hits me on the shoulder with it.

My jaw drops and I rub my sore shoulder. "What the hell was that for?"

"For saying mean stuff about yourself. You upset me."

For a long moment, we stare at each other, but I look away first, not wanting her to see the tears beginning to gather in my eyes.

"So, Amira actually *is* crazy," Julieta says, "but she is also right."

"Damn straight I am," Amira jumps in. "You are so amazing and funny and sweet, and if I weren't related to you, I would date the shit out of you. I swear, you wouldn't be able to walk the next morning."

I cover my ears with my hands and gag. "Amira, you are so nasty."

Amira laughs and leans over the bar, kissing me on my cheek before sticking her tongue out and licking the side of my face. "I would do things to you that you didn't even know were possible."

"Oh, gross, Amira," Julieta shrieks, protectively wrapping her arms around me. "We love you, Lulu, and you are an amazing woman. Please be kind to yourself, okay? And if you like this guy, maybe consider going out with him again. But you don't have to do anything you don't want to, okay?"

I reach behind me and squeeze Julieta's arm. "I love you, Juli. Thank you for being the normal one in the family."

Amira laughs and rolls her eyes in response. Before long, all three of us are back to laughing like hyenas, loudly enough that our aunt comes out and yells at us all to get back to work rolling silverware. Although I sometimes want to strangle my sisters, I have to admit that on days where I don't feel my best, or when the mean bitch who lives rent-free in my head starts listing all my flaws, I love having them as the team behind me, cheering me on.

Chapter Twenty-Two

 *Lucy*

WHEN I WALK INTO school on Monday morning, Nia instantly assaults me, almost dislocating my shoulder as she tugs me toward her classroom. Once inside, she shuts the door and turns to face me. "Details. Spill."

I hold up my empty mug. "Can't I get my tea first?"

Nia props her hands on her hips and shakes her head. "You have to earn it. Now stop delaying. Spill."

"Didn't I already tell you everything over text?"

Nia rolls her eyes, holding up her cell phone. "All you texted was heart eye emojis. Like, a concerning number of them."

"Well, that pretty much sums it up."

"You're impossible," she groans. "When are you going out again?"

I bite down on my lip. "I don't know. He mentioned wanting to hang out again this weekend."

Nia looks at me sideways. "Why are you looking so confused?"

"What if he was just being polite?" I whisper, even though there is no one else in the room beside us. "What if he didn't really mean it?"

"Why wouldn't he mean it? You're a total catch."

I level my eyes at her. "Nia."

She returns my stare. "Yes, Lucy?"

"You're really going to make me say it?" I let out a frustrated breath. This is too much work before eight in the morning. "He is so out of my league! He looks like a Ken doll, and I look like a Bratz doll that accidentally went into the dryer at the hottest setting and melted into one amorphous blob."

Nia's jaw drops. "The way your brain works seriously scares me."

I sigh and collapse into an empty seat. "That makes two of us," I grumble.

Nia takes the seat next to me. "Lucy, try not to shut Fletcher down before he even gets a chance. You sometimes can be a little..." She pauses, clearly searching for the right word. "Judgmental."

I blink at her. "What?"

"You have a habit, *sometimes*, of assuming the worst of people," she explains. "And you push them away before they can have the chance to hurt you. I get it, trust me, I do. But I don't want you to miss out on something amazing because you're scared."

Before I can respond, the bell rings and we both stand. Nia has a class, and I have an empty mug that needs caffeinated tea. As she walks me to the door, she playfully swats my arm. "Just let yourself enjoy this, Lucy."

I replay my conversation with Nia in my head as I walk against the swell of students making their way unenthusiastically to their classrooms.

I know that I can often be my own worst enemy. My

self-esteem is a sliding scale between "I'm a dumpster fire that doesn't deserve love so I'm going to lie in bed all day and stare at my ceiling" and "I'm a moderately interesting person and am very talented at baking a variety of fruit-filled pies." And because of that, I assume that everyone else sees me that way, and I have a nasty habit of suspecting that the people in my life see me as a burden.

After all, I'm always the one in some kind of crisis—usually over absolutely nothing. Like I'd told Fletcher, anytime I have a to-do list with more than five items, I feel too paralyzed to tackle any of them, which sends me into a spiral of shame, self-loathing, and exhaustion.

Over a list. That's always a fun one to dissect with Dr. Zhou.

So for me to even fathom that there is a successful, gorgeous, funny, amazingly sexy guy out there who wants to take me on a *second* date after I hadn't even put out on the first? Yeah, that is a hard one for me to grasp.

Apparently, it is for Georgia, too, because the second I step into the teachers' lounge, she is on me like the lice I got that one time I slept over at Kayla Polillio's house in fifth grade.

"I heard someone had a date with Fletcher this weekend," she says, with a smile that looks so forced, it's giving me major Jack Nicholson à la *The Shining* vibes. Which isn't good, because there are axes strategically located throughout the building by all our fire extinguishers, and there is no way I would ever be able to outrun Georgia. My legs are just too short.

I decide to go nonverbal and give her a nod as I pour water in my mug. Now that I know her history with Fletcher, the last thing I want to do is rub our new relationship in her face. Georgia and I have never been close—mostly because tall, beautiful blond women completely intimidate me, but I don't want to unnecessarily hurt her, either.

"So what did you do?" she probes.

Instead of answering, I take a long sip from my mug.

As long as I am drinking, I don't have to respond. Is it possible to shotgun tea? I guess we'll find out.

Eventually, though, I do run out and have to lower my mug. "We just, well, ran some errands," I finally answer. I can't help but feel a little embarrassed at my answer. *Ran some errands?* That sounds so…boring when I say it out loud, but I stop myself from overthinking it. Yes, it was a rather simple date, but it felt so special and uniquely *me*. Fletcher read the anxiety radiating off of me and designed the perfect date that made me feel seen and appreciated and cared for, and it feels wrong to call it boring when it was anything but that.

Her eyes pop open with surprise before her shoulders slump inward. "Well, that sounds…really nice," she responds, her smile now completely gone.

Shit. This is exactly what I wanted to avoid. While it still feels surreal that, in a competition for a guy between me and Georgia, *I'm* the one winning, it's not a victory I want to gloat about—especially when she carries her hurt so visibly on her face.

I stand, rooted to the ground, unsure what to say next. She doesn't move for a long moment as she stares down at her red high-heeled shoes, which would give me blisters for weeks. But when she does eventually look up, her eyes are glassy and full of moisture.

And then, without a second's notice, she begins to cry. Not just a few scattered tears, but full-body sobs, making her shake like a bare tree in the middle of a tornado.

I freeze, unsure what to do. I've never seen Georgia cry, and I know it's partly my fault. And as much as I want to run away and deny Georgia's pain, my gut—and my Jewish guilt—demand I stay. "Um, are you okay?"

The question is barely out of my mouth before she wails, "My life is falling apart!" She hiccups and looks down at me, tears racing down her cheeks. "I'm going to be alone forever."

I take a tentative step closer. "I'm so sorry, Georgia. Do you want to talk about it, or I can go grab one of your friends or—"

She collapses into an empty chair before I can finish. I take that as a yes and hesitantly slip into the seat opposite hers.

"Why am I never enough?" she moans as more tears stream down her alabaster cheeks.

I reach for a small pile of napkins and push them toward her. "I'm sorry, Georgia, but I'm not sure I understand."

She looks up at me. "I'm so sick of never measuring up! I am *never* good enough for anyone!"

I have absolutely zero idea what Georgia is talking about, considering she is a flawless human specimen and, despite her tears, her eyeliner is still intact. "Georgia, what are you talking about? You're perfect."

"Perfect? Are you kidding?" she scoffs as she wipes away the moisture from her cheeks. She glances at me, her brow rising higher and higher as she sees the obviously confused expression on my face. "You're *not* joking, are you?"

I toy with the hem of my blouse, purposefully looking down to avoid her intense stare. "I mean, you're gorgeous," I mumble.

"So because I look good in a skirt, my life must be perfect?" she asks with a sharpness in her voice that I deserve.

"Well, no. I mean…" I can feel my cheeks heat with

embarrassment. Why *had* I made that assumption? I mean, Georgia is right—it is pretty rude of me to assume that just because she is conventionally beautiful, her life must be amazing as well.

I wince and offer her an apologetic smile. "You're right. It is kind of messed up that I thought that. I'm sorry. I guess I just always assumed you had this perfect life because beautiful people always seem to."

"Ugh, that is so ridiculous—especially coming from *you*."

"Coming from me?" I ask, utterly confused. "What is that supposed to mean?"

"You want to talk about perfect?" she shoots back. "How about you? All the teachers and students idolize you. You have this tight-knit family that always supports you and stops by all the time to bring you food because they adore you, you have a cool best friend, *and* you have the hot boyfriend. But let's see, because I have blond hair and a nice rack, *I'm* the one with the perfect life? Do you realize how much I want *your* life? How jealous I am of *you*?"

I swallow, shocked at her confession. Georgia is jealous of *me*? For years, I've compared myself against her, never feeling like I measure up. She's always so elegant, beautiful, and graceful.

When I saw her, all I could see were my own flaws.

"I never knew you saw me like that. I mean, I'm jealous of *you*," I admit. "I'm such a mess, and you're always so perfectly put together."

She rolls her eyes. "It's all an act to hide the fact my life is a disaster. I'm so swamped with my student loans and need to find a second job. My mom is constantly on my back about me being thirty and unmarried, and every available guy out there is just looking to get laid, and the second I mention any type of commitment, they disappear!"

"Well, I can relate to that," I tell her. She eyes me skeptically and I continue, "Well the student loan and disappointing dating pool part. Luckily my mom isn't *too* concerned about marrying me off quite yet."

She lets out a sound that is a mix of a laugh and a sob. "My mother has been up my ass about getting married since I was in college. Of course, it doesn't help that both my younger sisters are married. And to doctors," she adds with an eye roll.

"Well, you know, sometimes these things just happen when you—"

"Least expect it? Yeah, I know. God, if I had a dollar for every time someone told me that, I wouldn't be stuck here teaching."

"Yeah," I respond, cringing, remembering too late how much I hate that particular piece of advice when I'm on the receiving end. Shame fills me, so I straighten my spine. I can do better than that. Georgia clearly needs a pep talk, and after all, I didn't build my platform of nearly half a million followers by spitting out unhelpful clichéd advice.

I try to think about what @TheMissGuidedCounselor would say—but then, as I remember how often I really have had to hear that particularly awful advice, I go out on a limb and say what *I* have always wanted to hear.

"Honestly," I start, "I think it sucks and is really unfair that your mom ties your worth to whether you're in a relationship. That's not a healthy way to think, and I should know, because it's how I used to think about myself, too. Like if I was single, it meant there was something wrong with me or I wasn't good enough for anyone to want to date. And I'm not going to lie, sometimes I still feel that way." I don't include that sometimes can be as recent as yesterday because, well, I'm trying to be helpful.

"But it helps to have my sisters, or Nia, or my family remind me that those mean voices in my head are wrong—I am enough. So, if you ever need a reminder, feel free to hit me up."

Georgia inspects me, her blue eyes assessing me with an intensity that I find incredibly intimidating. "You never even gave me a chance, you know?"

I blink, taken aback by her comment. "What do you mean?"

"I wanted to be friends with you. We started working here the same year, and we were around the same age, so I tried to talk to you a bunch of times. And you always just…blew me off."

I frown, not remembering *any* of this. "What are you talking about?"

"I always tried to invite you out for coffee or to sit together at lunch, and you always came up with some excuse not to and then ran off, like a scared puppy."

I shake my head, looking back with a different perspective. "I was just so scared my first year here. It was my first job out of grad school, and I *was* super anxious—though I disagree slightly about the scared puppy characterization. Truthfully, I never thought someone like you would actually want to be friends with someone like me."

Her jaw drops as she crosses her arms at her chest. "Has anyone ever told you that you are super judgmental?"

I cringe, thinking back to the conversation I had with Nia a short fifteen minutes ago.

And the numerous conversations I've had with my sisters, my therapist, Dr. Zhou, and that one lady I had accidentally cut off in the grocery store line about my tendency to judge others.

I know I do it mostly as a defense mechanism. After all, if I judge someone and push them away first, they'll never get the chance to do it to me. Even if it does mean losing the opportunity to let people in.

Like I said, Lucy Logic 101.

"Maybe once or twice," I mumble. I look up at her. "I'm sorry for not really ever giving you a chance. And for everything with, you know, Fletcher."

At his name, a wistful expression crosses her face. "Yeah, I really messed up on that one." She swipes away the remaining tears off her cheeks. "He's a great guy. Don't screw it up like I did."

I nod, and we settle into an awkward silence. I toy with my sleeve while Georgia rips the napkin in her hand into tiny shreds.

"So, does this mean we're friends now?" I ask, needing to break the tension and not entirely ready to discuss my hopefully new boyfriend with *his* ex-girlfriend. "Should we get matching tattoos?" I waggle my brows, hoping to coax a smile out of Georgia. "Or maybe make each other our emergency contacts?"

Georgia rolls her eyes, but I catch the way the edges of her lips curve into a slight smirk. "Let's not get too ahead of ourselves here."

I offer her a conciliatory high five and she reluctantly gives in, slapping her palm against mine with a quiet chuckle. With my depression, I sometimes feel like no one can truly grasp the depth of my sadness. And yet, here's Georgia, experiencing the same anxieties of never feeling good enough, thinking she's being judged by others, and plagued by loneliness. We have far more things in common than things that divide us, something I never allowed myself to see because I was too busy pushing everyone away.

But I don't want to do that anymore.

With Georgia, I think I *may* have a new friend, which feels great. Better than great. And not just because I am *finally* one step closer to nabbing that "bring eight friends, get the ninth one free" promotion at Smithy's, but because I am beginning to realize that maybe I'm not so alone in this world after all.

Chapter Twenty-Three

 *Fletcher*

I STARE AT THE phone in my hands, debating what to do as I see another notification pop up that I have a missed call. From my dad.

The third one in the last hour.

Glancing at the clock on my car's dashboard, I let out a frustrated curse. I'm due to meet Lucy in just fifteen minutes with the Chinese takeout I had ordered for our Saturday evening date, which thankfully is already sitting on the passenger seat beside me. My entire day I've been anxiously counting down the hours until I can see Lucy again. Press my lips against hers, hold her soft curves against me. Being around Lucy feels like inhaling on a summer's morning—the air tangy, sweet, refreshing—after being stuck in a windowless, stuffy, dust-speckled room.

How could I not crave her every minute of every day now that I know the life she breathes into my own?

And because I know how much I not only want her—but find myself also feeling like I truly *need* her—I also know that I have to set things right. Everything has changed since I made the connection. Even if this is just the beginning for us, I don't want to rush things, especially when I'm holding this huge secret from her.

No matter how afraid I am of Lucy's reaction, it's not right to keep messaging Lucy as @BravesGuy93; it feels too skeezy and deceitful. And I can't keep blowing off Lucy online either—or worse, ghost her and hope she never finds out. I learned my lesson with Georgia—lying to avoid uncomfortable truths (and yes, possible disaster) can't come at the cost of hurting the ones I care about.

I owe it to Lucy to reveal who I truly am in person.

And I *will*. Tonight.

I'm still not entirely sure how I'm going to break the news to her, but that's one of the reasons I suggested our date tonight be at her house. That way, we'll have privacy and be on her home turf, so if Lucy needs the space to talk things through or time to process, she can do it in the safety and comfort of her own home.

But with my father calling more than usual, it's hard to focus on tonight's purpose. The suspense of not knowing why he's calling is weighing on me too heavily, peeling away at the confidence I tried to build up earlier in the day for this evening's discussion. More, I hate how a mere call from my father has the power to make me feel so anxious and sour my whole mood. Just one more reason I've avoided talking to him since moving home.

I glance at the clock again. *Shit.*

My little stress-out has already cost me five minutes, and I'm still ten minutes away from Lucy's. If I don't call my father back now, not only will the reason for all these missed calls be on my mind all night, but I won't be able to think clearly enough for this monumentally important conversation I need to have with Lucy.

Better to rip the Band-Aid off now. Just in case the call runs late, I shoot a quick text off letting her know I might be running a few minutes behind.

I unlock my phone and select his name from my contacts. Reluctantly, I take a deep breath as the call connects.

He answers on the second ring. "Aldrich," he says. "How are you?"

"I'm fine, Dad. You called?" Might as well get to the point.

"Yes." He clears his throat and I hear the slight squeak of him shifting in his favorite leather chair. "I'd like for you to come over for a lunch tomorrow. Matthew and Angelica will be coming, and I think it's time we, well, clear the air."

My guard instantly goes up. Why is my father so keen on clearing the air now? And clearing the air for *who* exactly? I have nothing against seeing Matthew or his wife, since I don't *completely* fault my brother for forgiving our father so quickly, considering he has to work with the man. Plus they've always had a closer relationship.

There must be another reason.

"Will *she* be there?" I ask, unable to keep the bitterness from seeping into my voice. This invitation must have something to do with her, because why else would my father even *care* about "clearing the air" with me? It's not like he's ever made an effort before.

"Yes," he replies, a hint of frustration in his tone. "*Amelia* will be there."

Well, that finalizes my decision.

The last thing I want to do is endure a Sunday lunch with

my father *and* his pregnant mistress. While I can't blame her entirely for the demise of my parents' marriage, I do hold her half responsible at the very least. And while I want to have a relationship with my future half-brother, I'm not sure I'm ready to have a casual family lunch with his mother quite yet.

"As lovely as this all sounds," I say, not bothering to hide my sarcasm, "I don't think I'll be able to make it."

"Aldrich, I think it is high time we put whatever issues you have with me to the side and try to act like a family again."

I scoff. Act like a family? Again? When the hell did he ever care about acting like a family when he was working every day till nine o'clock at night? He was always away on business trips every other weekend, jetting off to some exotic location while missing baseball games, birthdays, and holidays.

We can't act like something we never were.

"Yeah, I think I'll pass."

My father lets out a long sigh. He sounds...tired.

"Look, Aldrich," he starts. "I know I've made my mistakes. And I can't take those back. But I am getting a second chance at parenthood. One I know I don't deserve, and yet, I want to try to salvage our relationship before this baby comes."

"And you waited, naturally, until your mistress was in her last trimester?"

"Well, it's not like you've been taking my calls, Aldrich," he snaps.

He has me there.

When my mother called me, in hysterics, after discovering not only that my father was leaving her, but also that he had gotten his mistress pregnant, I *had* ignored his calls. I was too angry, too hurt, and had no desire to hear his excuses. Only after a few weeks, when my anger had started to thaw, did I start responding to his emails with terse one-liners. And only because of Matthew's urging.

I blow out a breath, frustrated at this entire conversation. Because as angry as I am at my dad, I wonder if he's right; perhaps it is time to start to mend the rift in our relationship. "So why now, Dad? Why this sudden need for us to act like a family?"

"This child..." He pauses and clears his throat. "And Amelia have shown me how I squandered too many years. I've focused too hard on building up the fund and not enough on my family. Your sister still isn't talking to me. Not a single word. And I want to make things right. I figure if I can get you on board, maybe you can help me win Liv over eventually, too."

"Liv's an adult, Dad. If she wants to shut you out of her life, that's up to her, not me."

"I know, I know," he replies wearily. "But it's not just about her, Aldrich. It's about you, too. Come to lunch tomorrow, son. Let's figure out how we can start this new phase of our lives."

I pause, anxiety already beginning to twist my stomach into a tight knot of dread. Is this something I am ready for? Probably not, but I think my dad is right—holding on to this anger doesn't serve anyone, least of all me.

I let out a long breath, hoping I won't regret this. "Fine."

I barely get a chance to knock on Lucy's front door before she is flinging it open, a mix of excitement and concern on her face.

"I'm so sorry I'm late," I say, forcing a smile despite dread pooling in my stomach. "Did you get my text? I tried calling, too."

She shakes her head and grabs one of the bags out of my

hands, heading toward the kitchen. "No, I think I left my phone in my office at school," she says, crinkling her nose. "Again."

"Shoot. I'm sorry for making you wait," I say as I follow her. "I had something unexpected come up."

She eyes me curiously as she tears open the bag, her big brown eyes inspecting me. "Something unexpected good or something unexpected bad?"

I blow out a breath. "Not sure." I pause, debating whether or not to explain. This night has so much riding on it already, with me finally telling Lucy the truth. I don't want to derail it or dampen the mood with my family drama. But I also want to confide in her, as my closest friend and the one person who *always* has the ability to make me feel better. Especially because a part of me wants to ask her to join me so I don't have to face my dad alone. I met her parents, so it wouldn't be that awkward, right? Even if my family isn't nearly as charming as hers.

"It was my father," I finally say. "We haven't...well, been speaking much lately."

Lucy reaches for my hand and rubs a thumb over my palm. It feels nice. "I'm sorry. Do you want to talk about it?"

I open my mouth to respond, then quickly snap it shut. Yes, I want to talk, have her comfort me like she's done dozens of times so I can unravel this anxious knot in my stomach and emotionally prepare myself for tomorrow. But that feels selfish, taking up space to deal with my family drama when tonight should be about *us*.

I rake a hand through my hair. "Yes, and no. It's kind of a long story."

She nods encouragingly. "Whatever you need, okay? I mean, I *am* a licensed therapist, so I can offer you all kinds of great advice. Free of charge, remember?" She offers me a reassuring smile. "Plus, you were there for me when I needed it, so I am happy to return the favor."

"My father just did something really..." I pause, wanting to share but not wanting to reveal enough details so she can connect the dots before I can tell her I'm @BravesGuy93. To play it safe, I settle with something vague, but accurate. "Shitty. And I'm having a hard time forgiving him."

She offers me a reassuring smile "While I don't know the details, I know that family is complicated. And just because someone shares DNA with you, that doesn't mean you're obligated to forgive them if they've hurt you."

I squeeze her hand, thankful because, like always, her words are exactly what I need to hear. "You're right, but...I don't know. He's made a lot of mistakes and said some crappy things to me, but he's never reached out like this before. He sounded, well, sincere. And I think he might be serious about trying to fix things, which I want. He's my dad and I want him in my life, but I don't want to get my hopes up and be disappointed. Again."

She nods thoughtfully. "Well, did you tell him that? About how you feel?"

I chuckle wryly, shaking my head. "We don't talk about our feelings."

"So how did you end things?" she asks.

I dig my hands into my pockets and rock back on my heels. "Well, he asked me to come over for a little family lunch tomorrow." I leave out the part about Amelia being there.

Lucy arches a brow. "You want to go?"

"I think so? I mean, yes. I think I should try. It's been

months since I've seen my dad, and I haven't caught up with my brother much since moving back. But I'm not going to lie, the idea of this whole thing is making me anxious."

Furrowing her brow, Lucy asks, "Wait, the brother who—"

"Georgia cheated on me with?" I let out a breath. "The one and only. But we're good now," I reassure her. "I mean, we make a point not to talk about it, but Matthew's my only brother, so we've found a way to move on."

Lucy nods in understanding. "So does having your brother there make this lunch easier, or harder?"

"Easier," I answer immediately. "My brother knows how to talk to him and can translate, since my father and I apparently speak two different languages. It's just that we were never able to have the kind of relationship he has with my brother. He was always disappointed in me—nothing I did was ever good enough. And then when I 'squandered' my opportunities by deciding to be a teacher? It was like he lost all respect for me."

I pause, catching the concern in her eyes, and silently kick myself. This was exactly what I wanted to avoid, making this night about me and my family baggage. And even though it's probably unfair, a kernel of resentment unfurls at my father for his part in derailing this important evening.

"Look, I'm sorry. I don't know why I'm unloading on you like this. This is a terrible date." I move to grab the rest of the now lukewarm takeout containers from the bag.

She laughs and surprises me by leaning forward, brushing a soft kiss to my lips. "It's not a terrible date. And I'm proud of you for being brave and seeing your father. I wish I could be there with you and support you."

I bite down on my lip and catch her hand. "Well, it's funny

that you mention that, because I kind of was hoping you could come with me."

Like all her emotions, Lucy wears her panic so clearly on her face. "To lunch? To meet your judgmental and scary-sounding father?"

"Did I mention there's free food?" I ask, waggling my brows, trying to not appear *too* desperate despite how much I really do want Lucy there with me.

"I don't know," she responds. "I mean, parents scare me. And we *just* started dating."

Guilt hits me. "Of course, you're right, that wasn't fair of me to ask. I'm sorry. And this isn't what tonight was even supposed to be about and—"

"No," she interrupts. "I mean, yes." She shakes her head. "Yes, of course I will go with you to lunch. I mean, you met my *entire* family on our first date, so I think I can handle this. I *know* I can handle this."

"No," I hold up my hand, not wanting to pressure her. After all, if the tables were turned, I would be just as wary as her. "You don't have to—"

"I know," she says, cutting me off. "But I want to. Just ignore what I said earlier. I want to come."

I eye her skeptically. "You *want* to come?"

She tugs her bottom lip with her teeth and flashes me a guilty smile. "So, maybe not 'want' exactly, but I do want to support you. So same thing, right?"

Unable to resist, I capture her hand and bring her palm to my lips, dusting a soft kiss. "Thank you."

She twists her hand to interlock our fingers, and we sit in silence for a few long moments as I work up my courage, steeling my resolve. This is it. *This* is the moment I need to tell Lucy everything and not let there be any more secrets between us. Whatever the fallout is, at least she will know the truth.

I let out a steadying breath. "Lucy, there's something I need to tell you."

Lucy shifts in her seat, her surprise at my serious tone evident on her face. "Sure, of course."

"It's nothing bad," I rush to reassure her. "Well, I don't think it is, but—" I let out a raspy chuckle, scrubbing my hand over my jaw. "I don't know if you'll feel the same." I pause and run my clammy palms over the front of my pants. "It's just, well, I have really, *really* enjoyed getting to know you these last few weeks and, well, there's something about me that I've been… not necessarily keeping a secret, but just trying to find a way to tell you. I've just been afraid it will change how you think about me. And well, now that you're meeting my family tomorrow and things are getting more serious, I think it's time I tell you."

To my surprise, Lucy lets out a whoosh of air and laughs nervously. "Oh my God, you scared me there." She does a little shoulder shimmy, relaxing. "But I think I know what this is about, and I agree it's a good idea to talk about it now."

I arch a brow. She already knows? "You do?"

She nods. "Yes and I think we should talk about it so we're on the same page. I mean, this shouldn't change anything between us, I would hope."

"Oh, wow. Yes, I agree. Absolutely. Okay, well," I blow out a relieved breath, infinitely grateful at how easy this is turning out to be. "How did you find out?"

"I googled you," she says, blushing. "Well, I googled your family and found your dad's Wikipedia page and then did a *very* deep dive into him. And well, I know your family is kind of, well, *very* rich. I've wanted to talk to you about it, because, well, it's hard to talk about, isn't it? The whole money thing. And I don't want you to think that it changes my opinion of you at all, because it absolutely doesn't." She laughs and lets her shoulders sag. "I have felt so guilty about not telling you! I felt so, like, creepy knowing this secret side of you and not sharing it. I can't tell you how much better I feel now."

I rub a hand over my jaw as I process everything she's shared. She's talking a mile a minute, so quickly that even if I wanted to get a word in, I wouldn't have the opportunity. When she spots my wide-eyed surprise, her nervous smile slides away and she rises to stand at my side.

"I am so sorry for not saying anything before," she continues. "If it makes you feel better, I *do* run background checks on every guy I go out with. And who my sisters date, too. Well, who Amira dates, when she tells me. Julieta like *never* dates. I have a great deal on this website where you only pay forty dollars and get six reports. But I didn't run one on you. I mean, Google kind of was all I needed with all the info out there about your family. And I'm so sorry I didn't tell you immediately. I never wanted to keep this from you and always planned to talk to you about it, but you never brought it up, so I was worried you didn't like talking about it. But I feel like since I'm meeting your family tomorrow, we should." She lets out a nervous giggle, but I can see the moisture gathering in the corner of her eyes. "I mean, is there a secret rich-person handshake I should know?"

My stomach twists at the lopsided smile she's fighting so hard to keep on her face. I can read her like a book, and I see all the fear and worry and guilt written into the lines of her face. It only intensifies my own emotions because as bad as she feels for keeping this "secret" from me, the one I am holding from her is far bigger, its impact far more meaningful.

"Lucy," I start, capturing her hands in mine, "it's okay. To be honest, I fully expected you to google me." She chuckles, her shoulders sagging in relief.

"And you're right," I continue, "it can be…uncomfortable for me to talk about. I worry people might judge me for it. But I can confidently say I never worried about that with you." I give her hands a gentle squeeze.

Lucy's lips curve into a smile, and I wish I could freeze this moment. My fear is back in full force. Once I do reveal who I truly am, Lucy may never look at me the same way again. I won't just be Fletcher anymore. What if the thrill and magic that accompanies a new relationship is gone for her? After all, there is so much we already know about each other. Maybe there won't be enough mystery and excitement for her. Maybe *I* won't be enough for her.

No. I can't let these lies continue. This needs to end. Now.

But before I can open my mouth, Lucy's eyes lock on mine and she says, "There's something I want you to know, too."

Chapter Twenty-Four

 *Lucy*

I CURSE UNDER MY breath at my colossal fail of an attempt to be seductive and alluring. Because instead of a husky, Scarlett Johansson–esque purr, my voice sounds like I should be the spokesperson on the dangers of too much nicotine use.

"What I mean to say," I continue, with much less confidence, "is that I would very much like to, well, *know* you, like in a biblical sense."

Fletcher raises his brows—clearly confused at my pathetic pickup line—and a fresh wave of humiliation washes over me. I am now fairly confident even my own vagina is horrified and will be detaching itself from my body to run away so as not to be forced to witness any more of this excruciating attempt at human interaction.

"Sex," I finally blurt out. "We should have sex."

"Wait, what?" Fletcher asks, understandably more confused than turned on at the moment.

I need to fix this. And quickly, because I would very much like to get laid tonight. Especially now that I know what lies behind that crisp wrinkle-resistant shirt Fletcher's wearing.

I blow out a breath and force myself to look into Fletcher's eyes. "I want this. With you. The sex. But I'm nervous. And it sometimes takes a while for me to, well, get the ship into the port, if you catch my drift."

Fletcher reaches for my hand and gives it a gentle squeeze. "I want this, too. Trust me, I've wanted you for a very long time." He pauses and my stomach sinks when I see deep creases form across his forehead. He looks conflicted, guilty, even. "Which is why—"

My body acts without any input or guidance from my brain and I, for lack of a better term, jump Fletcher, pressing my lips against his.

That expression had scared me. And whatever he wanted to say? I know it can't be anything I want to hear. Sure, talking is good, but I *saw* the way he was looking at me. He was more than concerned, almost afraid—he looked as if he was gearing up to gently turn me down after my embarrassingly poor attempt to initiate sex.

I *hate* that look.

It's the same look (albeit under *far* different circumstances) my parents give me when I tell them I'm capable enough to do something on my own. Like lower my medication dosage or take a solo weekend trip. A combination of concern, fear, and pity that says they *want* to believe I can do it, but their concern outweighs their faith in me.

And that's the last thing I want Fletcher to feel when he sees me—so yes, I cut him off with my lips.

Thankfully it takes Fletcher only a second to catch on, like a switch going off. Before I can pull back, Fletcher moves forward, lifts me by my ass, and pins me against the wall. My dress hikes up to my hips, and Fletcher is drowning me with kisses, like he can't get enough of me, his lips exploring everywhere, from the hollow of my neck to the sensitive flesh behind my ears.

He only pulls back once, pupils blown wide and breathing harshly, as he asks, "Lucy, are you sure?"

I rock against his pelvis and realize his pants are in my way. "Fletcher," I say and start frantically unbuckling his belt, shoving my hands around his *very* impressive penis, "*Please* don't stop."

I feel like I'm floating, and my brain cannot fully compute that sexy Fletcher is *here*, in my house, grinding his pelvis against me as I very clumsily jerk him off. When I fantasized about our first time, it always involved us in bed, slow and passionate as we make love to a curated playlist of sexy early 2000s jams. But this is frenzied, chaotic, and needy.

Luckily, Fletcher seems perfectly content with frenzied, chaotic, and needy.

I pump my hand over Fletcher's cock and he drops his forehead against mine, letting out a long moan. The sound vibrates against my skin, sending pure liquid heat pooling to my core, and I quicken my pace.

Fletcher groans his approval as he presses his palms against the wall, caging me. I lean forward and nip at his neck as I continue to stroke his length.

When I move to bite him a second time, he jerks away.

"Your room. Where is it?" he asks, his voice throaty and gravelly and utterly sexy.

I gesture upstairs, and Fletcher pulls my hand out of his pants with a pained expression before wrapping his hands around my waist and hoisting me into his arms. I squeal as Fletcher practically runs up the stairs two at a time. When we reach the top landing, I direct him to the first door on the right. When he reaches my bed, he deposits me on it, and I land like a very bouncy sack of potatoes. We both laugh, but then Fletcher's gaze heats as he catches a glimpse underneath my dress.

He inhales sharply and then surprises me again by pulling me toward the edge of the bed, falling to his knees as he settles my legs onto his shoulders. I prop myself up on my elbows, content to watch him.

He keeps his eyes locked on mine as his hand slowly trails up my calf, then to my thigh before pushing the red fabric of my dress up to my hips. He sucks in a breath when he sees the black lace waiting for him.

He hooks his fingers into the band of my panties, sliding them down and briefly lifting my legs off his shoulders to toss them on the floor. He inhales my scent, something I never had quite realized was so sexy, and presses a kiss on my inner thigh.

"I want to taste you," he says.

I'm not entirely sure what to say, or if I am even capable of forming whole sentences at this point, so I just nod. The corners of Fletcher's lips curve into a devious smile as he continues his trail of kisses up my thigh until reaching the mound of dark curls I painstakingly spent the afternoon grooming.

He darts the tip of his tongue over my clit and hums with approval when I jerk at the touch. He goes for a second taste, this time longer and slower, and keeps his hands firmly rooted to my thighs, holding me in place.

I writhe on the bed as he continues his gentle assault, licking and sucking as his fingers dig into my soft thighs. And while past sexual encounters have mainly involved me finalizing my grocery shopping list in my head, being with Fletcher is different. It's all-consuming. Between his scorching touches and his soft grunts of approval, it's impossible to think about expired yogurt or empty cereal boxes.

I let go, giving myself permission to fully check out and hand control over to my body. Because with Fletcher, I feel safe enough to allow myself this escape.

My hips roll, grinding against him as he takes his fill, his tongue lapping greedily as he tastes me, over and over. My nerve endings feel as if they have all begun to fray and every touch shoots sparks of electricity from my toes to the top of my head. Fletcher has discovered the map of my body, something I have yet to accomplish, pinpointing every pleasurable spot, teasing and manipulating to bring me breathlessly close to the precipice of an orgasm that will undoubtedly be life-*fucking*-changing.

With the medication I'm currently on, orgasming isn't exactly the easiest task. It can be a frustratingly long process that involves smutty erotica, a backup stash of batteries, and the thermostat set at a cool sixty-eight degrees. But Fletcher seems anything but rushed, almost like he's savoring me as I get closer and closer.

When the pants and groans coming out of my mouth grow more and more frantic, Fletcher growls and nips at my clit with his teeth, far less gentle than he's been to this point, and exactly what I need. I shout my release and my entire body goes rigid, every muscle in my body contracting at the exact same instant.

There are orgasms and there are *orgasms*—the kind that make you believe you might have actually transcended your physical form and burst into a thousand tiny shards of pleasure, like a dinner plate at a Greek wedding. The kind that make your head spin, your heart race, and your toes curl. They usually come after too long chasing that elusive cliff with my trusty vibrator—not an easy task when your antidepressants make your libido feel like the grand prize in one of those arcade claw machines that are eternally rigged so you lose.

But with Fletcher? He didn't just bring me to the cliff, he tossed me right off the damn thing.

A heavy thump lands on the bed, and I turn my head to see Fletcher beside me. He's wearing a satisfied and slightly cocky smile on his face, which he has entirely earned. And he looks so gorgeous. Even more so after giving me that incredible orgasm. How the hell did I land a guy this good-looking *and* with such a skilled tongue?

"You okay?" he asks.

I turn to look at him and as much as I want to say how appreciative I am of his oral expertise, I'm not quite sure my brain is capable of forming coherent sentences yet. So I just give him a thumbs-up.

Fletcher laughs. And then I laugh because he's laughing and also because I'm still coming down from the world's best orgasm. Fletcher pulls me toward him so my head is resting in that comfortable nook between his shoulder and forearm. His fingers play with my hair.

"I'm really falling for you, Lucy."

I tilt my head to find him looking down at me with such tenderness, my breath catches in my throat. His honesty is so refreshing, so comforting, and it makes me want to be honest in return.

"I am, too," I say as I dip my head toward his.

This time, our kiss starts off slow and sweet, but as soon as I wrap my hands around his neck, pulling him closer against me, that switch flips back on. His kiss turns urgent, needy, and desperate. And I match his intensity with the same visceral need.

Hands caress, stroke, play, and tease as we take our time exploring one another. My dress comes off, as does everything underneath. Fletcher's shirt goes next, me doing my best to gently toss it on the chair by my bed so it doesn't get too wrinkled. His shoes, socks, and pants all follow—albeit with less care as they are unceremoniously dumped onto the growing pile of clothes at the side of the bed.

And then we're naked. Together. In bed. And even though he's not even inside of me yet, it feels different, even more intimate now.

"You're so beautiful." He says it almost as if he cannot believe that I am lying there beside him. He rolls to his side and kisses me fiercely—that primal, possessive side of Fletcher is back. And for once in my very anxiety-ridden life, I'm relieved at the loss of control. I trust this man, and I want him to destroy me tonight.

As his hands rove over my body, fingers digging into my soft flesh, I let go. Let go when his hot, wet lips take my hard nipple into his mouth, sending waves of electricity through me. Let go when his fingers trail down my stomach, finding their way into my folds back to the sensitive bundle of nerves, shooting slivers of pleasure through me as my body shivers beneath his touch.

And when he pulls out a condom and asks if it's okay to continue, I tell him yes, and within minutes he's inside of me, stretching me to a level of painful pleasure that makes me beg for more. For faster. For harder.

He complies with every command, grunting with exertion as his forehead drops to mine. Our hot breaths intertwine, our moans of pleasure now coming out in tandem. My nails are digging into his back, my legs wrapped around him as I lift my hips to match his thrusts. His body tenses, his grunts turn into groans, and I know he's close. His head drops to catch my nipple in his mouth, nipping with his teeth. There are too many sensations, too much pleasure, and I explode for the second time, coming with a shout that is quickly followed by his own release with a much more reserved, but equally contented, groan.

He collapses on top of me, our bodies both glistening with sweat. It takes us a full minute to regain our breath before Fletcher rolls off to lie on his back beside me. He instantly reaches for my hand, though, weaving his fingers between mine.

He's *definitely* a hand holder. And it's something I really like about him.

There's a lot I like about Fletcher. His kindness, the way he can quiet my anxieties with a simple squeeze of his hand, how he makes love to me and the way he looks at me as if I'm the only person in his whole entire world. I continue to mentally catalogue everything about Fletcher that I like, as he drifts to sleep with his hand still entangled with mine, and I find that the list only keeps growing longer and longer. That my feelings may be stronger than like.

It's only when I'm also drifting asleep that I allow myself to imagine what it would feel like to love and be loved by a man like Fletcher.

I decide that it's a feeling I like. Maybe even more.

BravesGuy93
Today at 8:16 AM

TheMissGuidedCounselor
Hey, are you alive?
Haven't heard from you in a few
days…it's the longest we've gone
without talking.
Did I do something?
I'm really sorry if I did—please just
tell me so I can make it right.
You're one of my best friends and I
really miss you.
I really, really hope you're okay.

Chapter Twenty-Five

Lucy

"YOU CAN STILL BACK out, you know."

We're currently on the highway, about fifteen minutes away, so when Fletcher offers me an out, I'm sure he doesn't mean it literally, like he'll deposit me on the side of the highway like a discarded tire. Though that doesn't feel like a terrible option, either, when compared to lunch with his father. When I googled him, I had gone twenty-three pages deep in the image search without finding a single photo of him smiling. Meeting your significant other's parents is already intimidating, but knowing they have their own Wikipedia page and a net worth that is the same as Gambia's annual GDP (yes, I looked it up) brings a whole new level of trepidation.

But the last thing I want to do is add to Fletcher's worry. I can practically see the anxiety radiating off him. So, I smile, shake my head, and continue tapping my foot a thousand times a minute. It's a nervous tic, but I'm counting it as my cardio for today.

Fletcher reaches for my hand, giving it a gentle squeeze. "You don't have to be nervous. I'll be by your side the whole time."

"I know." I give his hand a squeeze back. "Thank you."

I reach for the phone on my lap and slide to unlock it, instantly opening up my Instagram app. I frown when I see that @BravesGuy93 clearly viewed my last message from early this morning but didn't respond.

What the hell? He's never gone more than a few hours without messaging me and definitely never flat-out ignored me before.

With a frustrated grunt, I close the app and lock my phone.

"Everything okay?" Fletcher asks, tilting his head to inspect me.

"Yeah," I say, blowing out a sigh. "I just…it's nothing."

The last thing Fletcher needs right now is to hear about my friendship problems, especially when I'm not even sure how to explain them to him in the first place. Because what I could say? *Hey, so I have this online friend who I've never met but we chat every day. And he's one of my best friends and knows all this stuff about me and is a great listener and always lets me vent or talk about my day. Except I don't know his name, and he doesn't know mine. I also don't know where he lives or works or even what he looks like. But, like I said, despite all that we're really great friends, and recently, he's been ignoring me, and it's making me feel a weird combination of angry, concerned, and frustrated.*

None of that would make sense to Fletcher. As far as my internet sleuthing skills go, I couldn't tell if he's even on social media at all. How would he understand the power of the friendship that @BravesGuy93 and I share?

"You sure? You know, you can talk about it with me."

I offer him a grateful smile and nod. "I know. It's just, well, hard to explain I guess."

But I take a deep breath and try. "I have this friend, and it's a bit weird, but I don't know him in real life. We became friends online—really good friends. And we talked every day for months. And now he's not responding to me. I know in my gut he wouldn't ghost me—he's too good a person to do something like that. But I'm worried about why he's ignoring me. I can clearly see he's read my messages, but is just choosing, I guess, to not respond? It's not like him."

Fletcher doesn't answer for a long moment. He stares straight ahead, but the tiny muscles in his jaw clench. He looks tense—probably about the lunch with his dad. And here I am dumping my problems on him when he already has enough on his own plate.

"Look, I'm sure it's nothing," I say, hoping to reassure both of us equally. "He's probably just been busy. He started at a new school this year—he's a teacher—so, well, if anyone knows how chaotic that whole thing can be, it's you." I force a laugh to try to lighten the mood, but it seems to have the opposite effect on Fletcher. His hands squeeze the wheel until his knuckles turn white. *Great job, Lucy.*

"Can I come to your house after lunch?" he abruptly asks. "There's something I've been meaning to talk to you about."

Well, that doesn't sound good. I think back to last night, how I had silenced his attempt to talk by throwing myself at him. Not my classiest moment.

I had been scared that he wanted to slow things down, worried that I wasn't ready to move our relationship further. I thought I'd shown him I was, but now, seeing the way Fletcher continues his death grip on the steering wheel has me breaking out in a cold, anxious sweat.

"Um, okay," I respond, trying not to sound as panicked as I feel. Talks are usually *never* a good thing, but I also don't think he would be breaking up with me, considering he's introducing me to his family, right?

"It's nothing bad," he quickly adds.

That makes me feel a *teensy* bit better, but not a lot. Maybe this is a define-the-relationship talk? From my vast conversations with the Konfident Kids Klub ladies, I know that DTR talks are a *big* deal.

I haven't been a girlfriend in a *very* long time, and I'm not entirely sure I would be any good at it. But for Fletcher, I want to try. I can't deny that the feelings I have for him are much more than like, which was evident last night when we made love—because we definitely did not have good old-fashioned sex. Sex doesn't usually involve, at least in my experience, so much kissing, caressing, and tenderness.

What happened between us last night felt more like a Marvin Gaye song brought to life.

Fletcher drums his fingers on the steering wheel as he turns off the highway. He's nervous but trying to not look it—because he knows I'm already nervous? But the combination of both of us in the car, tapping our fingers and shaking our legs, just seems to heighten my anxiety. I admire Fletcher trying to make small talk on the drive over, but it's still not enough to quell the tension bubbling inside of me. I'm like an Instant Pot full of frozen chicken ready to release.

And then…We're here. I think?

Fletcher deftly slides his Audi alongside the curb (also, why is it so sexy when men can parallel park? Is it just me?) and puts his car in park. I know I'm right when he slides the keys out of the ignition and announces, "We're here."

I'm not ready.

The traffic was unexpectedly light, and we are seventeen minutes ahead of schedule, which means I have seventeen fewer minutes to emotionally prepare, and my pep talks usually run around fifteen minutes on a good day.

Fletcher's hand comes to rest on my arm. "I'll give you one more out. I can get you an Uber home and it's not a big—"

"No, I'm fine," I cut him off, hoping I sound decisive and confident, when in reality I want to melt into the leather interior and just wait here for him, kind of like those kids you see in the supermarket parking lot with the window open just an inch as they wait for their mom.

But I push those feelings away and slap a smile on my face. "Let's do this!"

Fletcher eyes me warily. Too much enthusiasm. Okay, I need to dial it back.

To prove I am committed to this, I open my car door and step out onto the curb. We're in Boston—the nice part where the sidewalks are brick to match the gorgeous façades of the ivy-covered town houses. I look toward Fletcher, now standing at my side, before staring back up at the incredibly imposing, beautiful town house in front of us.

"Wow, this house is stunning and probably like ten times outside my income bracket."

He smiles uncomfortably, shuffling his feet. I forget how awkward and unfiltered I can be and make a mental note to rein it in for today's brunch. I have to remember that not everyone feels comfortable talking about money, though if I were him, I would want everyone to know. Like how Hannah Goldman bragged to everyone in our eighth-grade class that her father owned an entire condo building in Florida—which I later learned was just a time-share he had been suckered into buying in exchange for a free spa voucher.

I know we talked about it, but I hope Fletcher doesn't think I'm after his money. Should I say something to him? Will he want me to sign a prenup if we get married? And why am I even thinking about marriage right now? We've only been on a few dates, and yes, I am meeting his father, but that doesn't really count because I'm mostly going for emotional support—like those golden retriever service dogs in their bright-red vests.

I'm even wearing a red dress, so I really fit the part.

"Uh, Lucy?"

I tilt my head to see Fletcher watching me with a soft smile, his brows arched. I got lost in the monologue in my head again. I need to stop doing that.

"Yes?"

"I asked if you're good to head in?"

I nod. "Right. Yes, lead the way."

The way is only two more steps, then we are standing before an intimidatingly large wrought-iron door overlaying a mahogany door. It's very tall and makes me feel small, insignificant, and incredibly poor.

Fletcher rings the doorbell and within a few minutes, a man opens it and offers Fletcher and me a warm smile, instantly putting me at ease. *See, Lucy? Fletcher's dad isn't that scary!*

He doesn't look much like the pictures from Google, but don't all old white guys kind of look alike? And this version of Fletcher's dad smiles.

I feel instant relief. *He does smile!* And the way Fletcher greets him, wrapping his arms around him, warms my spirit.

Maybe this chasm between Fletcher and his father isn't so big after all.

Fletcher turns to introduce me, still standing on the doorstep in the massive doorframe. "Edward, I want you to meet my girlfriend, Lucy. Lucy, this is Edward, my father's house manager."

Edward? So, clearly *not* Fletcher's dad, and I mentally kick myself for the assumption.

I hold out my hand and shake his, comforted now in knowing that he's a mere mortal like me and not the millionaire who lives in this home with marble floors and statues of abstract art that my public-school education did not prepare me to understand. "Nice to meet you."

"Everyone is in your father's study to the left. You'll be having lunch out on the terrace today," Edward says, gesturing down the hall.

Fletcher nods his thanks and leads me farther into the town house, his hand firmly secured around mine. At this moment, I'm not quite sure who needs the support more.

When we near the study—apparently a room with not only a desk but a shit ton of books and mahogany furniture—I immediately identify Fletcher's father and wonder how I could have ever confused Edward with this man. Fletcher is pretty much his identical clone except less scary-looking and with fewer gray hairs.

As we enter, everyone stands, all eyes landing on me and Fletcher. They all smile politely and do these fancy head nods that I can't quite re-create, because I feel like I am bobbing like a buoy lost at sea.

Fletcher rests his hand on the small of my back as he

introduces everyone: his father, who offers me a curt nod, and his brother, Matthew, and his wife, Angelica, who both offer me friendlier-looking nods.

He does *not* introduce me to the young woman by his father's side, who is very clearly with child—perhaps a giant monster baby, because her belly is huge. From what little Fletcher has told me about his family, I know his parents are divorced, so she's definitely not Fletcher's mother. Also the math does not add up, because she looks younger than both of us, so, yep, *definitely* not Fletcher's mom. I wonder for a brief minute if it's the sister, Liv, he's mentioned. But then why wouldn't he introduce us?

The slight does not go unnoticed by Fletcher's father. He clears his throat, the veins in his neck protruding prominently as he glares at his son, who, to my surprise, does not even flinch. I am pretty sure if his father ever looks at me like that, I'll spontaneously combust.

"This is Amelia," his father says, gesturing to the woman, who looks just as uncomfortable as I do. She smiles and doesn't do the nod thing, so I think she's normal like me—thrust into this world with rules and head nods we don't quite understand.

Fletcher doesn't nod, and even I, who have only recently been introduced to the culture of this intensely rich family, know that this is an insult. I make a mental note to ask Fletcher why he has a beef with this woman, because from what little I know about his family, she seems sweet and out of place. His father looks livid, though, and I wonder what comes next.

I am assuming a duel with swords at dawn.

Instead, his father marches straight toward me. *Shit.*

"You must be Lucy." He extends his hand for me to shake,

which I do despite my disgustingly clammy palms. He then looks at Fletcher. "My son says you're a guidance counselor at this public school he now apparently teaches at?"

The way the words leave his mouth tells me this was less a question to get to know me and more a way to insult his son for working at a public school. And judging by the way Fletcher tenses at my side, I can see that he's coming to the same conclusion.

I nod, keeping my smile plastered on my face. If Mr. Fletcher wants to insult me, he's going to have to try a lot harder than that.

Fletcher's father lets out a grunt and rocks back on his heels, inspecting me. "And Galindo. What is that? Mexican?"

I nod again, though now my guard is up. "I am. Well, half. And half Moroccan on my dad's side." Because of the permanent scowl on Mr. Fletcher's face, I am not sure if that answer displeases him even more.

His hawkish eyes don't blink as he keeps inspecting me like some kind of painting at a modern art museum—the kind that you can't tell if you think is brilliant or was drawn by a five-year-old.

I *can* tell the second he spots the small gold Star of David dangling around my neck because he quirks a brow.

"And you're...Jewish?" he asks, his eyes narrowing in disbelief.

Ugh.

When people discover I'm Jewish, their first question tends to be "Oh, when did you convert?"

I don't fit into their Seth Cohen version of what they imagine I should look and act like. And because the USPS seems to have lost my Jew card in transit, I have to fight through my aversion to conversation around my identity to sum up my entire lineage in a ten-second soundbite: "My dad is Jewish, and my mom is Mexican."

Their eyes usually light up at that point as they will smile and go "Ah," as if I have just revealed the answer to a complex mathematical equation they had been stuck on for hours.

Fletcher reaches for my hand, weaving his fingers with mine. "Do you have any questions for Lucy that you can't find on a census questionnaire?" he asks, his voice laced with annoyance. Such a sassy question coming from Fletcher—a very unsassy man—lifts me up a bit.

He's defending me. I like it.

His father looks taken aback, and he clears his throat. "I apologize, but I was just curious about your new *friend*. I've never heard of a Mexican *and* Moroccan Jew. I can't imagine there's so many of your mixed heritage out there."

While Mr. Fletcher may just be "curious," I can't help but feel a prickle of annoyance. Because even if he *is* curious, the question is still rude. His tone is almost hopeful, as if waiting for me to reassure his anxious soul that there aren't more like me out there, roaming the streets in sombreros in search of Kosher-certified tacos.

And while normally I don't mind volleying intrusive or impolite questions in the spirit of educating others, I am feeling less generous today.

"Well, usually you can find our kind at the Museum of Anthropology," I respond, biting back a laugh as I see how Fletcher's dad's cheeks burn red. I would normally be on much better behavior when meeting my boyfriend's parents, but I can't help but feel protective over Fletcher and want to score him a few more points over his father. "But ever since we were declared almost extinct, they've allowed us to return to the wild so we can seek mates and repopulate to build up our species a bit more."

I hold up my hand, still entwined with Fletcher's. "After careful analysis, it seems like your son is really the strongest candidate. And after a few test runs, I think I've made a good decision in my future sperm donor. Wouldn't you say so, Fletcher?"

Fletcher is watching me with a look of amusement and pride, nodding vigorously before looking back at his father and shrugging. "I'm just grateful I was even considered, despite my disease-ridden European lineage."

Mr. Fletcher's face is impossibly red. Like "could he be having a heart attack?" kind of red. But he's not—his son and his son's girlfriend are just giving him a taste of his own medicine, and I don't think he likes it.

Not one bit.

Unfortunately for him, I am enjoying it immensely. A quick side glance at Fletcher confirms he is, too.

"So, how about we start heading over to the terrace for some lunch?" Fletcher's brother, Matthew, interjects, an amused grin on his face as he pats his belly. "I'm starving."

Fletcher's dad nods curtly in agreement and exits the room. We all follow behind in silence, with his lady friend rushing after him and sliding her hand into the crook of his elbow.

Matthew wraps his arm around Fletcher's shoulders. "So glad you could make it!" He turns to me and offers me a warm smile. "And it's a pleasure to meet you, Lucy. It's always nice to see Dad humbled, right, Fletcher?"

Fletcher rolls his eyes and shrugs away from his brother. "Not like you've ever stood up to Dad."

Matthew's smile dims, and he lifts a shoulder. "Not so easy to do when he signs my paychecks." He says it with a forced brevity, but I catch the flash of frustration crossing his face. And while Fletcher told me that any lingering resentment between him and his brother had long gone, I can't help but wonder if perhaps that's only true from his perspective.

"Anyways," Matthew continues, "I'll see you both outside."

I tug on Fletcher's sleeve as we follow his brother outside. "Who is she?" I ask. "The pregnant lady?"

"My dad's mistress," he tersely answers.

I'm not sure how to respond. I had thought Fletcher's parents had been divorced for a while, but maybe his father had cheated while they were married? I make a mental list of questions to ask Fletcher later.

We arrive at the terrace, which is apparently the rich people word for a patio, and it's basically the size of my entire downstairs—including the overstuffed hallway closet that I haven't been able to open in two years for fear of being crushed to death by my mountain of random crap.

Tiles line the patio—*terrace*—and there's even a small fountain in the corner. Lush trees and plants cascade over trellises to offer privacy. The table is set beautifully, and there are at least two different forks by each plate.

I am not deterred: I took an etiquette course in college. Mainly because it included free meals in exchange for learning how to properly sip on soup. I am ready for this. I've been trained.

We all sit, in an order that seems to have been prearranged

without any official announcement. Fletcher's dad takes the head of the table (obviously), with his baby mama at his right side. Matthew, the heir, is to his left, his wife at his other side. I think she may actually be nice because, one, she smiles, and, two, I think I recognize her bag from Macy's and it cost well under $300, so she's frugal for her kind of folk.

That leaves the seat by the baby mama and the seat across from Fletcher's dad open. I very well might be in love with Fletcher, but not enough to spend an entire God-knows-how-many courses lunch being stared at by his father while I chew microscopic bits of salad in an attempt to look sophisticated. I slide into a chair next to the baby mama, and Fletcher takes the other seat.

I actually think he's relieved to not be sitting next to his maybe-soon-to-be-stepmother, so I decide this was a selfless move and pat myself on the back.

Then our meal begins, and I realize no amount of etiquette classes could have ever prepared me enough for lunch with the Fletcher family.

Chapter Twenty-Six

 *Fletcher*

LUNCH STARTS OUT EASILY enough.

The server brings out salads for everyone, arugula and mâche topped with a lobster tail and drizzled with vinaigrette. Lucy looks a bit disappointed and asks, in a whisper, if we are going to be having a soup course because she only has two forks.

When I shoot her a puzzled look, she sighs and shakes her head, muttering "all that practice for nothing" before stabbing the lobster unapologetically with her fork.

I can see my father staring at me—he's making zero effort to hide it. A silent battle wages between us, and we both know the score. It was stupid and immature of me to ignore Amelia. I thought I was prepared to see her, but when the moment came to actually *talk* to her, the words just wouldn't come. I froze and because of our history, my father retaliated by humiliating Lucy. And while I hate how he spoke to her, I have to admit I'm impressed with how well she handled him.

It's a hell of a lot better than what I would have done, that's for sure.

Matthew and Angelica make small talk, doing their best to ease the tension. But there are only so many times you can comment on the "delicious salad" and the "unseasonably warm weather." I notice that Amelia doesn't seem to say much. She looks the most uncomfortable out of us all, and though it's petty and mean, it does make me feel better.

After a few long lapses of silence, my father clears his throat, instantly putting me on full alert. It's coming.

"Aldrich, why don't you all tell us about this new job of yours that your brother told me about?" He shakes his head. "Though for the life of me, I cannot fathom why you left your job at Kenton for a public school."

I hear Lucy let out a small gasp, her fork midway between the plate and her mouth. I love that she looks horrified. She doesn't even know that this is my father just shooting the breeze.

He hasn't even warmed up yet.

"Well, I'm teaching US history to sophomores and juniors. And the reason I left Kenton, which I'm surprised Matthew didn't fill you in on"—I shoot an annoyed glance at my brother, who, for his part, is finally beginning to look very uncomfortable—"is to be closer to home and be there for Mom. Since she's understandably going through a tough time right now."

That shuts Dad up.

But I have to be careful about what I reveal in Lucy's presence. She knows so much about @BravesGuy93's life—especially my father's affair and the breakup of my parents' marriage. For months, she's been the rock I've leaned on, the person I share all my anger and frustration with, and she has spent hours helping me process it.

But the secret ends today. It should have ended last night, but after Lucy kissed me, it had been hard to focus on anything other than how good it felt to have her in my arms once again. I could have done more to slow things down, but she had looked so vulnerable, so sincere, I was scared to hurt her with my confession.

So yeah, I had been selfish. But no more. Today I am going to explain everything until she understands and forgives me.

But first we have to make it out of this lunch alive.

My father's face turns red, almost as if he's vibrating with anger. Good. No one ever has the courage to go up against my father.

Matthew sure as hell never does—not that I can totally blame him. Working for my father is a nightmare, and I know he needs to choose his battles. Meanwhile, Liv has completely cut Dad out of her life.

And though I don't want to admit it, from what I'm seeing of Amelia, she seems more like my father's Stockholm syndrome–stricken captive than the conniving mistress I imagined.

"Right. In your eyes, what I've done is unforgivable," my dad says. He stands up, throwing his napkin on the table. "In that case, I see no reason to continue this charade. You're free to go, Aldrich. If you hate me so much, then ignore me like your sister. I clearly mean nothing to either of you."

He storms away, disappearing back into the house. Amelia slides out of her seat and chases after him, admirably fast for woman who is eight months pregnant.

A heavy silence takes their place. Lucy's hand slips underneath the linen tablecloth and rests on my thigh, giving me a reassuring squeeze.

Matthew finally drops his head into his hands and expels the sigh I imagine he's been keeping inside since Lucy and I arrived.

"Did you have to do that?" he asks, turning to look at me.

"Do what? Say the truth?" My tone comes out a bit sharper than I had meant for it to.

"Do you think Dad needs it thrown in his face how much he fucked up, Fletch? Do you really feel better for sticking it to him? Reminding him about all he's lost?"

Now I'm pissed.

"All he's lost?" I echo incredulously. "You mean the thirty-four years of marriage he threw away? For his *secretary*? He's not the victim here, Matthew. I know Dad signs those six-figure paychecks of yours he's always holding over my head, but how can you sacrifice your morals like that? You've seen how he destroyed Mom! She's been an absolute mess these last few months. How the hell can you stick up for him like that?"

Lucy's hand leaves my thigh, but I hardly notice. I'm boiling with anger, outraged that my brother is so staunchly defending our father.

"He's still our dad, Fletcher. And he's not perfect, sure. He fucked up. Majorly. But he's trying the best he can!"

Lucy stands abruptly, shaking the table and surprising us all. I look up to find her eyes, wide and filled with an emotion I've never seen from her before.

"I need to step outside." She turns, then shifts uncomfortably and gestures to the door. "Or step inside, rather. I just need to get out."

The shakiness in her voice douses my anger, and I toss my napkin on my plate, standing.

"Of course. Let's go." I reach for her hand, but she sidesteps me and rushes into my father's house. Worry ignites in my chest.

"Wait, Lucy, can you just hold on a second—" I call out as she reaches the front door.

Before I can finish, she spins on her heel and faces me, her dark brown eyes alit now with visible fear.

"Thirty-four years?" she asks. "Your parents were married for thirty-four years before they divorced?"

I nod as realization begins to dawn.

I was so caught up in anger at my father that I had done the one thing I had been worried about doing: inadvertently revealing to Lucy I was @BravesGuy93. Because, sure, cheating spouses may not be the most unusual or unique situation.

But a cheating spouse after thirty-four years of marriage? Much less common. Especially when you add in all the other coincidences, like I had: The visibly pregnant girlfriend-slash-former-secretary. My disapproving father. The ex-girlfriend at a new job. And my crush on an unnamed guidance counselor.

All of which Lucy knows about thanks to the hours she's spent listening to me vent about my life and family drama.

I hold up my hands and take a cautious step toward her. "Look, I can explain."

Her brows crinkle in confusion before her eyes widen and she lets out a little gasp. Pressing her back against the door, she shakes her head. "Just tell me the truth. It's you, isn't it?" Her chin trembles as she locks her eyes on mine. "You're BravesGuy93?"

The look on my face is enough to answer, and her expression crumples.

"This isn't how I wanted you to find out," I say, hoping she will give me a chance to explain.

She laughs sharply. "What is this to you? What am *I* to you? Is this some weird game or—"

I reach for her hands. "No, nothing like that, Lucy. You have to believe me."

She snatches her hands away from mine. "No, I don't!" She wipes away a stream of tears from her cheeks. "How long have you known?"

"I didn't mean for it to happen, Lucy. I swear to God." I push a hand through my hair. "I only figured it out a few weeks ago. When you told me—well, when you told BravesGuy93—about seeing Georgia kissing me," I finally confess.

I didn't want her to find out like this. The whole reason I didn't tell her sooner was *because* I didn't want to hurt her.

But every tear falling down her face is *my* fault. It doesn't matter that I was planning to come clean later this afternoon. It's too late. The damage is done.

Only in this moment do I realize how selfish I was in not telling her sooner. I'd told myself this time was different—that I wasn't running away from confrontation but choosing the right moment to give our relationship the best chance.

Instead, I betrayed the woman I've completely fallen in love with.

She throws up her hands. "Why didn't you say anything then?" Her voice cracks as more tears stream down her cheeks. "Is this why you…disappeared? Stopped responding to my messages?"

I nod. "I was so scared that you were already so angry with me because of that kiss with Georgia. I wanted to win back your trust first as me, and not risk manipulating or deceiving you more as BravesGuy93. I kept trying to tell you, but then, it seemed like every time I tried, the moment would pass and—"

I shove a hand through my hair and fight the instinct to lie, to say whatever might make this situation somehow better. But lying has only hurt the people I love, and I can't—I *won't*—do that to Lucy anymore. I take a deep breath and center my gaze on hers, my chest caving in as I see the tears snaking down her cheeks.

"But the truth is, I chickened out every time. I should have told you, I know that now. I just…I knew how protective you were about your online identity, and I was scared that if you knew who I really was, you would push me away. And I couldn't risk losing you. You're my best friend, and—please, you have to believe me. Hurting you is the last thing I wanted." Desperation drives my next words, though as soon as they're out of my mouth, I know it was the absolute wrong thing to say—no matter how true it is. "I'm in love with you, Lucy."

She takes a step back, holding up her hand to warn me off when I move forward. "You do not love me, Fletcher." She groans. "God, how can you even say you love me? You've been lying to me all this time!"

She turns and tries to leave, grunting with effort as she heaves the door open. I panic—I can't let her go. She has to understand how much she means to me. How much I *don't* want to ruin the best thing to ever happen to me. Not to mention—we're in the middle of Boston, and we drove my car.

"Lucy, please!" I call out as she storms down the steps to the sidewalk. "At least let me drive you home. We can talk and—"

She pauses and looks at me, angrily swiping away the moisture on her cheeks with the back of her sleeve.

"There is *nothing* to talk about, Fletcher. Whatever this was"—she waves a hand between us—"is over. You know, maybe I would have pushed you away, Fletcher. Maybe yeah,

I would have completely freaked out. But at least I would have known the truth and could have made a decision for *myself*."

She takes a deep breath, looking like she's bracing herself. "You know the reason I'm so protective over my online identity? The *real* reason? It's because it's the only place *I* get to be in control. It's the only time I get to show the world how I want to be seen. Where I can be the funny one or the one who gives the best advice and is always there with a comforting word. Where I can be the one who has my shit together. And sure, maybe it's not one hundred percent real, but it was *mine*."

She throws her hands up in frustration then continues. "Do you even get that, Fletcher? Do you understand why someone like me—who has panic attacks over a stupid phone call and who sometimes can't get out of bed for days because I'm so goddamned depressed for no reason other than my brain is kind of an asshole with a major serotonin shortage—would want just *one* place where they could pretend that they were a normal human being? That instead of being the depressed and anxious burden that everyone else had to take care of, *I* could be the one taking care of everyone else? *I* could be the one who had my shit together."

Her shoulders drop as sadness replaces her anger, shrinking her body as if her muscles are folding into themselves. "And now, because you know who I am—who I *really* am—all of that is gone. All of that is just…It's gone."

I take a step toward her, every inch of me craving to comfort her, but she holds up her hand again, stopping me. When she turns and walks away, the silence that follows in her absence feels deafening.

This time, my feet stay glued to the brick sidewalk as

I fight the impulse to chase after her. She's right—about everything—and I need to respect her need to be alone if I don't want to push her away even more.

I fucked up in the worst way possible.

There's no defense for lying to her like that.

I collapse onto the front steps of the building, dropping my head into my hands. The door clicks open behind me, and Matthew takes a seat beside me.

"Care to explain what the hell just happened?"

I shake my head. "I've fucked up. Epically."

"Yeah, clearly." He pats my back with his hand. Clearly trying to lighten the mood, he adds. "But it's also not a Fletcher family gathering until half the table storms off."

I appreciate the effort, but I feel physically sick. All morning I was anxious about this lunch, and then I was so caught up in my anger with my dad that I lost the one thing that matters most to me in this world.

"If Dad just hadn't made me so angry, I could have avoided all of this. I was planning to tell her today after lunch, for God's sake! At least then she would have gotten to hear my side of things."

"Look," Matthew starts, his voice firm but patient. "I have no idea what that fight was about, but you cannot blame Dad for this. You can blame him for a lot of things, but that"—he gestures in the direction Lucy had run off in—"*that* was not Dad's fault."

I turn my head to look at him. "You saw the way he acted! How rude he was to Lucy and the way he talked down to me, like he always does, and the way—"

"Look, I am not denying any of those things, but whatever

happened between you two has nothing to do with Dad. This," he continues, his voice softening, "is on you to fix, not him. Because you're the one clearly in love with this woman."

I bark out a laugh, frustration sharpening my words. "And where was this advice when you found out Dad was cheating on Mom? How come you didn't tell *him* to fix things?"

Matthew scrubs a hand over his jaw, blowing out a breath. "You don't think I told Dad that? You don't think I was angry—*am* angry—for what he did to Mom? You weren't here, Fletcher, when Dad told us everything. I had no idea he and Amelia had been sneaking off together. I don't even work on the same floor as him, and he's avoiding the office these days, anyway."

He pauses, his face darkening. "And who am I to lecture Dad about cheating when I've done the same? I know better than anyone how fucked up it is, how it can destroy relationships. You went over a year without talking to me, and it was the worst year of my life."

He holds up a hand before I can interrupt. "I am not," he says, "playing the victim here. I fucked up, and I deserved every bit of your anger. To this day, I am still ashamed of how selfish I was back then. But when it came to holding Dad accountable for something I had also done, yeah, I struggled."

I sit in silence for a long moment, digesting Matthew's words.

I know I've spent too long letting anger at my family consume me—I said today I'd be willing to try, but at the first chance, I lashed out. Can I blame Dad for doing the same? And Matthew's right: I can't blame Dad for what happened with Lucy—I made the decision to lie all on my own.

How can I expect—or even ask—Lucy to forgive me for my actions when I won't take a single minute to put myself in anyone else's shoes? I wasn't here when our family imploded. I can't critique how everyone survived the fallout.

"You're right," I say, breaking the silence between us. "I just…I don't think I've ever been this lost before." I turn to face him. "I can't lose her, Matthew."

"So," he says, draping a comforting arm over my shoulder, "how are you going to fix this?"

I drop my head back into my hands. "I have no fucking idea."

TheMissGuidedCounselor
Today at 3:13 PM

BravesGuyIsSorry
Lucy, it's me. Fletcher.
I know you blocked my number, but
please let me explain.
I know I hurt you, and I promise that
was the last thing I ever wanted.
Please, just let me explain.
Please, Lucy.

You can no longer send messages to this person.
<u>Learn more</u>.

Chapter Twenty-Seven

 *Lucy*

"SHE DOESN'T LOOK SO great."

"Well, she's heartbroken, Amira!" Julieta snaps. "What do you expect?"

"But if this Instagram guy and Fletcher are the same person, what's the big deal? Shouldn't we be happy?" Amira counters. She crosses her arms indignantly, though I know it's her defense mechanism.

When I told my family what had happened, I had to explain the situation from the *very* beginning—including when I first started @TheMissGuidedCounselor. And, of course, they all immediately opened their phones to look up the account, liking every post from the past year while guessing which posts were not-so-secretly about them.

"Amira!" Julieta hisses. "He *lied* to Lucy. That is super sketchy behavior. And don't you find it kind of creepy how he ended up at *the* same school as Lucy? That's kind of stalker-y."

"Or is it fate?" Amira pushes back.

"Well, even if it is," Julieta argues, "he lied to her and betrayed her trust."

"But what if it really is because he was scared the truth

would make Lucy run away?" Nia chimes in. "I mean, we *all* know Lucy sometimes tends to…well, how do I put this?"

"Freak the fuck out?" Amira adds, finally prompting me to speak up.

"Enough!" I shout. "You all need to stop talking about me like I'm not literally sitting right in front of you!"

Their barrage of unhelpful advice finally slows to a stop. Julieta places a hand on my arm. "Lulu, we just hate seeing you like this. We want to help, that's all."

"I know, I know. It's just…some things can't get fixed so easily. And sometimes—"

I'm interrupted by a commotion from downstairs and the sound of overlapping voices. I sit up in bed and glare accusingly at my sisters. "Which one of you told *her*?"

They both deny it, but it doesn't matter: it's too late. My mother's hurried footsteps, followed by another, slower-paced pair, advance up the stairs. She pauses in the doorway to my bedroom and clasps a hand to her chest. Behind her, my father offers me an apologetic look, having clearly lost in his attempts to keep my mother away.

"Lulu, you look terrible!" my mother exclaims as she rushes toward me, pressing a kiss to my temple.

"Ma," Julieta says, turning to glare at her. "Lulu's having a rough enough day as it is."

"I know! That is why we are here." She elbows Amira off the corner of the bed and grabs my hands, cradling them in hers. "Tell me what you need, mija. Tell me what will make you smile."

I wish I could give her an answer, but I can't. Because I don't think there is anything right now that could make me smile. My heart feels like it's been ripped out of my chest, stomped on a thousand times, and thrown into a woodchipper *Fargo* style.

I shake my head. "There's nothing, I'm just…I feel sad," I explain, though *sad* doesn't quite capture all these feelings whipping around inside me like an uncontrollable tornado. I'm not just sad. I'm devastated. I feel betrayed in a way that I'm not sure I've ever experienced before.

My father clears his throat and looks at me. "Do you want us to call Dr. Zhou?" he asks.

My father is the one who first connected me to Dr. Zhou. Years ago, he did his residency with Dr. Zhou's wife, and they became close friends. And yes, it is super weird having your psychiatrist over for dinner.

I consider his offer and shake my head. While depression is hard, this feeling is different. I'm heartbroken, and you can't fix heartbreak with a pill.

He responds with a lopsided smile and leans against the doorframe, a bit of the weight of worry off his shoulders.

"Is there anything we *can* do for you?" Julieta asks.

"Besides teleporting me out of here, finding me a new identity in another country, and erasing my memory?" I ask, hoping to lighten the mood a bit. My joke doesn't land, and I wonder if they are seriously contemplating how to accomplish this for me.

"Are you going to go to work tomorrow?" Nia thankfully changes the subject.

I shrug. "I guess. I don't want to waste my sick days or PTO on Fletcher. I also have the Konfident Kids Klub."

"Well, if he wants to talk to you," Nia says, "he'll have to get through me first."

I give her a grateful smile, knowing that Nia means every

word. Weirdly enough, though, I'm not scared about tomorrow. I'm not looking forward to seeing Fletcher, but I'm a pro at avoiding unwanted confrontation. I know every shortcut and hidden nook of that school like the back of my hand.

The murmur of voices picks up again, and I sit up, trying to look assertive in the stained oversized T-shirt I threw on when Nia brought me back home after picking me up in Boston. "Look, I appreciate everyone's concern, I really do. And yes, I'm sad, but I'm okay. Really."

And I mean it. I *am* okay—and truthfully, it feels kind of nice to just be sad. Usually when I'm feeling this way, it comes with an extra serving of despondency and despair, so this is a welcome change. I'm sad because of *something*, and not because my serotonin supply is on major backorder. Having my family and friends' support makes me feel even safer to fall apart because I know if I can't put myself back together, they will step in to help.

"But," I continue, "I need a few hours to myself. I have to get ready for work tomorrow, and I could use some alone time."

When my mother opens her mouth to object, I add, "But I promise to call if I *do* need anything, okay?"

My mother sighs but nods in agreement, as do my sisters. Nia rises off the side of my bed and leaves with a wave goodbye, Amira and Julieta following behind. Amá looks torn, but when my father gently pulls her to the door, she acquiesces.

"I left food in the fridge for you. And you call me if you need anything, entiendes? I will be at the restaurant, so call me there. Or on my cell phone." She pats her pocket. "I will keep it on the loud setting for you, okay?"

I smile and dutifully nod. "I promise to call if I need you."

She comes back to cup the side of my face, squeezing my cheeks and giving me another kiss, followed by a second kiss from my father. "We love you, Lulu. And I'm very proud of you."

I don't know exactly why, but my mother's parting words bring tears to my eyes. I only shed them once I hear the door shut behind her. I've spent most of my life shouldering so much shame and guilt that it felt like I was carrying this invisible backpack stuffed full of giant boulders. I was ashamed that I couldn't be happy when there was literally nothing to be sad about, ashamed at the worry I caused my parents each time I would fall into a deep depressive episode, and ashamed at feeling like I was more of a burden to them than a daughter.

With a lot of therapy and even more self-reflection, I've learned to shed most of it, though some days that backpack is a little heavier than others. And though my parents tell me countless times how proud they are of me, hearing it again, in one of my weaker moments, reminds me how far I've come and how strong I am. I've been battling invisible demons that live inside my head, sinking me to levels of melancholy so deep and heavy and *exhausting*, and I keep coming out stronger on the other side.

I got through those dark days, and I'm starting to realize I'll get through this one, too.

Yes, my heart is broken, but that doesn't mean it can't be put back together again. Sure, it will take time for me to heal, but I'm finally understanding I deserve the same grace and kindness I implore my students to extend to themselves.

My worst fear has happened, and instead of being devastated, I just feel determined.

I can't keep hiding behind my computer screen instead of being the woman I want—and *need*—to be.

I don't want to be afraid of saying no anymore, of being too timid to speak up in meetings—like when I found it absolutely ludicrous that the administration was suggesting rationing students' bathroom visits to four a semester. I deserve to be heard, and I am tired of standing in my own damn way.

And though I don't want to admit it—and even though he violated my trust, and I don't know how or if to forgive that—a part of me is so unbelievably glad that he saw me, all of me, and in doing so, showed me that I am enough, just the way I am.

It is time for me to stop hiding and tell the world who the real Lucy Galindo is.

Just…starting tomorrow.

Chapter Twenty-Eight

♡ *Fletcher*

WAITING FOR THE CHANCE to beg the woman you love to either forgive you or cast you from her life is depressing. It's especially challenging when you work together, and your entire day revolves around trying to catch glimpses of her between your classes and meetings.

At this point, maybe I should go and work for my father. Even his disapproval and constant critique would pale in comparison to how painful this is.

And it's only Monday.

The thought of having to do this for the remaining seven months of the school year feels impossible. I can't manage a single thought without coming back to Lucy. For months, she's hovered on the periphery of my mind. Whenever I heard a funny joke or had a frustrating day, it was always @TheMissGuidedCounselor I wanted to go to. She had the best advice, the funniest distractions, and the kindest words.

And then when I finally had the chance to hold her in the flesh? I just knew. This was it. She would be the last woman I ever loved. I don't want to imagine a life now with Lucy not in it.

I'm a zombie as I go through the motions of the day—not really able to do much other than the bare minimum. Apparently, my misery is noticeable enough to grab Brodie's attention, because he finds me in the hall between classes, a concerned look on his face. "You aren't looking so good there, mate."

I'm not sure I'm in the mood for a Brodie intervention today, but that doesn't matter because Brodie easily has a good six inches on me and has *literally* cornered me. I am a captive.

"I'm fine," I respond, forcing a tight-lipped smile.

Brodie shakes his head, his forehead furrowed with concern. "No, I can see the sadness just emanating off of you. Have you ever tried crystal healing? I think I have some pink opal in my desk I can rummage out for you. Matter of fact, I was *just* using it this morning!"

I shake my head. "I don't think there's a need for—"

I'm cut off when Brodie's hand lands on my shoulder, forcing me to look up at his *very* troubled face.

"You need to be practicing self-care, friend," he says. "You cannot fill anyone else's cup if yours is empty. And self-care is an art, mate, not a science. You need to try different things to see what sticks. So after the crystals, we could try some breathing exercises, eh?"

I gawk, unsure of what to say. I guess I must look like real shit if Brodie is lecturing me on self-care. "I'm really okay, Brod—"

"Shh," he interrupts, lifting his finger to his lips. "You don't have to be strong around me." And then two arms are wrapping around me, pulling me tightly against Brodie's very solid chest.

At first, I hang there limply, though he seems to have no trouble holding up my dead weight. But when I open my mouth to protest, I hear Brodie let out a deep and peaceful sigh and mimic him instead. I lean in, reluctantly reciprocating his hug, and realize I'm enjoying it, too.

I'm not sure if I've ever hugged someone nonromantically, outside my family—and never for this long—but in Brodie's arms, I do start to feel better.

"This feels good, Brodie," I say with my cheek pressed against his chest. "I am feeling a lot better."

I swallow when I feel a sharp, hard bulge hit my stomach, right above my belt. I quickly pull back and instinctively look down, my cheeks red with embarrassment. Had I...excited Brodie?

"Ah!" he says, victoriously, as he pulls out a light pink crystal from his pocket. He smiles as he twirls it in his hand, before lifting a triumphant brow. "You see? The healing power of the pink opal crystals!"

After Brodie's self-care session—after which he forced the pink crystal into my pocket—I have one more period to go before finishing the day. While I have, admittedly, been phoning it in for my other classes, AP History is a harder task. We're in the middle of the Salem Witch Trials, and I'm half tempted to wheel in the A/V cart and throw on *The Crucible*.

But I settle for the next best thing: a pop essay quiz. It should take them the whole class to finish, and because I'm not a total monster, I allow it to be open book.

While my students work, I stare at a blank sheet of paper for forty-five minutes, running through—and dismissing—various ways to apologize to Lucy. Every once in a while, I'll pop my head up to see if they have questions. I don't know if it's my overall demeanor or if I've been teaching them so well that they genuinely don't need any help, but no one takes me up on the offer.

The final bell rings, and I let everyone take their quizzes home to finish. It's an easy A, so no one argues. As I pack up my own bag, Sophia joins me at my desk and grabs the stapler, attaching three pieces of lined paper with dark ink covering every available inch.

"I finished early," she says, handing it toward me. I don't doubt it—she's one of my brightest students.

"Great, thank you."

She doesn't leave immediately, and I stop packing my bag to look at her. Her expression is solemn.

"Is everything okay?" I ask.

She nods. "I just wanted to thank you. You know, for the other week with Ms. G."

"Oh, right. There's no need to thank me. It was all Lucy—I mean, Ms. Galindo."

It hurts for her name to leave my lips and serves as yet another reminder of how close she is, just a two-minute walk down the hall physically, yet so far removed from my life.

She tilts her head, studying me. "You know, you both kind of look like shit today."

"Language," I remind her. I wonder what it is about Harview High that both students and teachers alike feel so free to comment on how terrible I look. Maybe they should test the lead levels in the water.

"Okay," she whines. "You both look kind of miserable. Like super blotchy, and you both have these really deep bags under your eyes. Especially you. There's a cream for that, you know, to rehydrate the skin."

"I'll keep that in mind," I say as I swing my bag over my shoulder.

"Okay, okay. But before you leave, I just want to let you know that I'm really grateful you came and got me." She shudders. "I don't know what would have happened if you hadn't. And I'm done wasting my potential, as Ms. G would say. I've decided that I'm going to college. With my AP classes, I'll probably be able to graduate by the time I'm twenty."

I gape, impressed. She has her shit together way more than I currently do. She has a four-year plan, while I don't even know what I'll be doing in a few months. "I'm really proud of you, Sophia. I think you're going to do great things."

She beams and flips her blond hair over her shoulder. "That's what Ms. G told me, too. Before...well, everything. She told me to not settle for being some guy's girlfriend and that I'm smart enough to stand on my own. I did some research, and if I follow a law track, I can start making six figures by the time I'm twenty-three so I won't need some loser guy to buy me stuff."

I nod approvingly. "That sounds like a great plan. Have you, uh, told Ms. Galindo?"

Pink stains her cheeks, and she shakes her head. "I saw how upset she was with me after that meeting with my mom. And I felt so guilty that I've kind of been avoiding her." She bites down on her lip.

"What? No way. Sophia, she was never mad at you. She was more angry with herself and upset that you were in that situation. She just wants the best for you—and she believes in you so much."

Sophia blinks back a few tears. "I'm just embarrassed that I fell for him. I thought that he would be sweet and like, my Prince Charming, but he was really just a creep."

"Don't get too down on yourself. But also take this as a learning opportunity. We all make mistakes, and you were lucky Ms. Galindo was there for you. And I think it would mean a lot to her if you told her what you just told me."

Her lower lip quivers. "She'll be disappointed in me."

I shake my head, knowing that Lucy could never be disappointed in her. She's in awe of Sophia and is both saddened and excited to see one of Harview's brightest students leave for college next year. "No, she won't, Sophia. She just wants the best for you."

She pauses to consider my words. "You're right. Even if she's still mad, she should know that I'm going to learn from this." She smiles guiltily before adding, "And I also really need a letter of recommendation from her, so I guess I should probably talk to her sooner or later."

"Sooner sounds like a good option," I respond.

She rolls her eyes. "Okay, well, I guess it's off to Konfident Kids Klub I go. It's *still* social suicide, but I feel like I owe Ms. G to give it a try." She shakes her head as she walks out the door. "That is going to look *terrible* on my transcripts. We really need to change that name."

She walks out the door, and I consider following her. Maybe I could "run into" Lucy, and we'll talk. I can finally apologize. But I know that it would be unfair to put her on the spot like that.

And truthfully, I need more time to think, to find a way to communicate to Lucy how sorry I am and how much she means to me. How her online friendship saved me, a life raft in the middle of a dark, cold ocean when it felt like I couldn't tread water for another second. And how, when I had the gift of meeting her in real life, she ignited a spark inside me that I had thought long extinguished. She taught me how to laugh again and reminded me how fulfilling it is to let someone in, to trust another to bravely show me all their cracks and imperfections so I could share mine in turn.

That vulnerability should be cherished, a present to be protected and valued, not a weakness.

But how do you show that to someone? Especially when they don't want to talk to you.

Instead of the hollow silence that usually greets me, the soft sound of music is drifting through the air when I step inside the house. I follow the soft jazz—and the smell of garlic, roasted tomatoes, and simmering onion—to the kitchen, where I find my mom closing the door to the oven. She's dressed, no longer in her usual uniform of stained yoga pants and oversized shirts, and her blond hair is pinned in a low bun at the nape of her neck.

"Lasagna?"

She spins around and smiles. "Yes! It should be ready in about an hour." She steps to the sink, where she washes her hands. As she dries off, she pauses to look at me and frowns.

"I take it she's still avoiding you?" she asks, her voice sympathetic. When I nod, her smile drops. "How are you doing?"

After the disastrous lunch yesterday, I returned home and recounted the entire ordeal to her—starting from the very beginning, when, under anonymous aliases, we grew our friend-ship, to that fateful first day at Harview, when a scalding-hot cup of tea led me to meet the woman who captured my interest and then quickly my heart.

I shrug and push a hand through my hair. "I'm good." I'm lying, but my mom is going through enough, and I don't want to add to her stress.

She walks over and places her hand over mine. "You know, you don't need to be strong all the time. And you definitely do not need to protect me. I know…"

She pauses and sucks in an unsteady breath. "I know I haven't been easy these last few months. And I put too much on you and your sister, which wasn't right. I just…sometimes I wake up and think that I'm in some kind of alternate reality—or wish that I were. For too long I've just been feeling sorry for myself without ever thinking about how it was impacting you. I'm sorry for that."

She pulls her hands off mine and drops her head into her empty palms. "I mean, you quit your job to come home and take care of me! What kind of mother does that to her son!"

I pull her hands away from her face and cradle them with mine. "Mom, you don't need to apologize. I chose to be here. Besides, that job was killing my soul, and I had already been looking for new teaching gigs for a few months. I'm much hap-pier here."

She smiles. "Is that because of your job or because of Lucy?"

"A little bit of both," I answer honestly.

I may have only been at Harview for two months, but I love my students. Padmesh is a great—if overly enthusiastic—boss and believes in his teachers, which is a welcome change. There aren't any entitled parents threatening to sue because I gave their precious Philip an F on his plagiarized paper. I've even begun to enjoy Brodie's long and rambling monologues and self-care pep talks.

And yes, there's Lucy.

She's the first thing I think about when I wake and the last thing I think about before I fall asleep. I've been so lucky to work in the same school and to be able to see her every day and invent small excuses to find myself in her office or sneak a new tea into her cubby for her to try.

"I really messed up, Mom." I drop my head into my hands. "I guess I'm more like Dad than I realized."

"Hush." My mother swats my arm. "You are *not* your father. You made a mistake. All that means is that you're human."

I look up at her and shake my head. "It was a *big* mistake."

She smiles wryly. "Big like 'cheating on your wife and getting your secretary pregnant' big?"

I chuckle. "Okay, not *that* big. But still, I lied. I kept a pretty big secret, and I broke her trust in me."

"Okay, so what are you going to do to fix it?"

"I don't know. She's avoiding me at school and blocked me online."

My mother nods thoughtfully. "Sounds like you need to show her how you feel, rather than tell her."

"How do I do that? She won't talk to me!"

My mother rolls her eyes. "You kids and your text messaging. I said *show* her. You work with her, don't you? You see her every day!"

"She's going to keep avoiding me."

"And let her, for a few days at least. Give her space to process how she feels. And then you find a way to speak to her."

"You make it sound so simple."

"Sometimes it is," she blithely responds.

"You haven't forgiven Dad," I remind her.

"You're right. I'm angry," she says, her voice pensive. "But it's beginning to fade, and I can't help but feel this overwhelming sense of…"

She pauses and looks at me, her brow furrowed as she picks the right word. "Relief? Is that a weird thing to say? I feel like for the first time in quite a long time, I get to put myself first. My babies are all grown, and even though I can't seem to get rid of Liv, you're all doing well for yourselves and forging your own paths."

"I'm happy for you," I say. "I just wish you didn't have to go through all this shit."

She shoots me a stern look. She hates when I swear. "Sometimes you have to muddle through the *sh*—the poop—to get to the good part."

I shake my head. "I just need to get out of the poop part."

"Well, if you were to put yourself in Lucy's shoes, how would *she* know that she could trust you again?"

I think her question over as memories of Sunday's disastrous lunch replay in my head. In particular, the moment Lucy shared that the reason she started the account was because it was the one place where she could show the world who she was on *her* terms.

It was where she could be the woman she wanted to be, one who always knew the right thing to say, who had all her shit together and didn't have to live with anxiety or depression. And I understood how comforting that shield of anonymity could be—because wasn't that what I loved about @BravesGuy93?

But what Lucy doesn't know, what I didn't have the chance to show her, is that while I'm eternally grateful to @TheMiss-GuidedCounselor for being the best friend I could ever ask for, it's Lucy I am in love with. It's Lucy, with all the flaws and baggage she hides as @TheMissGuidedCounselor, that truly stole my heart.

Because I don't want some perfect, curated version of her. I want all of her. I love *all* of her.

"I think," I start, voicing what I haven't been able to say until now, "she would need to believe that I love her for her. And that the reason I lied wasn't because I was afraid to scare her off, but…because *I* was afraid of what might happen. So I let my fear get in the way of doing the right thing."

My mom tilts her head. "Well, why don't you start there?"

I nod, an idea about what to do forming, and grateful for the push in the right direction. "Thank you, Mom."

She pulls me into a hug, kissing my cheek. "You're a smart kid, Fletcher. I know you'll figure it out." She pauses. "And I hope you resolve things with your father, too. I understand that you're angry—trust me, I get it—but he's your father. He made a mistake, and he broke our marriage vows, but that doesn't mean he will ever stop being your father. He's not a bad man, Fletcher. He just made a bad choice. In a way, you have to admire how he chose to stay and raise the baby with her. A lot of men would have walked away without a second's thought."

I cock my head to look up at her. "Really? Admire?"

She chuckles. "All I am saying is, there's a child coming in a few weeks that could use a smart, caring, sweet, and loving older brother."

I nod and thank her again before heading up to my room,

promising to return when the lasagna finishes. It's good to see my mother returning to herself. She's always given the best advice, and tonight is no exception.

Because my mother is right—I *know* Lucy, and I know I can show her that I wasn't trying to hurt her. I made a stupid choice, but I'm hoping she can forgive me, because I am hopelessly in love with her. *All* of her.

Now all I need is to find a way to show her.

Chapter Twenty-Nine

 *Lucy*

I AM *NOT* IN the mood for a Konfident Kids Klub meeting today.

I barely slept, and I look like a drowned raccoon, with circles under my eyes and my hair haphazardly gathered into a messy knot at the top of my head. I am not the confident, fearless leader that my students need right now. But I cannot ditch our meeting.

No matter how much I really, really, *really* want to.

I grab my binder from underneath my desk, heft it into my arms, and take a cautious step into the hallway. Thankfully Fletcher has been giving me my space, and I haven't seen much of him today—just the quick glimpse I dared to sneak of the back of his head before darting into my office to hide.

But before I can step into the classroom, Padmesh spots me from the end of the hall and jogs over to reach me. I fight the urge to run inside and lock the door behind me. While I like Padmesh and find him a generous principal, I'm not really in the chatting mood today.

"Are you off to influence the next generation into making wise choices?" he asks, beaming at the binder in my hands.

I mumble out a cross between "yes" and "sure," which seems to satisfy him, and he gives me a big thumbs-up.

"Keep rocking it!" he says.

I am about to turn into the classroom myself when I stop. If I want to be serious about stepping out from @TheMissGuided-Counselor's shadow, then I need to start now.

Today.

"Actually, well, *no*."

While I am sure @TheMissGuidedCounselor would speak in a loud and authoritative (and probably British) voice, mine comes out squeaky, betraying every ounce of doubt roiling inside of me. I'm not @TheMissGuidedCounselor. I'm not effortlessly brave like her. I don't have an endless supply of amazing advice in a handy list format like her. I don't have inspirational quotes at the ready like she does.

I'm *not* her.

But I did create her. And obviously a part of her comes *from* me.

Maybe I'm not as well spoken or witty as @TheMissGuided-Counselor, but that shouldn't stop me from speaking up. Especially when I know I am in the right. This curriculum sucks, and if @TheMissGuidedCounselor wouldn't tolerate teaching this out-of-date, useless, and sometimes downright offensive curriculum from the nineties, I shouldn't either.

Padmesh's megawatt smile drops as he arches a bushy brow. "Sorry, what is that, Lucy?"

"No, I don't want to rock it anymore." I hold up the binder until my muscles scream. "This curriculum is antiquated and does not provide the resources these students need to really excel. I have emailed several times that I think we need a new curriculum for this club, and each time, I'm told there isn't enough funding." I think of the abandoned equipment that hides the cry closet and all the "staff enrichment" activities Padmesh funds and feel my voice grow louder.

"Well, how come there's funding for our football team, which hasn't won a single game in two years? Or funding for the karaoke machine that, trust me when I say, no staff member has touched once? We have at least a decade's worth of old gym equipment just sitting in a back hallway we could sell that would more than cover the cost of a new curriculum for the Konfident Kids Klub—preferably a curriculum that didn't share its initials with a hate group."

I'm on a roll now, and it feels *good*.

"The students in this group are some of the most caring and thoughtful people in our school. We should be investing in them with a quality curriculum that will enrich their lives and help them continue to succeed, not embarrass them and waste their time by forcing them to role-play scenarios straight out of an episode of *Saved by the Bell*—which yes, was a fantastic show but, please, I do not have the mental fortitude to explain for the hundredth time what 'getting jiggy with it' means."

Padmesh stares at me, wide-eyed. To be fair, this is the most I've ever spoken since he's hired me. He takes a second to process my words and then nods. "You know what? You're right. Why don't you send me some recommendations for what curriculum you would like instead, and we will make room in the budget."

Now it's my turn to stare at him. *That* worked? After being tasked to lead this group nearly two years ago, getting stuck with all the jokes about its name and how embarrassing the curriculum was, all I had to do was…say something?

"Um, yes, great," I manage to stumble out. "I will do that."

Padmesh's signature grin reappears, and he claps me on the shoulder. "Thanks for speaking up, Lucy! We're lucky to have you on the team."

He continues down the hall while I take a second to process his words. I did it!

Not only am I getting a new curriculum, but I spoke up for myself, and it didn't kill me. In fact, I feel a little bit of a rush, like I've just snorted an entire line of Pixy Stix. Is this what taking drugs feels like?

With a new confidence—the kind I'm not sure I've ever possessed—I step inside the room for our to-be-renamed meeting. Immediately the chatter between the girls comes to a stop. They all have their hands neatly folded on their laps, not a single cell phone is in sight. They look at me, with pleasant smiles, waiting for me to begin.

I am instantly suspicious.

"What's up with this *Stepford Wives* shtick?" I ask, taking my seat.

I'm answered with the familiar blank faces I often get when I forget that I'm utterly ancient and reference anything pre-2015. "Never mind," I mumble.

I dump the binder on the desk and move to grab an empty chair to drag into the semicircle but pause when I see an unoccupied chair. I scan the room, doing a quick headcount, and suppress a tiny squeal of excitement at seeing Sophia among the rest of the members. All the students are accounted for. Then it hits me.

The chair is for me.

They set up a chair *for* me. In the semicircle of trust.

I've made it.

I walk toward the chair and sit down, unable to suppress the smile dancing across my face. I can't help it. First I was able to finally confront Padmesh, and now my students have finally—*finally*—welcomed me into the semicircle of trust.

"Okay, so I have some good news," I say, crossing my hands on my lap. "We will soon be getting a new curriculum, which means we can pick a new name for our little club."

"We know," Trina says, pointing to the door. "We literally just heard you talk to Principal Padmesh."

"Oh, right." I guess in my passionate state, I hadn't been the most careful about modulating my voice. "So, is there anything special you want to talk about today?"

With the homecoming dance finally past and the Halloween one approaching, I'm hoping there will be enough to talk about to kill forty minutes. I'm fully prepared to sprinkle in my nods and *uh-huh*s, but I don't know if I have much more than that in me. As victorious as I feel after my conversation with Padmesh, it did little to boost my sullen post-breakup mood.

To my surprise, Sophia's hand is the first to shoot up in the air, directing my attention to her. "Sure, Sophia. What's up?"

We haven't spoken since the emotional meeting with her and her mom. It was a difficult one for all of us, and I know that Sophia needed her time to process. I was a bit saddened that she hadn't come and talked to me one-on-one, but I am heartened to see her today. I was worried she wouldn't come.

"Well, I just want to share that I made a *really* stupid decision to meet up with this DJ that I follow on Instagram with like, all those followers," she says, surprising me. I'm impressed and touched that she wants to share with the group.

"I had been so excited when he started to message me, and I felt so special," she continues. "So when he asked me to meet up, I agreed. He knew I was in high school and only sixteen, so he even made sure to tell me not to let my parents know where I was going. He said it was because they wouldn't understand our relationship, but now I realize he had been grooming me."

She pauses and looks up at the ceiling, blinking tears back. "Like, I always knew I was smart. I never had to study for tests, really, and I never got bothered about stupid high school drama. But then I let myself get talked into meeting some random stranger online. He made me believe I was special, and then when I got there, he treated me like garbage. And I just wanted you all to know that even though I think this club is totally dorky, I still care about you all. And if someone smart and super pretty like *me* can fall for it, then it could happen to any of you, too."

Trina reaches over and pulls Sophia into a hug as the rest of the club form a circle of support around her. It's sweet, and I am so proud of Sophia for sharing—even if she also low-key insulted them at the end.

As everyone returns to their seats, Sophia turns her attention to me. Tears trickle down her face, but her makeup stays pristine. She really does have it all together.

"And Ms. G," she starts with a sniffle, "you were there for me when I needed you most. And you never judged me or lectured me, and I really appreciate that." She takes a deep breath. "And Mr. Fletcher wanted me to tell you that I'm not going to settle for some loser. I am going to go to college and be a boss bitch all on my own. And I'm really, really sorry. I would never want to hurt you."

I want to cry. I'm *going* to cry.

Sophia is one of the smartest students to pass through Harview's doors. Her intelligence is effortless, and she's never pretended to be anything she isn't. She made a mistake, and she is owning it. That is something I *still* struggle with as a grown adult, and she has it mastered at the ripe old age of sixteen.

"Sophia, you don't need to apologize. Trust me, we *all* make mistakes. And you didn't hurt me; you just got me a little scared. I would never want anything bad to happen to any of you."

"But I did something that hurt you," she insists.

I shake my head. "But you didn't mean to," I tell her. "You just made a mistake."

"So you don't hate me? You forgive me?"

I lean forward in my seat. "Sophia, of course I don't hate you. And there is nothing to be forgiven. I'm really proud of you." My voice cracks, and tears are ready to pour out and ruin my non-waterproof mascara. "You inspire me."

I look around the room. At Trina, with her talent for painting, who is hard at work creating new pieces for the end-of-semester art exhibition. At Poppy, who last year wasn't able to say more than a few words without looking like she wanted to keel over and vomit, but this year regularly participates in discussions with enthusiasm.

"You all inspire me." I smile.

I've cried before all these students before, and while I would much prefer not doing so again, I'm not quite strong enough. The tears come, bursting out of me like a broken dam. And then the students are back out of their seats, arms extended as they come to comfort me.

They know the drill. As embarrassed as I am that I am back

in this seat, crying ugly tears *again*, I remember Fletcher, and how he had comforted me when I had confided in him that I was worried about crying in front of my students.

He reassured me, telling me that maybe my students seeing me upset was a good thing. Both Fletcher and @BravesGuy93—who I guess is now Fletcher, or rather, was Fletcher all along—*always* assured me that I was a great guidance counselor and good at my job. He believed in me, without hesitation. Even when I couldn't always believe in myself.

And despite being *so* angry at him, I can't deny I also miss him. A lot.

That sends another flurry of tears down my cheeks. I hope Fletcher was right that it's good for my students to see me being so emotionally vulnerable, because in the six weeks we've been meeting, I have comfortably demonstrated more variety of emotions than most adults tend to express over the course of a year.

After a few moments, and a few more tears, I settle and give a school-sanctioned hug (a one-handed side hug that is a step more conservative than the full-frontal, but with hips fully thrust back) to all my students.

"I'm so sorry I'm a mess today, guys. I've just been…" I shrug and force a smile. "Life stuff. I'm really thankful you were all here to support me and create a safe space for me to express my feelings."

The students all bob their heads in understanding and return to their seats. All except Sophia. "You know, he looks miserable, too."

I wipe my cheeks and look at her. "What do you mean?"

She rolls her eyes. "Mr. Fletcher. I saw him before coming

here. He looks like a sad dog, like the ones you see at the kennel. But like, more pathetic."

"Sophia—" I start to warn.

"Fine, fine!" She tosses her hands in the air before reclaiming her seat. "I just thought you might like to know that he's looking miserable. I mean, I always like to know when my exes look like garbage. It makes me feel better."

"He's not my ex," I say, a little too passionately, and quite a few brows shoot up to the ceiling. "I mean, we didn't...we aren't..."

My voice falters.

Yes, I broke up with Fletcher—or, well, implied I was breaking up by avoiding him in person and blocking him online—but the idea of him being an ex turns my stomach upside down. *Ex* feels cold and impersonal, and that isn't who Fletcher is to me.

But then, who *is* he to me?

He's the hot new teacher I have feelings for, the one who is an amazing kisser and who held my hand and comforted me through panic attacks and took me to the grocery store just to spend time with me. He is also @BravesGuy93, the friend I've spent months messaging with about everything from our weird food preferences to our frustrations with our families.

There wasn't a subject we hadn't touched—except, of course, our names and where we lived. And he always respected my boundaries, despite expressing that he wanted us to meet and possibly be more. The idea that the man I was falling for in real life and the friend I cherished online are one and the same should make me happy, right? Maybe I would be happier if I didn't feel overwhelmingly betrayed at how easily he had lied to me.

Though that wasn't exactly true, was it? Fletcher had said he did what he did because of how scared he was to lose me—and well, I know what that feels like.

"Uh, Ms. G?" I look up to see Sophia, and all the other students, watching me. I had zoned out. "Do you remember how you told us all, like two minutes ago, that we all make mistakes?"

I nod, still distracted by my own thoughts.

"And that I still deserve forgiveness for hurting you? Even though it had been a mistake?"

I nod again, growing a bit more wary about the direction Sophia is taking.

"So don't you think that *maybe* you should consider forgiving Mr. Fletcher? If he made a mistake but hadn't meant to hurt you?"

"And what makes you think it was Mr. Fletcher that made the mistake?" I counter.

Sophia rolls her eyes. "Because he's a man, Ms. G. It's *always* their fault."

I choke back a laugh and shake my head. "Sophia, I don't know where you get this."

She shrugs and picks at her nails. "Too much daytime TV. But"—she looks back up at me—"that whole bit about forgiveness? I got that from you."

Chapter Thirty

♡ *Lucy*

I DIDN'T THINK I would make it to the end of this week, yet somehow, I did. Only after my impromptu therapy session with the to-be-renamed Konfident Kids Klub, I've been even more confused about my feelings.

Am I ready to give up Fletcher—and @BravesGuy93—because of a single, albeit pretty big, lie?

But also, how can I trust him—or his feelings—after this?

What I need is to be with my family tonight. They never sugarcoat the truth, and enough time has passed since Fletcher's betrayal that I can talk about him without bursting into tears.

A few minutes before the final bell, I shut down my computer and pack up my bag, remembering to take my cell phone with me this time.

I scurry to my car in the parking lot. I've been sneaking out a few minutes early each day to avoid running into you-know-who. But as I approach my car, I see a package waiting for me. It's a wooden box, plain and brown, just a bit bigger than the Konfident Kids Klub binder. Attached to it is a white cardstock tag with my name written in black ink.

I stare at it, frozen, as if my feet have sunk into a giant pit of cement.

"Do you think it's a bomb?"

I jump with a loud squeal when I see Georgia standing beside me, inspecting the box with my same intensity. I was so caught up in my thoughts, I must not have heard her approaching.

"You scared me!" I say, recovering my breath. "And no, I don't think it's a bomb. Why would you say that?"

She shrugs and leans forward to look at the box more closely, yet still keeping her distance. "I've watched enough *Dateline* to know that if you see a mysterious package on a car, you run."

I stare at her, not entirely believing that my former arch-nemesis is a fellow crime junkie. "*You* watch *Dateline*?"

"How else am I supposed to unwind after a long day?" she asks. "Who do you think it's from? Have you pissed off anyone recently?"

I let out a long exhale. "It's from Fletcher."

I don't even need to look inside to know. I recognize the dark scribble of his handwriting from the note attached to the tea bags he had left for me in my cubby. "I think it's him trying to apologize for lying to me."

Georgia's brows shoot up. "Oh, wow. Well maybe you should hook up with his brother for revenge." When she catches me gaping at her, she playfully elbows me. "It's okay, you can laugh. I joined Tinder and have like eight guys in my DMs. I've moved on from your boyfriend."

"Ex-boyfriend," I mumble.

"Oh, so he *fucked* up, fucked up? Hope there's some diamonds in that little box."

I turn to look at her. "I mean, yeah, he did fuck up. But...I don't know if I'm overreacting, either."

She sucks in her bottom lip. "Well, if you want my advice—well, even if you don't, I'll give it—Fletcher usually wants to do the right thing. His execution, though? Totally sucks. But you have to realize he didn't exactly grow up with the best role model, either. His mom is lovely, but his dad? Kind of an egomaniac control freak obsessed with working and checked out for most of Fletcher's life."

"Yeah, I kind of got a preview of that."

She nods. "I'm not saying you need to forgive him. *Especially* not before getting some major apology jewelry first, but maybe cut the guy a *tiny* bit of slack. He's one of the good ones."

I take a moment to process her words before tilting my head up to look at her. "You're kind of a good person, too, you know."

Georgia grimaces, her face contorting like she just swallowed something disgusting. "Please never let anyone hear you say that." She straightens her jacket and pulls her keys out of her purse. "Anyways, just in case that *is* a bomb, I'm going to drive out, because I just got my car detailed and do not want your Hyundai shrapnel ruining my car."

She hurries away, and I grab the box, tucking it under my arm as I unlock my car. I toss my bag on the passenger-side seat and then place the box beside it. I can't decide if I want to open it or not, when I know opening it is likely going to unlock the emotions I've been barely holding back.

I need my sisters.

I'll bring the box to dinner tonight and we'll open it together. Or rather, I will make them open it while I hide in another room until they say it's safe for me to come out.

The adult decision.

The box stares at me the whole ride home. I decide it's wiser to keep it in the car until Shabbat dinner, because if I bring it inside, my lack of impulse control will lead me to open it, and I need my emotional support sisters.

I try my best to distract myself with cleaning until dinner. I make it seven minutes.

Then I sit through an episode of *Love Island* and instantly regret it when there's a character who mentions his love for bungee jumping. Fletcher mentioned once he had gone bungee jumping. Too painful. I decide to take a nice, relaxing shower. I could use one, and it might be fun to dress up for dinner tonight. Usually, I just show up in work clothes and call it a day. But tonight, I want to make an effort.

Look good, feel good, right?

The shower turns out to be a bad idea because that *also* reminds me of Fletcher and how sweet and thoughtful it had been for him to help me fix it a few weeks ago, when everything between us had been so simple and easy. But now everything is so much more complicated, and I'm too alone with my thoughts, so I drag my Bluetooth speaker from the kitchen and prop it on the bathroom counter to listen to my latest murder podcast while I shower. If listening to a serial killer cannibalizing his victims can't pull me out of this funk, nothing can.

That seems to do the trick for a bit.

Luckily, it's a two-parter and carries me through to drying my hair and spackling on some makeup, concentrating under my eyes so Amá doesn't make *another* comment about how I look exhausted before trying to shove an off-brand Ambien into my pockets. I pull on a dove-gray dress and tights, and when I look in the mirror, I do actually feel a bit better.

Not enough to forget Fletcher or that doomsday box waiting for me in the car, but enough to remind me that I am pretty hot shit. Even with a broken heart.

Enough time has passed that I decide to see if either of my sisters is already loitering at my parents' place so I can convince them to open the box for me. I head outside and grab the box. It feels heavier.

When my father hears me, he calls out from the back sitting room. "Come! I got some new mint tea in from my cousin!"

I lug the box, which is getting heavier and heavier with each passing minute, and join Amira on the couch. I place my phone and the box on the coffee table, where my father has placed five small, ornately decorated tea glasses, all in a different color, with a gold-etched design. A glass teapot sits in the center, an amber liquid inside with three mint leaves floating on the surface. The smell is fragrant and comforting.

My father drinks three to four cups a day, but only particular brands and *only* how he prepares it. He's a bit of a snob when it comes to his tea and is scandalized by my Lipton collection.

Julieta rushes in a second later, her cheeks flushed red with indignation. "I swear to God, I almost just killed someone!" she exclaims as she takes off her coat. When she sees our shocked faces, she adds, "Like, not on purpose, obviously. But he cut *me* off and then had the audacity to flip me off! God, I hate Boston drivers!"

My father pats the empty chair beside him. "Come and sit. Relax a bit."

Julieta moves to claim the chair, but her shoe catches the

leg of my father's chair, and she stumbles forward, arms flailing. She lands on the coffee table with a loud *oomph*, sending the tea glasses to the floor and turning the teapot on its side.

Amira and I jump up from the couch as the hot liquid splashes on us. Instinctively, I grab the box, clutching it to my chest. Julieta rolls off the coffee table, deftly avoiding getting any tea on her despite somersaulting straight into it.

"Oh, shit!" she exclaims when she's back on her feet. She winces and looks at Papa. "I'm so sorry."

He shakes his head. "It's just tea, and luckily Hassan sent a whole box." He bends over to pick up the teapot. "Girls, can you run into the kitchen and grab some towels?"

I drop the box onto the couch and follow Amira into the kitchen, where we gather a pile of towels. When we walk back into the room, Julieta is holding up my phone, pinching it with her forefinger and thumb as it dangles over the table, dripping liquid.

"No!" I cry out. I grab the phone from her and wrap a towel around it, but it won't turn back on. I had been so preoccupied with saving the box—the box of what, I still don't know—that I completely forgot I left my phone on the table.

"Rice!" Amira says, pulling me into the kitchen again. She reaches for a bowl and then grabs the giant plastic container of rice and pours it into the bowl. "Put the phone in the bowl, and the rice will absorb the liquid. I saw it on a TV show, it will totally work."

"Not too much rice!" Amá scolds as she finishes cooking. "I need that for tomorrow."

I dunk the phone in the bowl, and we both stare at the soaking-wet phone submerged in rice. Amá and then Papa join us. Nothing happens, so Amá returns to cooking and Papa fills the kettle with cold water to start a new pot of tea.

I look at Amira and she shrugs. "Maybe give it a bit longer?"

I groan. This day sucks. This week has sucked, and because I wasn't thinking, I chose to save a wooden box, which would have easily survived the hot liquid, instead of my phone. It's hard for me to not feel personally victimized by tea at this point. First the teapocalypse with Fletcher, and now this. Was the universe trying to tell me something? Punish me for my unsophisticated tea palate?

Amira loops her arm around my waist as we walk back to the sitting room. Julieta gives me a guilty smile. "I'm so sorry, Lulu."

I shrug. It's not like I have dozens of calls or texts waiting for me. Fletcher has given up texting me, and Nia's never offended when it takes me two or three days to respond. "It's okay, Juli."

She gestures to the box on the couch. "So…what is that? Is that like a gift or something?"

I sigh. "It's from Fletcher."

"What's in it?" Julieta asks.

"I don't know," I admit.

Julieta's eyes bug out. "You haven't opened it yet?"

I shake my head. "I was waiting for my sisters."

"Then let's do it!" she says, clapping her hands. She is way too enthusiastic for this.

I take a step back. "I was kind of hoping you would open it and then just recap it for me after."

Julieta shakes her head. "No way. Sit. We'll all be here for you, but *you* need to do this."

I groan as I drop onto the couch. But she's right. I can do this. Julieta sits on my left and Amira on my right. Taking in a deep breath, I unhook the latch and open the box. There's no note, just a ruby-red scrapbook album. I lift it out and place it on my lap. It's big, with a creased spine, and stuffed to capacity.

I exhale and flip it open to the first page.

Lucy,

Thank you for accepting this box and not dumping it in the trash, though I would understand if that's where it ultimately ends up. There will never be any excuse for having lied to you. The truth is, I knew if you discovered I was @BravesGuy93, it would complicate what we had as Lucy and Fletcher. I thought you might not want me in your life at all, and the idea of losing you terrified me. I let my fear steer my decisions, and that hurt you more than the truth possibly could.

But please don't think my lies mean I don't care for you. Lucy, you consume my every thought, and it physically hurts when I can't open my phone to talk to you or share a funny conversation. I miss our inside jokes and the way you turn a bad day around with just a single "hello." In some of the darkest and most challenging times of my life, it's been you who helped me get through them.

I know you didn't believe me when I told you I love you, so I am hoping I can show you now. I do love you—every part of you. Even the parts you think you need to hide as @TheMissGuidedCounselor, because those are the parts of you I love and admire the most. But I know it might be hard for you to believe that from me right now, so I thought I would try to show you how our friendship grew to be so much more for me.

Because loving you isn't just effortless, Lucy. It was inevitable.

Love,
Fletcher

I pause, rereading his note a few times over.

When Fletcher said he loves me, I dismissed him. I thought he was just trying to get me to stay and listen to his excuses, and that he didn't truly mean it. But maybe I had been wrong.

Maybe Fletcher *does* love me.

A tear falls from my eye, blurring the ink of Fletcher's signature. I look up to find all my sisters watching me, gauging my reaction. Julieta wraps an arm around my shoulder. "You okay, Lulu?"

"I'm not sure," I answer truthfully. I flip to the next page and see a printed screenshot of a post I had written over a year ago, the dark, bold font over a pale blue background:

TheMissGuidedCounselor
Posted 408 days ago

In case no one has told you this, you have permission to change. To want more—or less. To take the leap or stay firmly rooted on the edge of the cliff (METAPHORICAL cliff, folks!). You only have ONE life, so live it in a way that makes you not only proud, but also fulfilled. Chase your happiness and don't let anything, or anyone, tell you that you don't deserve it.

Scribbled in the margins is Fletcher's familiar handwriting:

This was the first post of yours I read and the one that inspired me to start following you. A few minutes later, I sent you a direct message. I never thought you would respond, but I'm so glad you did. I was lost—miserable at my job and not sure what to do about it. I felt so alone. I knew that if I confessed how miserable I was to my family, my father would just rub it in my face, reminding me how idiotic he thought my decision to teach was. But then I found you. And I didn't feel so alone anymore.

I barely remember writing that post, but staring at the words now I feel them mocking me. *Chase your happiness.* When was the last time I had done that? When was the last time my fears and anxieties weren't holding me back?

I flip to the next page, where there's a second screenshot—of our private messages, starting off with the first message he had ever sent me, an exchange I had long forgotten about:

TheMissGuidedCounselor

BravesGuy93
Hey, I think I'm ready to take that leap off the (metaphorical) cliff, but I'm not so sure. How do you know when it's the right time?

In the margins, there's more of his writing:

We stayed up messaging back and forth till about two in the morning. And instead of leaping off the cliff, you helped me take a step back. To reflect and assess. To see that, even though I was miserable at my job, I wasn't ready to give up on teaching yet. I just needed to find the right opportunity. Little did we both know that the right opportunity meant finding my way to you.

I continue to flip through each page, realizing that Fletcher printed out every single one of our conversations, adding personalized notes in the margins of each one.

I look up at my sisters, my chest full of emotion. "He collected every message between us and wrote about how much they meant to him. About how much I mean to him."

Julieta clutches her chest. "Wow. That is so romantic."

I turn a page, and then another, skimming each note, knowing that I will be spending the rest of my life rereading every page of this album, tracing my fingers over the gentle swoop of his *l*'s and the slanted lines that cross his *t*'s.

Then I land on a conversation I do remember well—from earlier in the summer. The day that Fletcher had discovered his father's affair and messaged me, absolutely heartbroken at the betrayal.

 TheMissGuidedCounselor

We'll figure this out, okay? I'm going to stay online and we can keep talking for however long you need.

This is when I knew I wanted to have you in my life forever. You stayed up with me when I was so wrecked, I couldn't sleep.

But you were there for me. Always. In the good times and the bad. You are the only person who I've ever been able talk to about my feelings without worrying about being judged. Even though we had never met, you became my best friend then.

As I read his note, I realize not only is Fletcher also my best friend, but that I fell for him, in the same way he fell for me: first as @BravesGuy93 and then as Fletcher.

And I realize the truth has been there all along. Fletcher loves me. Fletcher *loves* me.

And I love him.

As I near the end, I flip to a page with no pasted messages. Instead, there is another handwritten note.

Lucy,

If you made it this far, I hope you've been able to see how much you mean to me.

I love you with every fiber of my being and every cell in my body. I was lost before you came into my life, and without you, I feel that same emptiness once again. I know what I did was cowardly and only centered myself and my feelings. I hope you can forgive me one day and know that until you do, I will be waiting. Please know you don't owe me anything—if you wish to forgive me, it is your choice alone. But I couldn't let you go without you first knowing how you have changed my life and for that alone, I will be forever grateful.

Forever your favorite follower—online and off,
Fletcher & @BravesGuy93

I close the book and hug it to my chest.

"He loves me. Like really loves me," I say, dumbfounded.

"Why do you sound so surprised?" Julieta asks.

I shrug and swipe away a tear. "I don't even know. I've just spent so much of my life feeling like I wasn't enough to be loved by anyone." I choke back a humorless laugh. "I mean, if I couldn't even love myself, how could I expect some guy to?"

I look down at the album, skimming my fingers along the cover. "But when I see myself through Fletcher's eyes, I don't know…I maybe get it. He sees me as this incredible, amazing, and inspiring person. He said it was so easy to fall in love with me. And it has been so *hard* for me to love myself. I guess I just…I guess I didn't know I was lovable. I mean, I know you all love me, too, but…I don't know. This feels different."

"Probably because we don't also want to bang you," Amira says, prompting an exasperated groan from Julieta.

"What she means to say," Julieta says, glaring at Amira, "is that not only do you deserve to be loved, but that you are the easiest person in the world *to* love. You're sweet and caring, and you're like the *only* person who stays on the line to leave good feedback after customer service calls. You always say 'please' and 'thank you' to Alexa even though she's basically a robot. Lulu, can't you see? You're the best of us."

Amira nudges me with her shoulder. "She's right. You are the best of us. And you deserve love just as much as anyone else. And if you had to fall in love with someone, why not the sexy teacher who also happens to be very, *very* rich?"

I choke back a laugh. "This is…are we sure he loves me?"

Amira groans, rolling her eyes. "Yes, you idiot. For being the most educated out of all of us, you certainly are also pretty dense! He *literally* wrote it all out there for you. The man loves you."

"But what do I do now?" I ask, panic settling over my chest like a heavy anvil.

Julieta throws up her hands in exasperation. "You call him and tell him you love him, too!"

"And then you have amazing makeup sex," Amira adds. "Like he has to do double duty on oral to make it up to you."

Julieta drops her head into her hands. "You are so gross, Amira."

I interrupt before they can start fighting. "What do I say when I call him?"

"You tell him you've read his gift, you forgive him, and you love him, too," Julieta responds.

"And you want to bang," Amira adds.

I leap up from the couch, ready to declare my love. But then the cold hand of reality slaps me across the face. "Oh no! My phone is dead."

"It might have dried by now," Amira says, pulling me into the kitchen. Julieta follows, and we stare at my phone in the rice. I pull it out and press the power button.

We all hold our breaths.

One second…

Two seconds…

Three…

"It's dead," I announce, completely dejected.

Julieta pulls out her phone. "Use mine!"

I shake my head. "I don't know his number!"

"Shit!" Amira murmurs.

"Would Nia have it?"

"No, she hates him after what happened," I groan.

"Okay, well then let's drive to his house!" Julieta suggests.

"I don't know where he lives!" I respond, growing more and more discouraged with each passing minute.

"How?" Amira asks. "Haven't you been dating for like, a few weeks now?"

I shrug. "I mean, yes, but he's been living at his mom's, so we never went over there."

Silence settles over all of us as we think. Until Julieta looks up and smiles. "Yeah, but we know where his dad lives, right?"

Chapter Thirty-One

 *Fletcher*

"YOU LOOK WORSE THAN Mom did," Liv says, as she dives onto the couch next to me. "And you didn't even get dumped by a sixty-eight-year-old billionaire."

I turn and glare at her. "Is there something you want, Liv?"

She shrugs. "Well, it would be nice to not live in a house of perpetually miserable people. First Mom was all up in her feelings, and now you. I cannot be the only normal one in this family. That is way too much pressure." She grabs the remote off the couch, switching the channel to something else.

"Hey, I was watching that!"

She eyes me suspiciously. "On purpose?"

"Yes," I glare at her. "Put it back. It's almost done, anyway."

She presses a few buttons, returning to the movie I rented earlier this week and have been watching on repeat ever since, unable to sleep or really do much of anything besides stumbling from home to work and back.

"Seriously? You're watching this *again*?" Liv asks. "Isn't this movie like eighty years old?"

I roll my eyes, crossing my arms at my chest. "It was *filmed* in the eighties, not eighty years ago. And it's a classic. Now be quiet so I can watch."

She falls silent and we watch a young John Cusack heft a boom box over his head, Peter Gabriel's "In Your Eyes" spilling out from the speakers.

Even though this is my fifth watch this week, the scene comforts me. It reminds me of Lucy, even if thinking of her turns my insides into a chaotic, tornado-like spin of emotion.

Before we can keep watching, my phone vibrates in my pocket. I pull it out, and frown seeing it's my dad calling. Again. Sending the call to voicemail, I drop it onto the couch. Liv picks it up and arches a brow. "Four missed calls from Dad in the last ten minutes? Do you think he's okay?"

I glance at her. "Since when do you care? I thought you hated him."

She shrugs and takes a bite from the half-eaten candy bar in her hand. "We actually made up," she says as she chews.

"Wait, what?"

"I made him take me to lunch at L'Oiseau Bleu the other day, and he basically apologized for everything, but I told her I was like so devastated and would never forgive him. I made a whole scene, which you know dad *hates*. So he ended up bribing me with an apartment in the city. Two bedrooms, in-unit laundry, *and* a pool in the building." She lifts a shoulder and frowns. "Not a bad deal, right?"

I look at her, horrified. "So that's it? You've forgiven him?"

She blows out a sigh. "Look, it sucks what he did, and yeah, I'm mad at him on Mom's behalf. But he's still my dad. And considering that she's going to walk away from this marriage with half his assets, I think Mom will get over him. I mean, she's got it made. Plus," she adds, sneaking in closer, "I saw her flirting with the guy who trims all the trees. And based on how they were talking, I think Mom got *her* tree trimmed, if you know what I mean."

I cover my ears. "You're disgusting, Liv."

She shrugs and finishes up her candy bar. "Whatever." She looks down at my phone, which is vibrating with another incoming call from our father.

"I'm sure he's fine," I say, though not fully convinced myself. My father isn't in the habit of calling this much, especially not so soon after we'd fought. "If he calls again, I'll pick up," I acquiesce.

A second later, the phone begins vibrating again. Liv holds it out for me. "You were saying?"

I grunt, taking the phone and sliding it to accept the call. "Yes?"

"Aldrich?"

"Yeah, Dad. What do you want?"

"I need you to, uh, come over to the house now."

"Dad, I've had a terrible week, and I'm not really in the mood for—"

"Well, your girlfriend and her sisters are currently occupying my living room and refusing to leave until you come."

I immediately sit up and grip the phone. "Lucy's there?"

"*And* her sisters!" he adds, exasperated.

"Tell her I'm coming," I say before jumping off the couch and running into the kitchen.

"Wait!" Liv calls out. "What's going on?"

"It's Lucy! She's at Dad's!" I shout in response as I grab my keys.

Liv jumps off the couch and runs toward me, shrugging on a jacket.

"What are you doing?"

She shakes her head. "You think I'm going to miss *this*?"

I pull into the first empty parking spot I find. It's technically not a parking spot but rather a sliver of street in front of a fire hydrant, but I'm willing to get a ticket or towed. I have no idea why Lucy or her family are at my dad's, but I'm about to find out.

I kill the engine, and Liv follows me as we march up to the front door. I don't bother knocking but push inside and follow the sound of overlapping voices to the living room, where I need to pause in the doorway and take the scene in.

There's a fire roaring and the sound of raucous laughter. Lucy and her two sisters are sharing a couch, giggling hysterically. Amelia has her own seat, her feet propped up on a nearby stool as her hands lie comfortably on her pregnant belly. And then there's my father, sitting on the smaller couch next to Amelia. His hands are animated as he tells a story, a rare smile on his face. He apparently lands the punchline, because Amelia, Lucy, and all her sisters burst into another fit of laughter.

I turn to look at Liv, who shares the same puzzled look. We've stepped into the twilight zone.

"Lucy?"

Every head in the room snaps to look at me. My father clears his throat and pushes up from the couch. Lucy stays seated, her teeth biting down on her bottom lip, revealing her anxious tic as she, and everyone else in the room, leans forward to watch as my father approaches me.

"Son," my father says. "Thank you for coming." He clears his throat and shifts his weight from one foot to the other, and I realize he's nervous. I'm not sure I've ever seen my father nervous before, and it's a bit unsettling.

"I hope we can, well, move past this unpleasantness and work on fixing our relationship." He holds out his hand for me to shake.

This is as close to an apology from my father as I will ever get, but I hesitate before offering him my hand. Before, I would have eagerly accepted his handshake in a desire to avoid uncomfortable conversations. But if this year has taught me anything, it's that hiding behind civility is a pretty shitty way to cope with things. It's how I hurt the people I care about and what lost me Lucy, and I'm not willing to let my fear claim any more causalities.

So if my father is serious about wanting to fix our relationship, then now is the time to prove it.

I steel my spine as sweat starts to coat the back of my neck. "Actually, I think I need to say some things first. I can't just pretend everything is okay with us. I know you don't respect my career choice, and I can't change that, but if you continue to insult or demean my job, I can't keep passively accepting that, either. I'm also not going to tolerate you being rude to those I care about."

I pause to steal a glance at Lucy. She's watching me, her mouth drawn into a tight line, and as much as I want to avoid this entire confrontation and focus on her, I know I can't fix my relationship with Lucy until I stand up to my father. "So, if you're serious about wanting things to be better between us, then you need to apologize to Lucy. And not disrespect her again."

I hold up my hand before he can respond, not wanting to lose my momentum now. Looking toward Amelia, I offer her a remorseful smile. "And I also need to apologize to you, Amelia. I was rude at lunch the other day, and I'm sorry. My anger with my dad has nothing to do with you, and I hope we can get to know each other better before the baby comes."

Amelia's mouth drops in surprise, but she quickly recovers and offers me a tentative smile. "I'd like that, too."

My father nods slowly in response. After a long moment, he says, "Okay, you're right." I don't know if I've ever heard him admit I was right about *anything* before. "I must say I don't understand your career choices, but you're correct that it is unfair of me to judge them." He turns to look at Lucy. "And I do owe you an apology. I would like for us to get to know each other more. I very much disliked how our first encounter went and take full responsibility for being a—"

He turns toward Amelia, who's still sitting with her feet propped up. "What did you call me, dear?"

"Oh, a rude and condescending bastard!" She smiles sweetly.

My father beams back at her. "Ah, now I remember! Yes, I apologize for being a rude and condescending bastard. I hope you can forgive me and that we can start again."

Lucy suppresses a laugh and nods. "I would like that."

"Very well," he responds before walking to Amelia and dusting a kiss on her forehead.

Finally, Lucy stands, and everything and everyone else fades away. Her cheeks are flushed with that familiar crimson I've come to love. Her hair is down, her familiar curls splayed over her shoulders. Her eyes are wide, and when our eyes lock, her bottom lip drops as she exhales.

She's beautiful. And when she smiles at me, my entire chest constricts and I know without any hesitation or doubt that this is the woman I want to spend the rest of my life with. Now I just hope to God she feels that way, too.

She steps closer, taking my hands and turning them, so my palms are facing upward, before interlocking our fingers.

"I read the album," she says, her brown eyes piercing mine. "And I saw myself how you see me. I'm trying to see myself that way, too."

She shakes her head in disbelief. "And everything you wrote was beautiful and sweet and honest and just…" She sighs. "Amazing. And I needed to let you know all that. But then I broke my phone and I couldn't call you and I didn't know where you live, I just know where your dad lives so we all"—she gestures to her sisters, who are watching with rapt attention—"decided to come here to try to get in touch with you."

She pauses and gives me a lopsided smile. "So, this is my grand gesture."

"Wait, shouldn't *I* be the only one doing the grand gesture? Since I'm the one who majorly messed up?"

She shakes her head. "No, I think you leaving the album qualifies enough as *your* grand gesture. So now the ball is in my court to do *my* grand gesture."

"Ah, of course," I reply, a smile teasing at the corner of my lips. "So where's the boom box?"

"Boom box?" Her confusion quickly clears as her eyes widen in surprise. "Did you watch it? *Say Anything?*"

Behind me Liv lets out a snort. "He's been watching it on repeat all week."

"You remembered that list?" Lucy asks, crinkling her nose as she stares up at me, her gorgeous brown eyes locking on mine.

"I remember everything, Lucy." I take a step toward her. "But you may need to remind me what happens after the grand gesture part."

"Well," she says, moving even closer so I can feel her breath grazing my cheek, "you would declare your undying love for me, and traditionally, you would then kiss me in a very passionate and expressive—"

I don't wait for her to finish before I swoop her into my arms and press my lips to hers. Her hands weave through my hair as I deepen our kiss, unable to stop myself from selfishly taking everything she's offering me. Everything about her—from her teasing touches that hold promises of so much more to the smell of jasmine in her soft curls—overwhelms my senses and I happily succumb to the feel of her body against mine.

I am hers, and she is mine.

There are whoops and cheering, and Lucy pulls back, her eyes wide with embarrassment, and buries her face in my chest. Her warm curves melt against my body, a key sliding into its lock. We fit. And though I wish I could go back in time and take away the hurt from before, I know I have the rest of my life to make it up to her.

After collecting herself, Lucy withdraws and curls her arm around my side. She turns back to face her sisters. "You done embarrassing me yet?"

They erupt into raucous laughter. "Nope! Not yet!" Amira calls out.

I give Lucy a gentle squeeze and pull her closer as her sisters get up from the couch and gather around us. I look down at her, not able to stop myself from smiling at the sight of her in my arms. "So, what now?"

"Now," Amira interrupts, "we've got to hurry back to Shabbat dinner." She holds up her cell phone. "Because according to Amá, we're all *very* late."

Chapter Thirty-Two

 *Lucy*

WE FORM A CARAVAN of cars as we drive from Fletcher's dad's town house to my parents' house: me, Fletcher, and his sister in his car; my sisters in Julieta's Volvo; and Fletcher's dad and Amelia in his very impressive silver Lamborghini.

Screw Fletcher's Audi, my father is going to lose his mind when he sees *that* car.

I get to know Liv on the thirty-minute drive because she doesn't stop talking the entire ride. She is exactly how Fletcher described her: a bit brash and a lot sarcastic. The only break comes when she calls their mom to invite her to dinner—even though Fletcher and Liv are also pretty sure their mom isn't *entirely* ready to sit down for a meal with her ex-husband and his new girlfriend.

It just didn't feel right *not* to include her.

"So," she says, ending the call, "Mom is beyond excited that you and Lucy are back together." She drops her phone on to her lap. "But as grateful as she is to be invited to dinner tonight, Lucy, she's going to have to pass. She also wanted me to tell you thanks for the invite…"

I share a disappointed look with Fletcher and give his hand

a gentle squeeze. After he pulls off the highway at the exit nearest my parents' house, Liv continues.

"*And* she wants dibs on dinner sometime this week with you two. Just not Saturday night because she has a date!" Liv squeals.

Fletcher brakes hard at the stop sign and swivels around to look at Liv. "Mom? A date? With *who*?"

"The guy who does all the lawn maintenance for the house. Remember? I *told* you they were flirting." She pumps her fist in excitement. "Mom is *definitely* going to be getting some dogwood planted in her berry bush, if you catch my drift."

"Ew, Liv." Fletcher groans. "I do *not* need that visual in my head."

I bite back a smile as she pats herself on the back, a victorious grin on her face. "I am so proud of myself right now."

Fletcher cocks a brow as he continues to drive, turning onto my street. "And why is that exactly?"

"Because *I* was the one who spent like three weeks interviewing different landscapers trying to find the hottest ones! Do you know how hard it is to find a sexy, single landscaper? It is surprisingly difficult!"

"Wait, why were you trying to find a hot landscaper?" Fletcher asks, his brow furrowing.

"To find a guy for Mom to rebound with. Obviously."

"Huh," Fletcher says, pulling into my parents' driveway. He puts the car in park and Liv jumps out to help a too-pregnant Amelia get out of the Lamborghini.

I slide a glance at Fletcher, who looks lost in thought. "You okay?" I ask.

He nods slowly and then shifts in his seat to look at me. "For weeks, I've been so annoyed with Liv. I thought she wasn't doing enough to help Mom. It felt like I was *always* the one who had to comfort her while Liv would disappear. But it turns out, Liv *was* helping her. In her own Liv kind of way." He grimaces. "I think I might have been too harsh in judging Liv. Again. I thought she was checked out, but she wasn't. At all."

"Well, as someone who sometimes has a bad habit of judging people prematurely, I can tell you—from experience—people often surprise us in the best ways possible."

Blowing out a breath, Fletcher chuckles and scrubs a hand over his jaw. "You're right. Like always."

I catch his eye and we share a smile. "I missed this. Just..." I pause, trying to find the right words. "Talking to you. It's always the best part of my day."

He twists his wrist, interlocking our fingers as he stares down at my hand, a thoughtful expression on his face. "My day, too." He looks up at me, his brown eyes focused so intensely on mine that it sends a spark of electricity up my spine. "I'm really glad you're in my life, Lucy."

My stomach squeezes at the raw tenderness in his voice and I know this is a moment I'm going to remember for the rest of my life. But before I can open my mouth to respond, to tell him how thankful I am he's in my life, too, there's a loud banging on my window.

"Hurry up, lovebirds," Amira shouts from outside. "I'm starving." At her side, Liv nods in agreement and gestures for us to get out of the car.

"We *may* regret introducing those two," Fletcher says.

"I already do," I say, flashing him a smile and giving his hand a tug. "Come on. We have quite the interesting evening ahead of us."

He turns off the car and we step onto my driveway where my parents have started welcoming their dinner guests. My sisters had called my parents on the drive over, alerting them with the updated headcount for dinner tonight. No doubt my mother has already cooked more than enough food to go around and sent Papa down to the basement to grab the extra leaf for the dining room table.

As we all step inside the house, my mother shuttles us all into the dining room. Tonight is a relatively small affair with just my parents, two of my aunts, one of my cousins and her husband, plus their three kids, and our neighbor from next door. Eight more seats are added for all of us as my cousin's kids are booted to a kids' table in the living room where they have *Doc McStuffins* blasting on the TV as a consolation prize.

As we sit, my father looks around the packed dinner table, and a broad smile stretches across his face. "What a beautiful table we have tonight. There's a saying when it comes to us Jews. If you have two Jews, you'll have three opinions."

He chuckles. "And with three daughters, you have a lot of opinions. As the only man in the house, it is sometimes hard to get a word in. But I am proud to be the father of such strong and independent young women, and I am grateful for the many new faces they have brought with them tonight."

Sweeping a hand over the table, he continues, "You all are helping us to fulfill one of the greatest mitzvot in the Jewish faith: hosting guests. But hosting guests is more than a good deed; it is a commandment. After all, we are commanded to treat others as we would treat ourselves. And when provided the opportunity, would we not invite ourselves into a home with a delicious spread like this?"

Humor glints in his eyes. "And when we treat others as we would treat ourselves, we begin to see things that remind us of ourselves. We share a common humanity and far too often we allow our differences to divide us. I ask that as we share this meal, we look for ourselves in each other and search for what unites us, rather than what is different. We are all pieces of a tapestry; our strings may all be of a different color, but when woven together, we create a beautiful pattern. And tonight, I see many beautiful faces at our table, and I am excited to see what amazing things we will create together."

At my side, Fletcher squeezes my hand, and we share a smile. We're two people, after all, with not very much in common, from very different backgrounds, who fell in love first online, and then in person.

A beautiful creation, indeed.

My father smiles and then reaches for the bottle of wine and pours it into the silver Kaddish cup, reciting the prayer, sanctifying the wine. He then takes the two covered loaves of challah and blesses them. Ripping off a large hunk, he passes it to our mother, who rips off a piece before passing it to my aunt beside her. As soon as my aunt passes it to her daughter, she is up alongside my mother, heading toward the kitchen to bring out the food.

Platters loaded high with cod simmered in a chermoula marinade, honey-glazed chicken adorned with twigs of mint, and colorful salads with beets, carrots, fennel, and shallots are passed around as my aunt personally carries the vat of couscous with sliced almonds and roasted vegetables she brought to each person's plate, piling it high to form a mini pyramid of couscous on everyone's plates.

Conversations flow as my cousin grills Liv about the tattoo on her wrist and Amira grills Fletcher about "his intentions" toward me. Amelia lists off the names she's picked out for their baby boy. She's currently stuck between Parker and Elias. Julieta tells her she prefers Parker.

My father and Fletcher's are deep in conversation about a proposed new health care bill that would cut off critical funding to the low-cost clinics where my father volunteers. Mr. Fletcher listens thoughtfully and promises to "make a few calls" next week. I don't exactly know what that means, but I think Papa's clinic might be just fine. Mr. Fletcher is a formidable man, and if he's anything like Fletcher, he'll have an equally formidable belief in helping others. I shudder at what a phone call with him would look like.

Looking around the table, at the different generations and cultures and languages casually sprinkled into sentences, I can't help but appreciate all the people here who made me who I am today. They're the different-colored threads of my own tapestry—my father, my mother, my sisters.

And then there is Fletcher. They all have taught me how to love and to be loved. That it's okay to be myself, no matter how messy or complicated, because I am loved for *all* of my parts. That I am safe to fall apart, because I will always have help putting myself back together.

As if sensing my thoughts, Fletcher's hand slides over mine. "You okay?"

"I'm great," I say, squeezing his hand. "This dinner is actually kind of nice."

"Tell me about it. I can't even tell you the last time we sat down as a family to eat without wanting to murder each other. And my dad seems to be getting along really well with yours."

"He's not that bad, you know." While waiting for Fletcher to arrive, I had the opportunity to sit down with him and Amelia. He was, of course, taken aback by my arrival—and my entourage of sisters—but he warmed up after a few minutes (and a few glasses of brandy).

He's brash and a little standoffish, but he's also someone who clearly cares for his children. And most importantly, he's *trying* to change for the better.

Fletcher shrugs. "Maybe this new baby will mellow him out a bit."

"She's thinking of naming him either Parker or Elias," I whisper.

"Elias? Ugh, I don't like it."

"It's better than Aldrich," I shoot back.

Fletcher laughs and squeezes my hand. "Well, considering I'm the fifth generation of Aldriches, you might want to get used to the name when we have a son."

I raise a brow. "Oh, we're talking babies already?" I hold up my hand, splaying my fingers. "I don't see a ring yet, so I think it's a tad bit early to be talking about our nonexistent future son."

Fletcher captures my hand, running his thumb over my bare finger. "Hmm, you're right. No ring."

He turns to smile at me with those dimples I just can't resist. Maybe if he passes on that gene to our future children, I'll let him get away with naming our son Aldrich. He weaves his fingers through mine. "I think I'm going to have to change that soon."

I can't help but smile as a blissful glow settles over me and a familiar feeling stirs in my belly.

They were back. Those damn butterflies.

TheMissGuidedCounselor
Posted at 11:33 AM

Hi everyone!

First of all, I want to say a huge thank-you to all the people who checked in with me these past few weeks. I know I went AWOL and haven't posted in a while, but I'm okay! More than okay, really. And as much as I have missed you all, this will be my last post as @TheMissGuidedCounselor.

I first started posting here when I was feeling lost and scared in grad school, and I wanted to practice applying my newly learned skills to the real world under the safety of anonymity. As I've shared many times before, I am a guidance counselor at a public high school. And as my fellow guidance counselors know, this can be a really, really hard job. And it can be even harder when you have depression, ADHD, and anxiety like I do.

These diagnoses often mean the day-to-day stress from our jobs can feel insurmountable. Regular staff meetings can lead to full-blown panic attacks. Simple tasks, like organizing my weekly meetings and commitments, can feel like an impossibly complicated and unsolvable puzzle. Hard realities, like knowing I have students who live in dangerous situations where the adults meant to love them the most have abandoned or hurt them, can break my heart and soul, sending me into a cycle of depression that requires me to use up all my sick time as I hole up in my bed.

As @TheMissGuidedCounselor, I've been able to pretend I am the perfect guidance counselor. I always knew the right thing to say and was never depressed or anxious or scared. I could curate the image I wanted to share with the world and become the perfect woman I desperately wanted to be. As @TheMissGuidedCounselor, I never had to worry if I wasn't good enough. Wasn't interesting enough. Wasn't worth being heard.

But now I've come to realize that thinking that way isn't fair to you—or fair to *me*. My depression makes me extraordinarily empathetic. My anxiety helps me to always be prepared and think ahead for my students, and my ADHD allows me to relate to my many students who live with the same diagnosis and struggle with their day-to-day tasks.

I'm not a worse guidance counselor because of my neurodivergence; I'm a *better* one.

And I'm ready to stop hiding behind @TheMissGuidedCounselor and for you to meet the real me. The one who struggles with depression and anxiety and ADHD. The one who is overwhelmed by her student loans but still impulse-buys kitchen devices she uses a handful of times. The one who takes two months to fix her broken shower because the task absolutely overwhelms her. The one who sometimes forgets to do laundry for weeks on end so will just buy a new pack of underwear at Target and spray her clothes with Febreze. The one who has to work two, sometimes three jobs to afford her mortgage. The one who cries at least once a week and who has few close friends because she's scared to let too many people in.

I am all of that *and* I am also a kick-ass guidance counselor, a loving sister and daughter, a loyal friend, and a new girlfriend to an incredible guy. I'm so many things—some messy and flawed, some beautiful and unique—and I cannot wait to share them all with you.

Hi, I'm Lucy.

Liked by **BravesGuy93** and **others**

TheMissGuidedCounselor The end. Or the start of something…more

View all comments

ACKNOWLEDGMENTS

Thank you to my agent, Jill Marsal, for seeing the potential in both this book and in me and for pushing me to create the best book I could. I am grateful for your vision and tenacity.

A debt of gratitude to my editor, Sam Brody, who believed in Lucy and Fletcher from the very first tweets I shared about my book and who worked tirelessly alongside me to make *Flirty Little Secret* the best book it could be.

A thank-you to the Forever team, including *the* Estelle Hallick, Carolina Martin, Caroline Green, and Kate Riley from the marketing team. And another huge thanks to both designer Caitlin Sacks and cover director Daniela Medina, for bringing Lucy and Fletcher to life in such a fun, vibrant, and beautiful way.

And a big thank-you to Carolyn Kurek and Marie Mundaca from the production and design team for carrying *Flirty Little Secret* over the finish line and getting this book into readers' hands.

A mere "thank you" feels so insufficient to my Pitch Wars mentor and dear friend Lyn Liao Butler. You believed in me when I didn't even believe in myself yet. You saw the potential in my embarrassingly rough first draft and brought out the beauty and humor and heart that has made *Flirty Little Secret* the book it is. I hope I can spend the rest of my life making you Canva graphics as thanks for everything you've given me.

And thank you to my Pitch Wars class for being the best cheerleaders, CPs, venting partners, and dancing cats procurers. We went through so much together and it has been a joy seeing you all succeed in your publishing dreams. I cannot wait to see what else we all accomplish and am so grateful I can be there to cheer you all along.

Thank you to my fellow 2024 Forever debuts, including Becky, Erin, Lauren, Lindsay, and Lucy. Publishing can be a scary and lonely journey and I am so grateful for our little group where we can anxiously await our debut year together.

Thank you to the Romance Shmooze group for fostering a safe, welcoming, and loving place for our Jewish romance author community. While I am often AWOL because Discord *still* confuses me, I am always grateful for our supportive community.

A huge thanks to my original CP, Noémie, who must have read this book ten thousand times. I am confident this book would have absolutely not been where it is without your valuable and kind feedback, and I hope you enjoyed this entirely different version of the first book you read.

Thank you to my dear friend Ruth Cardello, who has been a constant source of wisdom, guidance, support, and love these past few years. I am so grateful for our friendship, and me and my pizza slices thank you for your infinite wisdom.

A heartfelt gracias to my family and friends here in Mexico who not only helped read through my early drafts and offer valuable and hilarious feedback, but also welcomed me into their homes and their hearts. Huge, squishy abrazos to Clara, Juli, Vanessa, and Lupe.

Both a hug and a thank-you to Joan Kaplowitz, who inspired me to chase this publishing dream of mine so many years ago. Your unflagging support was the push I needed to step outside of my comfort zone, and I wish you could be here to see this book in your hands.

This book could literally not have been written without the support of my parents, who helped to watch my infant—and later toddler—as I wrote, rewrote, and edited (and edited again) this manuscript countless times through Pitch Wars and then submission and finally with my work with the Forever team. This book, my wildest publishing dream come true, is here *because* of you and I am forever in awe of everything you have done for me and love you both so much.

And to my husband, Pedro, who still has not a single clue about publishing but supports me without question or restraint. I hope one day I can write our love story…maybe then you'll read it.

And lastly, thank you, dear reader, for giving this debut author a chance and for picking up this book. I hope you saw a little bit of yourself in this story and see that you are enough, exactly as you are.

A LETTER FROM THE AUTHOR

Dear Reader,

I wrote the earliest draft of this book while I was attending an intensive outpatient program (IOP) at Woman and Infants for my postpartum depression. So okay, yes, not exactly the *sexiest* backstory for a romance novel, but hang in there with me because I promise this story also has an HEA.

Having a safe space within the IOP allowed me the opportunity to dive deep into who I was and the type of woman and mother I wanted to be. Encouraged by my therapist, I turned to writing and a story began to blossom inside me. One where, even if the main character was depressed like me, she could still find love and acceptance. A story where, yes, there was a beautiful romance, but also a strong family connected by love and understanding inspired by my own family. A story where life didn't have to be perfect to be wonderful. And thus, *Flirty Little Secret* was born.

And if you've read the book (no judgment if you skipped straight to the back because I do the same!), you'll see that a central theme for Lucy is the struggle around her identity and her mental illness—two things I struggled with growing up (and, well, let's be honest, *continue* to struggle with even as an adult). So many of the thoughts and anxieties Lucy voices in her book are ones I've grappled with myself. The panic attack scene, for instance, shows very real words I've said in the midst of a depressive episode. Even the closet is based on a secret cry closet a few coworkers and I shared at a previous job (though Lucy's is far cozier and more comfortable).

It took a long time for me to accept my mental health diagnosis, and even then it really wasn't until the birth of my daughter that I realized prioritizing my mental health wasn't optional anymore—it had to be the priority. And I took the leap, sat my family down, and told them I needed help. A few weeks later, I had quit my job and was starting my first day at the IOP. And it was because I got that help that I was able to write this book you're now holding in your hands. See, I told you there would be an HEA.

Thank you for taking a chance on this book, and on me as a debut author.

With gratitude,

Jessica

QUESTIONS FOR DISCUSSION

1. Lucy puts a lot of effort into creating "perfect" content for her @TheMissGuidedCounselor account. But she also works hard to keep her identity as @TheMissGuidedCounselor a secret. Why do you think Lucy put so much time and effort into @TheMissGuidedCounselor? At the same time, why do you think it was so important for her to keep her identity anonymous?

2. On paper, Fletcher seems to "have it all," but as seen throughout the story, money and appearances don't equal a perfect life. Why do you think having his anonymous online profile was so important to him?

3. Lucy, as @TheMissGuidedCounselor, shares quite a few tips and helpful lists throughout the book. Is there any post of hers that resonated with you? Why do you think it stood out to you?

4. Throughout the book, Lucy grapples with her identity and never feeling like quite "enough" of her different cultural and religious identities, which is a feeling I think a lot of children with intercultural or interreligious backgrounds struggle with. Have there ever been situations where you haven't felt "enough" and could relate to Lucy's struggles?

5. The Galindos' Shabbat dinners are a cornerstone for the family and all the family members take the tradition seriously, often missing plans with friends to prioritize the weekly Jewish holiday. Do you have a tradition that brings your family together? What makes your tradition special or unique to your family?

6. When Georgia confronts Lucy about being judgmental and not reciprocating her attempts at friendship, Lucy is initially surprised but soon acknowledges she has a tendency to both judge and push people away as a defense mechanism. Do you think her conversation with Georgia will change how she sees the world around her? And have there been times when your first judgment of someone was wrong? How did you handle the realization?

7. There are quite a few side characters who help both Lucy and Fletcher along the way, from Brodie rescuing Fletcher on his first day of school to Lucy's sisters, Amira and Julieta, who swoop in to remind her how amazing a person she is. Is there a particular side character you fell in love with? Who would you love to see get their own HEA?

8. Fletcher's main reason for not immediately revealing his true identity to Lucy is that he is worried he will scare her away and lose her friendship both online and off. Do you think if he *had* revealed his true identity to Lucy right away she would have run away or pushed him away? Why or why not?

9. Fletcher struggles with confrontation and having difficult conversations, which lands him in some pretty uncomfortable situations. But as the book progresses, Fletcher starts to realize his behavior can actually hurt those he cares about and he starts speaking up for himself. Though it doesn't work for Fletcher, do you think there are times it *is* better to hide the truth to avoid hurting people? Or do you think it will always backfire, as Fletcher experienced?

10. Do you think Lucy will one day return to social media? Do you think she will reclaim her @TheMissGuided-Counselor account and continue offering inspirational posts and advice? Or do you think she will start fresh, creating a more personal account that highlights her uncurated life?

ABOUT THE AUTHOR

Jessica Lepe is a former social worker turned website designer who spends her days writing, listening to murder podcasts, and wrangling knives out of her toddler's hands (sometimes all at the same time). She discovered her love for reading after sneaking romance novels in her Bible at her all-girls Catholic high school and in between the spines of her siddur at synagogue each Saturday, and she hasn't stopped reading romance since.

A proud and passionate advocate for mental health, Jessica writes romances with complex and flawed characters with multicultural and religious backgrounds that reflect the people she loves most in this world.

You can learn more at:
AuthorJessicaLepe.com
Instagram @AuthorJessicaLepe